THIS IS HOW

M.J. HYLAND

THIS IS HOW

■ HarperCollins*PublishersLtd*

Published by HarperCollins Publishers Ltd, by arrangement
with Canongate Books Ltd., Edinburgh.

First Canadian edition

HarperCollins Publishers Ltd
2 Bloor Street East, 20th Floor
Toronto, Ontario, Canada
M4W 1A8

www.harpercollins.ca

Library and Archives Canada Cataloguing in Publication

Hyland, M. J. (Maria Joan), 1968–
This is how : a novel / M.J. Hyland.
ISBN 978-1-55468-501-1
I. Title.
PR9619.4.H94T45 2009   823'.92   C2008-908013-0

Printed in the United States
RRD 9 8 7 6 5 4 3 2 1

Part One

I

I put my bags down on the doorstep and knock three times. I don't bang hard like a copper, but it's not as though I'm ashamed to be knocking either.

The porch light comes on and the landlady opens the door. She's younger and prettier than I expected.

'Hello,' I say. 'I'm Patrick.'

'I thought you'd be here hours ago.'

It's after ten and I was due at six. My mouth's gone dry, but I smile, friendly as I can.

'I missed the connection,' I say.

I've not meant the lie, but she's forced me.

'You'd better come in.'

We face each other in the hallway. I've got my back to the door and she's got her back to the stairs. I should say something, but I can't think what. I put my bags down again and my hands hang heavy.

'You'll have to meet the other boarders tomorrow,' she says. 'They've gone out.'

She takes hold of her long brown hair and pulls it over her left breast like a scarf.

'Let me take your coat,' she says.

'I'm not bothered,' I say. 'I'll keep it on.'

I want the pockets for my hands.

'There's a rack just beside you.'

'I've said I'll leave it on.'

'I thought you might feel more comfortable with it off. It's a very warm evening.'

She looks at me and I look at her and she takes a step back as though she blames the place where she's standing for the silence.

I want her to show me to my room and get it over with. I take my coat off and put it on the rack.

'There,' I say.

She coughs and I get to thinking maybe she's nervous, same as me. Maybe she thinks I'm all right.

'Is that all the luggage you have?'

I've got clothes in one duffel bag, my toolkit in the other.

'Yeah.'

My coat falls off the hook and, because neither of us picks it up, it's as though there's something watching us.

Beside the hallway telephone, a pen hangs from a piece of string. I flick the string and the pen swings.

She laughs, but it's not a mean laugh.

'What did you do while you waited for your train?' she says.

'I read a book.'

I cover my throat with my hand. I didn't read. I went to an off-licence and they had a four-for-two deal on bottles of beer. I drank three at the station to get in a better mood and I've still got one in my bag.

'Is it a good book?'

'So far.'

There are pictures of boats on the wall.

'I'm building a boat,' she says. 'Bridget Bowman's building a boat.'

I smile and she smiles right back. She's got a few stains between her teeth, like grout between tiles.

'That's good,' I say.

She points to the hallway wall, to a picture of a half-built boat in a dark shed. I should ask her what kind of boat it is, but I know nothing about boats and she'll think I'm an idiot.

I pick up the coat.

'I'll take you up now,' she says. 'You're on the first floor.'

My room's small, but it's at the front of the house and I'll bet it has a good clear view of the sea.

There's a single bed, a sink, a draining board, and a rack for cups and plates. Under the window, there's a table and a wooden chair.

I put my bags down under the sink, go to the bed, and sit. I wouldn't mind a ham sandwich and a cup of coffee. After that, we could lie down together and I could put my head in her lap, or the other way round. It'd be up to her.

She comes over, stands close to me. 'What've you got in the big bag?' she says.

'My toolkit.'

She looks at it.

'Do you want me to open it up?'

'Never mind,' she says. 'I was just curious.'

I stand.

'Is the room okay?' she says.

'It's more than okay.'

She smiles. 'How long do you plan to stay?'

'Indefinitely.'

'You've come here for good then?'

'Or bad.'

She laughs, takes a step back. 'We'd better go down to the office now.'

I follow her down the stairs and she takes her time, goes too slow, keeps turning back to look at me, tells me the ins and outs of the running of the boarding house.

Three weeks ago my fiancée Sarah was standing at the top of the stairs when she said, 'I can't marry you, it's over,' and when she was halfway down, I called out her name, but she didn't stop, didn't so much as look at me, just said, 'Please don't follow me.'

I wanted to push her down the stairs, make the kind of impression I didn't know how to make with words. But I didn't, and when she'd closed the front door I said, 'Okay, then,' and, 'Goodbye, then.'

Afterwards, I played the scene over and over, imagined how I planted my hands in the middle of her back and pushed hard enough to send her flying.

And I got this sentence in my head, over and over, 'You broke my heart and now I've broken your spine.' It was something I'd never say, not like anything I've ever said. I've never done any serious violence to anybody, never even thought about it all that much.

The next day I set about looking in the papers for work and lodgings down south near the sea and three weeks later my bags were packed and I was on the train.

I'm here now, a hundred miles away, and that's the past. Sarah's the past. It's done with. I don't have to think about it again if I don't want to.

At the bottom of the stairs, Bridget takes a left turn to her office. The writing in the frosted glass says: *Do Not Enter.* She unlocks the door, goes in and sits behind her desk. There are more pictures of boats and her black-and-white wedding photographs on the walls and a pile of books about boats on the desk and a vase full of white flowers on top of a filing cabinet. I wonder where her husband is.

'You'll need to pay for the first two months and a six-week bond in case there's any breakage or malicious damage.'

4

I've only ever heard my father use the phrase malicious damage and I expect it from him because he's a miserable factory foreman, always on the lookout for thievery and wrongdoing. She's too pretty to be saying it.

'Right,' I say.

I open my wallet and take out a wad of notes and without so much as blinking I give her the money. I bet she'll think there's a lot more where that came from.

She looks at the notes and frowns.

'Wait,' I say. 'Let me count it for you.'

I've given her all she's asked for and I've only got a hundred and fifty pounds left.

'Is everything all right?' she says.

I nod.

'You're just tired.'

'Yeah, it's been a long day.'

'Of course.'

She wants more.

'I'm sorry I haven't been more friendly,' I say. 'I'll be a new man in the morning.'

'We'll do the paperwork and get you a set of keys tomorrow then.'

'That'd be good.'

She moves round to the front of her desk. 'Well, goodnight then, Patrick.'

She's lovely.

'Goodnight.'

I reach the first-floor landing and she calls up.

'Breakfast's at seven-thirty on weekdays and eight-thirty on week-ends.'

I call back, 'Okay, thanks. See you tomorrow.'

'Sleep well,' she says.

'You too.'

There's a good atmosphere made by our voices calling up and down the stairs, something like the mood of being on holiday, just me and Bridget, alone.

2

I'm asleep when the front door slams.

It's half-midnight and the other boarders are home. Somebody's fallen against the wall outside, and there's laughter.

I get out of bed and open the window, try to hear what they say, but all I hear is a tomcat crying for sex.

'Fuck you,' I say.

I dress and put my shoes on, try talking myself into going down, but change my mind and take my shoes off.

The other boarders, two men, they go on laughing and talking.

I put my shoes back on.

'Forget it,' I say. 'You'll meet them in the morning.'

I've not meant to talk to myself and, if I've done it now, maybe I've done it before and not known it.

I take my shoes off again, undress, get back into bed.

But I don't sleep, don't even close my eyes.

When the men come up the stairs, one of them laughs and says, 'The new boy.'

I wake at 4 a.m. The man in the next room's farting, a sound like sausages bursting in a frying pan. I'm wide awake now and staying in bed's a waste of time. I won't sleep.

I get up and dress.

I'll go out and walk by the sea, watch the sunrise and be back in time for breakfast.

I go down quiet as I can and take one of the keys hanging on the hooks beside the coat-rack.

I cross the empty road to the promenade and walk down to the water's edge. The only light comes pale from the moon and a few of the unbroken orange lamps further down the esplanade. Waves roll to the sand and suck as though for food and the sound of the sea is like applause.

I walk towards the town. By the time I reach the main street, my tongue's sticky with thirst.

All the shops are closed. I go on further, down to the train station at the junction. It's about twenty minutes from the boarding house.

There's nobody at the station, no attendant, no cleaner, and the buffet's closed. I climb over a barrier and go out to platform 2. The air here's cold and there's a smell of stale ash and engine oil.

I turn back.

When I reach the boarding house, the sun's risen and the light's foggy and blue.

I go straight up to my room, open my big bag, take out the toolkit and put it safe under the bed, grab a towel and go to the bathroom at the end of the hall. I lock the door and undress for a bath, but the water runs cold. I try both taps, adjust the pressure, but still no heat. I take the plug out of the bath, wrap the towel round my waist, go out to the hall and check the closet for a meter or a boiler. There's neither.

I pick up my clothes, go back to my room and get into bed.

When I wake, it's quarter past eight. I've almost missed breakfast.

I wash my face in cold water, tuck in my shirt, wipe the muck off my shoes, then go down.

When they hear my fast feet coming down the stairs, they'll know I'm fit and keen to make their acquaintance. Going quick's a trick that helps kill some of my social nerves.

There are two men in the dining room. They sit together at a table under the bay window. There's another table, set for one, in the middle of the room.

I go in, put my hands in my pockets.

'Good morning,' I say.

One of the men stands. His hair is jet-black.

'Hello,' he says, 'I'm Shaun Flindall.'

Flindall's got a posh London accent and he'd have the looks of a movie star if not for his big ears.

'Hello,' I say.

The second man stays in his seat and he only bothers to nod in my direction. His arm's draped across the back of the chair and his long legs point out from under the table, crossed at the ankles.

He's not as good-looking as Flindall, but he's tall and he's got a thick head of blond hair and the kind of big blue eyes girls love so much. And he's got a tan.

'I'm Ian Welkin,' he says, his voice even posher than Flindall's. 'Why don't you sit here with me?'

Flindall doesn't protest, picks up his plate and goes to the table in the middle of the room, looks at me, then takes hold of the cigarette he's got behind his ear. I expect he'll smoke it, but he just moves it to the other ear.

I sit opposite Welkin.

'Welcome aboard,' he says.

'Thanks,' I say.

Both men have got their hot breakfasts.

'We were hoping to meet you last night,' says Welkin. 'We thought we could show you round the town.'

'I missed my train,' I say.

'And you've missed breakfast, too,' says Flindall.

'Bridget's gone into town,' says Welkin. 'But she'll be back soon.'

'She might make you a bacon sandwich,' says Flindall. 'If you ask nicely.'

'Good,' I say. 'I'm starving.'

Neither of them offers me any food. A piece of toast would do.

'Do you know she's a widow?' says Welkin. 'Her husband was killed by a train.'

'How?'

Welkin laughs without opening his mouth. 'He was in his car and got stuck on the tracks.'

'The train was running early,' says Flindall. 'Astonishing bad luck.'

Flindall moves the cigarette again, back to the other ear.

'When?' I say.

'Two years ago,' says Welkin. 'Imagine the carnage.'

'Now she's building a boat with the other woman,' says Flindall.

'The other woman?'

'Her husband had a passenger in the car,' says Welkin. 'A man he worked with.'

'The other woman is the other widow,' says Flindall.

'Jesus,' I say.

Welkin wipes his mouth clean with a napkin and Flindall cleans his teeth with a toothpick.

They both look at me.

Welkin's left two sausages on his plate and some black pudding. I wouldn't mind a bit.

'What did you read?' he says. 'At university?'

Bridget's been telling them the stuff I put in my letter.

'I didn't finish.'

'What did you take?'

'History and Psychology,' I say, 'but I left after a year.'

'That's a shame,' he says.

'That's too bad,' says Flindall, who's holding the cigarette, looking at it.

'I wasn't really bothered,' I say.

There's silence while they pour themselves tea.

'I was just telling Flindall earlier about my trip to Australia,' says Welkin.

I say nothing, can think of nothing.

'I was hoping to see a few sharks, but I didn't see a single one.'

'Me neither,' I say.

What I mean is that I've never seen a shark, but I'm not sure it makes any difference to him what I've meant. He goes on talking in his booming voice like he's on a stage.

'I think if sharks had arms,' he says, 'they wouldn't bother killing. They only bite legs off because they're curious. If they had arms they'd just—'

'Hug people?' I say.

Both men laugh and the laughter's in my favour and it's the first time they've looked at me like they think I'm not an idiot.

I'll relax a bit now.

Welkin leans across the table.

'Welcome to Vauxhall Street, Pat.'

'It's Patrick,' I say.

'Have some toast then, Par-trick.'

Bridget's come back and she's carrying a parcel wrapped in brown paper. Maybe she's got our dinner in there.

'Good morning,' she says.

I stand up to say hello.

'Did you have a nice sleep?'

'Yeah, thanks.'

'You've missed breakfast. Are you hungry?'

'I am a bit.'

'I'll get you a bacon sandwich,' she says. 'Will that do?'

'That's great, thanks.'

Flindall puts the cigarette back behind his ear and stands. 'I've got to get to work.'

We say our goodbyes.

Bridget puts the parcel down and sits where Flindall was sitting. I'll have to wait a while for that sandwich.

'Shaun's an architect,' she tells me. 'He's one of the head architects for the new pavilion.'

'Right,' I say.

'And Ian's a mathematician.'

'An actuary,' he says, 'actually.'

She smiles.

'But I'm on an informal sabbatical,' he says. 'I'm sick of the big smoke and I'm taking the sea air. A rest cure.'

'You been sick?' I say.

'Not exactly,' he says.

'Just a bit too rich and a bit too idle,' says Bridget.

Welkin nods. 'That's right.'

Bridget smiles, takes the parcel, leaves.

What's gone on between them looks like something that's gone on before.

Welkin stays with me while I wait for my food.

'Why doesn't Flindall light that cigarette?' I say.

'He gave up two weeks ago and he sticks one behind his ear so he's got something to play with.'

'Isn't that like torture?'

'Yes, but I suppose that's the very point. Don't you see?'

I don't see. I say nothing.

'Have you got work here?' he says.

'Yeah, I'm a mechanic. I'm starting at the place on the main road on Monday morning.'

'Is that the one that does vintage cars?'

'Yeah, and sports cars.'

He turns his cup round, looks at the tea leaves.

'Why did you give up university to fix cars?'

'I prefer it,' I say. 'You've got to do the thing you prefer.'

'Yes,' he says. 'I suppose that's the right decision.'

I hadn't asked him for his opinion on my decision.

'Anyway,' I say, 'it's a good line of work, and the money's not too bad. And I get to drive some very nice cars.'

Bridget's come back with my bacon sandwich.

'Here you are,' she says.

'Thanks.'

I start to eat and she stacks dirty dishes onto a tray at the next table. Welkin stands to help her and when the job's done she puts her hand on his arm and leaves it there, and they look at each other, longer than usual, and even though it's not me she's touching, the heat shoots through my legs. I hope she's not one of those women who can touch a man she hardly knows without meaning anything much.

'I'd better be going,' says Welkin. 'I've got to see a man about a dog.'

'See you later, then,' I say.

'You've finished your breakfast,' he says. 'Why don't you come up with me? You've got the room right next door.'

I'm not in the mood for more chat.

'I'll stay down here,' I say. 'I need to make a few phone calls.'

Bridget leaves and Welkin follows close behind. I'll be damned annoyed if it turns out they're having sex.

13

I wait for a few minutes, then go up to my room, get a towel, try the bath again.

The water's still running cold.

I go downstairs to Bridget's office and tell her, 'There's no hot water.'

'The best time is earlier in the morning.'

She's searching for something in the top drawer of the desk and looks at me as though she blames me for the fact she can't find it.

'I tried earlier,' I say.

'Oh.'

'Can I have my key?' I ask.

'Of course.'

She goes to the filing cabinet and gets two keys.

She looks at me.

'Don't forget to put your front-door key on the hook inside the door when you get in. This way we all know who's home and who isn't.'

'Okay.'

'Yours is the blue hook, which is the same colour as the number on your bedroom door.'

'Right. I won't forget.'

'We'll do the paperwork now.'

It's very formal, like she's a different person from last night. When I tell her I'm twenty-three, she tells me I look younger. She asks me if my parents are Irish, with my name being Patrick.

'No, but my grandad was.'

'But you're not confirmed? You're not a Catholic?'

'How can you know that?'

'You've put your full name down as Patrick James Oxtoby. You've got no confirmation name.'

I say nothing.

'I'll bet your mum will miss you,' she says.

I ask her why she's said that.

14

'You told me earlier you're the youngest, and you've left home for the first time.'

I shrug. 'She might miss me. She might not.'

I go to the door, then turn back.

'Have I done something that's bothered you?' I say.

'No,' she says. 'Not yet.' She smiles, just about the same sort of smile she gave Welkin in the dining room.

'That's good then.'

'Don't worry so much, Patrick.'

I don't see how she could know how much I worry or not.

I leave the boarding house and walk into town and on the way I get to thinking that my mum's probably worried sick and I should've left her a good long letter with some nice things said. She's been a good mum. I should've said thanks, or something that's the same as saying thanks.

My new workplace is on the corner of the deserted main street, two doors down from the post office. The metal sign outside is faded and rusted: *North Star Mechanics. Specialists in All Makes & Models. Vintage & New. Service & Parts & Repairs.*

I stand on the opposite corner and watch. I want to see what kind of business my new employer's got running, but nobody goes in or out. Friday should be a busy day for a mechanic. First thing I'll do on Monday morning is tell the boss to put up a new sign.

I walk on down the main street, towards the train station. I've got hungry again. I stop to buy fish and chips. I'm the only person in the chippy except for a ten-year-old kid and it takes a while to get the food ready because they've not had the oil on for long.

I go to the pier and sit on a bench and eat.

A fisherman comes in with his catch in a yellow bucket. He hasn't got much, a few small ones, the kind I thought they threw back.

When I'm finished eating, I walk a while and look at the old pavilion. I try going in, but all the doors are bolted. There's a sign down the back, one of those sandwich boards, someone's written on with chalk: *Closed Today*.

I go back to the main street, pass an old cinema called The Royale. There's only one film showing, a song-and-dance picture. I'd like to sit in the cool dark, but I've got no interest in song-and-dance. I want something with action and I'm in the mood for a pint.

I go to a pub behind the station called the Ducie Arms.

There's an old man sitting at the bar. He's got a lit cigarette in the ashtray, but he lights another and I get why he craves the start of things. All the hope that goes with the new thing. Coming to this town for a fresh start, I've got that feeling myself.

I order a pint and the barmaid sees me reading the chalk-board menu and asks me what I want.

'I'm not hungry.'

'You just go ahead and let me know if you change your mind.'

The door opens and I look round. I can't help it. I suppose I'm a bit jumpy.

I have another pint.

Two men come into the bar, both about thirty, and they sit together near the door, one of them with a suitcase and he's the one who gets the pints, then sits down again. But these blokes have nothing to say to each other. They just look out the window at nothing.

I'm not a heavy drinker, not by a long way, but I drink in bouts, and in these past three weeks since Sarah broke it off there's been one of those bouts. It's not that I want to get drunk, it's the pain-killer part of it that I want.

I've had a sore neck and sore shoulders since I was fourteen. I don't know why I've got the pains and the doctors don't know either. The only time I don't have the pains is when I've had a few pints and the edges soften a bit.

'Are you waiting for somebody?' asks the barmaid.

She's asked because I'm sitting with my back to the door and keep looking round at it.

'Yeah.'

I don't bother making up a lie about who I'm waiting for. She's a barmaid and she's obliged to talk to any old fool.

I order another pint and then another. Even though dinner's included in my bed and board, I've got a craving for a pub meal.

I order steak and chips and have another pint, then head back to the house.

It's nearly eight o'clock.

I check my toolkit soon as I'm back in my room, and I leave it sticking out a bit from under the bed, like I always leave it, with the handle facing out, ready for me to pick up in the morning when I go to work. I don't notice right away that the bed's been made and my things have been tidied, but soon as I realise I get a rush of good feeling. Bridget's been up here straightening and cleaning my things and it's like I've been promoted. I can't afford this life much beyond three months, but I'm going to make it good while it lasts, make it count.

I lie on the bed and smell the clean sheets, close my eyes. I'm in the mood to go down and look for Bridget and that's my plan, until the noise starts up.

Welkin's got a girl with him and the bed's drubbing the wall and they're talking while they're at it. I sit up and listen. Welkin groans loud at the end of the act, then laughs as though at a mistake somebody's made. I'm only glad it's not Bridget he's got in there.

To insult me further, a fly lands on my face. I swipe it, and it takes off, buzzes its dirty black body against the wall over my table, then comes back for another taste of my sweat. Once it's been at my face, it goes for a rest on the carpet, catches its breath, then comes after me again. When it goes back to the wall over the table, I throw my shoe and shout, 'Get out of my room, you fucking shit.'

There's more laughter in the next room and my neck reddens and my arms sweat, even my shoulders sweat. I lie down and cover my head with the quilt.

My mood's ruined.

I'll need a radio.

3

It's Saturday and I've woken too early to go down to breakfast. I kill a bit of time sitting at the table under the open window, look out at the shore and the sea, the dead flat horizon.

A child shouts, 'Bye Dad, bye Dad,' over and over, and when the child's stopped shouting, the first bus of the morning comes past, down the esplanade, and it turns the corner out the front of the boarding house. I listen to the sound of its brakes as it pulls in to stop, the hiss of the doors opening, the moan of the engine taking the hill.

I leave the window wide open, dress, and go down.

It's only quarter past eight, but Welkin and Flindall have already taken the table under the bay window. Flindall's hair is slicked back and he's wearing a flash pinstripe suit. Welkin's got his silk-lined jacket draped across the back of his chair. All I've got on is an oily T-shirt and my lank brown hair hangs down over my ears.

'Morning, Patrick,' says Welkin.

I get the sense I've interrupted something.

'Sleep well?' says Flindall.

I've no choice but to sit alone at the table in the middle.

'Like a baby,' I say.

My table's set with cereal and toast and I start eating, but feel a bit daft sitting by myself.

I pour a glass of water.

'Why don't you tell us a little more about yourself,' says Flindall.

I try to think what I might say.

'Maybe Patrick's too tired to talk,' says Welkin. 'He was probably kept up half the night listening to me having the time of my life.'

'Maybe that's it,' says Flindall, like a Greek chorus.

'I was enjoying,' says Welkin, 'the ultimate satisfaction.'

I was hoping for some good chat over breakfast and now I'd like to punch Welkin in the neck.

'Good for you,' I say.

He smiles. 'Tell us about life as a mechanic.'

'There's not much to tell.'

I sound like a man of few words, not like I want a fight with them.

Bridget comes with the hot food on a tray. She's wearing a yellow frock, just down past her knees, and she's got red lipstick on.

She's a doll.

'Good morning, Patrick.'

I stand.

'Morning,' I say. 'Do you need a hand?'

'No. Not at all. Sit and eat.'

She puts the tray of food down on the sideboard.

'You're paying me,' she says, 'not the other way round.'

'And it's a pretty penny, too,' says Flindall.

She folds her arms across her chest in mock anger.

'See if you can do better for less,' she says. 'I'll bet you can't.'

'She's right,' says Welkin. 'This is the best damn seaside boarding house in town.'

'It's the only seaside boarding house in town,' says Flindall.

She laughs and gives us each a plate of rashers, eggs, tomatoes.

'Has everybody got everything they need?' she says.

We say we're happy.

She leaves.

I eat my bacon and the fork hits my teeth.

I stop eating.

'How long have you both been here?' I say.

'Two months,' says Welkin.

'And me,' says Flindall. 'Two months.'

'Did you come together?'

'No,' says Welkin. 'Just a coincidence.'

Flindall moves his cigarette from one ear to the other. 'There was another man though.'

Welkin looks at Flindall. 'But he left.'

I'd like to ask them about the other man, but there's no time.

The doorbell rings and soon as the door's opened I hear that voice.

It's my mother.

I get up from the table and go out to the hallway, but it's too late. Bridget's let her in.

I stand by the staircase.

'Surprise!' says my mother.

Her dress is like a bus seat cover and it's the same kind of ugly thing she wears every day of the year.

'Hello,' I say.

She comes to me, throws her arms open wide and the wobbly white skin spills out. She looks happy, her blue eyes bright and big, like she's ready for a picnic in the sun, and I'm glad of that, but it would've been a whole lot better if she'd warned me. I'd have met her in the town. I'd not have let her come to the house.

'Is that all the welcome I get?'

The dining room door's open and I know Welkin and Flindall can see us but I've no choice except to move closer so she can wrap her arms round. When I let go and she steps back, I get a whiff of the hot nylon off her stockings. She's probably walked all the way from the station.

'It's good to see you, Patrick.'

'You too,' I say.

There's a coin on the carpet. I bend down to pick it up.

'Come into the dining room, Mrs Oxtoby,' says Bridget. 'Have a cup of tea.'

'Thank you,' says my mother. 'I'm parched.'

Bridget goes into the dining room. My mother turns round and flashes me a quick smile.

I follow them in.

Welkin and Flindall stand and, soon as she's been introduced, my mother takes a chair and sits down at the table with them.

'I had a lovely train journey,' she says.

'You must have left home awfully early,' says Welkin.

'I stopped last night at my god-daughter's house.'

It's two hours by train, only one change, but it means she must've booked the train soon as I told her I was leaving.

'Jennifer's house in St Anne's?' I say.

'Yes,' says my mother. 'She says hello.'

Her handbag falls from the table. I pick it up and put it in her lap.

'I'll be back in a minute,' I say.

I go up to my room and take a pillow and get the ball peen hammer out of my toolkit. I put the pillow on the floor and put a towel over it and bash good and hard. And I count: *one fucking stupid bitch, two fucking stupid bitch, three fucking stupid bitch, four fucking stupid bitch.*

She's as good as followed me here and she's going to be staying not ten miles away.

I hoped when I saw her waving goodbye at the train station, that'd be the last time for a long time.

I go to the table under the window and sit, but I can't get my breath back. She'll be down there telling them her hospital stories and they'll know by now that she's head surgical nurse, one of the most experienced nurses in England. Jesus. I can already hear her laughing and she's made them laugh, too.

She's smart and, if she's worried they're not impressed enough, she'll find a way to tell them that she studied medicine for a year before her youngest son came along rather unexpectedly seven years after two miscarriages, but not unwelcome, of course, not unwelcome.

I go to the bed and lie down and close my eyes and wait for as long as I think it'll take her to tell her story and drink a few cups of tea. I'll not begrudge her the story, but I'll not sit through it either.

I go back down, stand in the dining room doorway.

'Mum?' I say.

'Yes, Patrick?'

Welkin's got a dirty smirk on his face and Flindall's sniffing at his unlit cigarette. He looks pretty amused.

'Let's go for a walk along the sea,' I say. 'It's a nice day.'

She looks at Welkin as though for his approval.

'If you're staying in town, Mrs Oxtoby,' says Bridget, 'why don't you come back here for tea?'

'That's a good idea,' says Welkin. 'Come for dinner.'

Welkin'll not have the evening meal known as tea.

'Maybe I will,' says my mother.

'You must,' says Welkin.

My mother stands and runs her hands along the front of her dress, removes the biscuit crumbs.

'We'll see you back here for dinner, then,' says Welkin.

'I very much hope so,' says my mother.

'Promise you will,' says Flindall.

They like her, have liked her instantly. She hardly needs to speak and she has everybody liking her.

'All right,' she says. 'I will.'

Bridget walks us to the door.

'Don't forget to show your mum the old pavilion,' she says. 'It's very jolly this time of year.'

I take my mother to the bus-stop, left of the boarding house, away from the sea.

'It's good to see you,' she says.

'And you,' I say.

I should say a lot more nice things and make her feel welcome, but she's got to know I don't want her here.

'It's a very nice house.'

'Yeah.'

'It must cost a fortune.'

'I'll be getting good pay,' I say. 'Nearly double what I was getting before.'

What I've said is true, and it feels good to say it.

'That's great news, Patrick.'

She reaches for my hand, takes hold of it. I don't mind her doing it, and I like her warm touch, but I let go sooner than I would've at home. It's different now.

'The sea's down that way,' she says.

'We'll walk back that way later.'

'But it's such a beautiful day. You said so yourself.'

'It's better if we catch the bus to town first and then come back.'

'I'm not an old woman yet,' she says. 'I'm well able to walk.'

'You could run a marathon,' I say.

She laughs and punches my arm, soft, affectionate. And now she's got the laughter going she's got trouble stopping. My father hardly ever laughs, only snorts as though he's criticising something. I've never minded her laughing.

I smile at her.

'You sound like the seagulls,' I say.

'It's nice to be near the sea, isn't it?'

'That's why I came.'

She looks down the road. There's no sign of a bus.

'Why did you leave?' she says.

'I'd left the tap on upstairs.'

'That's not what I meant,' she says.

I say nothing.

'Don't treat me like a fool,' she says. 'You know I'm not.'

My mother collects porcelain animals and she always gets them on birthdays and at Christmas. She's got hundreds of them and she dusts them every other Saturday afternoon.

I came home from the pub one night and she was sweeping up broken bits from the living room floor.

My brother Russell was helping.

'What's gone on here?' I asked.

Russell took me to the kitchen.

'Dad lost his temper and he went and threw two new horses against the wall.'

I went back into the living room and looked at my mother. She was down on her knees, collecting small shards and she turned and looked at me.

'He did it right in front of her,' said Russell.

Dad's temper must have been bad for Russell to speak against him. They've always stuck together.

And now, as we stand by the stone bus-shelter and wait, I see that same look on my mother's face.

'I want to know why you left home,' she says.

'I told you why. I left because of this new job. I'm not going over it again.'

'You left in an awful hurry,' she says. 'You only gave us a day's notice and we hardly had time to say a proper goodbye.'

I say nothing. She moves her handbag from one hand to the other.

'And what about Sarah? We were all very sad to hear about that, you know.'

I shouldn't have told them about Sarah. I could've lied and said it was my idea to finish it.

'End of story,' I say.

She looks at a bus travelling the other way as though she plans to go into the middle of the road and wave it down and ask the driver to turn around.

'We could be waiting here a month,' she says, 'let's walk.'

'What did you talk about while I was upstairs?'

'Nothing you'd be ashamed of.'

'So what was said? What did you talk about?'

'Those two lovely young men told me how much they enjoy living in the house.'

'That's good.'

'They said you're fitting in very well.'

'Fitting in?'

'Getting along.'

She puts her hand on my arm.

'The good-looking one,' she says, 'the dark-haired one with the cigarette behind his ear—'

'Shaun Flindall.'

'He's very good-looking, but I'm not sure that he knows it. He seems a bit biddable, the way he hangs off every word of the other one. The blond one. I'd bet he'd steal the blond one's personality if he could.'

She thinks what I think. It's pretty much always been that way. But I can't say this now. Not now. She can't stay here. She's got to go home.

'And the blond one? What's his name? I've forgotten.'

'Ian.'

'He studied maths at Cambridge. He's very self-assured, one of those arrogant but friendly types. A strange one, but at least you'll not be bored.'

'I know.'

She looks down the esplanade for the bus. There isn't one.

'They're both quite posh.'

I say nothing, don't even smile. I don't want to be hard on her, but she's left me no choice.

'And Bridget's building a boat.'

'I know.'

'What kind?'

'A clipper,' I say, though I wouldn't know a clipper if I fell over one.

'Maybe she'll take you sailing in it when it's finished.'

I sit up the back of the bus.

'Why sit up the back where the hooligans sit?' she says.

'I get sick up the front.'

'I didn't know that.'

I've left a space between us and she puts her handbag there and looks at it as though to check if it's comfortable.

'I wish you hadn't left in such a hurry,' she says.

'Is that why you followed me here?'

'You left with hardly any warning. You just walked out. You broke it off with us.'

She thinks she understands it, but she doesn't. She thinks I was hurt by Sarah and so decided to hurt them. That's not it. I left so I could start again. I don't want her thinking I need her.

27

'You shouldn't have followed me here.'

Two old women get on with tartan shopping carts and, even though there's a whole empty bus, they sit two rows in front of us.

'I was hoping we could talk in your room at the boarding house,' she says. 'I was hoping to see your room.'

'You can see it later.'

She won't see it later. As soon as I've finished with her, she'll get straight on the next train.

'Why don't we go down to the sea?' she says. 'We could get an ice-cream.'

'Haven't you just eaten a packet of biscuits?'

'I had two biscuits. You're a terrible exaggerator.'

She's right.

I say nothing.

We get off the bus at the top of the main street and I take us in the direction of the station, but I stop outside the pub I saw yesterday, two doors down from the cinema.

'It's too early for the pub,' she says.

'Is it?'

'You're not drinking at this hour.'

She sits on the bench outside the pub.

I don't sit.

She opens the clasp of her handbag, takes out a tissue.

'Let's go to the sea. It's only just over there. Let's get some fish and chips and watch the waves.'

She's spoken now like a small girl and I wish I could join her in the fun.

'I'd rather not,' I say.

'Let's find a café then.'

'I fancy a pub meal,' I say. 'I didn't get to finish my breakfast.'

She looks round the street but the only witnesses are the two old women with tartan shopping carts from the bus and a man walking a small white dog and, across the road, two teenage boys leaning on either side of a pole, smoking cigarettes.

The end of a hot summer, a seaside town, and it's nearly deserted.

'Look,' she says, 'I think there's a café over there. See? Just past the pharmacy.'

I want to speak and not to speak. I want the both, for it to be better than it is, and to make it worse so as she'll leave. If I could be alone with her, alone in a room, not in the street, not where we can be seen, then I'd want the chat with her. I've never minded the chat. But I don't want to start here with her walking too close beside me.

'Let's go there,' she says.

She takes the lead and we're crossing the road side by side, close enough for my arm to touch her arm. I don't move away.

We go into the café, sit at a table near the window.

'I want you to be a bit nicer to me,' she says. 'Can you do that?'

I want that too, but it's not the only thing I want.

'I'll do what I can.'

'Don't be sarcastic.'

I look at the menu.

'Why do you have to behave in such a contrary way?' she says.

'I'm not being contrary. It's just that what you want isn't the same as what I want.'

4

For my tenth birthday my parents gave me a brand-new Sting-Ray Schwinn because I'd topped my class. There's only me and my brother, Russell, and he's seven years older. He didn't ever show any promise at school, left after his O-levels and he's ended up working in the chocolate factory with my father and he'll soon be the head parts-importer and he wears a shirt and tie, always a white shirt, always a blue tie, just like my father.

After the red Schwinn, my parents paid me even more compliments for doing well at school, but in the very next breath there'd always be jabs from my father about my mutant genes, about missing adoption papers and the whereabouts of Einstein at the time of my conception. I knew he loved me, 'course I did—every night he used sit on the settee in his thick socks and watch the TV and have me sit up close and he'd put his feet on my legs and I'd massage his feet and then he'd do the same for me—but he got my back up with the hot and cold, with encouraging me one minute and teasing me the next.

Even without effort I was always close to the top of the class, and when it came time to sit the grammar school exam I gave it my best and passed easily and I think I did it because I could stomach the idea of failing even less than the idea of passing.

In my third year at the grammar, when I was fourteen—the year I noticed Sarah—I started getting the pains in my neck and shoulders and the dread of tests put knots in my gut.

And then, one weekend, the Schwinn's gears got jammed and I took the bike apart and spent the whole day and half the night building it again. When I'd put it back together, it was perfect. I danced around in my bedroom all light-footed and shadow-boxing like Muhammad Ali.

I started reading mechanics magazines. At first I borrowed them from the library, but then I saved some of the money I earned working on Saturday mornings at the corner shop, and I bought my first tools too, started my toolkit with adjustable spanners (a ten inch and a six inch), needlenose pliers and side cutters, then I got a set of box spanners, a ball peen hammer with a flat cold chisel, and a centre punch and some multi-grips. I knew what I needed and liked looking for the best pieces.

A few months before I fixed the Schwinn, I'd told my mates Geoff and Daniel that I wanted to run off to join the French Foreign Legion after school, or maybe as soon as I turned sixteen. I don't know why I told them. I wasn't even sure it was something I wanted to do, but I wanted to want to do something and maybe I wanted them to see me as a bit tougher.

Geoff liked the idea too and went off to ask his uncle about what kind of man could get into the Legion and his uncle told him all about it and also told Geoff that I wouldn't make the height requirements and it turned out he was right.

The night I'd spent fixing the Schwinn had given me a good confidence boost and I didn't care so much about the Legion any more.

The next Sunday I went round to my gran's house to share the good news. She always took my side in things and she said I had a good spirit and my father and my brother were like 'two tall drinks of water', but that there was nothing watery about me.

She took me to Dublin with her for a weekend when I was twelve, just me and her. We stayed in a hotel near Phoenix Park and we went down to the sea.

As soon as I was standing inside her hallway, I said, 'Gran, I think I want to be a mechanic.'

'And why do you think that?' she said.

'Because I fixed my bike last weekend and it was fun.'

'Fun is good,' she said, 'but what makes you think it's what you want to do with your life? There must be more to it.'

'I don't know how to say it.'

'See if you can.'

She waited.

'When I was doing it,' I said, 'the time flew like magic, like the world didn't exist. I thought I'd only spent an hour doing the fixing, when it turned out it was the whole afternoon. And when I was doing it, I didn't have any worries about school or anything. And the pains were gone.'

She didn't say anything, just opened her arms and gave me a good strong look and waited for me to embrace her, and when she was holding me she said, 'Dear Patrick, you've found the thing you love to do.'

She took hold of my hand then and we went in and sat on the soft blue settee and had cake and tea by the fire. It was lashing rain outside and her cat Samantha sat on my lap and we spent a very good day.

When it got dark, she had a brandy and let me take a few sips and she taught me how to play gin rummy and how to bluff at poker.

When it was time to go, I asked her to keep what I'd told her a secret.

'Of course,' she said.

'I'm not even going to tell Geoff and Daniel,' I said.

She took hold of my hand. 'It's good to sometimes keep something completely for yourself.'

Then she laughed. 'Except for me. You must tell me everything.'

She died two weeks later of a heart attack. She was sixty-five and she died on her feet. She was getting ready to go to Mass and she had her best dress and shoes on and she died, probably about to go to the dressing-table to finish putting powder on her face.

When I got the news I rode my bike to the new estate being built around behind the chocolate factory and dug a hole in the ground and screamed into it. I screamed about how fucking stupid the world is.

When I left for university, my parents and Russell came to the train station to say goodbye, and my father called me 'Professor' and 'Doctor' and 'Judge' but he laughed and shot my brother looks when he said it.

I didn't want to go to university but I didn't want to stay at home either. Leaving seemed easier than staying on, easier than talking about why I didn't want to go. They'd not like that I wanted to become a mechanic and they'd not understand it.

During the first term, I took up smoking, drank beer and improved my snooker game. I bought a set of arrows for the dartboard and played alone at night in the common room after most of the others were asleep or out on the town. By the end of the second term, I knew I was going to fail and my mood turned sour. I had stomach cramps and bouts of nausea and most days I slept till the afternoon.

My room-mate tried to cheer me up, saved jokes he'd heard down the pub or student union, but he gave up when I stopped him halfway through a joke to tell him I'd heard it before.

'What's the punch line then?'

'I can't remember,' I said. 'But I know I've heard it before.'

'When's the last time you laughed?'

'Yesterday,' I said.

I hadn't laughed for a long time and his question unnerved me.

After that, when my room-mate came back to our digs at night, I usually went straight out, and it didn't much matter where. I didn't have anything to say to him and he'd stopped talking to me anyway.

I took long walks, drank alone, or played darts.

Near the end of final term, I saw posters advertising *The Merchant of Venice*, one of the plays I studied at the grammar, and a girl I'd met when I won a snooker game was acting in it. The night I won the snooker, she came over to congratulate me and told me her name was Amanda. She was with her boyfriend then, but I got to wondering if she might be single by now.

Next time I saw her, I told her I was going to see her play.

'That's great,' she said. 'Maybe you could come to the party afterwards.'

I went alone to the theatre, but soon as I went in, I saw some students I recognised from my dorm standing in the foyer. There were five of them, three girls and two boys, all dressed very smart. I felt all right and thought I could make up the sixth member of the group.

I went over to them.

They reminded me of their names and I reminded them of mine and they did their best to include me. I wanted them to like me and it pleased me the way they counted me in.

'How long does a show like this drag on for?' I said.

One of the boys laughed and so did one of the girls.

'Do you have to be somewhere afterwards?' said the boy who'd laughed.

'No,' I said. 'I just want to be prepared.'

'You've just said the thing everybody wants to say but nobody has the courage to say,' said the girl who'd laughed.

'That's because I'm nervous,' I said.

34

She laughed again, but not viciously. It was as though I'd done something charming, as though they all liked me for being honest, as though it was part of a clever act I was putting on.

When we went into the theatre, the girl who'd laughed sat next to me, good and close, and she made movements like somebody snuggling up in bed. She draped her coat over her knee like a blanket and a bit of it went over my knee too.

I was bored by the play and a bit nervous about the girl and I stopped paying any attention for a good while, but that only made my restlessness worse. I wanted a drink to calm my nerves and thought I'd probably leave before the intermission and down a pint.

But when an actor on stage said:

I am a tainted wether of the flock,
Meetest for death; the weakest kind of fruit
Drops earliest to the ground, and so let me

tears came and clogged my throat.

I tried to swallow, but the tears forced their way and pushed through and even more tears came. I didn't know why I was crying, but I cried as though I had good reason. I didn't know then that a wether is a castrated male sheep, but I put my hands over my face to stop the noise my throat and mouth were making. I couldn't stop. I couldn't stop the noise and tears.

The girl put her hand on my arm and whispered, 'Are you all right?'

I got up without answering and left the theatre. When I got outside, I stood a while and I realised that I was waiting for the girl. I hoped she'd follow. I waited for a good while and it was cold. I let myself get cold, didn't even move to keep the blood flowing, just stood and waited and waited for her to come.

She didn't come.

The next week, I sat my only exam and about ten minutes into it I tore my unfinished paper in half. Maybe I wanted witnesses to see that my failure was deliberate, but the fact I'd not lifted a finger to succeed didn't make it any easier to fail.

After the exam, I went back to my room, sat at my desk, and wrote a letter to my parents to tell them that I was quitting, that I'd soon be home. They didn't write back, didn't even phone me, and when I got home my father didn't get out of his chair in front of the TV. He said, 'So what are you going to do now?' I told him I didn't know. I expected him to be angry, but I didn't expect him to keep looking at the TV.

5

The walls of the café are covered in faded striped wallpaper and the net curtains are stained yellow and smell of burnt toast.

'It's a bit grim,' says my mother.

The only other customers sit in a booth near the back, a man and his girl. Both have pimply skin and dirty hair.

'It'll do,' I say.

The waitress comes and she's nicely dressed, a white shirt with pink flowers on the collar and a straight black skirt. She belongs to a cleaner, brighter place.

'Good morning,' she says. 'Are you having something to eat?'

She's lovely and tall, with long dark hair and she's tanned. She's old enough to be married, but I can tell without looking at her wedding finger that she's not. It's the way she looks at me, more curious than the usual.

'I've a craving for burnt chops,' says my mother. 'Do you have any? Or is it too early for chops? And I'd love a good cup of tea.'

'That's easy,' says the waitress. 'I can make you some chops.'

'Burnt?'

'Consider it done.'

My mother rubs her hands together as though she's cold.

The waitress looks at me.

'I'll have sausages and chips,' I say. 'Not burnt.'

She smiles.

I watch her walk to the kitchen.

'It's a small town,' says my mother. 'I thought there'd be more to it.'

'It's just what I want,' I say. 'It suits me fine.'

She thinks a while.

'I've always thought,' she says, 'that a small seaside town would be just the right kind of place to start a family.'

Like starting a fire, starting a car, starting a fight.

'Leave it,' I say. 'Leave it.'

She folds the corner of a napkin. I've stopped her dead in her tracks. She won't be talking about Sarah now, and if she starts up again in that direction she'll be wasting her time.

When I came home from university, my father told me he didn't understand me, told me that my brother had a knack for happiness and he asked me why I didn't.

I took a two-year motor mechanics course and, by the time I was ready to start an apprenticeship, Russell's wife, Julie, was expecting twins. The talk at Sunday dinners was of babies and nobody wanted to talk about what had happened to me at university. This suited me fine. Instead of talking so much, my mother touched me a lot more than she used to. When we sat at the table to eat, she'd put her hand on my hand, or her hand on my arm. My father talked less too, but smiled more. It was as though both of them had decided I didn't care about words.

Even when I started working for a local mechanic, nobody was much interested in talking about it. The talk that Sunday was of the fact that Russell had decided to go to night school to do a course in management and that same night, after we'd been watching TV and eating liquorice allsorts, I walked my brother to his house and he said, 'At least one of us is going to use his brains.'

I didn't care. I wanted to leave home, buy a car, save a deposit for a house. I was getting on well with my boss, I'd already been given a raise and I had two customers who drove more than fifty miles to have their sports cars worked on by me.

And then, one Friday afternoon in April, Sarah came to the garage in her father's car. I remembered her from the grammar school and she remembered me. She looked even lovelier now, with her long blonde hair tied in pigtails, and she wore a red corduroy skirt and flat red shoes to match. She had such long legs she didn't need heels. And she always stood so straight, too. I liked that.

'Hello,' I said. 'You look well.'

'I suppose I am,' she said. 'I mean, I'm not sick or anything.'

'I meant you look good.'

'So do you,' she said.

And just like that, in two sentences, we'd got far and my mood soared.

Sarah was shy at school, but she was in the drama club and it impressed the hell out of me that somebody shy could walk on stage the way she did. She once played the part of a Martian in a musical written by four other students and she had to sing, dressed head-to-toe in a gold body suit. It would've killed me.

I stopped working on the car's engine and offered her a milk crate to sit on.

'I'm happy standing,' she said.

'I'll wipe it clean for you.'

'No bother.'

I did it anyway.

We chatted for a while and I found out she was single. I didn't tell her I'd never had a girlfriend or about the Irish girl at the local pub I'd been chatting to lately. It wasn't important.

'You don't stare at my birthmark,' she said.

She was talking about the leaf-shaped mark covering half of the left side of her face.

'I like it,' I said.

She laughed.

The sound of her laughter and the way she put both hands over her face to hide…well, this and a lot of other things made a big impression on me and I was very glad she was in the garage on that sunny day in April, twirling one of her blonde pigtails and liking me, and I was glad that nobody else had got a hold of her.

I asked her to come to the pictures with me and after two dates we were straight away very easy and relaxed in each other's company and we went out with each other as often as we could.

One night I picked her up at the bank where she was training to be a manager and as we walked to the pub she stopped dead on the footpath, took hold of the sleeve of my shirt, and she said, 'I like you a lot. You make me feel calm.'

I wanted to say, 'Is that all? You only like me because I make you feel calm?'

But I didn't say this or anything like this and I was too stupid to see what was coming.

When we had sex, it was the first time for both of us and, after a few awkward tries, the sex was easy and good and when we'd finish we'd stay wrapped up together in the bed, her in front and me behind. I liked it. I liked everything about it. After just one month together, I proposed marriage, and I think now that she said yes because she didn't know how to say no, because I took her by surprise.

We were engaged for two months and I thought we were very happy. I was on top of the world. I quit smoking, took up running, drank a whole lot less and stopped spending Saturdays and Sundays sprawled on the settee watching snooker or football on the TV.

I didn't want to tell my family that Sarah had ditched me until the day before I left home, not because they'd be sorry for me, but because they'd be ashamed. The girl with the birthmark had broken it off, the girl they all said was so brave and strong, 'a perfect angel' according to my father, and the wedding plans were down the toilet.

I got to thinking that Sarah had only been practising on me, getting her confidence in sex and romance and gathering up some extra nerve so she could move to another man. I got to thinking that I'd filled her full of hot pride, that she'd saved it up to use against me.

She said she was breaking up with me because I didn't know how to express my emotions. The thing is, I didn't have that many. As far as I was concerned, it was pretty simple. I was in love with her and I liked our life and we laughed a lot and it felt so good to be in bed with her and have her touching me. I liked what we had.

The waitress brings a pot of tea and, when she's gone, my mother says, 'So you think you'll be happy then?'

'I don't know yet,' I say. 'How could I know?'

'But you think so?'

''Course I do. Nobody thinks he won't be happy. Nobody plans that.'

'You'll not miss home?' she goes on. 'I mean, won't you miss Daniel and Geoff and—?'

'No.'

She draws her chair further in under the table.

'I'm just a bit concerned that with all the money that boarding house costs.'

One interfering idiot. Two interfering idiot. Three interfering idiot.

'I have it sorted.'

'But the board must be at least three-quarters of your wage.'

'That's my business,' I say.

'It's my business, too. I'm your mother.'

'I won't stay on at the house forever,' I say.

'You have a plan then?'

'Yes.'

She's silent a moment.

'You don't seem happy that I've come to see you,' she says. 'Did you not want me to come?'

If you'd told me, I'd have said not to come. If you'd asked, I'd have said no.

'No, Mum,' I say. 'I'm glad you've come.'

She smiles and reaches for my hand.

'That's good,' she says. 'I care about you very much.'

'Same here.'

The waitress brings our food and some water and, when she puts my plate down, she looks at me, smiles.

'Are you just passing through?' she says.

She's caught me by surprise.

'No,' I say.

'It's just I haven't seen you before.'

'I've just got here,' I say. 'But I'm going to be living here. I start work on Monday at North Star Mechanics.'

She's looking at me and the warmth floods my chest.

'I knew I hadn't seen you before,' she says.

'I bet lots of people tell you this,' says my mother, 'but you look a bit like that actress on the telly. What's her name?'

'Do I? Which one?'

I don't want my mum to be getting into any chat. I look at my watch.

'Thanks for the water,' I say.

The waitress laughs. 'Water's free.'

She's got the hint and leaves us alone. She isn't stupid. Far from it. She's understood that I don't want my mother breathing down our necks.

When we leave the café, the sun's shining strong and my mother's not trying to walk so close. There's a bigger space between us and my mood's better for it. Just another hour and she'll leave me be.

'Will we go back to the house now?' she says.

She goes right ahead and wrecks the mood by linking her arm through mine. It's too public what she's doing.

I look at my watch.

'I can't,' I say.

'Why not?'

'I have to go into work soon.'

She takes a hold of my wrist, looks at my watch.

'It's only Saturday. You're not starting work till Monday.'

'I've got to meet my new boss.'

'You didn't mention this before.'

'I forgot.'

'Can we meet tomorrow? I'll come and get you at the boarding house.'

'Are you staying another day?'

'I might stay for a few days.'

I walk on and she follows. It's unbearable this, her walking so close and thinking her son's a liar when she's gone and provoked the lie in the first place.

'You know I just want you to be okay,' she says.

I turn back to look at her.

She wipes lipstick from the corner of her lip with her thumb.

'Let's go to the pier,' I say.

We walk to the pier, go out to the end, stand and listen to the sloshing sea, the dark echo of water beneath.

The only other people at the end of the pier are two young lads leaning against the railing, next to a sign pointing to the petting zoo and they're smoking cigarettes as though there's still novelty involved, both holding the fags between thumb and index finger, looking at the fags as though in awe of them.

I stand close to the edge and look down at the water. It's about a twelve-foot drop.

She links her arm through mine and, as I look at the water, I imagine how she'd sink and her ugly short dress would float up and surround her head like a jellyfish.

I step back and pull her back with me.

'Are you all right, Patrick?'

'Yeah. Sorry Mum.'

She squeezes my hand. 'Your broken heart will mend. It'll take time, but it'll mend.'

'It's already mended.'

'Nobody's going to judge you if you're a bit sad. You loved Sarah and she loved you.'

I take my hand away.

'She didn't love me. You don't know. You only think you know.'

'I don't know why you blame us.'

'You never asked me if I wanted to go to university, then you hated me when I didn't stay.'

'Nobody hated you. We felt for you.'

There's pity in her voice and I can't stomach it.

I walk away.

I don't know if I've even had the thought to do it, but now I'm walking away I can't stop. I don't look back at her. I expect her to call after me but I don't turn back. I keep walking and listening out for her voice.

She doesn't call after me.

Before I cross the road, I stop on the kerb. The clouds are low in the sky and there's a wind rushing over the tops of the trees on the esplanade. The only car on the road is travelling slow, but I go on waiting on the kerb. I've got an awful, sad feeling, a feeling as though I might fall.

I've an urge to sit. If I stay here, maybe she'll come after me and we could patch things up.

I want this and I don't want this, and there's a feeling in me like I'm sorry for the way I've been to her and there's another feeling that I've no notion what I'll do next. Today, tomorrow or the next day. I don't know where I'll go, or what I want to do, a feeling like there's nothing I've got to look forward to.

I stop and look back along the pier. I see a woman, about my mother's shape and size, but it's not her.

I wait a bit. If she comes to me, there's nothing I can do about that, but I'll not go to her. I'll not reverse.

She doesn't come. She's probably down there inside that fish place at the end of the pier, probably drinking tea, chatting to everybody she meets. I hope she'll be all right.

I go to the train station bar and order a pint of beer, sit in the corner and drink fast, like it's water for an aspirin. After the pint, I go next door to the Whistle Stop Shop and buy a bottle of lemonade and a small bottle of gin, go to the toilets, pour most of the lemonade down the sink and mix in the gin.

I take the bottle with me and go round the corner to the bus depot.

I've been sitting for about ten minutes when a bus driver having a fag comes over.

'You shouldn't sit here drinking,' he says.

'Why not?'

'You could be run over by a bus.'

'Don't you think I'd see it coming?' I say.

He walks away and I only leave when he's back in his bus.

I get to thinking about the waitress at the café. I should get back there soon and ask for her name. She looked right at me.

45

6

It's four o'clock when I get back to the house.

I hang my key on the blue hook and see that Welkin's home.

I go up to my room, check my toolkit, take off my clothes, fetch my towel and head for the bathroom.

There's still no hot water.

I go back to my room, get into bed and try for some sleep, but there's too much noise. The pipes in the wall are clicking and squealing.

I dress again and go down.

Bridget's in her office, at her desk, and she's got a pile of receipts and a calculator.

'There's still no hot water,' I say.

She stops working, puts the calculator in the drawer, looks at me.

'That's no good,' she says.

'I need a hot wash,' I say. 'And I think Welkin's been leaving his taps running.'

'That can't be right.'

'There was none yesterday either.'

'Give me a minute, Patrick. I'll adjust the thermostat as soon as I'm finished here.'

'I can do it,' I say. 'Just tell me where it is.'

'No. I'll do it for you. Just give me a minute.'

I don't know what I'll do next. I don't want to go upstairs and listen to Welkin or the pipes creaking, and I don't want to go back out.

I stand by the coat-rack and read the messages on the pad by the phone. There've been six calls for Welkin and one for Flindall. I pick up the pen and write, *Patrick. Sarah called* but cross it out. I take the phone off the receiver, listen to the dial tone, put the receiver back again.

Bridget's left her office. She's on her way to the kitchen and she's seen me.

'What are you doing?' she says.

'Just looking at the carpet.'

I've tried to be funny but it hasn't worked.

'Where's your mum?'

'She had to go home.'

'Are you at a bit of a loose end?'

'Not exactly.'

'There's a good cinema in town,' she says. 'If you want something to do, I can give you a list of things to do.'

What I want is a list of reasons why she's giving me the cold shoulder.

'I like it here,' I say. 'It's a nice boarding house.'

'That's good.'

'And the food's very tasty.'

'Thank you.'

I step away from the phone.

'It's worth every penny,' I say.

'Goodness,' she says. 'And here I was thinking you weren't happy.'

47

I'm standing close and wish she'd just go ahead and touch me. I bet if I were Welkin she'd put her hand on my arm.

'I'm not unhappy,' I say.

'I'm sorry you've had no hot water,' she says. 'I'm going to adjust the thermostat now.'

She walks to the kitchen.

I think to follow her so as we can keep chatting, but my breath's got short.

I won't say the right things.

I go upstairs, sit at my window and look out at the sea. It's only just gone five o'clock and I get to thinking I should take a swim. It's still warm and there's a good clear sky and lots of light.

I've changed into my togs and I've got my towel in my bag but on the way out I meet Welkin coming up the stairs.

'Hello,' he says.

'Hello.'

I scratch my shoulder so as to have something to do with my hands.

He steps round me. 'May I take a look in your room?'

'Now?'

'If that's all right with you.'

I open the door and he walks right in. His trousers are hitched high and there's a lot of length between his crotch and belt, but he stands next to my bed as though he's king of the world.

'It's the same as my room, only a bit smaller,' he says.

'I'd rather have the view,' I say.

'I can see your point,' he says. 'With the sky outside and the view of the sea, it doesn't so much matter if the room's small.'

'Right,' I say.

I put my hands in my pockets then take them out again.

He's having a good look round and he sees my toolkit.

'What's that?'

'My toolkit.'

'Did you paint it yourself?'

'Yeah.'

'You like fire-engine red then?'

'Yeah. When I was younger I did.'

'It's pretty big.'

'It's a complete set.'

I've got everything in that kit. More than five years worth of collecting. My adjustable spanner, ball peen hammer, pliers, socket set, hackshaw frame, feeler gauges and distributor contact spanners.

'May I take a look?'

'Maybe later,' I say. 'I've got to get going now.'

He leaves.

I'll not bother with the swim. The pain in my neck's come back. A drink's what I want, and after a few I'll go back to the café and see if the waitress wants to chat.

I lock the door and undress to my underpants, get on the floor, do fifty press-ups, fifty sit-ups and, after a quick wash and shave in cold water, change into a clean shirt and trousers.

On the way out, I look in the long mirror that's inside the cupboard door. I'm skinny but I'm not a runt and I've got good strong arms and a bit of character in my face. I'm not as good-looking as Flindall, but I'm not ugly either. When my ears are covered with my hair and when I straighten up, put my shoulders back, and smile a bit, I'm definitely better looking than Welkin.

If all goes to plan, I'll ask the waitress to the pub. We could eat a pub meal together, and if she wanted to come back here it's a better place to bring a girl than my room at home and she's sure to like the fresh linen and the full English breakfast that I'll bring her while she's still in bed.

I go the long way into town, down by the sea. The waves are bigger than they were yesterday, there are more people on the beach and the sun's bright and hot.

Before the café, I go to the pub across the road.

It's noisy and dark and I'm surprised to see so many people standing at the bar. My heart pumps faster.

The barman nods. 'What'll it be?'

'A double whisky, no rocks.'

The girl on my right turns to face me.

'You sounded like an American when you said that,' she says.

She must be drunk. Her bare arm's touching mine.

'I like saying it,' I say.

She's young but she wears too much make-up, a bit like a prostitute, but I don't think she is one. There's a smell of soap coming off her short red hair and she's fair-skinned with a few dark freckles on her nose.

The barman gives me the drink and she watches me like she's watching the TV.

'Have you been to America?' she asks.

'Not yet.'

I should ask her name.

She puts her left hand up to her mouth and holds it there for no good reason except to show me she's not married.

'I haven't seen you before,' she says.

'And I haven't seen you.'

The barman takes my empty glass. 'Another?'

'Yeah,' I say. 'Same again.'

'Same again, Sam,' says the girl.

I look at her properly, in the eyes, and smile, but not too much, not so as to make an arse of myself.

'What're you drinking?' I say.

'I'll have the same as you if that's all right, but lots of rocks for me.'

She talks like she's used to having attention paid to what she says.

I hand the money over to the barman for both drinks.

'Not necessary,' she says.

She reaches for her purse.

The barman's twenty-odd, with a shaved head, like an army geezer. He pours two doubles and, soon as the drinks are on the bar, he starts chatting to the freckled girl like he owns her.

'Here's one you'll not have heard before,' he says. 'Did you know that coconuts kill more people than sharks?'

The girl laughs and so do the two men standing on my left.

'How many get killed?' I say. 'How many people get killed by coconuts?'

The barman doesn't answer and the girl turns away from me, turns to her friend.

'He's always got the most amazing facts,' she says to her friend, then to the barman, 'you've always got the most amazing facts.'

The barman smiles and nods.

I'm ready to ask for another double, then once I've had it, I'd better work on grabbing the girl's attention, or head over to the café. One or the other.

But I don't get that far.

Welkin comes from behind and hits me hard on the arm with a clenched fist.

'Fancy meeting you here,' he says.

I put my hand on my throat so I can speak without him seeing I've got to swallow my nerves.

'Just got here,' I say.

'Looks like the whole town's here tonight,' he says.

'Is this your regular?'

'There are only two pubs here. This one, or the Ducie Arms with sticky carpet behind the station.'

51

'So this one's better, then?'

'Much better. Better ale and better whisky and better everything.'

He looks over my shoulder at the freckled girl.

'But since you're all alone,' he says, 'why don't you come over and sit with me and Flindall?'

'All right.'

This might be the time we clear the air a bit, get some friendship going between us.

I sit opposite Welkin and Flindall so I'm facing the bar and can watch the girl talking to the barman.

'What kind of car does a mechanic drive?' says Flindall.

They can't have been here long, but Flindall's already got bloodshot eyes from the drink.

'I don't have a car yet,' I say, 'but if I count my pennies I should have one soon.'

I've sounded like an old woman.

'I used to have a car,' says Welkin, 'but my kid brother smashed it.'

We talk for a while more about cars and car crashes and the chat's easy and my mood's good.

Welkin gets onto the subject of Bridget.

'She's not had a man since her husband got killed.'

'That's what she says,' says Flindall.

'She's not a fashion model,' says Welkin, 'but she's got serious grace.'

'And considerable charm,' says Flindall.

I ask them if they think Bridget likes her job. Welkin makes a crack that she must do because she has an endless supply of young men, and they laugh.

'What was the other boarder like?' I say.

'He had to leave at short notice,' says Welkin.

'What happened?' I say.

'It was personal,' says Flindall. 'He wouldn't tell us.'

'When he left he did it in an awful hurry,' says Welkin. 'In the week before he left, he went about the house like a ghoul.'

'He just stopped talking,' says Flindall.

'Anyway,' says Welkin, turning to Flindall, 'he was a bit like that schizophrenic who got sent down at Cambridge. Remember the one I told you about?'

I look over at the bar and see the barman's put his hand on the girl's arm.

I try to get back into the conversation with a bit more chat about cars and they both seem impressed enough with my knowledge and the whisky's killed the pain in my shoulder.

'What kind of car are you going to get?' says Flindall.

'A Triumph TR4.'

'Right,' says Welkin. 'That's a very nice car.'

'Yeah,' I say.

They start up about London again and I don't bother trying to get back in.

I can see the girl's leaning in close to the barman, her breasts squashed right down on the bar so as she can reach over to him.

'I've got to go,' I say. 'I've got to meet somebody. I can't stay.'

'So soon?' says Welkin.

I stand. 'See you back at the house.'

'All right, Patrick,' he says. 'See you later.'

'Bye now,' says Flindall.

They ask me nothing, not interested in who I'm meeting, where I've got to go.

I go down the main street and cross over to the café. My heart's beating pretty fast, but I'm ready now, and I'm keen to see her again.

I go in, and there's a different waitress. She's about fifty and she's wearing a dirty apron. I sit and order a coffee.

The coffee comes, but there's still no sign of the other waitress.

The new waitress asks if I want anything to eat.

'No, thanks.'

I get up to pay the bill before I've finished the coffee.

'I was wondering where the other waitress is,' I say.

'She's taking a few hours off.'

'Right. What time does she come back?'

'She'll be back in the morning.'

I nod.

'Do you want to leave a message?'

'No. I'll come back tomorrow.'

I go round to the pub behind the station and stand at the bar and drink another whisky, but my mood doesn't go back up to where it was when I was first chatting to the freckled girl or crossing the road to see the waitress.

The two women in here are too old and dried up from the fags and booze and their voices are sharp and loud.

I speak to nobody and drink for an hour, walk back to the house, go in quietly, straight up the stairs to my room.

I'm in bed and near sleep when they come crashing through the door. I've forgotten to put the latch on.

I sit up, pull the sheet over my chest, try to make my face look more awake.

'He's in the bloody bed,' says Flindall.

They've switched the light on.

'Come down with us to the sitting room and have some more beer,' says Welkin.

'You could've knocked,' I say.

'Dead right,' says Welkin. 'But Flindall couldn't find the knocker.'

54

'Turn the light off,' I say.

'It was already on,' says Flindall.

'What time is it?'

'Half-eleven.'

'I might give it a miss,' I say.

'We absolutely forbid you from staying alone in your cot,' says Welkin. 'You can't go to bed before midnight. It's obscene.'

'The very opposite of supreme,' says Flindall.

'Supreme's enemy,' says Welkin.

I'll not get back to sleep now.

'What've you got to drink?' I say.

'Three bottles of beer.'

'One each,' says Flindall.

'Come on,' says Welkin. 'Have a beer with us.'

I get out of bed and they watch me put my shirt and trousers on. We go down.

Welkin takes the settee and Flindall sits in the armchair facing him.

I sit in the second armchair, between them.

Welkin and Flindall are pissed and talking shite and there's a load of in-jokes about mutual friends from college and the more exciting stuff that's going on down in London.

I'm damned sick of being counted out of the London talk, but I know a man's got to show he can stomach being cut out and I can't say I'm going back to my room.

When I was a kid I stayed for a night at Daniel's house. Geoff was there too. There were two single beds, one of them a foldaway that his mother had wheeled in, and when it was time to sleep Daniel said, 'You have to choose, Patrick. Who do you want to sleep with?'

'I think I'll go home,' I said.

They laughed at me.

'Just choose where you want to sleep,' said Daniel.

I chose Geoff, but once I'd made my decision he didn't seem sure he wanted me to share with him. He looked at the floor as though that's where I should go but I stripped down to my underpants and got into bed with him, my head near his toes, and he turned to face the wall and had nothing more to say to me.

Welkin and Flindall are still talking about London and their college days and I go on trying to add to the general thrust, but the beer's run out, my tongue's tied. I can't get back in. I've no choice but to clear out.

'I think I'll hit the sack now,' I say.

They don't protest.

Welkin escorts me to the door.

'What happened to your mother?' he says. 'We thought she'd be here for dinner tonight.'

'She wasn't feeling well.'

'That's no good,' he says. 'I was looking forward to a few more blood 'n' guts hospital stories.'

'She'll be all right,' I say.

'Good,' he says. 'Perhaps she'll come another time. She's a handsome woman.'

'A damned sight more handsome than yours,' says Flindall.

'Not that you'd know,' says Welkin. 'She's not ever followed me here, has she?'

Welkin laughs without opening his mouth.

I don't laugh.

'Thanks for the beer,' I say.

'Don't mention it,' says Welkin.

When he says this, the way he says it, it's as though he's my friend, as though he wants me to stay, as though he likes me.

I get into bed and close my eyes but I won't sleep till they've finished.

About a half-hour's gone when they come up the stairs.

They stop outside my door, the two of them there, silent, as though waiting for something.

I get up, put my trousers on, turn on the light. I'm ready for them. When they come, I'll ask them what the hell they think they're playing at.

But they don't bother me.

They go to Welkin's room.

I get into bed and try for sleep, but can't. They've got more booze in there and the two of them are laughing and shouting.

If Bridget's home, they'll have woken her.

I dress and go out to the hall and knock on Welkin's door.

He answers. 'Hello, Par-trick.'

'You're making an awful racket,' I tell him.

He says nothing and this makes me say more than I've wanted.

'I don't mind if you have a bit of fun, but I have to get up for work tomorrow.'

He laughs through clenched teeth. 'Tomorrow's Sunday.'

'Right.'

He smiles. 'Why don't you join us?'

'I'd rather not,' I say.

'Come on. Have some fun. Relax for once.'

Fuck you.

I go back to my room, slam the door so hard it ricochets open and I've got to slam it a second time. A few minutes later, there's silence.

It worked.

They've shut up.

I've shut them up.

I sleep a good sleep.

7

I've woken at half-six.

At home, I used to sometimes wake at dawn and listen to the first bus pull up outside my window. I'd daydream about getting on board with that airport mood I had when I went to Dublin with my gran, with my bags all packed and ready to go, but now I've got on a bus with my bags all packed, I don't bother with that line of thought. It's not something worth imagining any more.

I go down for breakfast.

Bridget's setting the tables.

'Good morning,' I say.

'Morning.'

I sit at the table under the open bay window and listen to the sea, the gulls squealing.

'It'll have to be a cold breakfast,' she says.

'Why's that?'

'Breakfast is served at eight-thirty on weekends. You're too early.'

'I thought you said I could have breakfast early if I wanted to.'

'I don't think we agreed to that.'

'I wake early,' I say. 'I always eat breakfast before eight o'clock.'

'I'm as busy as a frog in a sock,' she says.

I stand.

'I'm sorry,' I say.

I've told her I'm sorry when I've nothing to be sorry for.

I go to the front door without saying goodbye, as though this is the way to show my strength.

It's a cold, bright morning and I walk along the water's edge with my hands outstretched. There's nobody but that old man with his small white dog to see me.

I go to the café.

There are four people, each of them alone, at four separate tables.

I stand by an empty booth and the lovely waitress comes from the kitchen carrying two plates.

'Hello,' she says.

'Hello.'

It takes me too long to realise I'm standing in her way.

'Take a seat,' she says.

I sit.

A few minutes later, she comes back.

'Your mum was in here yesterday evening.'

'Was she?'

'She came for her tea with another lady.'

Jennifer.

'Right.'

'She wanted to know why I wasn't an actress. She was very sweet.'

I fancy the waitress, and my mother's sniffed the air and realised it.

'Don't worry,' she says. 'She said she was going home this morning.'

My mother's already gone then and I don't feel too great about it. I wanted her to go, and now she's gone it's like rejection, feels like it was her idea and not mine.

'What would you like to eat?'

'Sausages and eggs.'

I read the newspaper while I wait.

The waitress comes with my breakfast, four sausages, two eggs, two pieces of buttered toast.

I take my time eating and read the paper, start at the back, then work my way to the front.

When she comes to clear my plate, I look at her and smile.

'This is a nice café,' I say.

'I'm glad you like it. My dad owns it.'

'Why doesn't it have a name?'

'It does. It's called The Harvest, but the sign's being re-painted. It used to be called Powell's, but we all hated that name. We changed it four years ago.'

'Who's Powell?'

'That's the family name. But it's a boring name for a café.'

'Harvest is good.'

'I agree.'

She's got blue eyes and, as far as I'm concerned, blue eyes are more real than any other colour.

'How long have you worked here?' I ask.

'Four years.'

'You changed the name first chance you got.'

'That's right.'

'Is it fun working here?'

'Listen,' she says. 'I need to serve a few tables. I'll come back to you.'

I want to say more, something smarter than the things I've said, one more thing before she walks away.

'I'll be here,' I say. 'When you come back.'

'Where else would you be?'

'Right,' I laugh.

I watch her serve tables.

She's not only tanned, but she's got small nostrils to match her small nose and everything about her is neat and in proportion.

I stall at the counter when I'm paying the bill.

She gives me change, but I'm not ready to leave. Sunday's a lonely day, and if a man's lonely on this day people will probably think he's always lonely.

I'll have her think I'm busy.

'I'd better go,' I say.

'Are you late?'

'Only a bit.'

'Time flies when you're having fun,' she says.

I put the change in my pocket, but go on looking at her.

We give each other a smile and it seems a pact's been formed. How quickly it happens when it happens.

'I might come again tomorrow,' I say. 'I like it here.'

'Good,' she says. 'I'm open till ten o'clock.'

I turn to leave, but I've got to go back and ask her name. I take a deep breath and turn round.

'What's your name?'

'Georgia.'

'I'm Patrick.'

'Nice to meet you, Patrick.'

'And you,' I say.

I kill some time down the pier. The pavilion's open and I play arcade games and slot-machines and win a few quid. I buy a hamburger for lunch and sit on a bench and watch a fisherman untangle his net, watch the couples walking together arm in arm. I get to thinking I'll go back to the café tonight, before closing, have a good chat with Georgia and offer to walk her home.

At four o'clock, the air cools and dark clouds threaten a storm.

I get back to the house just as a heavy rain starts up.

Bridget's already started making the dinner and there's a good smell of roasting chicken.

I go straight to the office.

She's doing sums in a red ledger.

'I'd like to use an iron,' I say.

'You'll have to get it from Ian,' she says. 'He was using it this morning.'

I go to Welkin's room, but he's got company. The radio's turned up loud, but not loud enough to cover the sound of the grunting and giggling.

'I'm busy,' he says.

I go back to my room and sit at the table and without any warning I've a vision of Welkin with his trousers round his ankles. He's not bothered to undress, wears his shoes, and his girl lies on the end of the bed, her hips on the edge of the mattress, her legs round his waist, her hands grabbing at his hair.

He's got my blood boiling.

I go back down.

Bridget's in the sitting room putting flowers in a vase.

'Welkin's got company,' I say.

'Has he?'

'Yeah.'

'Did you get the iron?'

'No. He has company.'

I put my haunches on the edge of the settee.

'Well,' she says. 'You can get the iron later.'

'I'm going out tonight,' I say. 'I want to iron my good shirt and trousers.'

'Can't you get it later?'

'So, it's okay then?' I say.

She picks up a cushion, holds it to her chest.

'Within reason,' she says. She looks at the door. 'As long as the girl's gone by midnight and so long as there's not too much noise.'

I say nothing.

'We're all grown-ups, Patrick.'

I shift my weight too quickly on the settee and it rocks.

'Whoops,' I say, like a child.

I smile weakly, don't bare my teeth.

'You seem worried about something,' she says.

'Do I? I'm not.'

'Good.'

She steps closer, the cushion still hiding her chest.

'Where're you going tonight? Have you got a date?'

'Yeah. I met her on the bus.'

'When?'

'On Thursday. On the way here. After I got off the train.'

'Is that the real reason you were late?' she laughs.

'No. I missed my train.'

'That was quick work,' she says.

'She's a teacher.'

'Ian's girlfriend is a teacher.'

'It's not the same one,' I say.

She looks at me as though she thinks I'm an idiot.

'Well,' I say, 'of course.'

She smiles.

'I better go,' I say.

I go, but stand out in the hallway a few minutes, turn back to the sitting room.

'Who was staying here before?' I ask.

'Before you? In your room?'

'Yeah.'

'A young man from Belfast,' she says. 'He left a few weeks ago.'

'How long was he here?'

'A short time. A few weeks.'

'Why did he leave?'

'I can't give you his personal information.'

'Right.'

I go on looking at her.

'Right,' I say again.

She'll not say any more.

I go up to my room and I want to get into bed and nap a while before dinner, so I'll be rested for tonight. If all goes to plan, I'll have a late night at the pub with Georgia.

But the phone rings downstairs, a blasting ring so loud it can be heard all through the house.

Bridget shouts up the stairs. 'Patrick, it's for you. It's your mum.'

Welkin's sure to have heard, and Flindall too.

I take my time going down.

The phone receiver's hanging and I want to rip it from the socket but instead I pick it up and put it gently back in the cradle and then I loosen the connection. I can't talk to my mum now, not when I'm standing in this hallway when they're all here and probably listening.

Welkin's in the sitting room. He calls out to me.

'Par-trick!'

I go in.

He's on the settee and leans forward, puts his elbows on his knees.

'Why don't you come in and close the door,' he says.

I close the door and stand with my back to it.

'Was that your mum?'

'Yeah. But we got cut off.'

'We shouldn't have made fun of her last night.'

64

'I hadn't noticed.'

'Listen,' he says. 'I think we haven't got off to the best of starts.'

'I wouldn't say that.'

He stands and offers his hand.

'Well,' he says, 'I think it's time you knew that I'm glad you're here.'

His hand is cold and strong and mine is damp, but I press firmly and make sure not to be the first to let go. I hate to shake another man's hand, but it's got to be done.

'We don't want you to feel unwelcome,' he says. 'It's only that Flindall and I have become as thick as thieves.'

'Not to worry,' I say.

'Don't feel as though you're the third man,' he says.

'I don't.'

I know a fair bit about being the third man and I can't stand it. When we were kids and we went on a rollercoaster, Geoff and Daniel sat together up front and I sat a few rows back with some other kid.

As soon as the three of us started going down the pub, it was the two of them who said where to sit, what music to listen to, and what to do after closing. My jokes were as good as theirs and they always laughed with me, but they were the ones saying what we did and how we did it.

The same again with my father and my brother and my father made it worse by saying things like, 'Patrick, what do *you* want to do?'

'That's that all sorted, then,' says Welkin.

'No problem,' I say. 'But I've got to go now.'

'All right.'

'Will you tell Bridget I'm not stopping for tea?'

'All right,' he says. 'Bye then, Patrick.'

I don't say more, don't say goodbye, won't use his name the way he's gone and used mine. The thing is, I can't speak, not now. I've got to swallow the lump out of my throat and my mouth's clogged up and all because he's decided to make this advance to friendship, or whatever the hell it is, and he's patronised me and it riles me and it also makes me feel good and it's hard to say, but I suppose I want his friendship more than I don't, and what he's said has got me in the neck.

I go out and walk along the promenade. The storm's ended and the sun's shining bright and warm. When I reach the pier, I take off my jacket and hang it over my shoulder.

I go into town the longer way, by the water's edge, and I get to thinking that I don't have the stomach for Welkin's games, that we've nothing in common and nothing much to say to each other, but I know I want things clear and straight for a change and I suppose I want his friendship but I don't want the hot and cold threat of it all and I haven't the mind for being ignored, even when it's somebody I might just as easily send to hell.

I go to the pub behind the station for a quick pint. I'll soon go to the café.

I sit in a snug and an old man with the swollen nose of a drunk sits down opposite me.

'I'm saving that seat for my girlfriend,' I say.

'Where is she, then?' he wants to know.

'She's a nurse,' I say. 'There must have been an emergency at the hospital.'

I get away from him, play some pool, win five pounds after straight wins, but lose it all when I double up and go in-off the black.

I go to the bar to get another pint and the same old man comes to get his next pint, then turns round to face me.

'Yer shirt buttons are done up crooked,' he says, as though to tell me I'm in a worse state than he is.

Even with all the beer he's had, his breath stinks of sour milk and I'd like to punch the crooked teeth out of his mouth. I take a good look

66

at his dirty face and clench my fist and just thinking about punching him I can feel the crack of his teeth under my knuckles and when I run my tongue across my teeth I get a taste of blood off my gums.

'Mind your own business,' I say.

I'm not in the right mood now to go to the café. I won't see Georgia tonight. I'll see her tomorrow in the fresh, clear day.

I take my time getting home and stop to collect pebbles on the beach. When I've got two pockets full, I go out to the pier and sit with my legs over the side and throw the pebbles one by one into the sea.

I walk slowly back to Vauxhall Street.

8

It's eight on Monday morning and I'm a half-hour early for my first day at work. There's a middle-aged man standing out front, smoking a cigarette. When he sees me come through the gate, he turns and goes inside. I stall outside a few minutes, then follow him in.

He's sitting behind his desk in his small office, doesn't look at me when I walk in, and he doesn't stand.

'Hello,' I say.

There's no window in here and it's near dark as night.

'Oh,' he says, checking his watch, 'good morning.'

It's as though he's surprised, might have forgotten I was coming.

'Good morning,' I say.

He looks at me, but not for long, then down at his desk, flicks through the pages of a big RAC appointment book.

'I'm Greg Hayes,' he says. 'You must be Patrick Oxtoby.'

I stay in front of his desk.

'That's right,' I say.

'Dean had nothing but good to say about your work.'

'Thanks,' I say.

Dean's my old boss and he's also one of Hayes' brothers-in-law.

When I told Dean I was leaving, he said he'd miss having me around, and he offered to help me find a new job. He didn't ask me why I was leaving town, just said he hoped it all worked out. He told me to stay in touch.

'Take a seat,' says Hayes, 'and call me Grey. That's what they call me.'

I sit in the swivel chair that's covered in the kind of carpet put on the floor of cheap cars.

'I've been running this business for twenty years,' he says.

He looks at the wall, at the dusty clapboard smeared with oil. He's got the same kind of trouble making eye-contact that my father has. I bet if I blindfolded him now and asked him to describe what I look like, he'd not have a clue.

'Right,' I say.

'Do you have a nickname? Or is it just Paddy?'

'No,' I say. 'It's Patrick.'

He looks at the other wall, and I look where he looks, at a nude-girl calendar, torn and faded.

'All right, Patrick. I'll show you where everything is, then you can get to work on Mr Hancock's car. It's a 1966 MGB convertible, only a few years old, but the clutch is sticky and the steering's slack.'

I've worked on at least a dozen MGBs and I know how to fix just about anything that's wrong with them.

'There are some overalls on the back of that chair,' he says. 'Grab them on the way out to the garage.'

'Okay.'

'They're not yours to keep, but you can borrow them.'

'I've got overalls with me,' I say.

I reach for my duffel bag, but it isn't by my feet.

'I've left my toolkit somewhere,' I say.

'You won't need it. I've got everything here.'

I've got everything in that kit. My brand-new torque wrench

and my brand-new double-ended set of spanners. The whole lot. More than two hundred quid's worth. I can't lose it. I couldn't bear to lose it.

'I'm a bit worried I might've—'

'Lost it?' he says.

The panic's spread to my throat and I've gone red hot.

'Yeah.'

'Where?'

'I don't know, if I knew where, then—'

Hayes looks at the wall behind me, says, 'You won't need them.'

'I prefer to use my own tools,' I say. 'So I wouldn't mind—'

'I've got everything you'll need here,' he says.

He'll not let me reach the end of a sentence.

'In my experience,' he goes on, looking at a torn poster on the wall for the 1961 British Grand Prix and Von Trip's Ferrari 156, 'it doesn't pay to sweat over lost things. They pretty well always turn up, and in the rare case when they don't, it's because they've been stolen or lost for good.'

He's said these things as though they were wise and smart.

'Yeah,' I say.

'If you're that worried,' he says, 'go ahead and use the phone.'

'I'm not worried,' I say. 'I'll get started.'

It takes me a good while to stop thinking about the kit, but after I've spent a few hours fixing and aligning the steering on the MGB, I've calmed down enough to take it for a test drive. It's a lovely car, primrose-yellow, not the colour I'd get, but it still feels good to be driving it. A few miles out of town, I put the radio on and wind down the window. I drive along the esplanade road and stop for some fish and chips and sit on the promenade wall. I keep looking over at the MGB parked in the street and I get to thinking it won't be much longer before I've saved enough to get a car of my own. Nothing as flash as the MGB, but something nice all the same. Maybe six months, a bit less if I'm careful.

Hayes has left me a note and stuck it on his locked office door. He wants me to look at the ignition circuit in a Peugeot 504 Saloon that's misfiring.

I finish the work in a couple of hours, then take the Peugeot for a drive. It's running perfectly, and when the distraction of work's gone I get to worrying about my toolkit again.

I take a tea-break.

Hayes comes out of his office and we meet at the sink in the tea room. It's a dark and windowless room and he stands so close I can smell the onion sweat coming off his hairy neck.

'You can go home early if you like.'

This suits me in one way, seeing as I can go home and look for the toolkit, but it's only half-three and I'm meant to be doing a full-time job.

'I'm happy to go on,' I say.

'No need,' he says. 'There's nothing left to do.'

He walks away before I've a chance to ask him if he's pleased with what I've done with the MGB and the Peugeot. When I worked for Dean, he used to give me a pat on the back when my work was good.

I catch the bus home and talk myself through what I did this morning before I left the house. I'm pretty sure I left the toolkit by my bed, that I had to put it down to get my key out to lock the door.

When I've settled my head, I get to thinking I'll come back into town after tea and ask Georgia to have a drink with me. I should've gone to the café last night and we would've gone for a nice meal together instead of me drinking alone at the station pub.

Welkin's at the front gate with a girl. She looks to be about eighteen, wears red-framed glasses. She's very pretty. He sees me and grins, his mouth plump with happiness.

'*Bonjour*,' he says. '*Comment ça va, Par-trick? Je suis ravi!*'

The girl and Welkin, they've got the same kind of hair, blond and healthy, and they've both got blue eyes.

Welkin puts his hands under the girl's armpits, lifts her high, spins her round. She's wearing a tight T-shirt and a short skirt and she's got a nice body, small firm breasts. She dangles from him, laughing, happy for him to throw her round even though it probably hurts.

I say nothing and go past.

The girl laughs, 'Do it again,' she says, 'but mind my glasses.'

So, she's having some fun all right.

On the way upstairs, I get a whiff of the food Bridget's making. Smells like roast beef and onion.

I go to my room and see that my toolkit's right inside the door. My relief's so good I get my appetite back straight away. But I've got a lot of time to kill before tea, so I might as well go to the window and watch them.

I open the curtains, stand well back, and look down. Welkin's much taller than the girl and he leans down, says something into her ear. She turns round and he grabs hold of her wrists, rough and hard, pulls her body into his and thrusts his hips in and out.

It's like seeing a dog all over a rabbit.

I close the curtains and go to my bed.

I'm down ten minutes early for dinner and sit at the table under the bay window.

Bridget comes in. She's wearing a low-cut blouse and she's got her hair tied back in a red-and-black polka-dot scarf.

'You'll need to tell me when you're not stopping for dinner,' she says.

'I told Welkin last night.'

'Did you?'

'Yeah. I told him to tell you.'

Silence.

'Shaun's gone to London,' she says. 'He's got a business meeting there.'

'Right,' I say.

She stands opposite, smiles, looks right at me, makes proper eye-contact.

'And Ian's not coming down tonight. He's going out for dinner.'

'It's just me and you, then.'

'Yes,' she says. 'I'll go and get your tea.'

When she comes back in, I'll get some chat going.

She comes back with my food.

'What is it?'

'Steak and kidney pie, mash, peas and carrots.'

She puts the plate down, careful.

'Thanks,' I say.

'Happy?'

'Happier than a pig in shit.'

She steps back from the table.

'Why do people say that?' she says.

'Sorry,' I say. 'It just popped out.'

'I'm not offended. I just wonder why people say it. Are pigs so happy?'

'No,' I say. 'But sometimes they roll onto their backs and when somebody rolls round like that we think they're happy.'

Jesus. I've just embarrassed myself, made my ears and neck go hot.

'And their tails are curly,' she says. 'And they snort like people do when they laugh. Maybe that's why.'

She's not embarrassed. It's only me.

'Yeah,' I say. 'You're dead right.'

She pours me a glass of water, gives me a napkin. I've got a chance here to use one of the biggest words I know.

'It's called anthropomorphism when we do that,' I say. 'When we compare the things animals do with the things humans do.'

'I haven't heard that word since school,' she says. 'It's a nice one.'

'But hard to say.'

'You said it perfectly.'

This is good, this is.

Her mood's friendlier with me now, a bit more like it was on the first night, and she looks at me longer than usual, like she's fond of me.

The sun's coming in through the window and her face is all lit up. She looks lovely.

'I'm happy,' I say.

She puts her hand on her heart and gives me a big smile and I'm reminded of when I told the girl in the theatre foyer that I was nervous and how the truth got a good reaction out of her as well.

'People hardly ever say that,' she says. 'They'll soon enough tell you when they're not happy, but rarely the other way round.'

'Yeah,' I say.

But now, just like that, smack in the middle of the good, warm feeling, the chat's suddenly stopped and she looks away and it's like a cloud's passed over.

She picks up the tray and holds it in front of her chest.

'Don't let your tea go cold,' she says. 'Go ahead and start.'

I cut the pie open, but she doesn't leave.

She moves things on the sideboard.

I wish like hell I could think of something new to say instead of this silence and eating alone, with her in the room, not watching, but listening.

I should tell her I like being mothered by somebody who isn't my mother, that I like the way she puts her finger between her teeth when

74

she can't find something, that I like that she's spending a lot more time in here than she needs to. I'd like to tell her she's got one of the most beautiful faces I've ever seen and that I love the way her breasts don't wobble even though they're big.

'You could open your own restaurant,' I say.

'Thank you,' she says. 'But this is enough cooking for me.'

I should ask if she'll have a drink with me. And why not right here? We don't need to go out to the pub. Flindall's gone and Welkin's leaving soon. We can stay here, just the two of us.

She's finished stacking the plates on the sideboard.

'Do you have everything you need?' she says.

I've a mind to rush to my feet and kiss her on the neck.

'Yeah,' I say.

'I'll leave you to it then.'

'You don't have to go.'

'I've some things that need doing.'

'Right,' I say. 'Busy as a frog in a sock.'

'That's it.'

She leaves.

No matter.

We'll soon be alone.

I could go out to the off-licence and buy a nice bottle of sherry or port for us to share. I'll bet she likes sherry and port.

After I've eaten the pie, I go up to my room to wait for Welkin to leave. I finish hanging my clothes in the cupboard and tidy my toolkit. When everything's in order, I put the kit back under my bed, but leave it sticking out a bit, like I always leave it, with the handle facing out, ready for me to pick up in the morning.

It's half-seven when I've finished doing these things.

I should've got a newspaper. I don't know what to do to kill time indoors. I've never been good at it, have always been bad at doing

75

nothing, even worse at waiting.

I lie on the bed a while and look up. I keep on looking even though there's nothing to see but a freshly painted white ceiling.

It's eight o'clock.

Welkin's still in the house and the pipes in the wall are squealing.

I go out.

The bathroom door's wide open.

He's not here, but the hot tap's running. The bath's near full and the air's full of steam. He's got it working and I can't.

I turn off the tap and go back down the hall to my room and sit on the bed and do nothing but listen to the pipes clicking and groaning.

Welkin's door opens and closes.

I go back out, pass his room, down the hall to the bathroom.

He's leaning against the sink and he's got the bath plug in one hand, the other hand down the front of his pyjama bottoms.

He takes his hand out.

'Hello, Par-trick,' he says. 'How go things?'

He's waiting for the bath to empty.

'Hello,' I say. 'Things go well.'

I've made my voice posher like his.

He takes a clean towel from the linen closet and spreads it across the tiled floor and stands his dirty feet on it.

'Why didn't you take that bath? I say.

'The water went a bit cold. I like it nice and hot.'

I say nothing.

'Well, then,' he says. 'I'll see you tomorrow. I've got a date.'

'Yeah?'

'She's about six foot tall and she's got the best pair of pins I've ever seen and the most gorgeous olive skin. A Spaniard, I think. We're going to a flashy restaurant.'

Georgia?

I've got short of breath, like I've been running.

'But what about the girl outside? The one I saw you with earlier.'

He laughs. 'She had to go back to school. She's a bad girl and she's got detention.'

'What kind of hair does she have? The girl you're seeing tonight?'

'Who cares what colour hair she's got? She's tall as an Amazon and she's got great pins.'

'Right.'

He passes the bath plug from one hand to the other.

'But I must admit,' he says. 'I usually prefer the shorter ones. Nice and portable.'

'Right.'

He throws the bath plug at me.

I catch it neat.

'Good catch,' he says.

I throw it back.

He catches it neat.

I leave.

On the way back down the hall, I stop to look inside Welkin's room. It's bigger than mine and he's got two single beds, pushed together but made separately.

At the end of one of the beds he's got a white screen like doctors have in surgeries, made of a thin and papery material.

I go back to the bathroom.

'Have you got anything to drink?' I say.

'Sure, my friend. In my bar fridge. Help yourself.'

My friend.

'Right,' I say. 'Thanks.'

'And I've a few bottles of the hard stuff in the cupboard under the sink. We'll settle the bill later.'

He's got a half-dozen bottles of beer in his fridge, a bottle of champagne and a box of chocolates. In the cupboard, three bottles of whisky and two of gin.

I take two bottles of beer and the champagne to my room and put the champagne in the sink after I've filled it with cold water, then bring the beer down to the sitting room.

I take a copy of yesterday's newspaper from the magazine rack, but I can't concentrate. My legs are hot and restless. I change to the armchair by the window, but all I can manage is a short article about a snooker tournament. John Pulman's won again.

I finish the first beer fast and it's doing a good job of getting rid of the pains in my neck and I'm starting to feel better about the night.

The phone in the hallway rings.

Welkin runs down the stairs and answers it.

I've got the door closed and can't hear what he says.

He hangs up, comes into the sitting room.

'Oh,' he says. 'I was going to turn on the TV.'

Bridget's coming down the hall and neither of us speaks while we wait for her.

She comes in, but she doesn't look at me, only looks at him. She's got her hair out loose and she's got red lipstick on.

She speaks to Welkin. 'I thought you were going out on a date, love?'

'She just cancelled,' he says. 'And she fed me a rotten lie about a sick cousin.'

'Maybe it wasn't a lie,' she says.

'It's the second time she's cancelled.'

'Were you keen on her?'

'I'm afraid so.'

'Ah, love,' she says. 'What a shame. And you were looking forward to going to that lovely new restaurant.'

Welkin pouts.

'I won't cry,' he says, 'unless you tell me there're plenty more fish in the sea.'

'Well, there are.'

'I don't want fish.'

'Poor dejected monkey,' she says.

Welkin laughs, then stands, goes to her.

'Want to hug a monkey?' he says.

She thinks on it.

'A poor dejected monkey?'

They go ahead and embrace, and me sitting right here.

Bridget's got her back to me and Welkin's facing me and he's got his eyes open with a hard stare and, when he pulls her in tight, he's looking right into my eyes, one hand high on her back, one down the bottom of her spine.

'Mmmm,' he says.

He takes hold of her hair like it's a piece of rope.

'Mmmm,' he says. 'You're a lovely one for hugging.'

'Okay,' she says. 'That's enough.'

She turns away and she's blushing crimson.

'I'd better go,' she says.

She goes out.

Welkin looks at me and shrugs.

I go up to my room, close the curtains and sit at the table. I take off my trousers and I've thoughts of holding Bridget, without speaking, grabbing hold of her as she walks by, and for a minute we're at it against the banister.

But it's no good. I keep seeing Welkin's dead eyes, the way he looked right at me while he held her. He's downstairs, but it's just the same as if he were standing inside my room, laughing without opening his mouth, then saying some cocksure thing in French.

The front door slams.

I open the curtains an inch and watch him leave, walk towards the bus-stop.

I dress, wash my hands, wait a few minutes, then go down.

Bridget's sitting on the settee, her stockinged feet up on a pouf. The TV's on, the sound turned down low.

'Hello, Patrick.'

'Hello.'

She takes her feet off the pouf, slides them back into her flat shoes. She was wearing heels when Welkin hugged her.

'I thought you were busy,' I say.

'I'm just taking a little break,' she says. 'There's a picture I really want to see starting in a few minutes.'

She looks back to the TV.

'Mind if I join you?'

'Not at all.'

'I think I'll just read the newspaper for a while,' I say.

Although it's still light out, she's drawn the curtains. The air's stuffy and there's the smell of sweat from her feet.

I turn on the lamp and sit in the armchair nearest the window.

The TV's tuned to a game show. She turns up the volume.

'I like watching people win things,' she says. 'I can always tell I'm in low spirits if I can't be happy for somebody winning something.'

'I know what you mean,' I say.

The contestant's a middle-aged man with a stout belly. He sits on a backless stool and his feet don't reach the bottom rung. The prize is a fridge and it spins to the sound of tinny music on a slow carousel in the middle of the studio floor. He doesn't win the fridge and I don't feel sorry for him.

'What a pity,' I say.

'It was only a fridge,' she says.

She stares at the screen.

80

I wish she'd talk more.

There's a blowfly and it's buzzing behind her head and it circles her face, goes after the sweet soft skin on her cheeks, but she isn't bothered. It's just as though she doesn't notice.

I get up and go after the fly with a newspaper, hit the lampshade.

'Leave it,' she says. 'It's not bothering me.'

I sit.

'I can't stand flies,' I say. 'I can't be in the same room with them. They take up so much...'

I fold the newspaper.

'What?' she says.

'They take up so much of everything, they take the air out of the room, with their noise and the beating of their fat bodies all over the walls and sucking on your skin.'

She goes on looking at the TV.

'They don't bother me,' she says. 'And they only tickle. They don't suck.'

She won't look at me.

I move forward in the armchair, so I'm closer to her.

'Who knows what flies are doing,' I say, 'when they land on your face or hands and twitch their legs and make their wings vibrate. They're probably sucking. For all we know, that's exactly what they're doing.'

She ignores me, watches the commercial break.

Somebody's yelling at us about soap powder, shouting that it makes whites whiter than white.

At last, she turns to face me.

'Patrick. If I didn't know better I'd say you've been drinking.'

'I haven't.'

'You're in a strange mood.'

You all want me to talk more, and when I do this is what happens. I can't keep up with life.

81

'It's only that I don't like insects, especially flies. I wouldn't take it personally.'

She laughs, but it's not a nice sound. It's nervous and brittle.

'I didn't take it personally,' she says. 'I only thought it was a bit of an outburst. That's all.'

'There must be things that get on your goat,' I say.

'I suppose.'

'Give me an example.'

I know she likes being asked questions. Everybody does.

Sure enough, she looks at me, smiles. 'Let me think.'

I let her think, stop myself filling in the silence by counting the knobs on the TV.

'Okay,' she says. 'I suppose parents being cruel to their children, you know, when they hit them and scream at them in the street and your blood boils just knowing that right in front of you a life's on its way to being destroyed, then the next generation and the one after that…'

'I know what you mean,' I say.

She's ranted just like me and she's got to see now that we're not so different.

'Is there anything else?' I say.

She looks back at the TV.

'No,' she says.

'Nothing?'

'I think I'd like to watch this,' she says. 'And just have a quiet rest. Is that all right?'

Her voice's gone flat and cold.

'Of course,' I say.

I stand up.

She doesn't look at me.

'Enjoy the picture,' I say.

'Okay, Patrick,' she says. 'I will.'

There's no point staying if she's not in the mood and there's no point taking it to heart. She's probably tired from making the dinner or she's remembered her dead husband and she'll be wanting some distance between us now because of her embarrassment with Welkin.

I'll wait.

I go up to my room and undress and get into bed with the champagne and drink it straight from the bottle.

9

I wake at 5 a.m. I'm in a strange mood and my hand shakes when I take a shave. I've been thinking about Sarah and the first night we had sex, how she slept behind me with her hand on my chest and how I thought we'd always sleep that way. She said she liked it.

I don't go down for breakfast.

I want a walk in the fresh air to clear my head and I want to see Georgia and find out if she's been seeing Welkin.

It's a bright, warm morning and I walk the long way, cross the esplanade, climb over the low wall marking the edge of the promenade, go down to the sand.

My mood's good by the time I reach the café and even better when I see Georgia.

She's clearing a table, her back to me, and I watch her a while before I say good morning.

I get to thinking that I always liked Sarah best in the moment before I got to her, before she came to my front door, before she came to meet me after work. I always liked her more in the thinking of her. But it's not so with Georgia. I like her just as much when I see her.

Soon as she sees me, she turns and smiles.

'Hello,' I say.

'Hello. What've you got there?'

'My toolkit.'

Her cheeks are flushed and her eyes are as blue as the blouse she's wearing, like the colour in brochures showing swimming pools in fancy resorts.

'Have you started work?'

'Yesterday.'

There are five other customers. Three workmen wearing overalls who sit together by the window and two women in their forties in the back booth.

A man in the kitchen calls, 'Order!'

I didn't know she worked here with a man. I'd like to get a look at him.

'I think there's a man at the boarding house who knows you,' I say.

'Who?'

'His name's Ian.'

She says nothing, only looks at me.

'Do you know him?'

'I might do. If he comes in here, then I probably do.'

'He's tall and he's got blond hair.'

'I've got to get back to the furnace,' she says. 'Take a seat.'

She turns away. I call after her. 'Can I have the usual?'

She turns round. 'Sausages and eggs and coffee?'

'That's it.'

'I'll be right back.'

I take a seat in a booth in the middle, and face the door. There's a newspaper already on the table.

I've only read half the sports pages when she comes back with sausages and eggs and coffee.

'Here you are,' she says.

85

'Thanks.'

I swallow a bit of my nerves, then speak.

'I wonder if you'd like to have dinner with me?'

She looks toward the kitchen. 'Oh,' she says. 'That's so sweet.'

This probably means she'll say no.

'What do you think?' I ask.

She's making the tea-towel into a rope, twirling the length tight.

'I don't know.'

'Right,' I say. 'Never mind.'

She walks away.

I eat the eggs and sausages, but look over my shoulder whenever the kitchen door swings open.

When she comes back, she doesn't speak, just reaches for my plate, leans across in front of me and the closeness of her breasts makes my heart beat hard in my neck.

'Would you like more coffee?'

We both look round to the back of the café. One of the women has raised her voice in argument and she says, 'I'd be a lot bloody happier if you didn't keep telling me I look tired.'

I look at Georgia, make my mouth into a grimace, and she copies me. She's showing me that she likes me.

'I was wondering,' I say. 'If I borrowed a nice car from work, a sports convertible, would you like to go for a drive somewhere and maybe have a picnic?'

'When?'

'When it suits you.'

'Where do you want to go?'

'Could it be a surprise?'

'I suppose.'

She smiles. 'I've never been in a convertible. I could have my hair in a scarf and wear dark sunglasses.'

'So you would?'

'I could finish early one night.'

'What about Thursday or Friday night?' I say. 'It's bright till well after eight o'clock. What if I picked you up after work, around seven o'clock?'

'Are you allowed to take cars from the garage?'

'Yeah,' I say. 'I can get my hands on an MGB.'

She says nothing.

'So, do you want to?' I say. 'You don't have to.'

I'm nervous as hell and she looks at me for a good long while as though to check if I'm lying.

'Okay,' she says. 'I'll ask Michelle to spot for me.'

She picks up my cup and saucer.

Her hands are steady. She's not shaking at all, it's as though nothing's happened.

'Back to work,' she says.

I go to the counter and leave the money I owe next to the till. There's a pen on a pad of jotting paper and I get the idea I should write a romantic note for Georgia and leave it for her on the counter and she'll find it when she's least expecting it.

I lean on the counter and think what I might write, but when I look up at the clock on the wall I see I'm late for work.

There's no time. I pick up my toolkit and go.

Hayes is sitting behind his desk and doesn't bother saying good morning.

'Could you work on the Renault?' he says. 'I think you'll need to look at the tappets, they're really noisy. Check the whole lot. Cam, tappet, push rod and rocker arm.'

'Okay.'

I go out to the garage, use my own tools, and get the job done quickly.

At morning tea, we sit in the small tea room and talk about cars. It's the first proper chat we've had.

'You're a pretty good mechanic,' he says.

'Thanks,' I say.

Pretty good? I'm better than he is, better than most. Why doesn't he say so?

The phone rings in his office and he's gone a good while. I pour both cups of tea down the drain.

He comes back.

'I'd better get back to work,' I say.

'What did you do with my tea?' he wants to know.

'I thought you'd finished.'

'I'd only just started.'

'Sorry.'

At noon I take a break and go outside to the yard.

I've only been outside in the sun a few minutes when a Triumph TR4 drives slowly by. The driver's got his elbow resting on the open window and he looks damn well happy. He's got the radio turned up loud, his long hair flaps against his face in the breeze and his pale-blue polo-neck looks expensive, straight out of the shop, clean and new.

I go back in. I'm dying to take Georgia for that drive. I've got to ask Hayes if he has any customers with a TR4.

He's in the office, on the phone. I stand back from the door so he can't see me. I hear him say, 'Come in tomorrow, I'll have some work for you then.'

I step away, but I'm too slow. He's seen me.

'Patrick?'

'Yeah.'

'There's a message for you. From your mum. She sounds like a very lovely lady.'

He holds out the piece of paper and I've to go to him at the desk to get it. My hand's shaking when I take if off him. I want to know what she's said and I want to ask him who he was talking to about work and I want to ask about the car.

I'll start with the car, wait till my nerves steady before the other questions.

'I was wondering if I could get in touch with the owner of the MGB? Mr Hancock.'

'Why?'

'I'd like to ask him if I could borrow it.'

He frowns. 'That's not exactly company policy.'

His words have come out sharp. He's in a filthy mood about something.

'Okay,' I say. 'Not to worry.'

I'll ask the other questions tomorrow.

'Get to work on the Rover,' he says. 'It's just come in.'

'I didn't see it.'

'It's out the back.'

'Okay.'

I finish work on the Rover and Hayes meets me in the tea room to tell me to knock off early.

'I'm happy to stay on,' I say.

'No need.'

'The Rover might need a new clutch,' I say.

'Do an estimate for me tomorrow and I'll talk to the owner.'

'I can do it now.'

'It's a nice day. Go ahead and knock off early.'

It's only four o'clock but I'm in the mood for a drink.

I cross the esplanade and walk down to the end of the main street and go to the pub behind the station. I put my toolkit under the barstool and order a pint.

The two young lads who were smoking on the end of the pier yesterday are here. They're sitting at a table near the door and they've got pints of dark ale and in between drags on their cigarettes they look at their hands, same as they did at the end of the pier, as though in awe of the act of smoking.

I drink the pint and get to wanting a game of pool. My hands are steadier now.

I go to the lads and ask them.

'Mark'll play,' says the lad with pimply skin. 'He's better than me.'

'Yeah, I'll play,' says Mark.

Mark stands.

He's skinny and about five nine. Not much different in build from me.

We go over to the table and the pimply lad follows.

'Want to make it interesting?' I say.

'Yeah.'

'Can we play for pints then?'

Mark's a good player and he wins the first game, probably grew up on this table, but after that it goes my way. All I need to do is make it close enough to keep him interested.

'Want to play a quid a game?' I say.

He nods, slow and cocky.

'Yeah,' he says. 'You're on.'

Mark wins the next game, but he needs a few flukes to do it.

I win the next three.

Mark asks his friend for a lend so as he can keep playing.

I've had five pints now but I easily win the next, and the one after that.

'Better call it quits,' he says, 'or my girlfriend will have me bollocks.'

He's smiling even though he's taken a beating.

'Thanks for the games,' I say. 'You're a good player.'

'Ta.'

He shakes my hand, a good firm shake, then turns to leave.

'Hey wait,' I say.

He turns back.

I take five quid out of my wallet and put it on the table.

'Here's your money,' I say.

He looks at me like he feels sorry for me.

'Don't be stupid.'

'It's here on the table,' I say. 'Take it or leave it.'

I walk away, don't look at him again and go into the toilets, tell myself I'm getting out of his way, making it easier for him to take the money.

I go into a cubicle and sit on the toilet. I don't know exactly what goes wrong but, with the stink in here and the bright lights, I end up hanging my head over the toilet bowl and I'm sicker than the ale could've made me. I'm sick as a dog.

I stay hunched over the toilet bowl, my head resting on my arms, staring down into the dirty bowl, then it starts. The sobs hit me without warning, flood up from my chest, and I can't stop it, just like that time in the theatre.

I stay in the toilets a good long while, then go out to the basin and wash myself up with soap and toilet paper.

I walk the long way back to the house and go straight up to my room.

Nobody sees me.

IO

I wake with a hangover. My neck's sore as hell and I've got to breathe deep and slow to stop from heaving. Instead of going down for breakfast, I run a bath and the water's finally running hot and I stay in for a good while and the relief of the warmth makes me feel better.

When I get back to my room, and I'm ready to leave, I check in the usual place for my toolkit and realise I've gone and left it at the pub.

My back's soaked in sweat by the time I get to work and I mean to ask Hayes if I can use the phone to call the pub. But, soon as I arrive, Hayes stops me at the garage door.

'Let's put the kettle on and have a cuppa and a chat,' he says.

We go to the tea room and I reach for my cup.

'What about having a half-day off then?' he says.

'I've only just got here,' I say.

We both look up at the clock on the tea room wall. It's 9.30.

'No matter,' he says. 'There's nothing for you to do here today.'

Somebody's pulled up outside.

'See who that is,' he says.

I go out to the yard.

A man's pulled up in a Jaguar.

He parks and gets out, walks in my direction.

He's got a tidy moustache and he's wearing one of those pale linen summer suits, makes him look like he's just got out of bed, but rich at the same time.

'I'm Mr Hancock,' he says. 'I'm looking for the man who fixed my MGB.'

'That was me,' I say.

He smiles. 'I wanted to thank you in person. The engine's never run so well.'

'I'm pleased to hear it,' I say.

This is great, this is.

He'll give me his number now and I won't need to ask Hayes for it and I'll ask to borrow the MGB. I could offer him some free work in exchange, after-hours like, or I could dip into my savings and pay a hire fee.

'I'd like to tell your boss what a good new man he's got.'

'I'll go and get him,' I say.

Hayes is sitting behind his desk.

'Mr Hancock's here,' I say. 'And he wants a word.'

Hayes goes out and I follow.

'Mr Hancock,' he says, a big smile on his face. 'How's the MGB?'

'It's purring like a kitten. I came to thank the young man in person.'

'Thank you,' says Hayes.

Mr Hancock looks at Hayes' shoes and sees what I see: Hayes has small feet, and one shoe's bigger than the other.

'My wife will be bringing her Peugeot in next week,' says Mr Hancock, 'and my brother might bring his business to you as well.'

Hayes hasn't once looked over at me. 'Anything we can do for you,' he says. 'We're here to oblige.'

Mr Hancock looks at me.

'Here's my business card,' he says.

He gives the card straight to me and I put it in the pocket of my overalls.

I'm grinning ear to ear.

'Thanks,' I say.

'I've got to dash,' he says.

We say our goodbyes.

We go back in and Hayes stops outside the tea room.

'Let's finish that chat,' he says.

In spite of what's just gone on, he sounds cross.

'I'm sorry I was late this morning,' I say.

'Don't worry about that.'

'Okay.'

'Let's sit.'

We sit on kitchen chairs.

'Well,' he says. 'I suppose there's no time like the present.'

'Yeah?'

'I probably don't have enough work for you full-time. Part-time, yes. Full-time, no.'

'How many days then?'

'How about we stick to five days but you just work the mornings?'

My breath's gone shallow with the anger and the shock. It's not fair what he's done and there's a lot I want to say, but I'm in no position to argue. For now, at least, the only thing to do is take what he's offering and be a man about it.

'Okay,' I say.

'Good,' he says. 'Thanks for being a sport about it.'

'Did I do something wrong?'

'No, like I said. You're a good little mechanic.'

Little.

'Do you want me here today, then?'

'You can go home now,' he says. 'But I'll see you tomorrow morning.'

'Tomorrow, then.'

'Yeah. And thanks for being a sport about it.'

He stands when I stand and hands me a crisp tenner.

'Here's something for making Mr Hancock happy.'

I take it and say, 'Thanks.'

'Good man. When you get here tomorrow, we'll have a chat about splitting up the work between you and Ben.'

'Who's Ben?'

'My nephew. I thought I told you. He's starting his apprentice-ship.'

That's who he was talking to yesterday.

'Fair enough,' I say. 'Family's family, right?'

I've got to keep a lid on my anger.

'Yeah,' he says, 'but I'll look after you, too. Don't worry.'

I feel lousy and I've remembered my toolkit.

'Can I use the phone in your office?'

'You can.'

When I call the pub, there's no answer. I've got to get my toolkit back and I've got to do it tonight.

I leave the office and Hayes is standing right outside.

'You look like you've seen a ghost,' he says. 'Anything wrong?'

'I left something at the pub.'

'Yeah?'

'My toolkit.'

'There's really no need to lug that thing around,' he says. 'We've got everything you need here.'

I can't speak.

'Was there anything else?' he says.

95

'No.'

I leave.

On the walk home, I've got a churning stomach about the kit, an awful nervousness. I go over Hayes' words and this business with his nephew and the scenes with my mother and I get to wondering what Sarah's doing and my brain floods with all the sour things it's been storing up.

I've got to think my way out of this panic before it takes hold.

After I've called the pub again, I'll run a hot bath and relax a bit in my room, or maybe have that swim in the sea.

There are no keys on the hooks other than Bridget's. Unless somebody's forgotten to put their key on, it's just me and her.

I take a hat from the coat-rack and try it on. It's a brown trilby, with a band round the rim made of black felt, and I look at myself in the hallway mirror and I see that it might be true that a good hat can make a short man look taller.

I could wear this one for the drive with Georgia. I'll ask Bridget if I can borrow it.

'Well, don't you look a pretty picture?'

It's Welkin.

He's sitting on the landing and he's with the blonde girl.

I put the hat back on the hook. At least he's not got Georgia.

'Glad you approve,' I say.

'You look really well in it,' says the girl.

She's not wearing her glasses today.

'Why don't you leave your dirty overalls at work?' he says.

'Why should he?' says the girl. 'He looks good. He looks like a painter who paints with engine oil.'

Welkin's got nothing to say.

I smile at the girl and she smiles at me and I put my shoulders back a bit and head up the stairs.

When I reach the landing, Welkin takes hold of my trouser leg.

'Were you were thinking of stealing that hat?' he says.

'No.'

'I wouldn't have picked you for a thief, but then again, you're the inscrutable type.'

He's still got hold of my trouser leg.

'What's that supposed to mean?' I say.

'It means you're impossibly opaque.'

I've a good mind to knee him in the face.

'Fuck off.'

'Aren't you in a fine mood,' he says.

The girl stands, says, 'I've got to get going.'

'See you tomorrow,' says Welkin. 'I'll pick you up from school.'

They laugh.

'Bye bye,' she says.

We watch her go down to the front door, then Welkin stands and follows me up to my door.

'Flindall's leaving for London,' he says. 'He's got a new job.'

The last thing I want is to chat with him, but I've got no choice.

'When?'

'He had an interview with a big firm. He was offered the job on the spot. A big commission in London. He's the head architect on a new office building, a bank's headquarters, as far as I know.'

'Is he coming back to get his things?'

'He's coming back this evening, to say goodbye and all that, but he leaves again in the morning.'

'Right.'

I search for my key in the pocket of my overalls.

'Do you want something?' I say.

He stands close and when he stands close like this I've got to look up at him.

'Hey,' he says, 'steady on. I'm only having a bit of fun. Didn't your

97

grandmother tell you that being teased is a sure sign that somebody likes you.'

'No, she didn't,' I say.

I find the key.

'You're in a punchy mood,' he says. 'Anything wrong?'

'No.'

'How about a drink before dinner then?' he says. 'I've got a full bottle of whisky and we've got to give Flindall a nice farewell.'

Welkin's either making an offer of friendship or he's winding me up. I wish I didn't care either way. The thing is, I do.

'I'm a bit busy,' I say.

He sighs. 'That's too bad.'

I should've gone straight to the pub after work to fetch the toolkit. I could've had a few pints by now or I could've gone back to the café and asked Georgia to have some tea down the pub with me.

The key's jammed in the lock.

'Need a hand there?'

'Go on, then.'

He has it opened straight away.

'There!' he says. '*Là, ta porte est ouverte.*'

He walks into my room as though it's his room and I've no choice but to follow him in.

I stand with my back to the door, put my hands in my pockets, take them out again.

'Well, I'd better get on with it,' I say.

He doesn't bother to ask what I've got to do.

'Surely you've got time for a drink,' he says.

'No thanks. Maybe tomorrow night.'

'Listen, Patrick. I think you've got me the wrong way. Can we call it a truce?'

'What for?'

'I don't want you thinking ill of me.'

98

He holds out his hand and I shake it and I know he notices I've got a lot of sweat on me. He lets go too quickly.

'How about after dinner?' he says. 'Just a few drinks. And when Flindall gets back, we can toast to his success.'

I suppose I'd like to say goodbye to Flindall.

'All right.'

He smiles. 'Come to my room at eight o'clock.'

I go back downstairs and call the pub. There's no answer. I wait in the sitting room and watch some football. Half an hour later, I call again.

A woman answers.

'I've just come on,' she says, 'and I haven't seen a toolkit.'

'I'm sure I left it there last night,' I say.

There's hot panic come up from the pit of my stomach.

'I'll have to check out the back,' she says.

'I'll wait.'

'I can't do it now. I'm busy at the bar. I'll have to wait till somebody else comes on.'

'Could you check now? It's a good kit and—'

'I'm sure it is,' she says, 'but I can't leave the bar now.'

'I'll give you my phone number then.'

'No need,' she says, 'call us back in about an hour.'

I go up to my room and mean only to take a small rest, but fall asleep.

I've slept through dinner. Bridget's going to be cross with me because it's the second time I've not told her, and now I'm starving hungry.

I go down in hope of getting some leftovers, but the food's been cleared.

I go to the phone.

'I'm calling about the toolkit,' I say.

'Oh,' says the woman, 'we've found it. It was left in the toilets.'

'Right, I'll be in to collect it then.'

'I'll keep it out the back.'

'Okay.'

'You might want to keep a closer eye on it in future,' she says.

I hang up.

At eight, I go to Welkin's room, knock on his door.

'Come in!' he shouts.

I go in, but leave the door open behind me.

'Take a seat,' he says, 'and close the door.'

He's sitting on the bed by the left-hand wall.

'Has Flindall come back yet?' I say.

'He's decided to stay in London. He's not coming back.'

'What about his things?'

'Bridget's having it all sent down. His new firm's going to pay for it all. And they've given him a three-bed flat right near Green Park.'

'Right,' I say.

He picks the bottle of whisky up from the floor and pours me a glass.

'Take a seat,' he says.

I don't sit, but take the glass.

He pats the space next to him on the bed.

'I can't stay long,' I say. 'I've got to go out and meet somebody.'

'You don't look like you want to be here at all,' he says.

'Yeah, I do. But I've got to go soon.'

'Maybe we should do this another time then?'

'Maybe.'

'Oh, fuck it,' he says. 'Stay a while, Patrick.'

He sounds like he means it, like he wants my company, and I hate myself for being flattered.

'I'm sorry, but I can't tonight,' I say.

I take a sip of whisky, then hand back the glass.

He's got a glass in each hand now and he holds up both glasses and brings them together.

'Cheers,' he says. 'Bottoms up!'

He downs the whisky from both glasses.

He's smiling, but doesn't look happy.

I've got to admit I'm a lot more relaxed in his company now he's not so cocky.

'All right,' he says. 'Tomorrow night.'

'Sorry about tonight,' I say.

'Never mind. I'm sure I'll find something to do.'

'What about your girlfriend?'

'I'm rather in the mood for some male company tonight,' he says. 'Maybe a game of poker, maybe blackjack. That's the mood I'm in.'

I'm a reasonable poker player and there's a good chance I'd beat the pants off him.

'Okay,' I say. 'Maybe I could come back later. This thing I have to do, it'll only take an hour or so.'

His face lights up.

'All right. It's a date. I'll be here. I'll wait for you.'

A bus pulls away from the nearest stop. I make a run for it and the driver sees me and, even though he's a good fifty yards from the stop, he pulls over.

I get on. 'Thanks,' I say.

But he doesn't even look at me, only takes my coins and gives me the ticket.

He's an old bloke, about sixty, and he's got a tattoo on the back of his neck. Strange how when someone does a kind or good thing you expect them to be chatty and cheerful and not have tattoos.

'Anyway, thanks,' I say.

I sit down the back and can't keep my eyes off the driver. This old woman gets on and she's slow dragging her trolley up the steps and the driver shakes his head at her like he wouldn't mind speeding off and leaving her on the street.

It doesn't make any sense why he stopped for me and I get tight in my chest with the frustration of watching him and not having any idea what makes a man like that tick. I get to thinking the world would be a better place without the likes of him.

I get off outside the train station and go round to the pub.

'What can I get you?' says the barmaid.

She's much nicer to look at than I thought she'd be from the sound of her voice.

'I've come about the toolkit.'

'Oh yeah, you were the one on the phone.'

She yells for a man called Joe and he comes from behind the bar. He's middle-aged and bald, probably her husband. He's got a thick gold wedding ring on just like hers.

'All right?' he says.

They're both from up north.

'I'll get it for you now,' says the barmaid.

While we wait, Joe washes glasses and I peel the paper off a beer mat.

The barmaid brings the kit. She carries it in one hand as though it weighs nothing.

'You're right lucky, you are.'

She laughs and her laughter sounds like coughing.

'I know.'

'It were found in the last cubicle,' she says, 'squeezed between the wall and the cistern.'

I open the kit on the bar and check to see that everything's there.

'Right,' I say.

'You're dead lucky it weren't nicked,' says Joe.

'I know.'

'Are you stopping for a drink?' says the barmaid.

'No, I've got to meet somebody.'

'That's too bad. Maybe another time?'

'He might come back and fix some of the plumbing,' Joe tells her.

He's wearing one of those thin white shirts with silver lines running through it, like my father wears when he goes to work and, just like my father, his nipples show through.

'Maybe,' I say. 'But I'm not a plumber. I'm a mechanic.'

They both laugh.

I go home.

I'm looking forward to a drink and a game of cards with Welkin. I think tonight, when it's just the two of us, and him being in the humbler mood he's in, things might work out, and the chat might be friendly and straightforward.

I go upstairs and knock on his door.

There's no answer, but the door's not locked. I go ahead and open it. He's not in, but the bottle of whisky's on the draining board and it's near empty.

I go back to my room and wait.

About ten minutes later, he comes up the stairs.

I give him a minute to get to his room, then I go back out.

I knock, but he doesn't answer.

I try the handle. It's locked.

I call his name a few times, but he's not answering.

I go downstairs.

There's no sign of Bridget and her office door's locked. I try the kitchen door. It's open and I go in. She's not there.

I help myself to a few slices of thick white crusty bread and a lump of cheese, go to the sitting room and get a newspaper, then take the food and newspaper up to my room.

I get into bed, eat and read, get drowsy right away.

Somebody's knocking on the door.

I check the alarm clock on the headboard.

It's half-midnight.

'Patrick? It's Ian. May I come in?'

I get up, put my shirt and trousers on, open the door, switch on the light.

'Did I wake you?'

He's wearing his dressing-gown and he's got bare feet. He's pretty drunk, not legless, but drunk all the same.

'Yeah.'

'Sorry.'

He comes in, walks right by me and sits on my bed.

I cross the room, open the window and sit at the table.

'How are you?' he says.

'I'm not too bad.'

'I hope you don't mind my barging in like this.'

'No. I don't mind.'

'Nice day today. Even warmer than yesterday.'

'Yeah. It was pretty warm.'

He looks down beside the bed. 'What's that?' he says.

I get up and walk over. 'That's my toolkit.'

'It's huge.'

I'm sure he's seen it before.

'Yeah, it's got everything in it.'

He takes my pillow, sits back, puts it behind his back, makes himself nice and comfortable. I stay standing.

'Do you know a girl called Georgia?'

'I don't think so,' he says.

I go over and lean my back against the sink.

'She works in the café near the chemist.'

'Does she?' he says.

'Yeah.'

'I don't think we've met.'

'Have you been in that café?

'Yes, it's the only one in town.'

'Do you go there a lot?'

'Why don't you sit down,' he says. 'You're making me nervous.'

'I'm happy like this.'

He turns round and plumps the pillow.

'I've got this theory,' he says.

'Yeah?'

'I think every man is mistaken about the kind of man he really is.'

I say nothing.

'We never know how we seem to other men,' he says. 'I think it's time you and I did something about it. You tell me what kind of man I am, and I'll tell you what kind of man you are.'

'Right,' I say.

'I'm ready to hear it,' he says. 'I think the time's come for me to hear the truth about the kind of man I really am.'

I say nothing.

'What do you think of me, Patrick? I want you to tell me what kind of man I am.'

'Not now,' I say.

'Speak, Patrick.'

He lays himself down, sideways, his big hand on his face, supporting his big blond head, his dirty big feet on my sheets.

'Tell me,' he says.

I say nothing and go back over to the table, sit down.

'Come on,' he says. 'Tell me something true, then it'll be my turn.'

'I don't know what I think of you,' I say.

'Come on, man. Something. Anything.'

Funny thing is, I'm in the mood to say more. Maybe because he's drunk, it's as good as me being a bit drunk and I'd rather have him on my side than not, and it looks like that's what he wants too.

'I think you want everybody to like you,' I say, 'but you treat people like you own them.'

'More,' he says. 'More.'

'You're a bit of a pain in the neck,' I go on, 'but I wouldn't mind a bit of your confidence.'

'This is good,' he says. 'It's just what I need. Go on.'

I didn't plan to say this much and it's given me a sweat but I don't mind that I've said it because I've said some of the truth and now it's out and I see Welkin's face, all happy with approval, and my chest floods. Even though he's woken me in the middle of sleep, I've got a pretty good feeling right now.

I stand up from the table and go to the sink, lean my back against the draining-board.

Welkin puts his legs over the side of the bed, like he's ready to stand, but doesn't.

'That's the thing about you,' he says, 'you see through me.'

I nod as though I've thought the same thought.

'And I've never met anybody like you,' he says. 'There's nothing false about you. I don't think you know how to hide anything. And I think you're much smarter than you let on.'

My hands are on my hips. I change them to my pockets.

'The truth suits you,' he says. 'I like you even more now.'

He stands up from the bed, takes two steps forward.

He's standing too close.

'I like you,' he says again.

'That's good,' I say.

I move away.

'I didn't much like you at first,' he says, 'but now I think I'm getting the hang of Mr Oxtoby.'

'Well, that's good,' I say.

'Let's have a nightcap,' he says. 'I've still got a bit left in that whisky bottle. I'll go and get it.'

He goes to the door, but turns round.

'Don't go anywhere,' he says. 'I'll be right back.'

'I think we should call it a night,' I say.

He comes back, sits down on the bed again.

'So soon?' he says. 'Why not just one quick nightcap? I'm in a jolly fine mood tonight. How about a game of poker? I could go all the way. I could go till sunrise.'

'I've got to be up early for work,' I say, 'and I've got some things that need taking care of.'

He gets up off the bed and comes to me, stands close and leans his left hand against the sink and I'm leaning with my right hand and I expect the sink and cupboard to slide right through the wall, the whole room to crash down around us.

'Are you sure?'

'Yeah,' I say.

'You want me to go.'

'Yeah. I think so.'

'You think so?' He laughs. 'Well, that might be a bit ambiguous.'

'It's not. I want to go to sleep.'

He smiles. 'Okay, then. Goodnight, Patrick.'

'Okay. Goodnight.'

He goes to the door, but doesn't open it. He turns round, faces me.

'Are you sure you want me to go?'

'Yeah.'

He looks at the bed. 'You want to sleep?'

'Yeah.'

'Goodnight, then.'

'Goodnight.'

He leaves.

I lock the door and get under the bed-covers.

I I

I wake at 6 a.m. and go to the bathroom for a wash then put on a clean shirt and trousers and stuff my overalls in my duffel bag. I write a note for Bridget to tell her I won't be stopping for breakfast and put the note under the kitchen door.

I don't want to talk to Welkin and I've got to see Georgia.

Although I've walked the long way into town, by the sea, I get to the café at half-seven and have time to stop a few doors down to look at myself in the window of the pawn shop. I don't look too bad. I straighten my hair a bit and tuck my shirt in.

I'm the first customer and Georgia hasn't yet turned on the lights, not even put her apron on.

She looks lovely. Her face is clean, no make-up, and she's wearing a pretty summer frock, pink with yellow flowers.

'You're early,' she says.

'I like walking by the sea in the early morning.'

'Me too. Sometimes when I can't sleep I get up and just go for a walk along the promenade.'

'Isn't that a bit dangerous?'

'Because I'm a woman? No. Not here. I feel completely safe here.'

'That's good.'

She smiles and I sit in a booth facing the door.

'You've always got to face the door,' she says.

I laugh. 'Yeah. That's right.'

'My dad said there's a certain personality who has to do that.'

Her lips are big and red. She doesn't need make-up.

'Yeah?'

'Either a nervous person,' she says, 'or a domineering one that has to be in control all the time.'

'Neither of them sounds too good.'

She smiles. I wish she'd sit with me a minute.

'Breakfast will be about twenty minutes. Okay?'

'I'm happy with that. I'll read the paper.'

She goes to the door to get the papers that've been left out on the street.

I stand. 'No,' I say. 'I'll get them.'

She goes to the kitchen and I watch her walk and imagine we're lovers, that we've spent the night under covers together, that we've just woken and she's to cook my breakfast before I go to work. I imagine that I own my own garage and in a few weeks we're going on holiday to Spain and we're going to stay in a five-star hotel where we can have room service in the middle of the night and drink champagne in a big hot bath.

Once she's in the kitchen, and busy with the frying, I find a knife in a drawer near the till and get the bundle of newspapers from the street and cut them out of the plastic wrapping.

The headline says there's been a triple murder around the corner from my mother's house.

A man's killed his wife and two small kids and poured Mr Muscle down their throats.

I can't get my head round what order he would have done it in. Did he knife them, then pour the drain-unblocker down, or the other way round? And did he have to kill the mother first, or was it the mother having to watch him kill the kids first?

I can't turn the pages to get to the sports section, can't quit reading the story of the murder. I've read it a half-dozen times when Georgia comes back with my sausages and eggs.

'Here you are,' she says. 'The usual.'

I hold up the paper's headline for her to see.

Children Tortured in Brutal Triple Murder

'This happened round the corner from my childhood home.'

I've not meant to say childhood home, makes it sound like I'm a bit sentimental about it.

'Really?'

'Just around the corner from the house where I grew up.'

She sits down next to me in the booth and we both face the door.

She reads the article.

'This happened near your family home?'

'Right round the corner.'

'Do you think you might know the people?'

I shouldn't have shown her the paper. I want to talk about our drive and picnic. I've gone and botched it good and proper.

'I'm not sure,' I say. 'There are no names.'

'But the description? Do you think you might know them?'

'My brother Russell might, or my mum.'

She reads the article again.

'It's a terrible thing,' I say. 'Why would he stick Mr Muscle down their throats?'

'You should call your mum,' she says. 'You can use the phone out the back.'

I don't see the point. I can't change anything that's happened. I can't do any good.

'All right,' I say. 'Thanks.'

Georgia leads me out the back to a utility room that's full of mops and buckets, a stepladder, a small table, a locker, and a school desk piled with papers.

'Do I need a coin for this?'

I point to the old-fashioned black pay-phone on the wall.

'No, just dial.'

Georgia leaves.

I call and there's no answer. The sound of the ringing gets my heart racing.

I'm ready to hang up, but my father answers. He's always got to let the phone ring at least four times before he'll pick it up. Just like how he refuses to be a passenger in a car, always has to drive.

'Hello? Jim Oxtoby speaking.'

'Hello, Dad. It's me.'

'Hello.'

I turn to face the wall.

'How is everybody?'

'We're fine, son. How are you getting on?'

'I'm fine.'

He says nothing more. He's bad on the phone, always has been, but he's not even asked me about my new digs, my job, the cars I've worked on.

'So everything's okay, then?' I say.

'Grand. Everything's grand.'

'Can you put Mum on?' I say.

He doesn't bother to say goodbye, just puts the phone down.

He's come back. 'She's not here.'

'Right.'

'By all accounts you weren't exactly hospitable to her.'

My throat's got thick and I'm short of breath, but I've got to talk about what I said we'd talk about. Georgia might be listening.

'Isn't that murder round the corner a dreadful thing?' I say.

'What's that murder got to do with the price of fish and chips?'

'Is Mum all right over it?'

'You mean the murder?'

'Yeah. Who were they? The woman and kids killed?'

He takes a big deep breath, and I know he does it to stop his temper flaring, same as I do.

He speaks slowly. 'It were a young couple just moved up from Essex.'

'So nobody knows them?'

'I'm sure *somebody* does. But not us.'

'When will Mum be back?'

'I don't know, son. If I knew that, I'd have told you.'

It's like he hates my guts and I've got the pain in my shoulders and my neck as bad as I've ever had it.

'Right,' I say.

I want to talk to my mum. I want to tell her I'm sorry.

'I need to hang up now,' he says. 'I've got to see a man about a dog.'

He hangs up, might as well have kicked me in the head.

'Bye then, Dad.'

I put the phone down. Georgia's come back and she stands in the doorway.

She comes to me, puts her hand on my arm.

'Patrick, you're sweating.'

She points to the front of my T-shirt.

'Oh.'

'Is everybody okay?'

'Yeah. The dead people were strangers. They'd just moved from Essex.'

'Do you want to sit down?'

We go back out to the café, to where we were sitting before. She gets me a glass of water and I drink it down fast.

'Do you want another?'

'No.'

She sits next to me.

There are no customers.

'I'll reheat your food in a minute,' she says.

'I'm not hungry.'

I turn round to face her.

'Thanks for letting me use the phone.'

'You're welcome,' she says.

We're silent for a moment, both watch the door.

'I was wondering about that drive,' I say.

'Oh?'

'Do you still want to go?'

She moves the menu across the table.

'Okay,' she says. 'But I'll have to ask Michelle.'

'Good,' I say. 'I was hoping you'd say yes.'

I reach for her hand and hold it.

She takes her hand away, puts it in her apron pocket.

I've moved too quickly.

'Sorry,' I say.

She seems too calm, as though nothing's gone on, keeps looking straight at me.

I turn the menu round.

'You're about twenty,' she says.

'Twenty-four.' I add an extra year.

'I'm almost ten years older.'

'So?'

'I think it's better not to start anything.'

'Why?'

'Patrick, I'm too old for you.'

The way she says my name, it's like she's talking to a stranger, a different Patrick. When I found Sarah's letter under my bedroom door it was the same. *'Dear Patrick, I'm sorry, but I've got to end it...'* I thought the letter must have been meant for a different Patrick.

I stare ahead.

'I just don't want to start anything,' she says.

'I should go.'

'You can stay,' she says. 'You can stay if you want.'

As soon as she's said I can stay, she gets up from the booth as though to tell me to leave.

'I think I'll go,' I say.

We're standing close.

'I like you,' I say. 'That's all.'

'And I like you.'

'Then why not?'

A customer's come in. A woman and her small kid, hard to say whether the kid's a boy or a girl.

I get my toolkit and head for the door.

Georgia calls after me.

'Wait!'

I turn round.

'Come back tomorrow. Come early again. We can talk.'

'Okay,' I say.

'Good.'

I go out the door, then come back.

She's still standing by the booth.

'What about tomorrow night? What about we meet for a drink?'

She's flushed in the face and neck.

'What about lunch?' she says.

I smile. It's Friday tomorrow. I can work in the morning and leave at lunchtime.

'That's good,' I say. 'That's really good.'

'All right,' she says. 'I'll see you at midday?'

After all that, I've got a date with Georgia tomorrow and only one day to wait. I've got so light on my feet, it's like I'm flying.

Hayes is bent over, searching through the big black bin in the corner of his office.

'Sleep in?' he says.

'Sorry.'

'No matter.'

'I'm usually an early bird,' I say.

'Why don't you make yourself a cuppa?' he says. 'You look dead on your feet.'

'I'd rather get on with work,' I say.

'There's some work to be done on a Morris Mini and there's a Mercedes SL that's just come in.'

'What's wrong with it?'

'I don't know. You tell me.'

It's my lucky day and, if all goes to plan, I'll be taking Georgia out for a picnic in a Mercedes SL convertible.

I get started. The Morris is an easy job, some water in the distributor and with the Mercedes, a really beautiful car the owner's kept in great nick, the battery's not charging, so it's probably something like the regulator.

I get it all done in two hours. All I've got to do is tell a small lie about the Mercedes needing a bit more work and I can take it out tomorrow.

I go to the tea room and wash my hands with the cake of dirty yellow soap. I look in the small mirror above the sink and imagine it's Georgia looking at me. She doesn't think I look dead on my feet.

She thinks I look all right.

I go out to the garage.

There's somebody working under a car.

I go back into Hayes' office.

'Who's that?' I say. 'Is that Ben?'

'Yeah.'

'So he's started?'

There isn't enough work for three men. I could do it all alone. We don't need an apprentice.

'Yeah. You can say hello and all that when we have our tea-break.'

'Right.'

I get to work and finish everything that needs doing and I think I've proven the point that we don't need another man. When Ben comes back tomorrow, he'll see he's not needed.

Hayes comes to get me and the three of us sit in the tea room.

'This is Ben,' says Hayes.

Ben's the pimply lad who was with Mark, the lad I beat at pool down at the station pub.

'We've already met,' says Ben. 'This guy beat the pants off Mark playing pool the other night.'

'So, you're a shark on the pool table?' says Hayes.

'I'm better at snooker.'

'We should all have a game some time,' says Hayes.

'Can you teach me to play snooker?' says Ben.

'Sure,' I say.

'There's a place in St Anne's,' he says. 'We could go there during lunch one day.'

'The three of us,' says Hayes. 'I fancy some snooker. Haven't played in years.'

We drink our tea and chat about snooker. They ask me about the rules and such, and I answer all their questions and they're pretty impressed.

'Well,' says Hayes. 'Why don't we all call it a day?'

'I'm happy to keep on with the work,' I say.

'No need.'

I get my toolkit from the garage floor and leave.

But I don't go home right away.

I go to the corner and stand outside the post office and wait for Ben to leave.

But Ben doesn't leave. He stays back there with his uncle.

I walk home by the sea and the sky's full of low, dark clouds and the air's got a kick of that stormy chemical smell and I breathe it in gulps and walk with my hands spread out like a tightrope walker, my eyes shut. I want to get a good mood going so, when I get to the house, I'll have calmer nerves. I've got to be ready for the chat with Welkin.

I go straight up the stairs, but stop on the first-floor landing. Welkin's standing outside his room with a girl. Maybe it wasn't Georgia he was describing the other day.

'Welcome to the red zone,' he says.

She laughs. 'You're crazy.'

Welkin sees me.

'Hello, Par-trick,' he says.

'All right?' I say.

'Yes, I'm fine. And this is Isabelle. She's even finer.'

Isabelle slaps Welkin on the arm.

'Hello,' I say.

She steps forward to shake my hand.

'I'm pleased to meet you,' she says, her voice even posher than Welkin's.

'I've got to go,' I say.

'Where?' says Welkin.

'To my room.'

I put my toolkit under the bed and sit a minute with the pillow behind my head and close my eyes.

Welkin goes into his room with the girl and it's not long before they get started. I'll not stay in here and listen to the sound of them rutting.

I turn to check the time and see that my alarm clock's gone. I'm sure it was on my bedhead this morning, but it's not there now. I search under the bed, beside the bed, under a pile of clothes, in the cupboard. I search everywhere, but it's gone.

I go downstairs and knock on the kitchen door.

'Come in,' says Bridget.

She's cutting a loaf of bread at the big wooden table.

'Something's gone missing from my room.'

'What's missing?'

'My alarm clock.'

She laughs. 'Oh, that silly monkey.'

She stops cutting the bread.

'Ian said your alarm was making a terrible racket this morning and waking the whole house.'

'So you gave him the key?'

'He was worried about you.'

'You shouldn't have let him in my room.'

'I'm sorry, Patrick.'

I go to the door, don't mean to leave, don't know what I mean to do. I turn back and look at her a while longer, wait for something more to happen. But I don't know what it is I'm waiting for.

'I really am sorry, Patrick. Will you accept my apology?'

'Yeah,' I say. 'But it's him who should apologise.'

I keep watching her. She starts cutting the bread again, moves the knife back and forth across the bread but the knife doesn't cut through.

The knife's got more like the bread, the bread more like the knife.

'I can't concentrate,' she says.

'Fuck this,' I say.

I leave the kitchen, but stop outside in the hallway.

A moment later, she comes.

We stand together.

'You're right,' she says. 'I shouldn't have given him the key.'

She puts her hand on my arm, looks into my eyes. I'm shaking and hope she can't feel it.

'Okay,' I say. 'That's okay.'

She smiles. 'I'm glad.'

12

I go down early for breakfast. Bridget's set out croissants, sliced meats, two boiled eggs, a half a baguette, toast and jam.

She's also left today's newspaper and a note.

Good morning Patrick,

    I'm at the shed this morning. I hope you enjoy your breakfast. It's just like the one you get in a Paris hotel. If you want coffee, help yourself. It's all set up in the kitchen.

    Welkin won't be down this morning. He's gone to St Anne's for the day.

    Best wishes, Bridget.

I eat alone and make myself right at home. I feel like royalty with the dining room all to myself. I can breathe easier and eating's easier, too. I wish I had the place to myself every day. It would be just me and Bridget.

I get to work early, in a good frame of mind. At about half-eleven, I'll take the Mercedes out and pop down to the bakery and get a picnic for me and Georgia, some nice sandwiches and a few cakes, and pick her up at noon.

Hayes is sitting at his desk.

'You're early today.'

'Sorry I was late yesterday,' I say.

'There's another Fiat that needs looking at. Check the clutch and the pedal lash.'

He winks at me, says, 'And if you find anything else wrong, fix that too.'

But I won't do work that doesn't need doing. I'll only fix what honestly needs to be fixed.

I get to work and finish fast.

At eleven o'clock, I hear somebody out front.

I stop work and go outside.

Ben's hand-washing a car. He's wasting time with a bucket of soapy water, probably leaving scratches on the paintwork with that dirty old rag.

'All right?' I say.

'Yeah, and you?'

'Yeah. All right.'

I go back in.

I've nothing left to do, but I'll not stand idle.

I sweep the garage floor then go to the tea room, rinse the kettle and cups, wipe the biscuit crumbs from the draining-board.

I go to Hayes' office to ask if I can take a bit longer for lunch.

He gets out from behind his desk, and comes and stands next to me in the doorway.

'Why don't you go home,' he says. 'There's nothing left for you to do today. We have it all under control.'

He's talking about Ben.

'I don't think we really need anybody else,' I say.

He leans his hand against the doorframe, his arm a bar across the entrance. It's the kind of thing a man does when he wants you to know he's in charge.

'What do you mean?' he says.

I put my hands in my pockets.

'Your nephew,' I say. 'There's probably not enough work for him.'

'I think that's up to me to decide.'

He moves his hand lower down the door frame.

'Listen, you've still got a job and so has he. I've just got to keep all my commitments.'

I've nothing to say.

'And I'm paying you good money, better than you were getting before.'

'Yeah, that's true, but—'

He drops his arm, looks at his watch. 'I've got to go now. I'll see you Monday.'

'What about tomorrow?' I say.

'No need. Come in on Monday.'

'Eight-thirty sharp,' I say.

'Right. Or don't bother coming at all.'

I laugh as though what he's said is a joke and go straight out to the tea room.

I give my hands a good scrubbing with soap and hot water and get rid of most of the oil.

The Mercedes is ready to go and the keys are in the ignition. I take my overalls off, throw them in the back seat beside my toolkit, get in, start her up and drive out the back way.

When I stop at the traffic lights I use a bit of spit to get rid of some dirt on my good black slacks and I straighten my shirt collar.

I don't care if he's seen me drive out. Let him. He owes me at least this much. I'll have the car back in a few hours and in perfect condition.

It's a hot day and there are more people out on the street than usual, but I still get a parking space outside the bakery.

I stand behind a pregnant woman who's ordering a birthday cake and it's taking her a long time. She's got red arms from being out in the sun and right next to her, on the wall, there's an insect killer called Exocutor. It's zapping flies while she talks and it's got a blue light inside a metal cage.

To stop my nerves and cool down, I go to the ice-cream fridge and take a good look inside.

When the pregnant woman leaves, I buy two ham and salad sandwiches with extra beetroot and two sponge cakes and two vanilla slices and a big bottle of lemonade. I also get lots of napkins. Women always like to have napkins.

I get in the car, take the top off, put the radio on. I find a station playing jazz. If there's not much chat when she first gets in the car, at least there'll not be silence.

It's ten to twelve, but Georgia's already waiting in the street. She's not outside the café though. She's four doors down, outside the pawn shop, standing in the shade.

I pull up beside her.

'Hello,' she says.

'Hop in,' I say.

But I've not opened the passenger door and, have to lean over to open it for her. I should have got out and done it.

'What a lovely car,' she says.

She's wearing a pink dress with a big V-neck collar and, when she sits down, the skirt rides up.

'You look nice,' I say.

'Do I?'

'Really nice.'

'I thought we could go to the park,' I say. 'It'll only take about ten minutes to get there.'

'I like that park,' she says. 'It's got a big pond.'

As soon as we get off the main street, past the station, the road's empty. I want to put my foot down, open the engine right up, but that might make her nervous. I keep the speed steady and slow and turn the radio up a bit.

'Who owns the car?' she asks.

'I'm not sure. It came in yesterday and I've just finished working on it this morning.'

She's looking at me, smiling. She's been looking at me since she got in.

'What kind of car do you have?' she says.

'I've not got one yet, but I'll soon have a Triumph.'

'A convertible?'

'Yeah.'

The sun's streaming in and she's covered in sun. There's sun all over her legs and her hair's shining.

When we get to the park, I realise I've not got a rug. We've got nothing to sit on. I tell her and she laughs.

'Isn't sitting on the hot grass the best thing about a picnic?'

'Yeah, you're right.'

We find a spot beside the pond, right near where the ducks are. She sits with her legs tucked under her bum and I sit cross-legged. She's taller than me like this, so I move my legs under. It's not long before my knees hurt.

'If it starts raining,' she says, 'how long does it take to get the roof back on a car like this?'

'The lid on the Mercedes is back on in less than a minute,' I say. 'About forty seconds.'

'That's fast. It's like something from James Bond.'

'Do you like those films?'

'I haven't seen *From Russia with Love* yet, but I liked *Dr No*. Have you read the books?'

The chat flows easily and I don't even lie to her and tell her I've read the books. I tell her I hardly ever read and she seems not to mind.

She's put her hand down on the grass so the ants can walk over her fingers.

'You like ants,' I say.

'Yeah. They tickle.'

I get a crumb and put it on her hand and we wait. We watch an ant pick up the crumb and carry it all the way down her thumb, back onto the grass. We both smile and I'm not nervous. I'm as calm as I got to be after me and Sarah had been on two dates and this is only the first. It turns out Georgia hates beetroot but loves cake and she eats half of my vanilla slice as well as her own. I ask her how she stays so thin and she tells me it's because she only sleeps five hours. We talk about insomnia and lots of other things. We talk for about half an hour and there's no awkwardness.

I ask to look at her watch and when I move in closer and have hold of her wrist, I don't let go right away. She doesn't stop me holding her, doesn't stop me from touching her skin, but she doesn't encourage me either, and as soon as I move in a bit closer she takes her hand away and starts tidying up the wrappings, puts all the napkins inside the paper bag.

'I hope you won't be cross with me,' she says, 'but I've got to get back.'

'It's not even been an hour yet.'

'I couldn't get extra time,' she says. 'Michelle's got to leave at one.'

'Why?'

'I didn't ask her.'

'Do you want me to drive you back now?'

'If that's all right.'

She offers to give me money for the picnic and I refuse it.

There's more easy chat on the way back to the café and she looks happy. She goes on smiling at me and she laughs at my jokes and she seems to be having a good time. Maybe she wanted to stay longer like me. Maybe next time she'll let me kiss her.

'Drop me outside the pawn shop,' she says.

I pull over and when I stop the engine she stops smiling. It's as though she's worried I plan to stay here and make a move, but I was only going to get out and open the door for her.

Instead I turn the key in the ignition and the engine starts up.

She opens the door, smiles again.

'I've had a really nice time,' she says. 'I'm sorry I have to rush off.'

'That's okay.'

'Let's have another picnic,' she says. 'When I can get more time off.'

'All right,' I say. 'That'd be good.'

I stay parked by the side of the road and wait for her to turn round and wave at me. She doesn't.

I take the car back to the garage and park it out front, leave the keys in the ignition, honk the horn loud and sharp to let them know it's back, then catch the bus home.

I pay no attention to anything on the bus, couldn't tell you how many people got on or off, what the driver looked like. Nothing.

There are no keys on the hooks. I go up to my room, put my toolkit under the bed, change into a pair of jeans and a T-shirt and lie on the bed for a bit of a rest.

The pipes in the wall are groaning again.

I go down to talk to Bridget about the fact that Welkin's leaving his tap running.

She doesn't answer when I knock. She's on the phone.

I knock again when she's finished, but still she doesn't answer.

I try the door, but it's locked.

I go back up to my room and sit at the table, open the window and look out at the sea.

Bridget's coming up the stairs. I know it's her and not Welkin because she uses the banister and it creaks when she leans on it halfway up.

I rush to straighten the bedclothes and put my shoes on.

She knocks.

I open the door.

'Hello.'

'I forget to tell you,' she says. 'I talked to Ian last night about your alarm clock.'

'Yeah?'

'He said it's about time the three of us had a drink together.'

'Yeah?'

'He'd like to meet in the sitting room tonight. And he wants to apologise and he'd like us to have a drink and he's going to bring some Cuban cigars.'

'Tonight?'

'Yes. What do you think?'

I like the idea of sitting with Bridget, that's for sure, and I wouldn't mind hearing his apology, wouldn't mind knowing what the hell he thinks he's playing at.

'All right,' I say. 'That sounds good to me.'

'Eight o'clock then? In the sitting room?'

'Yeah.'

'Good,' she says. 'That's good.'

She turns and goes.

I eat dinner alone. Bridget's made me a fish pie.

She comes in right after I've eaten the last mouthful.

'How was it?'

'The best fish pie I've ever had.'

'I caught the fish myself,' she says.

I laugh.

'I'm not joking,' she says. 'I went out this morning at five.'

'In your boat?'

'Good grief, no. Mine won't be built for another six months or so.'

'Is yours a fishing boat?'

'It's a sailing boat.'

I nod.

'A twelve-foot, gaff-rigged sloop,' she says.

I don't know what a sloop is.

'That's a small boat?'

'But it's going to be a beauty.'

'Can I see it?'

'In the shed you mean?'

She thinks on it.

'You could come with me after breakfast on Sunday.'

I might have Georgia with me then. I've been thinking I could go to the café tomorrow night and ask her out for a drink. On Sunday morning we might want to stay in my room all cosy under the blankets after I've brought her up her breakfast.

'So, will you come?' says Bridget.

I suppose I could see Georgia on Sunday night. She might prefer that, might prefer it if I wait a while before asking her out again.

'Okay,' I say. 'Thanks.'

She picks up my dirty plate.

'Don't forget to be in the sitting room at eight,' she says.

I have a rest after dinner then wash and change into my best clothes.

At eight, I go to the sitting room.

I'm the first to arrive.

I open the window and sit in the armchair closest to the fireplace.

Bridget comes in.

'Good evening, Patrick.'

'Hello.'

'I like your blue shirt,' she says. 'You look dashing.'

She's wearing a knee-length black dress and high-heeled brown boots with pointy toes.

'Thank you,' I say. 'You look dashing too.'

She smiles. 'Shall I open the brandy now?'

'Good idea,' I say.

She looks at the clock, then goes to the cabinet.

'That dress suits you,' I say.

'Thank you. I bought it last week. It's not too short?'

'It's definitely not too short.'

She gives me a glass of brandy and sits on the settee.

'So,' she says, 'how's your new job?'

'It's first-rate,' I say. 'I've already got some praise from one of our best customers.'

'You must be doing a great job.'

'I don't know about that, but I like it when people comment on my work.'

'Yes,' she says. 'That's always nice.'

She looks at the door.

'Ian said he'd be back from St Anne's by eight.'

'What about you?' I say. 'Do you like your job?'

'Very much,' she says.

'Is there anything else you want to do?'

'What do you mean?'

'I don't know. A different job?'

'I've always liked taking photographs,' she says. 'I did a course a few years ago and I've thought about converting the box-room on the third floor into a dark room.'

'If you did,' I say, 'I could help you out. With the set-up and all that.'

'That'd be nice.'

She smiles at me, but has no more to say.

I do as she does and look at the door.

'What do you take photos of?' I say.

'Oh, the sea usually, and boats. Sometimes the sky. That kind of thing.'

'What about portraits?'

'I'm not sure,' she says. 'I don't think I've got the confidence for that.'

She gets up and pours us each another glass of brandy.

'I'll light the fire,' she says.

I hope Welkin doesn't come.

'Do you think it's silly to light a fire when it isn't cold out?' she says.

'No,' I say. 'I think it's a good idea.'

I watch her pile up old newspapers and sticks and briquettes.

'Do you want me to help?'

'No need.'

She has it done, sits again.

The front door opens and closes and there are slow footsteps going up to the first floor, the sound of somebody moving back and forth across the landing, from bedroom to bathroom, opening and closing doors. We both know it's Welkin, but we don't say it.

'Do you play the piano?' she asks.

'No,' I say, 'but I'm thinking of learning the guitar.'

'Ian plays the piano,' she says. 'Maybe he'll play something for us tonight.'

Welkin's not in the room but he might as well be. We're in the company of his absence.

'I think you should take portraits,' I say.

'I'm not sure.'

'I think you'd be good at it. You make people feel comfortable.'

The booze is warm in my throat and chest and the pains have gone.

'That's a very kind thing to say.'

'I mean it,' I say. 'Not only that, you've got grace. A lot more grace than most people.'

'Grace? What a lovely word. Hardly anybody ever uses it.'

'It's what you make me think. You make me think of it.'

She moves forward and sits on the edge of the settee so she can reach over and put her hand on my knee.

'That's just about the nicest thing anybody's ever said to me, Patrick.'

She keeps her hand on my knee.

'You just proved it,' I say. 'You're full of grace.'

She laughs and I laugh.

I don't want him to come. We're better off without him. If he must come, let it be now while we're laughing.

As soon as she's taken her hand off my knee, and we're silent again, Welkin arrives.

'Ah,' he says. 'Here we all are. And a fire, too.'

He doesn't apologise for being late and sits in the armchair nearer the settee, near to Bridget.

I should've sat there.

'I don't care how mild it is outside,' he says, 'an open fire with a stiff drink is perfection.'

He takes a box of Cuban cigars out of his jacket pocket and puts it on the coffee table.

Bridget reaches over and puts her hand on his knee, just like she did to me.

'But where are my manners?' she says. 'Let me get you a drink.'

She moves quickly and gives the impression that a party's begun, that the room's suddenly crowded with interesting people. She hums a

131

tune as she fetches Welkin's brandy and when she hands it to him she says, 'Cheers!'

He says, 'Yes, cheers,' and reaches into his jacket pocket and takes out my alarm clock.

'Here!' He throws it at me and I catch it.

'Why'd you take it?' I say.

He sprawls back in the armchair, his long legs pointed at Bridget.

He looks at her and not at me.

'Just one of those unconscious things,' he says. 'I was only half-awake.'

'Right,' I say.

'You took a degree in psychology, Patrick,' he says. 'You know how it is.'

'I didn't know you had a degree in psychology,' says Bridget.

'I didn't finish,' I say.

'That's a pity,' she says. 'Maybe you'll go back one day.'

'Anyway,' says Welkin, 'the point is, I shouldn't have taken Patrick's clock and I'm sorry.'

Welkin stands and pours himself another drink but he offers none to us.

He looks at me. 'What do you want to talk about?'

'I'm not fussy,' I say.

'How's the love life?'

'Healthy enough,' I say.

'Oh, yes?' says Bridget.

'Tell us more,' says Welkin.

I'll not tell them about Georgia. I'll only be giving Welkin ideas.

'She's a history teacher.'

'Where does she teach?' says Bridget.

My ears redden.

'I don't know.'

Silence.

'Let's have a cigar,' says Bridget. 'I've been looking forward to this. I haven't had a cigar since my uncle's sixtieth birthday.'

We light our cigars and Welkin stands.

'I'd love a glass of whisky,' he says.

Bridget looks at me. 'Patrick? Would you like a whisky?'

'If you're having one,' I say.

'All right,' she says. 'I'll open one of the bottles I got last Christmas. It's in the kitchen.'

Bridget leaves to get the whisky.

I start coughing up the smoke.

'You know,' says Welkin, 'you're not supposed to inhale cigar smoke. Have you not had one before?'

'No.'

'You should've spoken up sooner instead of sucking away like a baby on a cold tit.'

'Yeah.'

'Never mind,' he says. 'It's a bit tricky the first time.'

'Right.'

He stands and comes to me.

'Do you mind if I give you a bit of advice?'

'No, why would I?'

'All right. Let me show you.'

He takes a puff of his cigar and I look up at him and watch.

'Got it?'

'Course I have.'

'That's right. You've got it now.'

He smiles, a big friendly smile, just as though we're best mates, as though he loves me.

'Yeah,' I say. 'Thanks.'

'Don't mention it.'

Since he's standing and I'm sitting, he's made me feel like an idiot and, at the same time, in spite of everything, I'm glad of his attention.

Bridget comes back with the whisky and pours us each a drink. As soon as she's sitting, Welkin turns his chair round to face her. He's as good as turned his back on me.

'You can't get much more civilised than this,' he says.

My cigar's gone out again and Welkin throws the box of matches at me. I miss. The box lands on the floor.

'I'm delirious and stupid with happiness,' he says. 'I haven't felt so good in a long time.'

He goes to the settee and sits beside Bridget.

'Hello,' he says. 'Thought I'd pop over and offer you a shoulder rub.'

'There's no need,' she says.

'It's on the house,' he says. 'And I'm good at it.'

'Oh, all right,' she says. 'Why not?'

He takes the glass out of Bridget's hand, puts it on the floor. She turns round so her back's to him and he rubs her neck and shoulders, slow and gentle.

'Tell me if it's too hard.'

'No,' she says. 'That's nice.'

'I'm glad,' he says.

He slips his hands under her collar, starts on rubbing her back.

She laughs. 'That's probably enough,' she says. 'I think you're a little bit too merry.'

'I think so too,' I say.

She turns round to face me.

Welkin's got no choice but to stop.

He moves away from her, moves across on the settee.

Bridget clears her throat.

'So, Ian,' she says. 'Do you think you'll go back to work soon? Do you miss it?'

'In a while,' he says. 'I'm happy for now just taking a breath.'

'It's a long bloody breath,' I say.

'Well,' he says. 'I took a degree at Cambridge and got a first and then I worked for three years and I think I've probably earned all the breath I want.'

'No point working yourself to the bone if you don't have to,' says Bridget.

'That's my philosophy precisely,' says Welkin.

He moves in close again, puts his arm over her shoulder.

'Let's toast to the good life,' he says.

I stand.

'She doesn't want you sitting there with your hands all over her,' I say.

'It's okay, Patrick,' she says. 'He's not doing any harm.'

'Do you want him there?' I say.

Welkin kisses her on the cheek and she laughs, but I can see she's nervous. Her chest's going up and down too fast.

'I think you should leave it,' I say.

Welkin moves his arm round Bridget's neck so the tips of his fingers dangle like hungry worms near her breasts.

'Just having a little bit of fun,' he says.

'I know,' she says.

He puts his hand on her leg.

'Leave her alone,' I say.

'Why don't you make me?' he says.

He says this so as it's not clear if he's serious or joking.

I take a step closer.

'Patrick,' says Bridget. 'It's fine.'

'Is it?'

'Ian's going back to his seat now.'

'You're a bloody spoilsport,' says Welkin.

He gets up and goes back to his seat.

When he's sat down, he flicks cigar ash into the ashtray. The ash misses and goes on the carpet. I'll sit, but I'll not stay for too much longer.

135

'Don't worry, Patrick,' says Bridget.

Welkin drags his armchair across so that it's closer to the settee and reaches for Bridget's hand.

'I'm sorry,' he says. 'I got a bit carried away.'

'Never mind,' she says.

She lets him hold her hand and he moves in closer. He's narrowed his eyes. He's about to kiss her and she'll probably let him.

She's not as smart as she lets on.

'Let's play a game of truth,' says Welkin. 'Just you and me.'

Bridget looks at me.

'Can three people play?' she says. 'What about Patrick?'

'It's time I heard the truth,' says Welkin. 'Tell me what you make of me.'

She looks at me, but she's right back in it. He's got her right back in.

'All right,' she says. 'Let's try it.'

'Tell me what kind of man I am,' says Welkin. 'I don't mind if you mention the good with the bad.'

I get up and throw the dead cigar in the fire.

I look at them both, but neither of them looks at me.

I open the door.

'Fuck this,' I say.

13

I go up to my room, open my window, take in a few gulps of clean air, sit a minute, get the cool night breeze on my face.

When I go to the bed, I know I won't sleep, not till they've gone separately to their rooms.

I don't want it, but I get to imagining them having sex. Welkin's hands round Bridget's wrists, her chin crashing against his shoulder, Welkin grunting, Bridget crushed against the settee.

I get up and pace the room and my heart's pounding so hard the blood's beating in my teeth. To calm myself, I wash my face in cold water, drench my hair, wash my hands.

I listen out.

At last, Bridget's bedroom door opens and she goes in. She goes in alone.

Welkin comes up the stairs.

I stand near the wall and listen.

He changes, washes, gets into bed and then he's quiet.

I sit on the bed.

The only sound is of a few drunk lads out in the street, singing, one of them the leader, the other lads following.

I get down to the floor and do twenty push-ups and thirty sit-ups and, from the floor near my bed, I can see my toolkit's been moved, pushed too far back. It's not in the place I always leave it.

I pull it out from under the bed and check the contents and there's no doubt the tools have been tampered with.

Someone's been in here rummaging.

I take everything out to be sure, line the pieces up on the floor: SF and AF spanners, sealing pliers, grease gun and extension bars, the whole lot.

The ball peen hammer's gone.

I go to the desk and sit and think about what I've to do and it doesn't take me long to know.

I've got to go next door and wake him and ask why he's moved my toolbox and taken the hammer. He must've done it when he got back from St Anne's.

I'll not wait till morning to face him at breakfast with Bridget listening in and I'll not sit up the night without sleep and I'll not let him get away with it.

I go out to the hall and knock once on Welkin's door and say his name.

He doesn't answer.

I try the handle and go in.

The curtains are closed and the stuffy air stinks of his drunken skin.

It's too dark for me to see what I need to see.

I go out to the hall, switch on the light and go back in with the door left open behind me.

I look at his big body asleep on its back and listen to the wet gurgling in his fat throat. His right arm hangs down over the side of the mattress and his fingers are near to touching the mouth of the empty whisky bottle.

I stand close by his bed.

'Ian? Wake up. It's Patrick.'

He doesn't stir. He's deep inside a drunk's thick sleep and goes on snoring.

'Ian? It's Patrick. Wake up.'

He sleeps the untroubled sleep he doesn't deserve.

I go back to my room and sit on my bed, but now I've got a bad thirst, the parched hot thirst of a fever. I go to the sink and drink two glasses of water then kneel down beside the emptied toolkit and restack it. When everything's back where it belongs, everything but the ball peen hammer, I take the adjustable wrench and go to his room.

I stand beside his bed and wait.

I don't know why I wait.

I take hold of his shoulder and shake him.

He grunts, turns on his side, seems about to wake. I move back, take a step into the middle of the room. But he doesn't stir again and his heavy breath goes on dragging snot through his nose.

I step forward, lift the wrench in my right hand and bring it down. Only once, a good, certain blow to his temple, not heavy, and the wrench bounces.

I stand back and move the wrench from my right hand to my left, feel the heft of the handle, switch again, move it again.

His body shudders, his legs kick, right leg followed by left, then both legs at once, as though he's struggling to get out from under the weight of the blankets. His eyes are open, staring out, but there's no sign of pain. Two brief convulsions, then nothing.

He's stopped snoring.

I go back to my room, put the wrench in the sink, and close the window so as not to be woken by noise from the street.

I sleep.

I wake with my neck and chest covered in sweat, turn over on my side, look across the room to the window. Night will soon be morning and there's already a murky blue sky.

The pipes in the wall are groaning and I'll bet Welkin's left his taps running.

And then I remember.

I get up, dress, and go next door.

I knock on his door, soft, a few times, and when he doesn't answer I go in, stand next to his bed.

His eyes are open and the room smells of shit and something's changed. He's not moving, but there's something else, something that makes him seem small in the bed.

I hold my finger under his nose. There's no breath. I put my ear to his open mouth. No breath and no sound. I step back. I keep stepping back all the way to the second bed, then I sit.

I'm not sure of anything, of anything at all. I get up, go over to him, check for breath again, go back, sit down, stand again.

I go out to the hall and stand on the landing. My skin's gone cold.

I want more light, want the day to hurry up.

I go downstairs and turn on the lights in the hallway and in the dining room.

Bridget's bedroom door's locked.

I call her name.

My voice is shallow, there's not enough breath.

She doesn't answer.

'Bridget, it's me. It's Patrick. Wake up.'

My hands are numb, a tingling in my fingers, much stronger than pins and needles.

'Bridget, wake up. I need to talk to you.'

She's getting out of her bed now. She comes to the door, opens it.

'Patrick? What's wrong?'

She's in her dressing-gown.

I say nothing, look at her face.

'You're crying,' she says.

'I might have done something,' I say.

'What's the matter?'

'I think something's happened to Ian,' I say.

She reaches for my hand.

'What's wrong, love? What's happened?'

'He's not breathing. I think you should go and see.'

'Is he sick?'

'I don't know,' I say. 'But you've got to go up. He's not breathing. I might've hit him a bit too hard.'

It's sunk in.

'Oh, God,' she says.

'You've got to go to him.'

She goes back into the room for her slippers by the bed.

I go after her and grab hold of her arm, probably too hard.

She looks afraid of me.

'There isn't time,' I say. 'You have to see to him before it's too late.'

He might not be dead.

'You have to go now.'

She goes fast up the stairs and I watch her till she's out of sight then take my key from the hook and leave.

The air's cool, the first frosty morning for a long time. Summer's ended.

When I reach the water's edge, I look out at the horizon and walk in the sand towards the pier. There are two orange lights from fishing boats out at sea and I don't want to be seen by the fishermen if they come in.

I go back to the promenade wall and get a bit warmer under the light from the street lamps, but I've got that thirst again.

I'll go now to the train station.

There's a phone booth by the main entrance and I step inside. I think I'm only going in for some warmth. It's cold with only a shirt on but, once I'm inside, I put the coin in and call.

The phone rings a long time. At last, an answer.

It's my father.

'Hello,' I say. 'It's Patrick.'

'Hello?'

'Dad, I think I've done something stupid.'

'Hello? I can't hear you.'

'Dad, it's Patrick.'

'Hello? Hello?'

'I can hear you,' I say. 'Can you hear me now? Is Mum there? Can you please put her on?'

He's hung up.

I try again.

My mother answers.

'It's five o'clock in the morning,' she says. 'Who is this?'

'Hello, Mum. It's me. It's Patrick.'

'Hello?'

'Mum?' I shout now. 'It's me. I need to talk to you.'

She hangs up.

I don't know if she's heard or not and I've no more coins to put in the phone.

The buffet's closed and the waiting room's open but there's nobody here to help me and the drink machine's out of order. There's a handwritten sign on the front and the word THIS has been crossed out and someone's replaced it with the word TIME. It says: TIME MACHINE IS OUT OF ORDER and I stare at it for a while before I know what it means and I've got a sickness in my gut. I leave the station, go down the main street.

There's nobody out, only the newspaper man in his white van and a street sweeper. All the shops are closed.

I go past the café and look in and see the empty tables and say Georgia's name and I'd give anything for her to come now, to see her standing inside.

I want life to go back where I had it before.

Night's become day and my feet and hands are cold. I've not thought what I'll do. I've got no plan.

I check my wallet and all my pockets for money. I've not got much, twenty-eight quid, enough for a train journey, a night somewhere, maybe enough to clear a hundred miles. I could do a runner, find work in a garage in a far away city or on the continent. I should've packed a bag, should've got my toolkit.

I go fast in the direction of the station and see there's a motel across the road. It's called The Comfort Inn, and there's a yellow sign with plain black letters that say: Budget—TV—Weekly Rates—Daily.

That's where I need to go, just for a day to get my head in order, but I've not even got as far as crossing the road when there's a car pulled up beside me. I didn't even hear its engine, didn't see it coming.

It's the police.

The cop driving is in uniform and the cop on the passenger's side is in plain clothes and he winds his window down. I expect he'll get out to talk to me, but he just brings the window down and speaks to me through the gap.

'Are you Patrick?'

'Yeah.'

There'll be no going back.

Welkin's dead.

'Get in.'

I get in.

The uniform cop starts driving and the plain-clothes copper turns to me.

'I'm Sergeant Middleton,' he says, 'and this is PC Davies.'

Middleton's in his fifties. The copper, Davies, is about the same age as me.

'What's happened?' I ask.

'Were you in the bedroom of Mr Ian Welkin this morning?'

'Yeah,' I say. 'What's happened?'

'He's dead,' says PC Davies.

A heat goes down the front of my body and it's as though I'm standing by a fire, the heat of shock, and it spreads all over my chest and head.

'What's your full name?' asks Middleton.

'Patrick James Oxtoby.'

He writes it down, then asks me for my home address, my father's name, my date of birth.

'What's the date?' he says to Davies.

'August.'

'I know the bloody month. What's the date?'

'Twenty-ninth, sir. It's Saturday the twenty-ninth of August.'

Middleton's so tall his head is near the roof of the car. He makes another note, then says, 'Patrick James Oxtoby. You are being arrested on suspicion of the murder of Ian Gordon Welkin.'

I nod.

'Do you wish to say anything? You are not obliged to say anything unless you wish to do so but whatever you say will be taken down in writing and may be used in evidence.'

I nod again.

'We need to take you back to the house. You need to show us where the weapon is. Can you do that?'

We pull up outside as the paramedics are leaving with the stretcher.

'Just wait in the back,' says Davies.

Bridget stands on the street, looks at the ambulance with her hand up over her nose and mouth, watches the stretcher getting put inside the ambulance.

When the ambulance pulls away, Davies opens the door and lets me out.

As we follow Bridget inside the front door, he doesn't wipe his feet on the mat, but I do.

'In here okay?' he says.

'Yes,' says Bridget.

We go with her into the dining room.

I sit at the table under the bay window.

They all stay standing.

Sergeant Middleton stands against my chair and his gun-belt touches my shoulder.

'Where is it?' he says. 'The weapon?'

'In the sink.'

Davies leaves, goes upstairs.

'Should I get some water? Some tea?' says Bridget.

Bridget's not crying, but her voice shakes.

'No,' says Middleton. 'We'll be finished in a few minutes.'

My mouth's dried up but, now I've had some time to think, I'm not so nervous as I was before and I think they've got to realise there's been a mistake.

He can't be dead because of anything I've done and they'll soon work it out. I'm pretty sure I only hit him once and it wasn't hard enough to kill. I know that much.

There's been a mistake.

Davies comes back with the adjustable wrench in a plastic bag and he's got my toolkit.

'Why are you taking my toolkit?'

'We need to take the lot.'

Fuck.

'I'll just go up to my room and get my clothes, then,' I say.

'You'll not need clothes,' says Davies.

Bridget moves in, stands close to me.

'Can he take a toothbrush?' she says.

Middleton thinks on it.

'Okay,' he says.

Now Bridget has tears rolling down her face and into her mouth.

'What about a change of clothes?' she says.

She's crying hard now and Middleton looks at her like she's doing something wrong.

'No,' he says. 'He can't take any clothes.'

'She can get your things to you later,' says Davies.

'Her name's Bridget,' I say.

And then I remember. I might've left my ball peen hammer at work. I took it out when Hayes' nephew asked to borrow it. I gave it to Ben. He mightn't have returned it.

Davies gets a pair of cuffs from the hook on his belt and takes hold of my arms. He hold my arms out in front of my body, my palms face up, as though I'm about to be given something nice, puts my hands in the cuffs.

Bridget comes back with a toiletries bag.

'The prisoner's ready to go now,' says Middleton.

'We'll be out of your hair,' says Davies. 'And be sure not to touch anything in the deceased's room.'

'But the mess?' says Bridget.

'Leave it,' says Davies.

What mess?

Bridget leaves the room.

There's no goodbye.

We go out.

It's going to be a fine, bright day and I want to be included, want to stand near the water and look out at the horizon and smell the salty air. I want to swim and go and eat down the pier. I want going back.

146

'Get in the car,' says Davies.

I get in the back with him.

A small crowd's gathered and there's an angry old woman, her arms folded tight across her chest, her face lopsided and bitter and, the way she looks at me, as though she'd like to spit, it's like a blow from a fist to the neck.

I've a rush of tears clogging my throat and the old woman speaks to a woman with a pram standing close by but, whatever she's said, it's not meant for me to hear.

Part Two

14

We go through an entrance at the side of the cop station, then at the end of a long corridor through a door with frosted glass that says *Custody Office*.

We go to the counter.

'Just stand here,' says Davies.

The only window is high on the wall, a useless, murky porthole and the walls are covered top to bottom with posters for the missing and the wanted.

'What's happening now?' I say.

'You'll be put in a holding cell.'

'And then?'

'You'll be interviewed. You'll make a statement.'

'And then?'

'You might be charged.'

'Do I get a solicitor?'

'You're entitled to one.'

'And what about a phone call?'

'We'll get to that.'

The desk sergeant comes through a door holding a black mug

with steam coming off.

Davies stands close to me and I'm cautioned and put under arrest, the same as before.

'Patrick James Oxtoby, you are being held in custody on suspicion of murder and anything you say…'

And then it happens again. That same heat all over my chest as though I'm standing in front of a fire. I lean my elbows on the desk, put my head in my cuffed hands, close my eyes.

'You going to be sick?' says Davies.

I shake my head.

The desk sergeant takes a noisy slurp from his mug of tea, says, 'Give me your date of birth, address, and your father's name.'

'I already gave that,' I say.

'Give it again.'

I tell him.

'And your mother's maiden name?'

I've gone into Welkin's bedroom and I've hit him on the head. It was dark out, but getting light. He was on his side, facing away from me. I hit him on the right temple, not very hard. I hit him all right, but there was no blood. But maybe there was blood, and that's why the wrench was put in the sink.

'Your mother's maiden name?'

'Collins.'

Wait a minute. I'm not sure. Maybe Welkin wasn't facing away. If he was facing me, I must've hit him on the left temple. If there was blood, it came after. I don't know how long it all took. I don't know what the order was. I drank some water and then I think I slept.

'We can make that phone call now,' says Davies.

I give him my mum's number but, when I see it written on the page, I can't do it. I can't face it.

'I've changed my mind,' I say.

I give him the name of the café, and the desk sergeant looks it up.

'Can I have the cuffs taken off?'

'No.'

Davies dials the number, hands me the phone.

She takes a long time to answer.

'Georgia,' I say. 'It's me, Patrick.'

'Hello there.'

'Listen, I've gone and done something a bit stupid.'

'What's wrong?'

'I hit a man in the boarding house last night and he's dead. I've been arrested. I'm at the police station.'

'I don't understand.'

'I haven't much time,' I say. 'I just wanted to tell you I've been arrested.'

'You killed somebody?'

'No,' I say. 'I didn't kill him. I didn't mean to kill him, but he's dead. I only hit him once.'

'Was it an accident?'

'It's hard to explain,' I say. 'I just wanted to say I'm sorry I won't be able to see you for a while.'

'I don't understand.'

'I just wanted to tell you.'

'Do you have somebody to bail you out?'

'No.'

'Is that why you've called? Do you need somebody to come and get you?'

'No, that's okay.'

'Are you sure?'

'Yeah.'

'Have you spoken to your mum?'

I've got an idea.

'If I give you the number, could you call her for me?'

She waits, thinking. 'I'm not sure.'

'They won't give me another phone call.'

'Okay, I'll call your mum for you. If that's what you want.'

I give her the number. 'Will you tell my mum I'm really sorry.'

Another pause.

'It'd be better if you said that.'

'All right,' I say.

'You'll be okay,' she says. 'Don't worry. It'll all get worked out.'

If I say much more, I'll be sure to choke up and I'm glad Davies has stepped forward to signal that my time's up.

'I've got to go,' I say.

'Okay. Goodbye, Patrick.'

'Goodbye.'

I should've used her name like she's used mine. It was nice to hear it said.

Davies takes me back to the custody office and the desk sergeant's got the inkpad ready for my fingerprints. When I've pressed my fingers onto the print sheet, rolled them back and forth, the desk sergeant steps out from behind the desk and puts my cuffs back on.

There's a chair in the corner and I mean to go to it and sit, but I don't make it. There's no warning when it happens and it happens fast and it doubles me over. The sick that's come out of me is liquid, a bitter water, and there's lots of it.

'Get a bucket,' says Davies.

The desk sergeant comes with a bucket, says, 'Put your head over this.'

I go to the chair and sit and put my head over the bucket.

The desk sergeant gives me some water in a paper triangle and the paper goes soft in my hand.

Davies takes me back out to the corridor, holds me by the elbow.

'We'll set up an interview room soon as we can,' he says.

'What about some more water?'

'In a minute,' he says.

There are two empty cells, one a bit bigger than the other. In the smaller one there's a sluice in the middle of the floor and a rubber mattress sits on a low bench.

I won't go in.

'You're in the big cell,' says Davies. 'We've got a drunk 'n' disorderly coming in. I don't want you sharing with him.'

I don't go in.

'Pop yourself on the bed,' he says. 'Might as well take a rest.'

'I only hit him once,' I say, 'and there was no blood.'

'Best to wait for your brief,' he says. 'Get in and hop on the bed.'

But this is no bed. It's only a blue rubber mat about two inches thick and it sits on a bench that's bolted to the wall. Over the bench there's a window, six bars in, six out, and there's a crack in the glass letting the cold air in. In the corner of the cell, there's a squat three-legged wooden stool and a toilet.

'Give me your belt,' says Davies.

I take my belt off, give it to him.

'Now get in,' he says.

'I don't belong in here,' I say.

'Get in.'

I go in, get on the bench, sit with my back against the brick wall.

Davies takes the stool into the middle of the cell.

'Are you staying?'

'Yeah.'

'Why?'

'It's routine for an officer to stay with murder suspects.'

'I'm not a murderer.'

'It's routine.'

'Can I have these cuffs off?'

'Not yet.'

The rubber mat looks like a PE mat, but it's not soft and it stinks of rotten meat.

I hang my legs over the side.

'You can smoke if you want,' he says.

'I don't smoke.'

'There's a packet in my pocket, in case you change your mind.'

Davies flips through the pages of his pocket book and then looks over at me as though he's sure I'm about to do something interesting.

I get up, pull the bucket in nearer the bench, put my hands to my throat and breathe deep to stop myself being sick.

'You going to spew again?'

I say nothing.

He sits with me for an hour, maybe more.

The desk sergeant comes to the cell door, speaks through the opened hatch.

'The brief's gonna get here as soon as he can.'

'Okay,' says Davies.

The desk sergeant leaves.

'I'll get you something to eat in a minute,' says Davies.

'I'm not hungry.'

'I'll see if I can get something.'

Davies leaves the cell, slides the bolt across, locks me in.

I want him back.

So long as he's here, I'm not a prisoner, not yet jailed.

I go to the cell door, try to slide the hatch open.

It'll not budge. There's no hope of it opening.

I go back to the bench and stand on it, look out the window. There's a wall about four feet away and overhead there's a wire grille with cigarette packets stuffed into the holes.

When they let me out, I'm going for a long walk and I won't look at the ground in front of me. I'll pay more attention.

156

Almost a half-hour later, Davies comes back with a sandwich on a paper plate.

I smile when I see him.

I want to talk and I want him to stay. So long as he doesn't go away, there's still hope I might get out of here before dark.

'Here,' he says. 'Try and eat.'

I peel the bread back and look at the thick butter and slice of cheese.

'You don't want it?'

'No, but thanks.'

'Give it here.'

Davies eats the sandwich.

'What happens now?'

'We wait for your brief.'

I want him to know.

I want him to know there was no blood.

'I only hit him once,' I say. 'It wasn't hard and I didn't mean to kill him.'

'You'd better save it,' he says. 'You're being held for murder. You should probably keep your trap shut for now.'

It shouldn't take only a second to end a life.

'I'm not a murderer,' I say.

'That's not for me to decide.'

I wrap my arms round my knees.

'Are you cold?'

'Yeah.'

'I'll see if I can get a blanket.'

He goes out for the blanket, locks me in.

He comes back.

'Sorry, we don't have any spare blankets. I'll get you one later.'

I take a tissue out of my pocket.

He looks away, waits a bit, looks back. 'Okay?' he says.

He takes off his jacket and hands it over.

'Thanks.'

I put the jacket over my shoulders.

'I'll need it back,' he says. 'Soon as I can get you a blanket.'

I look down at the concrete floor and wipe my eyes and it probably looks to Davies like I've got a case of remorse. But I don't know about that, or guilt either. All I know is, I didn't mean to kill him.

It's three or four o'clock when the desk sergeant comes. He's got my solicitor. Davies leaves the cell.

My solicitor's about fifty and he's got curly black hair.

'We've got about ten minutes,' he says.

'I think I need help,' I say.

'That's what I'm here for.'

He sits next to me on the bench and opens a red notebook.

'My name's Keith Pearl. I've been appointed by the court. I'll be taking you through your statement and I'll sit with you when we go into the interview room. But you might not see me again.'

A jackhammer starts up outside.

'That's bad timing,' he says.

'Yeah,' I say. 'It was dead quiet before.'

'You'll have to speak up nice and clearly.'

'Okay.'

He tells me that Ian Gordon Welkin was found deceased in the room next to mine and that I woke the landlady by knocking on her door and informed her that I'd 'hit him too hard' and that I subsequently went for a walk but didn't resist arrest when I was found by the police about a half-hour later.

'I didn't hit him hard enough to kill him,' I say. 'And I didn't mean to kill him.'

'What did you intend then?'

'I don't know.'

He moves his red notebook from one hand to the other. 'But were you angry?'

'No.'

I pull Davies' jacket tighter round my neck for some warmth.

'Why did you hit him?'

'I didn't mean to kill him.'

He crosses his legs. 'All right, you'd better tell me what happened. Tell me about all the important details leading up to the event. Your actions, state of mind, who said what to whom.'

'What I tell you doesn't get told to the police, right?'

'Yes. What you tell me is privileged and you only tell me what you want me to know. Is that clear? I need to know the story as you want it told in your statement.'

'I could lie if I wanted?'

He crosses his legs again. 'I didn't say that. And I wouldn't advise that. I'm not advising that.'

I tell him the story, that Welkin got very drunk, that I went in to wake him and, when he wouldn't wake, I hit him on the temple.

'I can't remember now if it was his right or left temple but I know for sure there was no blood.'

'Didn't the victim steal something of yours?'

'Who told you that?'

He opens his notebook. 'The landlady, Mrs Bowman, made a statement to the police.'

'He took my clock but then he gave it back. I didn't want to get revenge or anything like that, if that's what you mean.'

I won't mention the ball peen hammer.

'What was the cause of death?' I say.

'We don't have a coroner's report yet,' he says, 'that'll take a few weeks.'

'Is that all you can tell me?'

The jackhammer fires up, and he raises his voice, moves his face in

159

close to mine and I can feel the heat of his breath.

'The preliminary report suggests that the cause of death was internal haemorrhaging caused by blunt impact. It appears that the time of death was about 4 a.m. That's all I can say at this stage.'

The jackhammer stops.

'I didn't hit him very hard,' I say.

He makes a note, then puts his notebook in his jacket pocket.

'That's what you keep saying,' he says. 'But I need a clearer picture of what you actually intended. I need to know your state of mind.'

'I wanted to wake him up.'

'Can you be a little more specific?'

I held the wrench in my right hand and struck a blow. I know that. Welkin slept, deep and drunk, and maybe I wanted to get at him while he couldn't move or talk or strike back.

I went to my room and he was still sleeping. I don't think I slept. I think I went straight down to Bridget.

I didn't want him dead.

'I'm not sure if I remember,' I say.

'All right. So, you hit him with a wrench, which you'd taken from your toolkit? When did you get the wrench?'

'I don't know.'

'Did you get it an hour before? Two hours before? Try to remember.'

'I told you. I can't remember.'

He crosses and uncrosses his legs. 'Okay. Did you have the wrench when you went into his room?'

'I think I went back out to get it, but I'm not sure.'

He makes another note.

'Why did he die if I only hit him once?' I say.

'Some heads burst open like grapes,' he says.

He smiles, shows me his big white teeth, straight and neat like white bricks.

I look at him but, as soon as we make eye-contact, he looks away.

'Do you want to tell this story in your formal statement, or do you want to exercise your right to silence? Perhaps wait until your memory begins to serve you a little better?'

He looks at his watch.

'Can I do that?'

'Yes.'

'Silence,' I say. 'I think I'll be silent.'

'Then we're agreed.'

He gets up, goes to the cell door, bangs on the hatch, two times with the side of one fist, twice with the other, and not too hard. He's done it a thousand times before and he'll not risk hurting his hands.

He leaves.

15

Somebody out in the station's eating fish and chips and the smell of vinegar's making me hungry.

Davies comes back. 'The interview room's not ready yet. There's going to be a delay.'

'How long?'

'Don't know.'

'But my solicitor's here.'

'He'll wait in the office.'

Davies sits on the stool and flicks through his pocket book and yawns with his mouth closed. His eyes water and his nostrils flare.

'Do you want your jacket back?'

'I suppose you'd better keep it for a while.'

'Could I have some food?'

'After the interview.'

He writes something and then takes his time putting the lid back on his ballpoint pen.

'I'm going to try and sleep now,' I say.

'If that's what you want.'

I lie on my back and look up at the dirty porridge ceiling.

I don't sleep.

There's somebody at the cell door.

Davies gets up, speaks in a whisper through the hatch, turns back to me.

'We're set to go,' he says. 'I've got to cuff you.'

I hold out my hands. 'Okay.'

'And you'd better give me my jacket.'

We go to a small, grey-walled interview room.

My brief's sitting at a small white table opposite two middle-aged men. There are four chairs, no window, and the dark brown carpet's scarred with cigarette burns. It smells like a chicken pen.

I smile at the men, smile like a man about to be interviewed for a job, forget that I'm cuffed, reach out to shake their hands.

'Just sit,' says Davies.

I sit at the table next to my brief.

Davies leaves.

'I'm Detective Inspector McCrossan,' says the man with a thick grey moustache sitting opposite me.

'Hello,' I say.

He pulls his chair in closer to the table and I get a whiff of the ashy stink that's caught in the bush of hairs over his lip.

'And I'm Senior Investigating Officer Watts,' says the other man sat opposite. This one has a thin mouth and small teeth like a row of dirty pebbles.

'You're being held and questioned on suspicion of the murder of Ian Gordon Welkin,' says McCrossan. 'Is that clear to you?'

My arms go cold, a blast of fear up from my gut, all the way to the ends of my fingers.

'I'll take down the exact words as spoken by you,' says McCrossan, 'and I'll only ask you questions which seem necessary to make the statement coherent, intelligible and relevant to the material matters.

I won't prompt you.'

'Okay.'

'When the statement's finished,' he says, 'we'll ask you to read it and then we'll type it up and make three copies.'

'I just want to say—'

My brief puts his hand on my arm, a light touch, like he doesn't want his hand on me, and he says, 'My client will be exercising his right to silence.'

'Is this what you want?' says McCrossan.

'Yeah,' I say.

'If you do decide to make a statement,' says McCrossan, 'you can make any corrections, alterations or additions that you wish. Then you'll be asked to write and sign a certificate.'

My brief takes a sheet of paper from Watts and writes: *Patrick James Oxtoby has elected to exercise his right to silence.*

He dates the page and gives it to me to sign then pushes his chair back as though he means to stand, but doesn't stand, just puts himself further back, away from me, away from the table.

'No, wait,' I say. 'I want to say that I didn't mean to kill him. I just hit him once and not hard.'

My brief sighs. 'It's up to you,' he says. 'It's entirely up to you. Are you sure you want to make a statement?'

'Yeah,' I say. 'I want to tell you what happened. I'm not a killer.'

Watts takes out a new sheet of paper.

'Write your name in the blank space and sign,' he says.

'I PATRICK JAMES OXTOBY wish to make a statement. I want someone to write down what I say. I have been told that I need not say anything unless I wish to do so and that whatever I say may be given in evidence.'

My brief folds his arms across his chest and I tell McCrossan and Watts what I've already told him.

When I stop to take a sip of water, my brief puts his hand on my arm, same as before, like he's afraid if he touches me properly he might get a disease off me.

'Are you satisfied with that?' he asks.

'Yeah,' I say. 'That's all I want to say.'

McCrossan shows me the adjustable wrench. It's wrapped in plastic and it's clean.

'It doesn't even have blood on it,' I say. 'Isn't that some kind of proof I didn't crack his skull open?'

'All we need,' says McCrossan, 'is for you to identify this wrench as belonging to you.'

I lift my cuffed hands to scratch my head, then put them back on the table.

If I say it's mine, is that like admitting to murder? Is it a trick?

I look at my brief.

'If it's yours,' he says, 'go ahead and say so.'

'Yeah, it's mine,' I say.

'What, for the record, am I holding in my hand?' says McCrossan.

'You're holding my adjustable wrench,' I say.

Davies comes in with four mugs of tea and a tin of biscuits on a tray.

The interview stops and we drink tea and eat the stale biscuits. When we're finished, the room's dark and the lights need to be switched on so I can read and sign this document:

I have read the above statement and I have been told that I can correct, alter or add anything I wish. This statement is true. I have made it of my own free will.

'Patrick James Oxtoby,' says McCrossan, 'you are formally charged with the murder of Ian Gordon Welkin.'

'That's it?' I say.

'We're finished,' says Watts. 'Take the prisoner back to his cell.'

My brief puts his business card on the table, stands, goes to the door, opens it and walks straight out. I look at his card. I'd forgotten his name was Keith Pearl.

Davies shakes his head, nice and slow, back and forth. 'He could have at least wished you luck.'

Davies takes me to the cell and uncuffs me.

'So I'm not going to be let out on bail then?' I say.

'We'll be taking you to the magistrate's on Monday morning.'

That's nearly two days away.

I sit on the rubber mat.

'I'll get you something to eat,' he says.

He leaves and comes back with two sandwiches, two shortbread biscuits, and a cup of tea in a polystyrene cup.

'Thanks,' I say. 'I'm starving.'

'You'll get a hot breakfast in the morning.'

'Thanks.'

He leaves.

I want him to stay.

After I've eaten one of the sandwiches, I go to the hatch and look out into the corridor. The wall opposite is covered in pictures of the wanted.

I call out through the wire mesh.

'Can somebody put the heating on?'

There's no reply.

There's a red button on the wall to the left of the door. I press it long and hard.

There's no reply.

I press it again, longer and harder.

There's no reply.

I press it again, keep it held down.

The desk sergeant comes. 'Stand back,' he says.

I stand back and he opens the cell door.

'Here's a blanket.'

He gives me a grey blanket and I take it to the bench. He stands by the cell door and watches.

The blanket's got four big holes in it. Somebody's burnt the holes with cigarettes and then stretched the holes good and proper.

'It takes a bit of getting used to,' he says. 'Best eat all your food. It'll make you feel better.'

'Yeah,' I say.

He leaves and after he's out the door I say, 'Thanks for the blanket.'

There's enough air for breathing but I'm short of breath, with a kind of panic, just the way it happens when you're locked in a cupboard or in a broken-down lift. Same thing, only this isn't for a few minutes and this isn't a joke somebody's played and there's no reversing it.

I want the cell door to open and for Davies to walk in and tell me they've decided to release me.

But nobody comes and the pain in my neck and shoulders is getting worse.

I lie down, try for rest, but there's cold air coming in through the crack in the window and the blanket's too small to cover me.

I stand and do about twenty star-jumps, the kind I've not done since I was in school and then I pace a while, count my steps, five across, seven from the cell door to the back wall, back and forth I walk, fast as I can, but when I lie down again I'm as cold as I was before.

I get up and look through the hatch.

It's dead quiet out there.

I go back to the rubber mat and sit.

But here it is, at last.

There's somebody out there.

At last, somebody's come, there's somebody walking in the corridor and there are keys jangling. A cell door opens.

But it's not mine.

I try to open the hatch, but it's been locked.

I bash my fists on the metal.

'I need another blanket.'

But nobody comes.

'I need another blanket.'

16

I wake in the early morning. It's still dark outside, dark enough for cars to have headlights on, a few people off to work. There's probably a moon in the sky.

When the sun rises, it's pale and cold. A car door slams. A copper talks on a CB radio. A siren starts up. The world's got started.

During the long cold night, when I sank into sleep, it was short and shallow and I saw what I did to Welkin, saw it over and over, and I was in a stupor so close to screaming that I went in the dark and slammed my fist on the cell door.

For a while I believed in magic and imagined that the door had opened and I walked out to the street and to an all-night café where the windows were lit by orange lamps and Georgia came to my table and I ordered steak and chips and then I caught the bus and walked by the sea and Bridget's sailing boat was finished, painted blue and waiting.

Then, as the sky began to fill with light, the birds sang it over and over, sang that I'd done it, sang that the world will go on the same way without me, without Welkin and without me, they sang that the world would go on just the same, that what I'd done made no difference.

I've been awake a good while and the sun's gone behind the clouds, the cell's dark again, and the rubber mat stinks even more of rotten meat. My feet are cold and I wish I'd been wearing thicker socks when they came to get me.

I try pacing to get some warmth and think all the time that I want to be counted back in, to go out there and join in with the sounds of the street, people getting in and out of cars, meeting family and friends, off to work and shops, cafés, cinemas and clubs, schools and houses and pubs, down the clean, carpeted stairs to full English breakfasts in boarding houses.

I had all that and what I didn't have I could've had.

Davies comes and he's got another brown paper bag. I sit up on the bench.

'Good morning,' he says. 'What've you done with the mat?'

'It's over there.'

I point to the corner.

'It stinks,' I say.

He comes right over to me, stands good and close, and he's smiling. He must be here to tell me I'm free to go.

'Are you letting me go now?'

'No. I've brought you a sandwich and a cup of tea.'

'I didn't mean to kill him,' I say. 'At most I'm guilty of assault.'

'Eat this,' he says. 'It's got chicken in it.'

I take the sandwich.

'I've got to stay until you've eaten that,' he says. 'And I've got to see you've had something to drink.'

He takes the stool to sit on.

'Some people can't eat after a murder,' he says. 'Some can't even hold down a cup of water.'

'I'm hungry,' I say. 'But that doesn't prove I'm a murderer.'

Davies comes to my cell early next morning. I haven't slept more than a couple of hours and every time I closed my eyes, I got to thinking about my mother, how she must be worried sick. In one of my dreams I explained what happened and she told me I had to go to work at a petrol station. I went to work at the petrol station and I got no breakfast. Every morning at the petrol station I had to lock up bikes. All I was doing was locking up bikes. Smell of petrol. No breakfast. The smell of petrol and an empty stomach.

'Get ready to leave,' says Davies.

'Where am I going?'

'Magistrate's court. *Habeas corpus.*'

'Can I make another phone call?'

'You've had your phone call.'

He cuffs me and we leave.

Sergeant Middleton drives and Davies sits with me in the back.

'What's going to happen?' I say.

'The magistrate'll decide whether you'll be remanded in custody or released on bail.'

'I've no money for bail.'

'That's not for you to worry about.'

It's a short drive to the court, about five minutes, but everything out there looks better than it ever did. The white of the clouds, bright like snow, the green of the trees lush and thick like paint, a woman's yellow umbrella shines like the sun.

As soon as we arrive outside the courthouse, Davies takes me through a side-entrance and straight down to a holding cell. Darkness again, and dank, ashy air.

Davies asks me to hold out my hands.

'I've got to check your cuffs.'

He checks that the chain's not loosened or broken.

'Okay,' he says, 'here's where I leave you.'

He doesn't say anything else, just nods, turns, walks away.

A copper opens the cell door.

There's no front wall, just a row of thick bars.

'Get in,' he says.

There are six other men in the cell, all of them give me the once-over, then get back to their business. One of them leans against the right-hand wall and he's eating a bar of chocolate. He eats it slowly, a kind of sucking. Another one's sitting, reading a newspaper. Another one's standing in the corner talking to himself, facing the wall, doing two voices.

I go to the back left corner and sit.

A few minutes later, the same copper comes.

'Patrick James Oxtoby,' he says. 'You're up.'

The copper takes me out, up a flight of stairs, into the court-room.

The copper takes me into the wooden dock.

'Stand here,' he says.

My brief sits on the other side of the aisle, turns to face me. He's got grooming oil in his curly black hair.

'We should be up next,' he says.

The magistrate announces my name and my brief goes forward.

I'm standing between two coppers and one of them cuffs me to the rail.

My brief goes to the table at the front and he says I'm pleading not guilty to murder and that he's requesting bail.

He sits.

The charge sheet is read out by a court official who's sitting below the magistrate, and the magistrate makes some notes.

He asks me how I plead.

'I'm not guilty,' I say.

'That's fine, but how do you plead?'

'Not guilty.'

He makes another note and asks for the police statement and witness statements to be handed up.

There's only one statement: Bridget's.

He reads the statement and takes his time.

Before he turns each page, he looks across at me, then back down.

He'll have to set me free on bail and first thing I'll do is call home and explain to my mother what's gone on and I'll call Bridget and Georgia and then I'll get on the next train home.

The magistrate passes the statement back down to the court official.

'I'm denying bail,' he says.

I've got a sick feeling, low and nervous in my gut, but not enough to spew.

He doesn't say why he's denying bail. He says nothing more.

My brief stands and tells the magistrate that I'm not a threat to the community and that this is my first and only criminal offence.

The magistrate ignores him.

'Patrick James Oxtoby,' he says, 'you're to be remanded in custody until a trial date set by the Crown.'

The magistrate asks for the next case to be called forward.

My brief steps up to the dock.

'I'm sorry,' he says. 'I did what I could, but bail's tricky with murder cases.'

He did nothing.

'Yeah,' I say. 'Sure.'

I'm taken by a copper down the steps to the holding cell.

When we reach the cell door, I turn round to the officer.

'This can't be right,' I say.

'Get used to it,' he says. 'You're about to be taken into remand.'

'Where?'

He tells me I'll be transported to a high-security prison to await trial in a crown court. He tells me where.

Both the prison and the court are in my home town.

'Are you sure?' I say. 'Why do I have to go there?'

'It's the nearest high-security prison and it's the nearest Crown court.'

'But we're a hundred miles away.'

'It's the nearest.'

I know the courthouse well, used to pass it on the way to school, a big red-brick building with a big white statue of justice outside. Somebody once spray-painted *fuck me* across her tits and it took only two days for the paint to be cleaned off.

'I'm going to be sick,' I say.

He says nothing, sends me back into the holding cell.

I go straight to the left-hand corner and sit, pull my knees into my chest. The only other prisoner here is the one who was talking to himself earlier.

My family might come to the trial, and they might not, and I don't know which is worse, not to see them, or to see them because they think they've got no choice and because of the pity.

In a situation like this, a man might be better off being an orphan, to not have personal witnesses. Right now there's still a way for me to think none of it's happened, that it might yet be undone, the facts reversed, that I might go back to where I was. But my family being around, seeing me, that'll only go and make it real.

'Fuck you,' says the prisoner.

He's facing the back wall, standing close, staring ahead. He jabs with his finger at the bricks, as though stabbing a shorter man in the chest.

He laughs, stops, turns round to face me.

'You're not insane, are you?'

I say nothing.

'Are you insane or not?'

'No,' I say. 'Probably not.'

'They'll make you pay for that,' he says. 'They'll make you suffer for that.'

He moves to the front of the cell, faces into the corner near the bars, goes on talking to himself.

The officer comes to the cell.

'The van's here,' he says. 'Get out.'

The van is white and as long as a bus, with dark windows. There are already four other prisoners inside.

Two cops cuff me to the bolts fixed to the partition wall.

There are metal seats along both sides and each seat is housed inside a narrow cubicle, fenced on either side by metal partitions. There's no wall at the front of the cubicles. The men opposite can see each other, but it's not possible to see the man sitting next to you.

When the van leaves the courthouse, I turn round so I can look out the window, look at the streets and houses and shops. I pay a lot of attention. It'll be the last time for a long time. Almost all the houses have chimneys. I've never paid any attention to the shape of them before but I see that most of the chimneys have two red-brick stacks poking out of them, like miniature versions of the smokestacks on ships. I see that the most popular colour to paint a door is red.

I don't believe in God, never have, but the few times I've thought of Him, when I was a kid and went to church for Daniel's confirmation in the Catholic church, and once to my cousin Megan's wedding, and I had the idea that He knows who I am and I thought that He probably likes me. And that's what I get to thinking now. As I look out the van's window I make Him promises. If He lets me free, I'll never sin again, and I'll live a proper life. But God's got a quick answer ready. He reminds me that things are never as good as I think they'll be and that I'm always disappointed and that when I've got something in my hands

175

I know how to wreck it or not pay the proper attention to what it is I've been given.

He says, *The best things in the life of Patrick Oxtoby were the things he remembered or the things he still waited for* and I know He's right, but I go on making pacts with Him, promise that, if He helps me now, the toast that turns up in the morning will be as good as the idea of toast in the morning and that I'll never again complain where complaining isn't called for.

We've been travelling for about two hours when we arrive in my home town, the city I grew up in, these streets the same ones I walked down two weeks ago to buy a mechanics magazine, and everybody I see looks like somebody I once knew, everything makes me think of something I want and can't have. The woman handing out pamphlets makes me want to take one and go and do whatever the pamphlet says and, worst of all, Riley's pool and snooker hall, where I once won a Friday night tournament, makes me want to sob. I might never have any of it again.

The van stops outside the Bootle Street police station to collect two more prisoners. They climb in the back, both cuffed. They sit in the two empty cubicles opposite and one of them asks the other for a cigarette, but he has no cigarettes and says, 'You smoked the last outside.' The one who asked for the cigarette bashes the heel of his shoe against the side of the wooden bench and when he stops bashing his shoe he starts tapping the glass of his watch with a match.

The van's stuck in slow traffic and it's got very hot inside, the first time I've been warm since I left the boarding house.

The other prisoners talk about what they've done or haven't done, the length of the stretch they face, how much time they've done before, which are the best prisons, which have the worst food. They say the one we're going to is Cat A. High-security. 'A bad place to do your bird. But a good place to do your nut.'

The windows are blacked and nobody can see me, but the people on the street waiting to cross at the lights, all of them look at the van with faces full of hate.

I close my eyes.

17

Everybody's stopped talking.

The gates open and the van drives into the prison grounds, stops at the edge of the yard.

'This is it,' says the prisoner who asked for the cigarette. 'The secured gates to hell.'

I've got that same feeling, a seasickness, a nausea deep and low in my gut.

This is it.

Four prison guards in grey uniforms open the back of the van, uncuff us, escort us through the yard.

I look at the two tall turrets at the corners of the high stone walls and remember the last time I looked up at those towers.

A summer's day, around the time of the first World Cup I'd got to see on a TV, and I stood with Geoff and Daniel and I asked Daniel if he thought the guards up there had a TV so they could watch the match. He said, yeah, he thought they did.

We're inside now, inside the main door, and there's another set of internal gates. We walk single file down a corridor lit by long fluorescent yellow lights and nobody speaks until we reach a room with a sign on the door that says *Admissions*.

We go in.

A guard steps out from behind a long, high counter.

'Strip off your clothes and put them in this box.'

The other prisoners strip.

I leave my underpants on.

'Let's have your jockeys,' he says.

I've kept the card the brief gave me and have it held tight in my hand.

I stand naked, like the rest of them. One covers his dick with his hand, one chews the flesh inside his mouth, one scratches his hand, the scab on his new tattoo.

Another guard comes through the door behind the desk. He wears a different uniform, green, with two epaulettes on each shoulder.

'Nine kits,' he says.

They give each of us a plastic yellow bag filled with prison-issue clothes and I copy what the others do, get dressed in the baggy green trousers and a long-sleeved green shirt, brown socks, and a pair of black, canvas, slip-on shoes. I'd expected the prison clothes to be tight, too small, suffocating. Instead, I'm dressed relaxed, as though for a holiday.

I stick the card my brief gave me in my shoe and then sign a receipt for my belongings.

We're given two prison-issue blankets with H.M.P. stitched on in large black letters. Both blankets are grey and heavy. We're also given a spoon and fork, each the colour of mud, made of a thick plastic, hard and stiff.

We hand our clothes over to be bagged in more yellow plastic.

'Follow me,' says the guard in the green uniform.

He takes me, only me, through two more sets of gates and we enter a long corridor, lit like the others with yellow fluorescent lights.

I've been singled out, taken away from the other prisoners. This could be good news.

179

We stop between two doors. The sign on one door says Day Ward, the sign on the other says Fit Cell. Maybe this is the room where mistakes are corrected.

'You're in here,' says the guard.

Here's where I'll meet the governor and he'll tell me I'm to be released. My father's petitioned for my bail and I'm going free.

We go into the Day Ward. It's a small room with a low ceiling and no windows. A tall man in a white coat stands up from behind a desk.

'What's your name?'

'Patrick.'

There's a gurney in the corner, a set of scales, two stethoscopes hanging from a coat-rack, an oxygen machine, a pile of kidney dishes, a blood-pressure gadget.

'Last name.'

When he speaks, he bends forward, lowers his head.

'Oxtoby.'

'I'm the nurse.'

The guard stands in the corner and the nurse comes closer to me. 'I'm going to give you an internal examination and I'm going to check you for the clap and then I'm going to take your blood pressure.'

'Okay.'

'Sign this form.'

He's got to know I'm not a murderer.

'What's a fit cell?' I say, like a man on a guided tour.

'For epileptics. Please sign the form.'

I look at the form, but the words swim.

'There's no need to read,' he says. 'It just says what I just said.'

'Okay.'

Why am I not given an injection for my nausea, a sedative? Where's the bed in a dark room, the curtains drawn, the doctor?

I sit and put my head between my knees.

'Stand up,' says the guard.

'I can't,' I say. 'Can I have a sedative or something?'

'Stand up.'

'There's been a mistake.'

'Stand.'

I stand.

'Undress,' says the nurse.

He steps forward.

'But I shouldn't be here,' I say.

'Undress.'

I don't do it.

'Take your clothes off.'

I've got trouble getting my arms free of the sleeves.

'Get a move on,' says the guard.

'Everything off,' says the nurse.

I take it all off.

The nurse takes a pair of surgical gloves from a box and crouches down in front of me, holds my penis, lifts my testicles, drops my testicles, lifts my penis and pulls the foreskin back as far as it'll go without ripping it right off.

'Now turn round and bend over,' he says.

I bend over and hit my head against the facing wall.

'Move back a bit,' he says.

He uses his finger to probe my anus, and when he's done he throws the used glove into a bin at the other side of the room.

The glove lands soft on a pile of other gloves.

'Now sit,' says the nurse.

I sit and my blood pressure's taken. The nurse says it's normal.

'Get on the scales.'

I'm weighed.

'Fine,' says the nurse. 'He can go.'

I dress slow as I can and get to thinking that, if I'm to have any hope of stopping this from going any further, I've got to act now. I've got to stop them, and I've got to speak up so they don't slam me into a cell.

I see there's a phone on the nurse's desk.

'Wait,' I say. 'Can I make a phone call?'

'You'll have to do that later,' says the guard.

'I just want to make one phone call. I've got to tell my family I'm here. They don't know.'

The guard looks at his watch. 'Okay. But it'll have to be quick.'

He asks me for the number, makes a record of my mother's full name, date of birth, and address.

He dials the number, hands me the phone.

My mother answers straight away.

'Mum? It's Patrick.'

'Oh, God,' she says. 'What's happened? Where are you? Are you all right?'

I can hear people talking in the background, sounds like a good crowd, like a party.

'I've done something really stupid,' I say. 'I've been accused of murder.'

'Oh God, Patrick. That girl called us. And then the police. I've been worried sick. Are you all right?'

She puts her hand over the receiver, shouts to the others, tells them it's me.

'Where are you?'

'I'm in prison. The magistrate refused my bail.'

'Why have they accused you?'

'I hit that man in the boarding house. But I didn't mean to kill him.'

'Which one was it? Did he hit you? Was it self-defence?'

'Not exactly.'

'Why did you hit him then? It doesn't sound like you, Patrick. Were you drunk? Did you have a fight?'

'Mum, it's a long story.'

'Oh my dear God, Patrick. What did you do? Did you kill him?'

'No,' I say, quietly, softly. 'I just hit him once.'

Somebody prompts her to ask me something. It sounds like my aunt Mary.

'But that man in the boarding house,' she says, 'he's dead. Is that true? Is it that one who went to Cambridge? The girl who phoned me didn't know who it was and the police wouldn't tell me. They only said the same thing, that you're on suspicion for murder.'

'I'm not a murderer, Mum. There's been a mistake.'

She's started crying and I let her cry.

The guard steps in close so I can see him. He taps his watch, then holds up two fingers.

'What happened?' she asks. 'Did you get in a fight? Were you drunk? Are you all right?'

'It wasn't a fight. I just hit him once.'

'This can't be right.'

'It's true.'

'How did he die?'

I should say I'm sorry, that I'd give my own life to bring Welkin back, but I wouldn't give up my life to bring Welkin back. I want my life more than I've ever wanted it. I want another go.

'I don't know why he died,' I say, 'but he did. And they've locked me up.'

'It makes no sense. Why are you being accused of murder? Do you know why?'

'No,' I say.

She's stops crying and blows her nose. Her tears end just as suddenly as they began.

'I don't understand, Patrick. How could you do this?'

Her voice has changed, it's colder now, calmer.

'I don't know.'

The guard holds his hand up again. One finger. I nod.

'You've destroyed your life. You've thrown everything away.'

183

'That's why I wanted to talk to you, so I could—'

'None of us slept last night or the night before and everybody's been here waiting to hear from you.'

'I didn't mean to kill him,' I say.

'It makes no sense.'

'You already said that.'

'You've ruined everything. You've thrown your life away and you can't even make an apology or own up to what you've done. What a horrible and selfish sacrifice.'

'Mum, listen—'

She sobs again, builds pain with pain, keeps on sobbing without breath or break, and her crying builds momentum like a kind of falling and it can't be stopped and it might even feel good to be falling.

My father takes the phone.

'Patrick,' he says. 'Your mother can't speak to you any more.'

'Yeah, but I was just trying to—'

The guard runs his finger across his neck.

'Just tell me one thing,' says my father. 'Did you hit that man?'

'Yeah.'

He hangs up.

I turn my back to the nurse and the guard. I don't want to have them see my face.

'Let's go,' says the guard.

I lower my head, but I'm not turning round. 'Yeah.'

The guard takes me to the toilet block and showers. The sign on the door says *Recess*.

'You need to undress again,' he says.

He watches me undress, gives me a towel and a toothbrush.

'Best be careful when you brush the back teeth.'

'Why?'

'A lot of men puke first time. Might not know how nervous you are until you stick that toothbrush too far back.'

I stop brushing and turn to the showers, but I can't find any taps.

He goes away and, when he comes back, there's water spurting from every nozzle in the shower stalls. I step under the water and turn my back to him and, in spite of everything, the hot water takes off some of the pain and my breath comes less sharp and less shallow.

'Now dress,' he says.

'I need to use the toilet.'

'Then use it.'

I stand over the urinal but my piss won't come and when it finally comes it hasn't got the same smell it usually has.

I zip up.

'Finished?'

'Yeah.'

He takes me back to the admissions room where he checks which wing I'm meant to go to.

'Get him to the barber on Thursday,' says the guard behind the desk. 'He's got hair like a hippy.'

Another guard waits at the gate at the admissions room exit and I'm handed over to him.

'This is Johnson,' says the guard. 'He's the officer in charge of daytime remand.'

They're officers, not guards.

'Right,' I say.

'He's your boss now.'

Johnson's a huge man, fat and wide, and he's leaning against the gate. He looks at my face, looks a long time, fixes me with his pale green eyes, as though to memorise me.

I look back, hold his gaze.

'Come with me,' he says.

He turns round, opens the gate and I follow him through to the other side. The corridor walls on this side are blue. They were green on the other.

He walks on ahead of me, keeps his left hand on a bunch of keys hanging by a short chain from his trousers. One of his trouser legs is caught in his sock.

'Hurry up,' he says.

We reach another set of gates, go through and walk down another corridor. This corridor is just like all the others, painted blue and lit yellow, and it stinks of cleaning fluid.

I've noticed that, before he opens the gates, he covers the top of the key with his hand.

'Why do you do that?' I say.

'Take a guess.'

'I don't know.'

He stops walking, stands close to me.

'There was a prisoner here once, he saw one of these keys and made a copy in the metal shop. He had a photographic memory.'

'Did he escape?'

'Never seen again.'

He walks on and I follow.

He stops again, turns to me.

'And you can't have chewing gum in here for the same reason,' he says.

'So you can't make copies of keys?'

'That's right.'

Johnson's my boss and I'd better get it right. He needs to know who I am.

'You'd need a lot of chewing gum to do that,' I say. 'And you'd also need a key print and a mortice cutter and a marking punch and—'

'You know something about this kind of thing then? But you're down for murder, aren't you?'

'Yeah, that's right,' I say. 'But I'm not guilty.'

'Another one who's innocent,' he says, and I think I've blown it, but he smiles. I might not have blown it.

We stop.

'Where are all the prisoners?' I say.

'It's lockdown. This is remand. You're in your cell twenty-three hours a day.'

'All day and night?'

'That's right. Except meals in the mess hall. And you're in C Wing. Remand,' he says. 'This part of the prison is E-shaped, with four main blocks, six wings in each block. Twenty-four wings all told. You're on the ground floor, known as the ones and down here there's four wings dedicated for remand. Upstairs, that's the twos. And then on the third floor, the threes. You're in the long part of the E. Make sense?'

'Yeah.'

It makes no sense and I don't care what shape the prison is. I want to know why I'll be locked up all day and night.

'Remand prisoners are kept separate from the rest of the prison population and there are four sets of gates between you and the rest. It's only a temporary wing though. The usual remand block is being fixed up on the other side of the prison, the other side of the yard.'

'Okay.'

'Everything's down here,' he says. 'The mess hall and rec-room and stores and workshops and chapel and library. You don't go up or down any stairs, or cross any bridges or go into any of the other wings or blocks.'

'Okay.'

He moves in close, softens his voice. 'I heard you went to university.'

'Yeah,' I say. 'For a year.'

'The first night's the hardest,' he says. 'But I'd advise you to stop looking so nervous. They'll soon learn you've never been in before, but don't let them know how soft you are. Do you follow?'

'Yeah, thanks. I appreciate that.'

'Six-thirty is slop-out and showers,' he says.

He's stepped away from me and his voice is hard and loud again.

'You have to be ready to leave your cell before the second siren. Your bed must be made and you must be dressed before chow. After morning chow you clean your cell. Lights out at ten o'clock.'

'Okay,' I say.

'While you're in remand, you won't be using the exercise yard and you won't be in the workshops or stores.'

He looks in through the observation panel of the cell door and then he slides the latch, lifts the bolt.

'You're sharing,' he says.

'What's he like?'

'Could be worse.'

'Okay,' I say. 'Thanks.'

He moves in close again, whispers, puts his hand on my arm. It feels good to be touched.

'Good luck, lad.'

He called me lad and the bones in my chest pull tight.

He waits for me to walk in, then slams the cell door shut, locks it, bolts it.

He doesn't say goodbye.

18

This is it. I need to shit and I need to cry and I can do neither.

I stand with my back to the door.

My cell-mate's sitting cross-legged on the floor between two single cots. He's about thirty-odd and he's got a bald head and he's got a book in his lap, a dirty paperback with red edges on the pages.

He doesn't look at me.

Aside from his fat gut, he's scrawny, and he can't be much taller than me.

He's been waiting for me and this is the way he's decided he wants to be seen. Just like Hayes sitting behind his desk and pretending to be busy on my first day at work.

'Hello,' I say.

He looks up at me, then down at his book.

'Yeah, hello.'

He lights a cigarette and his hand shakes when he brings the fag to his mouth.

I pull at the latch so I can call out to get Johnson back. I've got to ask him when I can see my brief. I should've asked him before.

'There's no way out,' he says.

He goes on looking at the book, but he's doing a bad job of pretending to read, turns too many pages too fast.

'I need the toilet,' I say.

'There's one in here,' he says.

He points to the corner, doesn't lift his face from the book, tries to act tough, but his hand's shaking again.

'Thanks,' I say.

I move forward. 'Which bed is mine?'

'The one nearest the TV.'

There's no TV.

'That was a joke,' he says.

'So, which one?' I say.

'Take the waterbed, I'm bored with it.'

I step round him and the small desk and sit on the cot against the right-hand wall.

'That's mine,' he says.

I get up and go to the other cot, take off my shoes, sit with my back against the wall, put my brief's card under the pillow, cross my legs.

The only light in the cell comes off a naked electric bulb. It's so dim it's probably only a thirty watt. There's a barred window, a view of a brick wall and no blinds.

Even a hearse has curtains.

There's no clock and I've no idea what time it is.

Somebody's got to come and tell me I've got bail after all, or that Welkin's alive or in a coma and, if he's dead, I wasn't the cause of it. They'll call me to the hospital and I'll see him in his bed and I'll tell him I'm sorry. But that's bullshit. The cell door's not going to open, Welkin's dead, and the pain in my neck and shoulders pounds hard, a throbbing that goes right into my ears as though there's not enough room in my skull for all the putrid thoughts.

My cell-mate puts his book down, looks up at me. His eyes are brown and dull, and I see what it means to say that somebody's got beady eyes.

'My name's Stevenson,' he says.

'I'm Patrick,' I say. 'Oxtoby.'

He nods. 'I know who you are. You killed a bloke 'cos he stole your alarm clock.'

He knows more than my mother does.

'Right,' I say.

He picks his nose as though he's alone in the cell.

'What about you?' I say. 'What are you in for?'

A siren rings, three long, high-pitched squeals.

Johnson opens the cell door.

'Get out,' he says.

Stevenson gets straight up, goes out to the corridor.

'Time for tea,' he says.

I haven't eaten since breakfast, but I'm not hungry. I only want to sleep.

'I don't want any food,' I say.

'You can suck on air for all we care,' says Johnson, 'but you have to go to chow.'

I go out and line up behind about twenty other men.

A lot of them have shaved heads and tattooed arms. I hold my shoulders back, stand tall as I can and brace myself for what's coming.

Some of the men turn to look at me, but they say nothing.

All of them have their shirt sleeves rolled up and most of them are big and built. I'm about the skinniest guy in the line.

I roll my sleeves up.

We go through two sets of gates and, at the second gate, a prisoner turns round.

'Hey, new boy!' he shouts. 'Did your nut over a clock!'

I clamp my teeth, square my jaw, give a nod I hope looks tough and follow the line through two more sets of gates and then wait outside the mess hall while the men from the blocks above cross the bridges and come down on the spiral metal staircases.

The mess hall door opens.

Stevenson touches my elbow as we go in and, now that we're standing close, I see he's a good two inches shorter than me.

'Keep your trap shut in here,' he says.

We line up with the others and collect our plastic bowls.

He touches my elbow again. 'Stop looking round like you're at Butlins. You've got to lay low, Oxtoby.'

A row of prisoners wearing white aprons spoon the stew out of metal vats, but there's no steam coming off.

I'm given a half-ladle, with potatoes, three slices of bread, a lump of margarine, and an orange.

I follow Stevenson and we sit side by side at a table at the back of the hall, facing into the middle of the room.

'If you look up there, you can see a bit of sky,' he says.

He points up at two barred windows. His hand doesn't shake so much now and he's got a different attitude, already sick of the earlier routine, or he's sussed me and decided I'm not a threat.

'At least there's some light in here,' I say.

There's a crack in my voice and he's heard it.

'The first day inside is the worst,' he says. 'But you've got to eat.'

He watches me while I try to cut through a bit of meat with the plastic fork, then points to a man sitting at the next table.

'He's new like you. An alky. Drugged to the eyeballs on Largactil.'

This man is waving his hands in front of his face and he's kicking at something under the table.

'He's probably got the DTs,' says Stevenson. 'Snakes and spiders.'

I look down at my plastic bowl. The dark marks round the rim have been made with cigarette burns.

I can't eat.

'Do you want my food?' I say.

'No. Eat it. Looks like crap, but you'll be glad you did. It's a long night the first night and you don't want an empty belly.'

I look down, wonder if I close my eyes my appetite might come back.

'You'd better get yourself a dog face,' says Stevenson.

'Okay,' I say.

'Fuck,' he says. He's eaten his slice of bread so fast he's bitten his lip.

'You don't know what a dog face is, do you?'

'No. I s'pose not.'

'It's a face you gotta wear in here. Show no expression. No emotion.'

'Right.'

'You look like somebody stole your kitten.'

He eats all his food and makes so much noise it's as though there's a microphone in his mouth.

'You know,' he says, 'some lifers only serve about ten years and then they're out on licence.'

'What does that mean?' I say.

'I'll tell you later.'

He sticks a segment of orange in his mouth. 'I shouldn't eat sugar,' he says, 'it gives me an itchy arsehole.'

I'd like to tell him that the sugar in fruit's not the same as the kind of sugar that might make his arse itch, but I don't know what he's doing time for and he's been pretty civil so far and I'd like it to stay that way. And I should be careful. Even with that fat paunch, he could probably do me some damage, or maybe he's connected to the people who do damage.

'Plastic spoons and tin spoons are just as dangerous as stronger ones,' he says. 'Know why?'

'No.'

193

'You can still make a shiv out of plastic or tin. It's dead easy. I can show you later.'

Suddenly, he stops eating.

There's a prisoner on the way over. He's tall and wide, walks slow, with his arms held out a bit from his body. He's got tattoos on his face, both cheeks covered with badly drawn crucifixes and a half a skull on his left cheek.

'Here comes the snout-baron,' says Stevenson. 'His name's Walsh.'

Stevenson moves his chair away from mine and Walsh comes up close, stands next to me and puts both hands flat on the table.

'If you need any snout,' he says, 'you see me. If you want credit, I can give you credit, but you pay me back double. If you go to somebody else or don't pay your debts, you'll wish you was dead.'

Walsh takes hold of my wrist and pulls my arm up high and hard behind my back. The pain shoots right through and my eyes water so fast there's nothing I can do to stop it.

'Got that?' he says.

'Yeah.'

When Walsh's back at his table, Stevenson moves his chair in close.

'Be careful,' he says.

'He can just do that?' I say. 'With officers in here?'

'Most of the screws are on his side. Some are on his payroll.'

I nod.

'If you cross Walsh you'll wish you was dead,' Stevenson says.

He looks down at the table, shakes his head.

'But you should've said something to him.'

'You told me not to say anything.'

'You look a bit of a nancy, so he mightn't bother with you. But I'd still be real careful.'

'What should I have said? What should I say next time?'

'I don't know. Walsh's bird-happy, so he's got nothing to lose.'

'What does bird-happy mean?'

'He prefers doing bird than being outside.'

The siren sounds and we line up, put our scraps into yellow buckets. As we move through the door, the room darkens. The sun's gone in again.

'You'll be okay,' says Stevenson. 'Stick with me and you'll be okay.'

In the cell, Stevenson sits on his cot with his back against the wall and lights one cigarette from another, then wipes his hands on his trousers.

'What are you in for?' I say.

'I knew you was going to ask that.'

'You don't have to tell me.'

He moves forward on the cot and he's got to sit up close to the edge so as his feet can reach the floor.

I wait. He says nothing.

'Tell me later, if you want,' I say.

'I'll tell you now,' he says. 'I'm in for sex assault.'

He checks his cigarette packet, realises he's already got one lit.

'Not rape mind, just underage girls.'

He moves right up to the edge of his cot and rests his elbows on his knees, sits like a man ready for a long heart-to-heart.

'How underage?'

'Listen, I don't want you getting the wrong idea. Will you try and hear me out and not jump to conclusions?'

'Yeah.'

He holds his hand out, as though he wants me to come over and shake it.

'You understand, mate. These are the kind of girls who look real mature for their age. Lots of make-up and kinda grown-up, well developed. You know, the type who don't even get asked for ID when they go to clubs and stuff.'

He puts his hand in his lap, sits back a bit on the cot.

'How old?'

'Thirteen, twelve was the youngest. Eleven and a half she tells the court. But I don't do children. I'm not a paedophile.'

I'm sick to the pit of my gut. I've got to take a deep breath to speak.

'What did you do with them?'

'Listen, if it's all the same with you, I'd rather not get into the particular details.'

I lie on my back, stare up at the ceiling, try to steady my breath, slow it down.

'Listen, Oxtoby,' he says. 'Basically, I get them into my car and usually they don't even put up that much of a fight and they're always wet once I get started. Know what I'm saying?'

As soon as I see Johnson tomorrow, I'm asking for a transfer.

'I'm going to sleep,' I say.

'But it's only eight. It's two hours till lights out,' he says. 'Want to play some cards or something?'

I want to sleep, to die for a while, wake up a million miles away from this pervert.

Stevenson gets up from his cot and comes over to my cot and sits right down next to me.

I sit up.

His breath's as bad as old vase water and his skin's parched and lined from heavy smoking, but it's oily too, like it's got resin all over it.

'I can kind of tell what you're thinking,' he says. 'But I'm not as bad as all that.'

My heart's thumping in my throat.

'No,' I say. 'You seem like a decent bloke.'

'I am that,' he says, as he puts his hand on my leg. 'I'm a pretty decent bloke.'

'I can see that.'

I want his hand off me.

'Thanks for telling me how to get on in here,' I say.

I look him in the eyes.

He takes his hand off my leg.

'We're mates now,' he says. 'We've got to stick together. You'll be in this cell with me for at least six months, maybe longer.'

'But I'm going to have a trial soon,' I say.

'It's never soon,' he says. 'It'll take at least six months, maybe longer.'

'Isn't that some kind of miscarriage of justice?'

'No, that's how the law works. Slow and painful.'

He goes back to his cot, lights another cigarette and flicks the spent match into the corner near the head of my cot.

'Listen, Oxtoby. I don't want to upset you or nothin', but you'll probably die in here.'

'I'm going to sleep,' I say.

'Suit yourself.'

Even when I cover my body with the two blankets, the cell's cold.

I finally drift into sleep, but wake in the middle of the night and the blankets have fallen off and I'm very cold and my thoughts are back to what I've done. I've killed a man and there's no going back. I did the thing regarded by the law as the worst of things and what I did adds up to no more than the act of raising and lowering a hand. My mind played hardly any part, but my body acted and, as far as the law's concerned, my body might as well be all that I am.

I move from side to side, my bones sore and cold against the thin foam mattress, but I sleep a while.

19

At 6.30 a.m., there's the siren, long and screeching. It takes me a few minutes to work out where I am and a few more minutes to work out that it's Tuesday morning, that what happened was in the early hours of Saturday morning, three days ago. Hayes will probably have heard by now, probably glad I've solved a few of his problems. It's just him and his nephew now, the one with my fucking ball peen hammer.

My neck hurts like hell and one of my teeth has come loose.

Stevenson stands naked by the toilet bowl waiting for his morning piss to come.

We don't speak.

His arms are thin, his arse is flat and saggy and his feet are big. He urinates with one hand on his bruised and skinny hip.

I dress and make my bed quickly, as though by moving fast I'll be able to stop the thoughts.

When I'm done making the bed, I wait by the cell door.

Stevenson dresses, doesn't look at me and I don't look at him.

An officer shouts, 'Slop-out!' and the cell door opens. I follow Stevenson outside and stand behind him in line-up.

'Welcome to the slammer,' he says. 'Slopping out, counting heads, and banging up.'

I need to shit.

I look up at the blocks above, another floor of cells and about a hundred men in line-up.

I see Johnson up ahead and fall out of line and go to him.

'I need to make a phone call,' I say.

'Get back in line,' he says. 'You can't stand anywhere you feel like.'

I go back to my place. Stevenson shakes his head and the prisoner behind me steps up close. He's short, about five feet flat, and he's got one of those homemade tattoos of a swastika on his arm.

'You better wait your bloody turn in here,' he says, 'or you'll be dead meat before you know what's hit you.'

I nod, slow and calm, wonder if I should thank him, nod again, then turn back round and wait for the gates to open.

When we're through the last gate, Johnson comes to the back of the line and stands close to me.

'The first night is the worst,' he says. 'Did you sleep?'

I look round to see if the prisoner with the swastika is watching. He's not. He's at the back of the line, talking to another short guy with a shaved head.

'Yeah. I slept a bit.'

Johnson moves in close. 'I bet you had good dreams.'

I say nothing, move back a bit.

'Did you?'

'I don't remember.'

We get to the Recess and stand in line-up waiting for permission to go into the open shower stalls.

The officer standing by the sinks shouts, 'Five minutes.'

I do as the other men do, undress quickly and step forward. The water sprays hard from a row of shower-heads. I stand between Stevenson and another prisoner. The water isn't hot enough and, when I say so, the prisoner next to me laughs.

'Count yourself lucky. We used to only get one cold shower a week.'

My neighbour's a young lad, maybe only eighteen or so, but he has warts on both eyelids.

'Name's Kirkness,' he says.

'Oxtoby,' I say, like it's the most normal thing in the world.

The water stops running and a prisoner down the far end shouts for it to be turned back on and when it starts again there's more pressure than before.

My neighbour's washing his penis now and, instead of looking at his own, he looks at mine.

I turn round to face Stevenson, but he stares straight ahead, towards the wall, his mouth open, as though in a dream.

Breakfast in the mess hall with about a hundred other prisoners and it's a bowl of cornflakes, two slices of bread with margarine, cold scrambled eggs and a blackened banana. I don't eat. I'm too busy watching my back and, every time a tray gets dropped or a man raises his voice, I think I'm going to get jumped. I calm down a bit when I realise there's nobody even looking at me and, when the siren goes and we all file out, I take an apple off the table. I don't have a pocket (no pockets, no belt, and no laces) so I try to stash the apple in my sock.

A kitchen screw stops me at the door. 'You can't take that fruit.'

'Can't I eat it in my cell?'

'Hand it over or I'll put you on report and you'll go on basic.'

I give it back.

When I turn round, he clears his throat, hawks up phlegm. He wants me to think he's going to spit on my back. I move forward in the line-up, but there's no spit.

I turn round to look at him.

He's gone.

Back in the cell, Stevenson takes the dirty paperback and sits on the floor.

'You went to university,' he says. 'That right?'

'Not for long.'

'Could you help me with a letter?'

'If you want.'

'I'm not too good at spelling and you got me thinking last night. I saw that look on your face and I felt a bit guilty, you know?'

I say nothing.

'I thought about writing a letter to the girls, you know, as part of that programme where inmates say sorry to their victims.'

'Sounds like a good idea.'

'How about I write it and then show you?'

'If you want.'

He sits at the desk and gets out a piece of blue airmail paper, begins to write with a red biro, bows his head so low it almost touches the paper, and he writes with his left hand, his grip tight, his wrist twisted.

I lie back on the cot and close my eyes.

He lights a cigarette.

'Will you read it for me now?'

I get up to get the letter, but the cell door opens.

Johnson's here.

'You can make that phone call now,' he says.

I get the card my brief gave me from under the pillow and put it back in my sock.

Stevenson doesn't look at me, goes on with writing.

Johnson takes me through three sets of gates. At each gate we stop and wait.

'It's a valve system,' he says, 'we can't go through until the gate behind is shut.'

We reach the final gate.

'We have to go up the stairs to the twos,' he says. 'The phones down here on the ones are all busted up.'

We walk up the metal spiral staircase to the landing above and, when we reach the top, Johnson's out of breath. He stops in front of me to rub the rolls of fat at the back of his neck. Where the rolls meet, there's a dark slit and he puts his finger in there.

'You need to give me the name and number of the person you're calling,' he says.

There are three phones, each of them surrounded by scratched Perspex. Two of them are occupied.

I give Johnson the business card my brief gave me.

'You don't want this,' he says. 'You're entitled to silk.'

'What's that mean?'

'You're entitled to a court appointed QC. That's Queen's Counsel. Anybody facing a murder charge is entitled. It's the law.'

I nod.

'Count yourself lucky,' he says. 'Not that long ago you'd have been hanged for what you did. If you were in America, you'd be up for the chair.'

'How do I get this QC?'

'That'll all be sorted out in due course.'

'Can't you call somebody now? Can you take me to see the governor now or something?'

He runs his hand down his neck.

'No, not now. It'll be sorted in due course.'

'I want to change cells.'

'You can't.'

'I want to see the governor then. I can't share my cell with him.'

'Listen,' he says. 'I know it's tough, but that's how it is.'

'Don't I have the right to see the governor?'

'In a week or so. You'll be notified.'

I nod.

'Stand up tall,' he says, 'You won't get through this if you can't stand up.'

He walks away. I follow.

We reach my cell and, before he opens up, he stands close.

'I'll get you an app,' he says. 'For the governor.'

'Thanks.'

'Try and stand tall.'

'It won't make much difference,' I say. 'They'll come after me if they want to.'

'Not necessarily,' he says. 'If you keep your nose clean.'

'How do I do that?'

'Don't grass, don't blank the wrong men, don't thieve another man's gear and mind your own business.'

He sends me in.

Stevenson's lying on his cot, staring up at the ceiling, smoking.

'All right?' he says.

'Yeah.'

I sit on my cot and close my eyes, but my head spins, my heart pounds, my breath's stuck in my throat.

I sit up.

'I think I need to go to the hospital.'

'You sick?'

'I can't breathe.'

'There's an alarm on the cell door,' he says. 'It's a call button. You can press it, but they probably won't come.'

I go to the cell door and find the button.

'Be careful,' he says. 'If it's a false alarm, they'll make you pay.'

'But I can't breathe.'

I want obliterine, something to knock me out and send me off to sleep. Not just for a night, but for a good long time.

'Maybe you should wait for sick-parade in the morning,' he says. 'You could report as special-sick.'

I sit on my cot.

'Maybe it's a panic attack,' he says. 'Feels like a heart attack? Feel your heart pumping everywhere? Even in your arsehole?'

I hate that I need this man and his advice and information and, even worse, that I need him for an ally.

'Yeah,' I say. 'It feels like a heart attack.'

'Ah, well,' he says, throwing his voice at me as though he were a doctor. 'It won't last. The symptoms only last about twenty minutes. We all get them.'

And he's right.

It doesn't last.

'You don't have to read that letter I wrote,' he says.

'Why not?'

'I decided it was a stupid idea.'

I say nothing.

'Don't you want to know why?'

'Maybe later,' I say.

Stevenson sits next to me during midday chow and I wish he wouldn't. Sooner or later I'm going to get jumped by another prisoner and it can't help that I'm keeping company with a nonce.

'I don't feel like talking right now,' I say.

'Because of why I'm in here?'

'No.'

'Yeah it is.'

'I just don't know what to say to you.'

'Oh snickety, snick, snick,' he says.

'I just want to sit and not talk for a minute.'

'You think you're so high and mighty.'

I say nothing.

'I'm not a sex-case,' he says. 'The baby-splitters are in wet cells and seg units with body belts. But not me. I'm here with you. I'm not a sex-case.'

I take up a mouthful of brown beans, put the spoon back down. My nerves are too bad for eating.

Stevenson brings his chair in closer. He's so close now I can smell his dirty clothes. He stinks of dried cum.

'I'm not proud of myself,' he says.

'No?'

'I have guilt just like the next man but I'm not the worst kind of man either.'

'I suppose not.'

'I used to do a good job as a janitor.'

'Where?' I say. 'In a primary school?'

'Fuck you.'

I break a slice of bread, roll the bits into balls to make it softer.

'For your information,' he says, 'I was a janitor in a hospital and the patients used to talk to me for hours on end. I did my fair share of good turns and I was good to a lot of people, specially the geriatrics.'

'That's nice,' I say.

I take a few balls of bread, dirty now from my fingers but not so dry after being massaged, and I stick them in my mouth.

'Some people have more choice in life,' he says. 'There's no such thing as complete freedom.'

'So,' I say, 'what you did isn't your fault?'

'No. Is it yours?'

We're silent for a while and Stevenson finishes off his plate of beans as though it were something tasty. The sound he makes with his mouth is like rubber boots lifting in and out of mud.

'You gonna answer me, or what?' he says.

'Can't you be quiet for a minute?'

I look round to see who might be watching, but there's nobody who gives a shit. About a hundred prisoners, almost all of them talking, some of them laughing, just a few sitting alone, two old men who sit together but don't talk, and the guy with the DTs.

'Ask me what my dad did for a living,' he says.

'What?'

'He worked in a paper mill. He was a foreman. I was a happy kid until he died in an accident when I was only four and then—'

'I don't want to talk,' I say.

Stevenson gets up. 'Where's your fucking sympathy?'

He's standing up but he's not going anywhere. He holds his tray out like it's got something valuable on it and looks down at me.

'Not even any sympathy for what happened to my dad,' he says. 'Didn't even let me get to the end of the story.'

'Sorry,' I say.

He sits down, speaks quieter, slower.

'The point is this,' he says. 'No girl at school would so much as look at me, never mind kiss me, and they told me I looked like a rat and I grew up hard and lonely and there's some stuff I could tell you about what happened to me that'd disgust you so bad your toes would fucking curl.'

'What?' I say. 'More disgusting than these beans?'

I smile and he looks at me, happy, his eyes wet, like I've done him something very fine.

Back in the cell, I lie down on my cot and Stevenson comes and sits on the floor right up next to me.

I wish I had a book.

'I did a crap yesterday that was as black as a pair of socks,' he says. 'And rock hard, too.'

'Right,' I say.

'You get real bad constipation in the nick,' he says.

I turn over to face the wall, put a pillow over my face, cover my body with the two grey blankets and try for sleep, but he's too close to me, I can feel him here, too close, desperate for talk.

I turn back round, look at him.

'It's cold today,' he says.

'Yeah. It's freezing.'

'Your body thermostat will adjust in a few weeks. But you still feel it, especially your feet and hands.'

'I've got to sleep,' I say. 'I've not slept properly for days.'

He lights a cigarette.

'When did it happen? The murder?'

'Saturday.'

'I didn't sleep for two weeks once. Nearly lost my mind.'

'I think I'll sleep now,' I say. 'That okay?'

''Course it is. You sleep.'

He pats my leg, gentle, like a parent, goes back to his cot. I'm surprised he doesn't tuck me in and I wouldn't stop him if he did.

I'm woken three times during the night. The first time when an officer opens and closes the observation panel, slams the shutter closed, crashes his keys against the metal. The second time when a prisoner shouts, 'Who's fucking your wife now, eh?' And the third time I'm woken by a dream. I'm in my room at home and there are two mice under my bed. One mouse is purple, the other green. These mice are longer and fatter than the usual and I pick both up and stroke their soft backs. Then I go to the window and hang them by their tails. I want to know if they'll die if I drop them from the second floor.

I wake before I drop them.

The blankets are on the floor.

On the way to showers, I daydream about Welkin. A mistake's been made and he's alive, sitting at the table under the bay window with Flindall. I look at them from the dining room door. He's waiting to go on a picnic with Georgia and he tells me she has a 'spare friend' and I'm invited, but that Flindall's not. He says Flindall's got a job to go to. I tell Welkin I'd love to come along and then I laugh.

Johnson catches up with me and as we pass through the third gate he comes in close.

'You need a visitor, Oxtoby. Why don't you call somebody?'

'I just want to see my QC and get out of here.'

'There's one on the way. I'll let you know when he gets here.'

'He's on the way now?'

'Not today. I don't think today. Tomorrow, the day after. Maybe the day after that. Maybe next week. I'll tell you when he gets here.'

The gate opens and the men ahead go through. Johnson puts his hand on my arm to stop me going forward.

'You need to do something to pass the time.'

'Like what?'

'Do you read?'

'Yeah.'

His eyes are on my crotch.

'Borrow some books then.'

'I'm going to.'

He moves in, puts his fat mouth against my ear.

'I'll sort out the apps for you.'

'Okay.'

'Pardon?'

'Thanks very much,' I say.

'Right,' he says. 'That's better.'

I take the open shower stall furthest from the door and after a few minutes I turn and see Johnson's standing by the sink looking at me, his fat tongue resting on his bottom teeth.

He's going to help me out and there's nothing will stop me getting out of here.

20

After midday chow two days later, there's a letter on my cot, first-class post, and it's already opened and the single page is folded in half and sits on a torn envelope.

I sit at the desk to read it.

Dear Son,

This is the hardest letter a father could ever be faced with writing. There's a lot I want to say and I don't know how to say most of it.

Your mother's in an awful state and I thought I should jot down a few words. You must be in a lot of pain too, just like we are. The news of what's happened has hit us all very hard and we're trying to find a way to understand, and a way to be compassionate to you.

I sat Russell down this morning and he said he wanted to see you, but I told him I think it would be best for now if we just got our heads round what's happened and come and see you when we're ready, in our own time. I've told him that I would write for all of us and come and see you when the time's right.

I'm sure you're suffering now and I don't want this letter to make you hurt any extra, but I want to tell you that forgiveness is going to take time. At the moment it is too painful and there's a lot of anger and hurt and I don't think we should come into the prison. I am also asking you not to phone us. I am asking you to give us some time.

Please be patient with us and be patient with your mother too. She is in a terrible state of shock but she still loves you as your mother.

Your father,

Jim

I go to my cot and lie face down and remember what my father said when I came home from university, that my brother has a knack for happiness and I don't. I suppose he was right and I hated him then, but not as much as I hate him now.

'You all right?' says Stevenson.

'Yeah.'

I read the letter again then go to the toilet, tear the paper in half, throw it in and flush it.

I go back to my cot and rub my neck.

I can't breathe.

'You don't look all right,' he says.

I pull the blanket over my head.

It's morning. The siren's not yet gone for slop-out or showers and there's somebody at the cell door. I jump up from the cot, my hands balled into fists. It might not be an officer, but time for a beating.

It's Johnson.

'Get dressed,' he says. 'It's time to go.'

'Yeah?'

I think he means it's time to walk free. Six days inside and they've finally worked out I shouldn't be here.

'Your QC's here.'

I dress fast and nick one of Stevenson's extra strong mints from the table.

Johnson takes me through to the admissions room. He signs me in and gets another set of keys and then we go to the corridor where the Day Ward and Fit Cell are. He opens the door to the Interview Room and we go in.

Johnson locks the door from the inside.

'Security regulations,' he says.

The room's small and grey-walled and there's a white table, four green plastic chairs, and a barred window. The wall to the right of the door is covered with Missing and Wanted posters and the Wanted are all men and the Missing are all girls, except one.

'Sit here,' he says. 'We'll wait.'

I sit facing the window and he sits next to me.

'How are you getting on?' he wants to know.

'Okay,' I say.

'Sleeping?'

'I keep waking up.'

'Bad thoughts.'

'Last night it was. . .'

There's somebody out in the corridor. We both look to the door, but whoever's out there only stops for a moment, as though to listen, then goes on walking.

Johnson's knee rests against mine.

'Last night?' he says. 'What was it last night?'

'I woke with the same thought going over and over.'

'What was it?'

'I can't remember.'

'Tell me.'

'I kept thinking: *I'm on my way out. I don't want to be on my way out.*'

'What do you think that means?'

'I don't know.'

Johnson looks at his watch. 'Your QC said he was coming before court. Must have got waylaid.'

Waylaid? I've got to keep the chat going.

'Who is he?' I say.

'Can't remember his name but he's a QC and he's appointed by the court.'

'Is he good?'

'Don't know, but he's a QC and that's what you need.'

He puts his hand on my leg.

I stand and go to the window but I don't know why I've bothered. I can't stop him if that's what he wants.

'Good view?'

There's only a view of a brick wall about ten feet away.

'Fuck all,' I say. 'I can see fuck all.'

At last, a knock at the door, the sound of a key rattling on a chain.

'Come in,' I say.

Johnson laughs, gets up and unlocks the door.

My QC enters the room.

'I'm Michael Perkins,' he says, moving at speed to the table. 'You must be Patrick Oxtoby.'

I stand and we shake hands.

'Yeah. Thanks for coming.'

'Let's get started.'

Johnson moves his chair to the other end of the table and Perkins sits across from me. He's grey-haired, somewhere in his fifties, and he has a deep dimple in his chin—the kind of bum-chin a boy at my school called Derek Blunk had. But it hardly matters what Perkins looks like. He's taking off his dark suit jacket and I see the silk lining and I know I'm about to talk to the man who's going to get me out of here.

'I'm just sorry I couldn't get here sooner,' he says. 'We don't have much time.'

His words slur, too much saliva in his mouth.

'I'm glad you could come,' I say.

In a matter of minutes, he'll deliver some good news.

'My car refused to start,' he says. 'Seems not to like the rain.'

'It's raining?'

'Yes. It was.'

'Heavy rain?'

'Yes.'

'What kind of car do you drive?'

'You're going to be tried for murder, so we'd better get on with it.'

'I'm not a murderer.'

'I'm going to do my level best for you. You've got a clean record and your character will stand you in good stead, but this is a difficult case.'

'I didn't mean to kill him, so I can't be found guilty of murder, right?'

'Yes and no. Everything turns on your intention, what's known as the *mens rea*, and the prosecution must prove beyond all reasonable doubt that you had an intention to do either grievous bodily harm or to murder.'

'I didn't intend either of those things, so they can't prove I did.'

'But the facts, as I understand them so far,' he says, 'point to a clear intention and we'll have to discuss the possibility of pleading guilty to manslaughter.'

He's supposed to fight for me, to get me freed.

'There's no way I'm doing that.'

'I'd like you to think about it. The police prosecutor might agree.'

'Who's that?'

'The solicitor appointed by the police to prosecute you. The Crown.'

'What if I don't plead guilty?'

'You should seriously consider it, because as it stands—'

'He must have had a pretty thin skull to die from one hit.'

'Even if he did have what's known in the law as an eggshell skull, it makes no difference. As far as the law's concerned you must take your victim as you find him.'

'I didn't want him dead and I can tell you now that there's no way I'm pleading guilty to anything. I don't see how I can be convicted of murder if I didn't want to kill him or even do serious injury. And you're already talking like you think I'm finished.'

'Patrick, you're not finished and I'm going to do my best for you. But I'd strongly advise you to plead guilty to manslaughter. Of course, if you refuse, if you want to leave your fate to the jury, you're entitled to do so.'

His double chin's covered in short black hairs, looks like a spider's fat gut.

'So I don't have to plead guilty?'

'No. But you're going to need a bit of good luck.'

'So it's down to fucking luck then?'

'Patrick, I appreciate what you're saying, but I want you to consider a plea. Maybe you'll change your mind once we've talked about your case a little more.'

'Sounds like you've already decided I'm guilty.'

'It's more complicated than a blunt equation of guilt or innocence,' he says.

'Right.'

'Let's get on with looking at your police statement and go over the facts. Then we can discuss our strategy.'

Johnson pulls his chair in closer to mine and Perkins empties his briefcase on the table and some of the documents fall. I help pick them up. The first page of one is headed: THE TABLE OF MAIMS. Beneath that title are these words: FINGER: £1000. LEG: £2500.

'What's this?' I say.

214

'You needn't worry about that,' he says. 'That's for my civil work. Nothing concerning you.'

He puts the documents away.

'How much is a head worth?' I say.

'That's funny,' he says. 'But you'd better keep that kind of humour under wraps during the trial.'

'Whatever you tell me,' I say, 'that's what I'll do.'

He looks at me as though he hates me.

'Okay,' he says, 'then listen closely.'

He talks in his flat, watery voice about the criminal law as it pertains to my case.

I tell him I can't be convicted of murder. I only meant to wake the bastard up.

Perkins shakes his head, slowly, as though he enjoys the fact I've failed to grasp the black letter of the law then he puts his chubby hands on the table, palms up.

'The problem here is that you applied a weapon to the victim's skull during the dead of night while the victim slept.'

He mimes the act of a man lifting a weapon and bringing it down on another man's head. His right hand holds the weapon, his left hand, formed into a fist, is the victim's head.

'But I only meant to—'

'You went to the victim's room in the early hours of the morning and hit him very solidly with a spanner, so you must have been thinking—'

'An adjustable wrench,' I say.

'Pardon me?'

'An adjustable wrench,' says Johnson.

'And when you hit him you intended to do *some* harm,' says Perkins. 'How much harm you intended to do is critical in this case and the evidence might point to a lot of harm—grievous bodily harm.'

'But I didn't want to kill him.'

'It may look as though you not only had the requisite *mens rea*, but that you had a motive, of sorts. Not a strong one, but a motive none-theless.'

Looks like the wrong grey man's been sent.

'What motive?' I say.

'He stole something of yours. Is that the case?'

'Yes, but—'

'It was a clock, if I remember correctly, and there's at least one witness prepared to say that you were very angry about this incident, and that you were heard screaming abuse at somebody the night before the incident.'

'I didn't scream abuse. I don't know what you're talking about.'

Perkins makes a note on a yellow pad. 'Perhaps we'd better return to that later.'

Johnson puts his hand near my hand, as though he means to touch me, but he doesn't touch me and takes his hand back.

'The blunt impact to the skull appears to have caused traumatic haemorrhaging,' says Perkins, 'which may have been made worse by the victim's alcohol consumption.'

'What are my chances?'

Pity me, I want to say. Help me.

'I'd prefer not to give you a percentage. But I am very encouraged by the fact that you are of good character with no history whatsoever of violent crime.'

'So there's hope?'

'Yes, there's hope. And, next time we meet, I'll know more.'

'That's good then, cos I definitely don't have this *mens rea*. I had no intent to kill, so I can't be convicted of murder.'

He takes a breath. 'The trial should take place in the New Year. We think mid-January.'

'But it's only September. I can't be kept in here that long.'

'Sit down,' he says.

I hadn't known I was standing.

'You have to remain in custody until the trial,' he says.

'Can't I get out on bail?'

'Bail's been refused and that's the end of the matter.'

I wipe snot away with my knuckles.

Johnson tries to find a tissue in his pocket, but he has none.

Perkins does nothing, just waits for me to clean myself up.

'This is fucking stupid,' I say.

Perkins looks at the door.

'Now,' he says, 'I'm afraid I must ask you to go over what happened, in your own words.'

'The same story as in my statement?'

'Yes. I need to hear it straight from the horse's mouth.'

He pulls his sleeve back from his wrist, checks the time again.

'And as briefly as you can, Pat. We haven't much time.'

'It's Patrick,' I say. 'My name's Patrick.'

And so, in five minutes flat, I tell the story from start to finish and Perkins writes it down and, as soon as I'm done, he stands, puts his jacket on.

'That should do us for now,' he says. 'Shall I see myself out?'

'I thought we were going to talk about strategy,' I say.

'There's no time now. We'll come back to that.'

I stand and Johnson stands.

'I'll get an officer,' says Johnson.

Perkins holds out his hand for me to shake.

'Thanks for being so cooperative,' he says. 'I promise I'll do my best for you.'

He's got a soft, damp hand.

'That's good,' I say. 'I appreciate that.'

Johnson gets an officer and the officer takes Perkins away.

I go over and stand by the window, look out at the brick wall opposite. Johnson comes up behind me.

'May I?' he says.

I don't turn round. He's at least a head and shoulders taller than me and he puts his hand inside my shirt, on my neck, fingers reaching down to my collarbone. I flinch a bit when he moves in so his chest is against my back, but so far it's not much worse than what happens on a crowded bus.

'I think you'll be okay,' he says, his voice quiet and soft. 'That man didn't know what he was talking about.'

I'm stuck at the window, can't move till he moves. His chest is pressed harder against my back now and he slides his hand further down my neck, past my collarbone, towards my nipple.

'Can you turn?'

'I'd rather not,' I say.

He takes his hand away, steps back.

I turn and look at his face and he looks at mine, and we're just standing, looking at each other a bit longer than people usually look.

'Okay,' he says. 'We're finished in here.'

Next morning, after breakfast, Johnson comes with more news.

'The Deputy Governor's given you a library pass.'

'Now?'

He runs his hand up his neck, pushes the flesh up towards his chin.

'Yes, now. I thought you said you wanted to borrow some books.'

Stevenson lights a cigarette.

'Yeah,' I say. 'Sorry.'

'Good. We'll go.'

The library's dimly lit and about the size of two cells and there are four shelves about six feet high, two desks, a long fluorescent light in the ceiling, black carpet, and one small window. But it's warm.

Johnson takes me to a shelf at the back wall. There's a handwritten sign pinned to the wood: *Prisoners and The Law.*

'You might want to start reading about this stuff,' he says.

'Okay.'

'Listen,' he says, 'you've only got an hour today and I'm not going to stand here like a midwife while you decide what to do.'

I take a book off the shelf, *Penology: The Arrangement of Types.*

'I want to read up on criminal law,' I say.

He goes away and comes back with a book.

'Take this one as well, then,' he says.

He hands me *Blackwell's Criminal Law and Commentary.*

He takes me to the desk under the window and tells me to sit.

'I'll be standing right outside,' he says.

I put the chair at the end of the desk so I'm closer to the radiator.

I read a bit of the book about prisoners first. I've got a few months to get ready for my trial and it's probably more urgent for me to work out how to get on in here.

The main types of prisoner are the inconspicuous ones who keep to themselves and stay out of trouble, the inmate who continuously schemes, always on the look-out for ways to make his life inside easier (usually at the expense of others), the persistently violent prisoner whose unpredictable behaviour often ends in segregation, the sadist or predator, the preyed upon, the litigious (a man always appealing his conviction), the inmate who leaks information to the officers, the inmate who peddles in the misfortune of other inmates and, finally, the inmate who's always planning his escape.

I get to thinking that I'm the inmate who lays low, the one who minds his own business, the safest and most common of the types.

Johnson comes back. It's not been an hour, only a half-hour at most.

'It's time to go,' he says.

'Can I borrow this book?'

'Not that one. Only the ones with yellow stickers on. This one's got a red sticker.'

On the way back to the cell I ask him if I can have some paper and a pen. I don't want to use the old red biro that Stevenson's been chewing on.

'If you're very good,' he says, 'I'll get you the apps.'

'Thanks.'

We're up the end of the walkway, between the lights, and there's nobody around. He leans in close, puts his mouth next to my ear and he gives me some of his breath.

'I've never wanted to see the back of somebody,' he says, 'like I want to see the back of you.'

'What's that mean?'

'It means I want you to walk. I want you to get out of here.'

21

It's near the end of September and my mood's rotten. My craving to get my old life back is desperate and I can't shake the daydreams about being back in the house with Bridget, that soft bed I had in my clean room, the smell of the sea, her smiling face, that good food. And every fantasy about my old life makes the cold and stink in this place all the worse.

If I'd not made that mistake with the hammer. Must have said this to myself a thousand times and every time the thought sends a sharper stab of poison through, and gives me the shakes.

Three days ago, at seven o'clock in the morning, just after slop-out, Perkins came to see me.

We sat for about half an hour in the interview room and we had a cup of tea and he said the same things over and over, every good thing cancelled by a bad thing, and he ate the ginger biscuits the officer brought us, went on eating just as though nothing important was happening.

He told me my trial date's been set much earlier than expected, and he told me that it's going to be a murder or nothing trial. He told me that the Crown has refused to allow manslaughter as an alternative.

The coroner's report has come in and the cause of death was an acute subdural haematoma, the result of a blow 'of considerable force'—or several blows—with a blunt instrument.

I told him again that I only hit Welkin once and not very hard.

'The coroner's report suggests considerable force,' he says. 'But I'll do my utmost to adduce evidence from the pathologist that there was only a single blow.'

When I asked him about my chances he said, 'If I had to lay a bet, I'd say fair to middling.'

When I asked him what that means, he said, 'I don't want you to give up hope. There's a very reasonable chance that with the right jury you'll be okay.'

I told him what I've read in the Blackwell's book, that murder is the killing of a human being with *malice aforethought*, and that I've found out that the jury is not allowed to infer my intention. I told him that the judge has to direct the jury not to infer my intention.

He said, 'Patrick, I know the law very well and the facts point persuasively toward the conclusion that you intended to do some harm if not serious harm. The evidence strongly suggests sufficient intention.'

He stood up from the table and offered me his hand. I shook his hand and he put his free hand over my hand and clasped me firmly, held me there, held me tight. I wanted to bawl.

'Listen, Patrick. I'm presenting things in the most pessimistic light so that you're prepared for the worst, but you mustn't panic.'

He held my hand for a good long while and we were both sweating and then he let go and went to the door and knocked sharply three times.

An officer came and took him out to the corridor.

He'd left a small, round black box on the table.

I rushed after him. 'You've left this,' I said.

'Goodness,' he said. 'My wig.'

'I'm not the only one losing hair over this,' I said.

He laughed at this and so did I, but I was in an awful state, and we both knew what I'd said wasn't funny at all and only stupid.

I was taken back to my cell and, just before midday chow when the door opened, I had a bit of what I suppose you'd call a breakdown, one of those panic attacks, like I had before, only much worse and the panic wasn't just about my trial and the feeling that my QC wasn't on my side and that he'd let me down, and it wasn't just about my sentence. It was also about being beaten and the almost constant fear of it, the way my body's always stiff with being on guard, afraid all the time I'm going to be jumped.

After I broke down, ended up on my cot, face down, hardly able to breathe, next thing I know I was in the infirmary and I was there for two days and I was given super-strength sedatives to help me sleep, enough for a few days, and I was given a docket so I can get more sedatives when I need them. They stop me from remembering so much.

While I was in the infirmary, Johnson came to visit and he gave me a bag of chocolate raisins.

'I'm not going till you've eaten them,' he said.

He sat with me and watched me eat.

'Turns out your victim came from a rich and powerful family.'

'Yeah,' I said. 'I know.'

'His father's the mayor of Brighton and his mum's a paediatrician.'

'Right.'

'You're pretty unlucky you are.'

'Yeah.'

'I think it's time you started calling me sir,' he said.

I smiled at him, hoped he was joking, but he wasn't.

'All right, sir,' I said. 'I will.'

When I got back to my cell *Blackwell's Criminal Law and Commentary* was on my cot. The yellow sticker was missing and there was a stamp in the back saying it's on loan till next June.

It's Sunday, midday chow, and I'm in the mess hall with Stevenson. There's a new prisoner standing in the corner and he leans his head against the wall and cries.

'Who's that?'

'Name's Trevor Rogers,' says Stevenson. 'It's his first time. A botched shop robbery. He was only an accomplice, but he'll serve a ten stretch at least. The other bloke killed the shopkeeper.'

I look at my plate.

'Want me to save my extra pudding for you?' he asks. 'You can eat it later.'

It's a bowl of green jelly.

'You eat it,' I say.

'Why don't you want it?'

'I'm not hungry.'

'But I'm offering you it.'

'I don't want it. Thanks anyway.'

'You still on a hunger strike?'

'I'm just not hungry.'

Stevenson eats his extra pudding, but stops when the commotion starts up.

Trevor Rogers is on the floor and being beaten by another inmate and he hasn't even bothered to put his hands up to cover his face and that's where the other bloke kicks him, his foot straight at Rogers' nose, and he's shouting, 'Stop your fucking bawling, you stupid fucking baby.'

Now it's the other bloke's turn for a beating and he knows it, just stands back and waits for the officers to pile on and restrain him and, when it looks like he's going to get off lightly, a fourth officer comes, a tall meat-head from Pentonville, and this one beats him with a metal bar, three blows across the back, a couple more across his shoulders, the back of his legs, and there's a new blow with the fall of every word: 'Not. On. Sun. Day. You. Worth. Less. Cunt.'

The bloke's dragged off and Rogers is left on the floor, his face bloody. Nobody goes to him. I want to go to him and I don't want to go to him. I don't know how to do it or when to do it. We're all of us just staring over at him and he's still there when the siren sounds. He's just left there on the floor, too beaten to bother crying.

Once we're all standing in line-up by the door, I turn back.

'Leave it,' says the prisoner behind me. 'Best leave it.'

We all file out.

We're woken, as usual, by the 6.30 siren, but there's no shower today, no slop-out, and there's no breakfast.

We're in lockdown.

A prisoner is dead.

I expect it to be Rogers, but it's not. His name was Kirkness, the one I met in the showers on my first day. He was nineteen and he had the cell two down, waiting for his trial for attempted murder.

Every other week his mother sent him plastic model aeroplanes and he glued them together and then crashed them against the walls of his cell.

The full story about what's happened doesn't get passed down the ones till somebody finds out from a screw and then the news gets sent along the cells by 'fishing'. Somebody ties a piece of paper to the end of a length of weighted string, and casts it out like a line to the door of the next cell where the note's collected from under the half-inch gap, then read and passed on.

The note says. *Kirk took bottle Nitric acid. Wanted city hospital. Died in sleep. Dumb fuck.*

By mid-afternoon we know that Kirkness thought nitric acid wouldn't kill him right away, thought it'd take days, maybe weeks, that he'd have a high fever and spend enough time in the city hospital to plan and execute an escape. But he took the whole bottle and choked on his vomit during the night. The prisoner who got him the acid is in the strongbox, probably in a body belt.

'I knew he were a complete barmpot,' says Stevenson.

'Yeah,' I say.

I liked Kirkness. Would rather have been bunked with him than with Stevenson.

'Yeah,' I say. 'Barmpot is exactly the right word.'

I get a few sheets of that airmail paper from Stevenson and go to the desk. It's been more than a month since my father's letter and I've definitely given him the time he asked for.

I want to tell them what happened, all of it, but I've got to be careful what I say in case it'll be used against me in court.

I've had a lot of time to think about what I can say. I think I have it worked out well.

Dear Mum and Dad

Nothing I say will change the fact that I did what I did, which was a very stupid thing, but I want you to know that I didn't want that man Welkin to die.

I can't say much in this letter because my trial's coming up and there'll be censors reading it, but I want you to know that I didn't hate him and I didn't want to kill him.

I'm feeling pretty optimistic that the jury will work out that I didn't intend to kill him and that I didn't intend to do GBH, because that's the truth. I didn't have a motive and it wasn't premeditated or planned in any way.

I've got Queen's Counsel to represent me and he's very good and I don't think I'll get convicted of murder. To get me for murder the law requires that the prosecution must prove <u>beyond all reasonable doubt</u> that I intended to do GBH or that I intended to murder.

I understand why you haven't written again and why you haven't come to visit me. It's an awful place to come and I know you're very upset and worried and shocked.

I just want you to know that I didn't want that man to die.
I liked him. He would have been my friend if I'd given him a
chance. That might sound mad to you, but it's also the truth.
Maybe that makes it even worse as far as you're concerned, but I
hope not.

I'm not a different person just because I did something foolish.
I'm still your son, I'm still Patrick, and I still love you both very
much.

Love, from C Wing, remand.
Your son, Patrick xxx

I've got tears on my face and a screw's come to deliver food to the cell, a half-loaf of bread and two lumps of cheese.

'How can I get this letter posted?' I say. 'I want it to go first-class.'

'Give it here.'

The screw takes the letter and leaves.

One lump of cheese is nearly twice as big as the other.

Stevenson's seen I'm upset and offers me the bigger lump.

'You have it,' I say.

'You look like a skeleton,' he says.

We sit up on our cots to eat and, as soon as we've eaten, lie down again.

I doze off, but wake to hear Stevenson in the middle of a coughing fit.

'Jesus,' he says.

I sit up. 'You all right?'

'Yeah.'

He goes on coughing, hawks up some phlegm and takes a good look at what he finds in the palm of his hand.

'My phlegm's not grey today. It was grey yesterday. Not today. Today it's clear.'

'Good news,' I say.

I lie down again.

'Have you ever noticed that the sicker you are the sweeter it tastes?' he says.

I say nothing.

'Yesterday,' he tells me, 'my spit was sticky and thick like glue.'

We're still banged up at teatime and Stevenson sits on the cell floor and eats prunes from one of the jumbo bags his sister sent in a hamper for his birthday. He's already eaten the peanuts and the chocolates and the crisps.

When he's finished eating the prunes, he farts, a loud and putrid marathon, and then he sits on the toilet and, when he's finished shitting, he leans in over the toilet bowl.

The stench is foul.

'More good news,' he says. 'Yesterday I had tiny black pebbles for shit, but today things are looking up. Yesterday I thought I had cancer. Today it looks like I'm fit as a fiddle.'

He crouches down beside the toilet and puts his hands inside the bowl.

'Please don't do that,' I say.

'You don't own this cell,' he says.

'I know,' I say. 'But you can't do that.'

'If I want to look at my own shit, I have every right.'

'I can't stomach it.'

'You don't have to look.'

'Where else can I look?'

'Put the pillowcase over your head.'

'Please flush the toilet.'

He flushes the toilet and, on the way back to his cot, cocks his arse and farts in my direction, then sits with his knees up, facing me, and goes on farting.

'I'm enjoying myself,' he says. 'Maybe you should join in. I have another bag of prunes. You can have it.'

'No thanks.'

'Don't you like the smell of your own farts?'

I say nothing.

'Do you or don't you? It's a simple question.'

'Not especially.'

'Everybody does.'

'Not me.'

'That's because you're repressed. I noticed it the first time I saw you.'

'Jesus fucking Christ.'

'You hate your own body.'

'Leave it out,' I say.

He wants me to laugh but I get up from the cot and undress with my back to him.

'I'm going to sleep,' I say.

'You don't even understand the basics of pleasure,' he says. 'Fucking, shitting and farting.'

I pretend to sleep and then Stevenson starts beating himself off. He waits a while before he starts, maybe thinks I'm still awake, and then he gets going. He starts off slow and says, 'Mmmm' just once and then the cot starts to rattle and he breathes faster and it takes him a good while to come and when he gets there he says, 'Fucking hell.'

I'm wide awake after he's done and so is he, and we stay like this for a long while, the both of us pretending to sleep.

Next morning, after Johnson's fetched me for the library, I sit by the small radiator and read more about the criminal law and more of *Penology: The Arrangement of Types.*

There's nowhere in the prison as warm as this small corner of the library and it feels safer in here. There's always an officer at the door and another lurking round the shelves.

After a few minutes, I put my head on my hands to sleep.

Johnson's standing beside me when I wake.

'You talked in your sleep,' he says.

'Yeah?'

'You said *poison*.'

'Did I, sir?'

He runs his hand down his neck, wipes at the sweat that's always there. It's as though he's in the tropics.

'And you said *friend*.'

I nod.

'And you had your tongue hanging out.'

'Did I?'

He looks at my lips.

'You're not being very good,' he says.

'No, sir. I'm not. I'm tired and I feel sick.'

'Still not sleeping?'

'I can't. And, when I do, the pervert wakes me with his shit-talk.'

'You should put in an app for sleeping pills.'

'I will then.'

'I'll get you the forms.'

'Why didn't nobody fucking tell me I could get sleeping pills before?'

'You're starting to sound like one of them. You've lost your manners.'

'Well I'm not one of them, sir. I'm just sleep-deprived. I'm desperate for some rest.'

'Let's go. It's time to go, time to leave.'

He has a habit of making it sound like I'm about to go on a journey, go somewhere good, get out of here.

'Get up,' he says.

He tells me to walk ahead of him, and that's what I do. He wants to watch. Let him.

Three days later, visiting hour, and Johnson comes to my cell after breakfast.

'You've got someone coming today,' he says.

'Who is it?'

'Jim Oxtoby.'

My heart's never pounded so hard.

Johnson takes me to the visiting room and puts me in box seven. There are eight boxes divided by sheets of glass and there are telephones on both sides, with two receivers on the visitors' side. Five officers stand guard, three behind the prisoners and two at the visitors' entrance.

My father looks nervous and he's wearing his usual white shirt and blue tie and his hair's parted down the middle and it's gone grey at the temples. He waits behind the glass, his hands flat on the bench and he speaks into the phone before I've had a chance to pick up the receiver.

'I didn't hear,' I say.

My throat's dry and tight.

'Hello,' he says.

'I'm glad you've come,' I say.

'You're keeping well then?' he says. 'You're well enough then?'

'I'm getting more used to it,' I say.

He reaches into his pocket, removes a newspaper article, reads some of it, then returns it to his pocket.

'There was this big article in the newspaper about the murder. Your mother saw it.'

Is this all he's come to say? Is that it?

'When was that?' I say.

'That's neither here nor there,' he says. 'It was a while back.'

'I just wondered,' I say.

He reaches into his pocket, glad to have something to do.

'I can check the date if you want to know it.'

'That's fine,' I say. 'It doesn't matter.'

He looks me in the eye for the first time.

'Turns out there are some people who say we should bring back the death penalty for murderers.'

I want to stop him. He's come only to punish me. I want my mother here. But she's not here so I'll say to him what I'd like to say to her. I'll say a good thing, try and soften him.

'I'm glad you've come,' I say. 'I'm glad to see you.'

He coughs for a bit. I wait for him to stop but he's started a proper fit. One of the officers by the visitors' entrance looks over, but does nothing.

I turn round to the officer behind me. 'Can't you get him some water?'

The officer goes out, comes straight back with a small plastic cup of water, unlocks a gate and passes the water through to the officer on the visitors' side.

My father drinks but, when he tries to speak again, the coughing starts up.

It's no good.

'I'm glad you've come,' I say.

He puts his hand on his throat.

'I'm really glad you came in, Dad,' I say. 'I'm really sorry about what I've done.'

He's stopped coughing.

'Anyway,' he says. 'It's because of your mother's heart.'

'Is she sick?'

'Of course she's sick. We're all sick.'

'What's wrong with her?'

'She's got angina, what killed your gran.'

'I'm really sorry, Dad. Can you tell her I'm sorry?'

'I'll tell her. But she can't come in to see you.'

'What about Russell?'

'He'll come after the trial. He said he'll come then.'

'But I won't be here after the trial.'

'We'll see.'

'Will you come?'

'To the trial? I'm not sure, son.'

The visitor next to my father laughs. He's a young bloke, maybe eighteen, with dark shades on and earrings. He's laughing pretty loud.

My father looks back to me.

'I might come,' he says. 'I'll probably come.'

'I hope you do, Dad.'

We're silent a moment. He looks again at the visitor next to him, seems to want to make him stop laughing.

'You look tired,' he says.

'They've given me pills to sleep. I'm not so tired but they make me look tired.'

'Be careful you don't get addicted to those things.'

He looks at the visitor on the other side: a young blonde woman who's crying and wiping under her nose with her fingers.

He looks back at me.

'A normal man,' he says, 'wouldn't have gone to another man's room like that with a wrench and attacked a man in his sleep.'

'I know that,' I say.

'Do you?'

''Course I know that.'

'And what about remorse? Are you sorry?'

''Course I am.'

'You didn't say much about that in your letter.'

I thought I had.

The siren sounds.

My father gets up.

The officer shouts 'Time!'

I want the doors to open for me, to go out the gate in my father's place.

I wish my mother had come. It's nearly two months since I last saw her and I'll bet she would've come if he'd let her. She'd have shown more sympathy. She'd have shown some love. She'd have wished me luck for the trial.

'Bye, Dad,' I say.

'Goodbye, son.'

It's less than a week before my trial and there are two other prisoners in the library today. One of them reads standing up and the other sits at the table next to the radiator and he's got a newspaper over his lap so as he can rub his dick.

I sit at the other table and turn my chair away from him, face the window. I read *Blackwell's Criminal Law and Commentary*.

And the more I read of the law, the more I get to thinking that there's real hope for me. The prosecution has to prove that I wanted Welkin dead or to injure him seriously. I didn't want those things so how the hell can they prove it? And the judge has to direct the jury on the law so they're not left to their own ignorant devices and he's got to remind them about the 'burden of proof'. The burden is on the prosecution. It has to be beyond all reasonable doubt.

There are too many doubts in my case and therefore my chances must be pretty good. I get to thinking that Perkins is just playing it safe, not wanting to get my hopes up. It's probably what he was taught to do. He probably signed something like a legal Hippocratic oath that binds him never to tell a man that he'll walk free.

22

It's 8 a.m., Friday, October the nineteenth. The morning of the first day of my trial.

Perkins comes to my cell with two uniformed coppers and they've got my civilian clothes in a yellow plastic bag.

'Take a seat,' he says, as though there's more than one place to sit. 'We've got a few minutes while we wait for the transit van.'

I sit on my cot.

'Can I have that newspaper?' asks Stevenson, pointing at the paper under Perkins' arm.

'No you can't,' says one of the coppers.

'I didn't fucking ask you,' says Stevenson.

Perkins takes his suit jacket off, turns it inside out, sits on it at the end of my cot, as far away from me as he can manage without falling right off.

'The most important thing in the first few days is that we get the right jury,' he says.

He stops talking, scratches the corner of his eye.

'We're going to be okay then?' I say.

'With the right jury we might do well.'

Stevenson lights a cigarette.

'What kind of judge have I got?'

'He's not the worst you could have.'

Johnson comes to the cell.

'It's time,' he says. 'The van's here.'

The cops cuff me.

'Steady on,' says Stevenson. 'He'll not fight you.'

Stevenson puts his cigarette out, even though it's not finished, stands, picks my shoes up off the floor and hands them to me.

'Goodbye, Oxtoby,' he says. 'It's been nice not knowing you.'

The cops take an elbow each and escort me from the cell and I'm halfway down the corridor when it hits me that I've not said goodbye to Stevenson.

Maybe I've been too afraid to risk hearing the sound of it. Maybe I'll never see him again and what difference does it make what my reasons are? Either way, I haven't said goodbye and it'll never get to be said, and Stevenson's back there in the cell, alone now, and he's just given me my shoes and somebody should have at least thanked him.

I'm taken through the yard and outside the gate to the transit van.

Perkins goes to his car, a beautiful Mercedes-Benz 250C Coupé. He must know I'm watching because he turns and waves before he gets in.

Two coppers get into the front of the transit van and a third takes me round the back.

'We'll be there in about twenty minutes,' he says.

He slides the door shut and fastens the bolts.

There are four other prisoners in the van, already cuffed to the bolts in the cubicles. I say nothing to them, and the feeling's mutual. We're silent.

I've taken two pills this morning and I'm drowsy. I fall asleep pretty much straight away and I'm only woken when the van stops outside the courtroom. Photographers shout my name and flashlights go off. I duck from view and sit with my head between my knees.

The van makes its way into the yard and when the door slides open I'm met by two new coppers. They take me down to a small holding cell below the courthouse. They lock me in and don't tell me how long I'll be here.

The holding cell is the smallest I've been in. There's a sluice in the floor for hosing out, two cots, but no blankets. I sit on the cot under the barred window and wait. About an hour passes before somebody comes. It's one of the coppers who was in the transit van.

'Your trial's not starting today,' he says. 'There's been a post-ponement.'

'When then?'

'That's not rightly known,' he says. 'Probably Monday.'

He's a redhead with a red moustache and he's got a missing front tooth. He looks as bad as the crims.

He closes the cell door and I go back to the cot. I wonder if any of my family have come to see me in court and, if they have, how they've wasted their time.

Hours pass and I'm given no food and nothing to drink.

I know prisoners have a right to food and water. Stevenson told me. There's a charter of human rights for prisoners.

I knock on the cell door and the officer takes his time coming.

'Can I have something to eat and drink? And a blanket?'

'Not now. You'll be fed and watered at teatime.'

'I need to go to the toilet,' I say. 'And I know I have a right to food and water and warmth.'

'There's a bog in the corner.'

'I want to wash.'

He sniffs the air with his flat nose.

'You feel dirty,' he says. 'I don't blame you.'

He opens the door, cuffs my hands and leads me down the corridor.

'Can I have the cuffs off?'

'No.'

'How will I wash my face then?'

'You'll figure something out.'

I turn on the hot tap, cup my cuffed hands under the water and splash my face. The first thing I'll do when I'm freed is take a long hot shower and use plenty of soap and after I've washed I'll eat steak and hot chips until I burst.

'Do you always talk to yourself like a nutcase?' asks the guard.

'I wasn't,' I say.

'You just blabbered some shit about using soap when you're freed.'

'I didn't say anything.'

At six o'clock he brings me a bowl of mashed potatoes, two sausages, and a glass of water.

He puts the bowl down by the foot of my cot and, before he leaves, he kicks it over. He kicks the water over too.

'Idiot,' he says.

It's Monday morning and I've hardly slept a wink all weekend. I've got to see if I can get more pills.

The same officer comes to get me and he's got Perkins with him.

'We're starting today,' says Perkins. 'And I've got something nice for you to wear.'

He takes a dark suit out of a dry-cleaning bag and a pair of black socks and he's got me a pair of black shoes in a shopping bag.

'He can't be given that belt or tie,' says the officer. 'You can give it to him up in the courtroom and we'll take it off him when the court's adjourned.'

'I know that,' says Perkins, 'but since I'll be with him on the way up I don't see what harm it can do.'

The officer shrugs and Perkins turns his back while I dress. The officer watches.

'You'll be moved in and out of the courtroom over the next few days,' says Perkins, 'and there'll generally be a lot of housekeeping.'

The shoes are too big, but the socks are clean and warm.

'Time to go,' says the officer.

'I was given a docket in remand,' I say. 'It's for more sleeping pills. I'm wondering if could get some in here?'

The officer asks where the docket is.

'I've left it behind.'

'I'll look into it,' he says. 'Leave it with me.'

I'm taken into the empty courtroom and up the three wooden steps of the dock. The dock's door is locked by a court official and I'm told to sit between two uniformed cops, both of them already sitting and waiting.

More court officials arrive and people stand in the aisles and chat. A pair of journalists take a look at me and make some notes. One of them makes a sketch and then they leave.

None of my family's here.

'They'll be back,' says one of the coppers.

He's talking about the journalists.

At 10 a.m., the court usher, who's dressed in black, shouts into the courtroom.

'All stand.'

The judge comes through a door at the back and sits on a throne-like seat on a long bench. There are five wooden chairs behind the bench, all of them with high backs and green leather seats, and he sits in the middle.

He's wearing a red gown and a white wig and a white collar and he's an old man, so stooped he's almost bent in half and he's got a big nose swollen with burst blood vessels and he's got a big old head and big old hands.

When he speaks, he doesn't look at me. Not even once. Behind him there's a royal coat of arms with the lion wearing a crown and the chained unicorn and the words underneath *Dieu et mon droit*.

The jury gets sworn in. The process begins with twenty people, eighteen men and two women, and they're all asked the same question, whether there's any reason they can't be impartial and whether they recognise any of the names of the witnesses and then I'm asked if I have any objection to any of the potential jury members and I say no and then twelve people, ten men and two women, are randomly selected from the original twenty and they're sworn in.

It takes half the day to do this and then the court adjourns for lunch.

I'm taken down to the holding cell and given a cup of tea and two chicken sandwiches. An hour later, I'm taken back up.

The usher says, 'Will the prisoner please stand,' and then the judge asks me how I plead.

I plead not guilty.

The copper in the dock tells me I can sit.

I ask him why there are only two women on the jury and he tells me I shouldn't talk now and that you have to be a property owner to sit on a jury.

The judge is talking to the jury about how the trial will work and the rules about not discussing the case with anybody except other jurors. Somebody in the gallery laughs and the judge stops talking, looks up. I turn round and I see my mother.

She's alone at the edge of the aisle, behind the dock, and she's staring straight on, head up, like somebody's told her this is how she's got to sit, and she's acting self-conscious like she does when she's having her photo taken.

I keep on watching her and cough a bit to get her to notice me, but she won't. I don't blame her, but I wish she'd look at me at least once.

If the judge would let me out of the dock for a minute, I'd sit beside her and tell her I'm sorry for the way things ended up, sorry for the way I treated her when she came to see me at the boarding house. I'd tell her that I was wrong to talk to her the way I did.

It's half-two and there's commotion in the courtroom. My mother's collapsed in her seat and she's being carried out.

At first I think she's had a heart attack and the fear goes through me, right through to my bowels.

They carry her out like a length of carpet, two court officials hold her head and shoulders and two coppers hold her legs. The middle of her body hangs down and her dress rides up her thighs.

I've got a sudden memory of a morning before school on a hot day when we were in the kitchen and it was so hot my mother hitched her dress up and tucked the corners into her knickers and I went bright red and looked away.

I go red like that now and the double courtroom doors are held open and the courtroom's dead quiet and when my mum's carried through the door she says, 'My bag.'

As soon as she's left, the prosecutor, Mr Nielsen QC, continues making his opening speech to the jury, keeps talking as though nothing's happened.

'Members of the jury,' he says, 'I'm going to provide you with the factual outline of this case, the skeleton, if you like, to which I will gradually add more flesh as we proceed and, when I have finished outlining the factual framework, I want you to consider this simple question very carefully.

'Why would a man, who says he had neither an intention to do grievous bodily harm, nor to kill, bring a heavy weapon into the bedroom of his neighbour in the dead of night and strike with sufficient force to kill?'

He speaks slowly, every word important and yet every word spoken as though he's bored, as though the conclusion is so obvious, the outcome so clear and necessary, that there's no need for emphasis.

'You will hear evidence,' says Nielsen, 'that the prisoner had a heated argument with the deceased and that the deceased had borrowed and failed to return the prisoner's alarm clock in a timely manner—'

Nielsen laughs, looks at the judge and the judge gives him a wry, tight-mouthed grin and says, 'I trust there was no pun intended.'

'None at all,' says Nielsen. 'In any case, the prisoner's response to this rather trifling matter was to reach a fever pitch of anger. You will also hear evidence…'

As Nielsen goes on, Perkins scratches his hands like a man bitten by fleas and, when he's not scratching, he's moving documents in and out of his black folders as though he hopes that moving them will erase what's there and replace his watery words with better ones.

Middleton and Davies have both been in the witness box giving evidence about my arrest and I've fallen asleep.

I'm woken by one of the coppers and the courtroom's empty again.

Perkins comes to the dock, three black folders in his arms.

'You should probably try and stay awake,' he says.

'I didn't sleep last night.'

'Why not?'

'It's too cold in the cell and I don't have my pills.'

'All right. I'll make sure you get some blankets and some pills. But you've got to stay awake during the proceedings. It makes a very bad impression on the jury if you fall asleep.'

'Okay.'

'I'll bring some blankets from home.'

'Thanks.'

He nods. 'I'll see you tomorrow.'

The coppers take me down to the holding cell.

The next morning I look round to the public seats and up to the gallery.

I want to see my mum again, want to see that's she's okay. I don't expect my father will come, but I expect her.

The gallery's full. Schoolchildren and university students, probably law students, most of them taking notes, being ushered in and out by teachers and told to be quiet, not to lean over the gallery rail.

The pathologist's in the witness box for three hours and the upshot is just like Perkins said. There was a blow to the right of the skull, the right temple, at least one blow—but perhaps more than one—and the blow was struck with a force sufficient to cause an acute subdural haematoma.

Nielsen gets the pathologist to go into graphic detail about the injury and how it might have taken as long as an hour for Welkin to die, that he might have been in agonising pain or paralysed from the neck down, unable to call for help.

Perkins tries to discredit the evidence about the length of time it took Welkin to die and all he manages to do is cut the time down by half an hour and, by going over and over how long it took, I think he has made it worse. And when Perkins asks, 'Is it possible that the defendant, Patrick Oxtoby, might have delivered only a single blow?' the pathologist says, 'Yes, but in my professional opinion it would have been delivered with tremendous force.'

'In your report,' says Perkins, 'there is a reference to only one contact point, one site of impact. This suggests, does it not, that there was only a single blow?'

'It might, or it might suggest accuracy of repeated blows.'

Perkins raises his voice. 'This seems an unlikelihood does it not? Two blows to the very same site? Two blows to precisely the same contact point?'

The pathologist looks at the judge and says, 'Yes. Perhaps that's unlikely. But not impossible.'

'Not impossible, but unlikely?'

'Yes.'

Perkins gets onto the subject of Welkin's drunkenness and the pathologist admits that it's possible Welkin's state of intoxication contributed to death. Marginally, he says, to a negligible extent.

Perkins says, 'No further questions' and the court's adjourned.

I'm taken back down to the holding cell.

There'll be no more today.

'You've got company,' says the copper who takes me down to the holding cell. 'His name's Gardam and he's on for murder.'

I go in.

My cell-mate stares at me and I wonder if it's finally time for a proper beating.

He's about thirty, muscular, and he's got tattoos on his arms and hands.

I sit on my cot which means I'm pretty close to him. Closer than I want.

'Hiya,' he says.

He goes on staring at me. The whites of his eyes are yellow with smears of red, like eggs with blood in them.

'Hello,' I say.

He doesn't say any more and he doesn't look interested in violence.

The cell's already a bit warmer with two men in it and, so long as he doesn't want any aggro, it'll be better to have mute company than none at all.

When dinner arrives, Gardam gets up from his cot and shouts at the officer through the hatch, 'We don't want any.'

I won't tell him I wanted the food. I won't cause any trouble until I know who I'm dealing with.

At half-eight an officer comes to the cell with Perkins and he's got two thick, woolly blankets with him.

'I hope you can get some sleep,' he says. 'Tomorrow's a big day.'

'Thanks,' I say.

'The landlady's going to be in court tomorrow,' he says. 'She's appearing for the prosecution, but based on things you've said earlier it seems to me that it's likely she's going to be very much on your side. Am I right?'

'Yeah. She is. She liked me.'

'And there was never any friction or trouble between you?'

'That's right.'

He looks at his watch.

'I'd better dash. See you tomorrow morning.'

He leaves.

I go back to the cot.

'Is that your brief?' says Gardam.

'Yeah.'

'He seems a bit nervy or something.'

'A bit.'

'Doesn't that make you shit yourself? That your brief's got a kind of lispy voice?'

'He's okay in court though,' I lie. 'I think he'll be good.'

He's silent for a minute, then says, 'Want to hear something funny?'

'Yeah.'

'Since the death penalty ended a few years back you're about ten times more likely to be done for murder.'

245

'Right,' I say. 'That's a laugh.'

We're silent for a minute.

'Do you want one of these blankets?' I say.

'He brought them for you, but.'

'I don't need two,' I say.

I stand and go to his cot.

'Well, if you don't want it,' he says. 'I might as well take it.'

I give him the blanket and go back to my cot, which isn't far away.

'I hate red,' he says.

He's talking about the colour of the blanket I've just given him.

'What did you do?' I say. 'What are you on trial for?'

'Killed my wife.'

'Right.'

23

It's Wednesday, day three of my trial, just gone 11 a.m. and already the courtroom's sticky with heat. The radiators are turned up too high and the jurors are wearing bright summery clothes, as though they've made a mistake, turned up out of costume, and they pay even less attention than usual to what's being said. They might as well be on an excursion, a day out to ride paddleboats or to picnic by the river. Worst of all is the foreman, a lanky man with a thin black moustache, who's wearing a shirt with flowers on it and he makes sure I'm watching when he yawns.

'Your Lord, if it pleases the court,' says Nielsen QC, 'I call Mrs Bridget Bowman.'

Bridget's brought into the court by the usher.

She's the fourth witness for the prosecution.

If I'd seen her in the street, I'd not have recognised her. Her face is bloated and her neck is wide and thick, as though there's a lot of fat stored there waiting to go down to the rest of her body.

She climbs into the witness box and the usher closes the door, making sure her hands and feet are securely inside, like he's closing the passenger door of a car.

After Bridget's sworn in, Nielsen looks at the jury and nods three times, slowly, as though to say, *Now, listen carefully to this. It won't take a minute, then you can go back to your boat ride.*

'Your full name please.'

'Bridget Jane Bowman.'

'Your title?'

'Mrs.'

'Your occupation?'

'Landlady.'

Bridget leans forward, puts her mouth nearer the microphone.

'You have been the proprietor at 128 Vauxhall Street for fourteen years? Is that correct?'

'Yes.'

'And you take in boarders who must stay for a minimum of four months and who each pay a bond equivalent to six weeks' half-board?'

She pushes her face forward, even closer to the microphone and says, 'That includes breakfast and dinner.'

'Mrs Bowman,' says the judge. 'We'll be able to hear you so long as you speak nice and clearly. There's no need to gobble up that microphone. We don't have many to spare.'

He smiles at her, hoping she'll like the joke, but she just nods and moves back in her seat.

Nielsen continues. 'Half-board, then?'

'Yes. And my boarders also have their rooms cleaned weekly and their laundry and—'

'Mrs Bowman,' says Mr Nielsen, 'please remain pertinent and relevant to the question in question.'

'Sorry,' she says.

'Mrs Bowman, when, in the early hours of the twenty-ninth of August, you went to the bedroom of the victim, Mr Ian Welkin, a young boarder at your premises, did you find that he was quite clearly dead?'

Some of the jurors look across at me soon as they hear the word *dead*.

Bridget nods.

'For the transcript, Mrs Bowman, and so that the jury can hear you, you'll need to say yes.'

'Yes.'

She turns round and looks at me. There's no anger about her. She's nervous, but she's made this effort to look at me.

I smile at her.

She looks back to the prosecutor.

'When you went to the room at—' Nielsen refers to his notes '—approximately six o'clock on the morning of Saturday, the twenty-ninth of August, you found Mr Welkin was quite plainly dead?'

'Yes.'

'How did you ascertain that he was dead?'

'I checked his pulse and then his breathing.'

There's a taste of dirt in my mouth.

'You also stated in your interview with the police that there was blood coming from his nose and mouth.'

'Yes, but—'

'And, after you tested for a pulse and for breathing, you found no signs of—'

The judge coughs. 'I think you might be labouring the point here, Mr Nielsen. I don't think the fact of death is in any dispute. We have a corpse and a coroner's report to prove it.'

Nielsen smiles. 'Yes, of course.'

It's Perkins' turn to cross-examine Bridget.

'Mrs Bowman, did you ever feel in any danger when you were in the company of the defendant, Mr Patrick Oxtoby?'

'Never,' she says. 'He was always gentle and courteous. He was very respectful.'

'And did you ever hear him threaten the deceased?'

'No. I thought they were getting along very well. Mr Welkin liked Patrick. He told me so. I was very shocked when I found Ian was dead.'

'And on the evening of the incident in question you spent some time with Patrick in the sitting room drinking brandy and talking?'

'Yes.'

'And the mood was courteous and respectful?'

'Yes.'

Perkins doesn't ask what the chat was about that night, but I know Nielsen will.

'The general demeanour of the defendant from the time he arrived at your establishment a week earlier, and up to and including the night in question, it was a good and cheerful mood?'

'Yes. Patrick was always kind and in good spirits.'

She goes on to say that I shouldn't be called a murderer: 'The prosecution makes it sound like it's his profession when they call him a murderer, but I know he didn't mean to kill Ian Welkin.'

One of the jurors, one of the women, whispers something to the man next to her and the man shakes his head as though to say *Only an idiot would believe that crap* and the foreman looks at me like he wishes I was dead.

Nielsen re-examines Bridget.

He gets her to mention the business with the missing clock, and that I said 'Fuck this' when I stood in the kitchen doorway, and that I said 'Fuck this' again on the night of the murder when I left the sitting room.

And then:

'Mrs Bowman, as I understand it, on the evening before Mr Welkin's death, the defendant had several cross words with the deceased. Correct me if I'm wrong, but I think I have this right. You and the prisoner were in the sitting room with the deceased and you and the prisoner were sitting very close together on the settee.

'As I understand it, the prisoner had his hand on your leg and then the deceased wanted to sit beside you and the prisoner shouted, "I'll kill you if you touch her" and then he stormed upstairs—'

'No,' she says. 'He didn't say that and it was Mr Welkin who was sitting close to me and he was the one who had his hand on my leg and Patrick lost his temper a little bit—'

She realises her mistake and stops.

'I have no further questions,' says Nielsen.

When Bridget's released from the stand, she walks by the dock without looking at me and it's pretty obvious to me she wants the jury and all the people in the gallery to know she's had no physical contact or association with me and never would.

I tap the shoulder of the copper on my right.

'I'm not well,' I say.

I've a terrible shooting pain in my head and I'm dizzy with a churning gut, a bit like vertigo. You might never before have thought of jumping, but when the ground swirls up, you have that sick urge to jump.

The copper calls for the usher so I can be taken down from the dock and an adjournment is called. As soon as the courtroom's cleared and I start to move, I'm sick in the dock.

'Oh shit,' says the copper.

I want to talk to Perkins and see if it's not too late to plead guilty to manslaughter and bring an end to this.

The copper takes me down to the holding cell, supports me under the arms, takes the steps slowly.

He's got a kind sort of face. He even smiles at me.

'Are you able to walk now?' he says.

'Yeah,' I say.

He takes me into the cell.

'All right?'

'Yeah.'

A few minutes later he comes back with water in a paper cone and a box of tissues so I can wipe myself clean.

'Knock on the door if you want to throw up again,' he says.

Gardam's come back from his day in the dock.

'How was it?' he asks.

'Bad,' I say. 'It's all turned against me.'

'Me too. There was a friend of my wife's in the witness box saying my wife never hurt a fly and she cried so hard they took her out of the box and she went out and probably had a fag and then came back right as rain. I don't think my self-defence story's going to work out.'

'Was it self-defence?'

'Not in the legal sense probably no.'

We both stop talking, stop and go stony quiet, but not because of what he's said. We stop because there's the smell of fish and chips outside. The smell of vinegar's strong and so is the smell of the salty batter.

I stand. I can't stay sitting.

There's somebody at the cell door.

'Stand back,' he says.

It's the red-headed officer and he's delivering fish and chips. He puts the tray down on the floor and I nearly cry out at the sight of it. Two big piles of hot fish and chips brought in from the local chippy and there's four pickled onions and two battered sausages. I grab my plate and sit on the cot to eat.

'If you get sick again,' says the guard, 'raise the alarm. Okay?'

'Okay.'

Gardam doesn't take his meal.

'You can have mine,' he says.

'You sure?'

'Yeah.'

I take his plate and set about eating both lots. I eat like a wolf, don't say a word while I do it and don't care that Gardam's going hungry. I lick my lips and my fingers and I lick the plates clean and I can't remember a meal ever tasting so good.

I lie down afterwards and so does he and I'm almost asleep when he talks again.

'Did you spew today?' he says.

'Yeah.'

'Everybody does it at least once.'

'Yeah?'

'And they usually also talk a lot.'

I sit up and face him.

'I got the impression you didn't want to talk.'

'Yeah, but then I realised you might be the last person I ever talk to.'

Gardam lights a cigarette and sucks the smoke so hard into his lungs there's hardly anything left to exhale.

'Do you want to talk now?' I say.

'I stabbed my wife,' he says. 'Knifed her at least ten times.'

'Right.'

'I did it with a kitchen devil.'

'That's a sharp knife.'

He looks at me like I'm an idiot.

'Why did you kill her?'

'I don't know,' he says. 'Maybe because she was a bitch.'

His cigarette's finished and he puts his orange finger in his mouth. 'Anyway, I feel like shit. My trial's nearly over and I'm going down for life.'

'I'm sorry,' I say.

'I want to die,' he says.

He's got a tattoo of a swallow on his neck and I want to ask him why it's a swallow.

'Still, I'm sorry,' I say. 'But maybe—?'

'Maybe nothing. I just want to die now.'

I say nothing.

'Ever noticed,' he says, 'when men get older, they laugh less and less?'

I shrug.

'Even a dog keeps wagging its tail when it gets older.'

I've an image of a man sewing his lips shut, a thick needle piercing the flesh and the white thread dragged through, but there's no blood, just the needle going through.

24

It's Thursday the twenty-fifth of October. Day four of my trial. Perkins comes to the cell to tell me there's a delay, an adjournment till tomorrow.

'How are you holding up?' he says.

'I hate the way the jurors look at me. They look like they hate me or they don't care.'

'That's normal. Don't take it personally. Some of them are probably intimidated by the formality of the proceedings.'

'Okay.'

'Are you sleeping?'

'I want to plead guilty to manslaughter.'

'I thought we'd gone over this. I told you then you needed to make your mind up. It's too late now. You'll have to let the jury decide.'

'And if they decide I'm guilty of murder?'

'Then we might consider an appeal.'

'And if I lose that?'

He puts his hand on my upper arm, squeezes a little.

'We'll cross that bridge when we come to it. I hope we won't come to it.'

'So you're still optimistic?'

'Yes.'

I nod. He takes his hand away and leaves a patch of warmth behind.

'I have to go now. Is there anything you need? Anything that can't wait?'

'Could you bring me some books?'

'What kind?'

'Maybe something about snooker or cars or something like that.'

'I'll do my best.'

He leaves.

Gardam's still up in his courtroom, the one across the hall from mine. This means I've got the cell to myself.

I get under both blankets.

An hour or so later, a doctor comes.

'Don't get up,' he says.

He crouches down beside me.

'I'm going to give you some pills for the next few days,' he says. 'The pink one is to stop you getting sick and the white one will help you sleep. But they're pretty strong. You might feel quite drowsy.'

'Thanks,' I say.

'You're welcome.'

'I suppose I won't be able to drink alcohol or operate heavy machinery.'

He smiles and pats my hand.

'Good luck.'

When he leaves, I get up and put one of the blankets on Gardam's cot.

I take the pills and sleep through till morning.

After breakfast, day five of my trial, the guard gives me four more pills, two of each.

'You'll get more tonight,' he says.

'Is my brief coming?'

'Yes, soon as he can get here.'

Gardam doesn't eat his breakfast, stays in his cot under the thick blanket.

He leaves his breakfast bowl at the foot of his bed and looks at me.

'Do you want one of my pills?' I say.

'Yeah. Good.'

'Don't you want to know what it is?'

'It's a drug, right? Something that'll take the edge off?'

'Yeah.'

'Well I want it then, who wouldn't?'

I go to him with the pill, but he's changed his mind. He holds his hands out for me, shows me how violent his shakes are.

'Maybe keep it,' he says. 'It's your pill.'

I put the pill down on the floor next to his bowl of cereal.

'You can have it later,' I say. 'But maybe you should eat first.'

He looks down at the pill.

'Maybe you could mix it through the cereal for me,' he says. 'That'll force me to eat a bit.'

I crush the pill between my finger and thumb and sprinkle it over the cereal.

'You'll have to mix it through,' he says. 'Or I might just eat the top.'

I mix the pill through the milk and cornflakes with the plastic spoon, then hand him the bowl.

'Hope I don't puke me guts up,' he says. 'I haven't eaten for days.'

The courtroom's packed and, just as I'm being cuffed to the rail of the dock, my father walks in.

He's alone and he's wearing a black suit and he sits at the outside edge of a wooden pew, close to the aisle. I swallow, but it's too late to stop my eyes from flooding and too late to stop the thought that, if I'm convicted of murder, I might not see him again, or only if I'm allowed a day's leave to go to his funeral.

I look at him, just keep looking, but he gets up from his seat and leaves. His chin is thrust forward at a strange angle and his feet take short, quick steps. Maybe he's only come so that he could leave, so that I'd be forced to watch him leaving and, in this way, even without speaking, he's told me he doesn't want to see me again, that he's seen the last of me.

I look at the jurors.

Nothing but contempt.

The court's adjourned till Monday morning.

I ask the copper for some paper and a pen and he gives me a page from his pocketbook.

I write a note for Perkins, *I need to talk to you*. It gets passed over.

He comes to the dock.

'What is it?'

'I want this to stop. I want to plead guilty to manslaughter or something.'

He shakes his head, takes no time to think it over.

'It's too late. I'm almost certain the Crown will refuse it.'

'Why?'

'It's too late.'

'What do you think of my chances now?'

'The same as before. No better and no worse.'

'Fair to middling?'

'Perhaps a little better than that. The landlady was a hostile witness.'

I frown.

'Although she was called by the prosecution, she took every chance to say things in your favour.'

'So, do you think—'

'Listen, Patrick, I've absolutely got to be going. I'm running very late.'

He's got my blood boiling.

'Do you have a dinner engagement?' I say.

He looks away, thinks a moment, then turns back, looks at me, hard and square.

'No, Patrick. I have a hospital to go to. My wife's taken quite seriously ill.'

'Shit,' I say. 'I'm sorry.'

I don't know if I believe him.

I've taken another pill and I've given the second to Gardam.

The heating's broken down and it's 2 a.m. and neither of us can sleep. We sit on our cots with our blankets wrapped round our shoulders and we've both got our arms wrapped round our legs.

We've been talking for a couple of hours. He suddenly gets weepy.

'Misery's made me a cunt,' he says.

'How so?' I say.

'My father was a fucking cunt too. He savaged me and I've gone and done the same. I once said to a bloke—we was stood outside a laundrette—I won't kill you but I will make you walk with a limp.'

I've no idea what to say.

'I've ended up here 'cos I was fucking miserable, and now that I'm here, I'm even more miserable.'

'I know what you mean,' I say.

I lie down, put my head on the pillow.

'Are you going to sleep now?' he asks.

'I'm going to try,' I say.

'You do that,' he says. 'I'll talk to myself.'

Gardam talks till late every night, and then at 6.30 on Monday morning we're both awake, seem to have woken at the same instant, both of us too nervous about the final days of our trials to get rest and last night there were no more pills to get us through.

'I'll warn you now about the last day,' he says. 'The courtroom's gonna be packed with onlookers. All the fucking ghouls will come.'

I open the book that Perkins gave me, a book about deep-sea diving.

'Like Houdini said,' Gardam goes on, 'they'll come to see you die.'

I close the book. 'You like Houdini?'

'You know,' he says, 'when men got hanged for murder the hangman used to fill a sack with sand and the sand was weighed so it was the same as what you weighed.'

'Why?'

'To make sure your head broke clean off your neck.'

A few years ago and that's what I might've faced.

I look at a picture of a deep-sea fish. It looks happier than me and a lot happier than Gardam.

'Look at this fish,' I say.

'And they put a big dish under the trap door to catch your shit,' he says.

I say nothing.

After the officer's come to the cell with our breakfast, Perkins arrives.

He's wearing a dark suit and a red scarf tied in a loose knot around his neck and there are crumbs on the scarf, as though to show me he's been wearing it while he had his delicious hot breakfast. I take this as proof his wife's not sick and dying in hospital.

'Good morning,' he says.

He turns his coat inside out and, with the silk lining face down, he sits on the coat, at the very end of my cot.

'The bed's not dirty,' I say. 'They wash the blankets.'

'I see,' he says. 'I went to the judge last night to have Georgia Powell struck out as a witness,' he says, 'but she's been subpoenaed because you used your phone call from South King Street police station to speak to her. Do you remember? You phoned her on the day of your arrest.'

'Yes.'

I'd forgotten her last name was Powell.

'You should have told me this. You really should have told me this.'

'Will it make any difference?'

'The prosecution will undoubtedly make something of the fact that you used your phone call to speak to a girlfriend and not your family.'

'I tried to call my mum that morning, but the phone was out of order.'

'You should have called your mother from the police station instead of calling your girlfriend.'

'Georgia isn't my girlfriend.'

'Be that as it may,' he says.

Gardam stands and goes to the cell door, slides the hatch across and shouts out for a packet of cigarettes.

'I need some fags!' he shouts. 'Somebody bring me some fags!'

Perkins reaches for his briefcase.

'I've got some purple Silk Cut,' he says.

'Can't stand them,' says Gardam.

Perkins stops looking in his briefcase.

A few moments later, Gardam gets up. 'You'd better give me one of those then,' he says.

Perkins finds the pack and hands it over.

'Take the pack.'

We both watch Gardam light up.

'But why is Georgia being called?' I say.

'Because of the things you said to her.'

'I hardly said anything.'

'Well, that's the prosecution's very point. It's what you didn't say that they'll endeavour to use against you.'

In his effort to hide the fact that he's irritated, Perkins speaks now as though he has a pen between his teeth.

'The prosecution will argue that what you didn't say further supports a verdict of murder. They'll say your silence evinces an intention to kill.'

The officer comes.

'Time to go,' he says.

Perkins gets up and goes to speak to Gardam.

'Didn't you ever learn how to say please and thank you?'

Gardam looks at Perkins like he's a fool.

Most of the morning the judge's been talking to the prosecutor, on a 'point of law' as they say, and the jury's been sent out and my mouth's dry and my tongue's hot. I've had this terrible thirst since the trial started and they only give me one glass of water in the morning and I usually have to wait until the midday adjournment for another.

I turn to the cop on my left and point to my tongue. He looks away, puts both hands on the rail of the dock like a man seasick on a boat.

'Water,' I whisper.

He ignores me.

'Water,' I say.

He does nothing.

The prosecutor calls a new witness, a girl by the name of Mandy. Nielsen introduces her to the courtroom as Welkin's future bride. I've never seen her before and I'd remember if I had. She's got long, straight blonde hair, all the way down to her hips, and she's got the face of an idiot.

According to Nielsen, the relationship with Welkin, although a long-distance one, was very strong. Mandy, he tells the court, was doing an apprenticeship at a hair salon. Instead of salon, he mispronounces the word as *saloon*.

'And is it not true that you would very likely have married?' he asks.

'Yes,' she says, 'that's completely all true.'

'Is it also true that the deceased was due to meet you at the hair saloon the day that he was murdered?'

'Yes. He was going to come on the early train.'

'And is it not also true that he meant to continue to discuss the prospect of marriage—'

'But he screwed other women. He screwed them like rabbits. He used them up like cheap whores. He probably screwed Georgia.'

The judge calls for order, asks the prisoner to stop shouting.

I hadn't known I was shouting.

Perkins cross-examines Mandy pretty well. He manages to establish that the couple were not officially engaged, that their relationship was not only long-distance but that they'd only spent a week together, that they had known each other for less than two months, that Mandy is as dumb as she looks.

Welkin's alleged future bride is released from the witness box and it's the end of the day's proceedings.

Perkins comes to reassure me.

'I don't think that did the Crown much good,' he says.

'Why not?'

'She wasn't very credible.'

'That's good.'

He flicks his cuff, looks at his watch, walks away.

It's Tuesday, day seven, and Georgia's in the witness box. She's wearing a black dress over black trousers and her long hair is tied in a neat, shiny ponytail.

Nielsen's examination-in-chief begins.

'What did the accused say to you, Miss Powell, when he phoned you on the morning of the twenty-ninth of August?'

'He said he'd done something mad. That he'd done something really stupid.'

'Miss Powell,' says the judge. 'You may relax in the seat. And please make sure you continue to speak clearly.'

She smiles at him and what a lovely smile, the first I've seen in court, the bright smile of a movie star.

The prosecutor goes on. 'And what did he say next, Miss Powell?'

'He said that he'd killed one of the boarders. He said he'd killed the man in the next room.'

'And what else did he say?'

'Nothing.'

'I have your statement here, Mrs…I beg your pardon, Miss Powell, and if you'd like me to refresh your memory—'

'He said he didn't expect to be in a cell. He said he wanted to be with me.'

She looks over at me and I want to look away. Yesterday I saw my face in the mirror in the showers and I looked ugly.

Mr Nielsen QC looks at the jury. 'But he wasn't upset, Miss Powell, or sad, or remorseful—'

'Yes. But—'

'Yes. And what did he say had made him so angry?'

'Because he'd been looking forward to all the things we could do together.'

'Including sexual things?'

'He didn't say that.'

'But he did speak, at some length, about the romantic things he'd been looking forward to doing to you?'

'*With* me.'

'Ah, I see, so it's true, Miss Powell, that he had romance on his mind?'

Perkins attempts to object on the grounds that the questions aren't relevant and his objection is overruled.

The judge goes so far as to roll his eyes.

Nielsen presses on. 'Did he have romance on his mind, Miss Powell?'

Georgia's got to speak loud now to be heard because there's rain falling hard and it beats like a drum against the skylight.

'That's not exactly what—'

'And in your statement, here on pages three and four,' continues Nielsen, 'you make it plain that he didn't mention the cold-blooded attack but only his disappointment that you wouldn't meet. He was angry, was he not, that your romantic tryst had been thwarted?'

Georgia sits up taller.

'Yes. I suppose he was a bit angry, but—'

'That'll be all, Miss Powell.'

She looks at me and when she turns back to Nielsen she speaks to him with a steady voice.

'Patrick is a good man and he's not a murderer and he wanted me to—'

The judge intervenes.

'That's enough, Miss Powell. Thank you. That will be all.'

Perkins begins his cross-examination of Georgia.

'I will also now refer to the statement you made to the police at South King Street. Could you please open that statement to page three.'

She does.

'Did you not say, Miss Powell, that when the defendant called you from the police station he said, "I didn't kill him. I didn't mean to kill him, but he's dead. I only hit him once"?'

'Yes. That's right.'

'And did you not also say, "He sounded sad and regretful"?'

'Yes, that's right. He kept saying, "I didn't mean to kill him."'

And on it goes like this and, for the first time, I get an optimistic mood going and when Georgia leaves the court and passes the dock we look at each other and she smiles and I'm sure we'll meet again and that we might meet again soon.

But this better mood is short-lived.

Greg Hayes is called next and the prosecutor asks only three questions. The first is this:

'Was there any reason, Mr Hayes, why the prisoner should bring his toolkit home?'

'No, not unless—'

'A simple yes or no will suffice.'

'No.'

Hayes doesn't look at me.

'So, he might as well have left his tools at work?'

'Yes.'

'Do you carry your tools home at night, Mr Hayes?'

'No.'

'That'll be all, your honour.'

Perkins cross-examines Hayes and he manages to get Hayes to tell the court that I was 'very particular' about my tools and that this might account for the fact that I carried them home with me. He also gets across the fact that I was a 'willing and capable' worker.

The jurors have started taking more notes.

Gardam's already in the cell and he's sitting on my cot, staring at the floor between his feet.

'I've a favour to ask,' he says.

I stand with my back to the door.

266

'What?'

'Can you smuggle your tie back into the cell on the last day?'

'But it gets confiscated on the way down.'

'You could roll it up and stick it in your pants.'

'I can't.'

'You mean you don't want to.'

'No. I don't want to.'

'You'd be doing me a big favour.'

'I can't.'

'It's my life.'

'I can't do it.'

Gardam hugs his knees to his chest. I want him off my cot, but he's not going anywhere. I stand with my back to the door and wait.

Shaun Flindall is called on day eight, first thing. He's dressed as though for a dinner party: a pinstripe suit.

'I heard him shouting,' he says. 'I heard him shout, "Get out of my room, you fucking shit!" and I heard him bashing the walls.'

'When was this, Mr Flindall?'

'A few days before the murder. I distinctly heard him shouting.'

'And who do you think he was shouting at?'

'I didn't hear Mr Welkin in the room with Mr Oxtoby, but it must have been Mr Welkin. There were no other boarders staying on the first floor and Mr Oxtoby didn't ever bring a guest.'

'Thank you, Mr Flindall, that'll be all.'

The cop on my right shrugs and points at his watch.

The next morning Perkins visits my cell. He's got another suitcase.

'I think you should take the stand tomorrow.'

'No.'

'I think you should.'

'I don't think I should.'

'It's very important that we try this. You must trust my instincts on this.'

I'd like to know why he's so blunt and forceful in this dark cell with me and why he's got no stones in the courtroom.

'If you don't lose your temper,' he says, 'I think the jury will like you.'

'Are you sure?'

'I'm positive this is the right strategy. If we play our cards right, the jury will like you. You've got to get their sympathy and this is the only way to do it.'

I take a minute to think on it.

'Okay,' I say. 'But will you help me out?'

Perkins opens the suitcase.

'Here's a clean suit and a decent pair of shoes.'

The suit's lined with silk.

'Yes,' he says. 'I'll help you out.'

He spends two hours with me.

25

On day ten, I take the stand. I'm the only witness for the defence.

The jurors look up at the hail pelting the skylight, shake their heads, probably worry about the fact they didn't bring their umbrellas.

Perkins asks me easy questions, the ones we went over yesterday. I get a chance to talk about how well I did at school and how I scored very well to get into the grammar school and then university and I talk about my work as a mechanic and I get to paint a picture of myself as a pretty upstanding member of the community. I get to say over and over that I've been misunderstood and that what I did was stupid and I say the same thing about twenty times, 'I didn't mean to kill him.'

The jurors don't take notes when I'm talking but they lean forward in their seats like the good bit of the movie's just started, and the people in the gallery move closer to the rails so they can get a nice close look at me, and the judge puts his pen and yellow pad away and picks his nose with his thumb and forefinger and, even though he sees that I can see him, he's not in the least bit embarrassed. It's not real. Not any of it. It's like a play and everybody's acting in it and, at the end, I'll walk out that big double door behind me and shake my head. But that's bullshit. This is as real as it gets. This is how it goes.

The prosecutor begins his cross-examination.

'I'm going to refer to your statement made on the twenty-ninth of August at South King Street.'

I've already drunk most of the water they've given me, and my mouth's bone-dry.

'Do you have a copy of this statement in front of you?'

'Yes.'

'I refer now,' he says, 'to page six of your statement. The jury also has a copy of your statement in their folders of evidence.'

He waits while the jurors find the page.

'In paragraph three of this statement you say, "I don't know why I hit him. He'd made me angry and it was just as though he was in my way." Is this what you said?'

What I did lasted just a few seconds. The time it took to raise and lower a hand.

I look at the jury. 'Yes,' I say. 'I think so, but I also said—'

'You think so? Could you please read the relevant paragraph and confirm for the court that these are in fact your words?'

I read: *I don't know why I hit him. He'd made me angry and it was just as though he was in my way. And I thought he'd got away with too much and he was treating Bridget badly and I wanted him to answer my questions and I wanted his apology. I wanted to wake him up. I wanted to make him face things.*

'Is this what you told the police?'

'Yes. I said this, but I also said—'

'And did you then explain this idea further in paragraph eight: "I wanted to get on with things and he (the deceased) was in the way."'

I want the skylight to crack open, let the water pour down, let it carry me out in a flood.

'Yes. I said that, but—'

'In your statement, you say you went back to your room, and took some time there, a few minutes, and in this time you made a decision to

270

return to the deceased's room with a weapon. You took some time. You said in your statement it was at least ten minutes. Time to drink a glass or two of water. Time to collect your thoughts. Why did you decide to return to the deceased's room?'

I can't respond to this. I don't remember why. I don't think I thought why I did. I don't know what I was thinking. It's possible I didn't think at all.

'I don't know,' I say. 'It was complicated.'

'It was complicated and yet it was simple. Is it the case that you had time to think and time to calm down but you returned to the deceased's room and you returned with a weapon?'

'Yes.'

'You also say in your statement that you didn't think a blow to the head with a heavy implement could kill a sleeping man. Is that correct?'

'That's right.'

'Perhaps I'm missing something obvious, but I don't see how you could have formed that view.'

'I didn't want to kill him.'

My throat's dry, but it'll go against me if I stop this to ask for water.

'So, you formed the view that a heavy and forceful blow to the unprotected skull of a sleeping man, with a weapon weighing more than two large hammers, couldn't kill a man?'

One of the male jurors laughs.

'I only meant to wake him up,' I say.

Nielsen smiles like the cat that's got the cream or whatever the hell that fucking expression is and he turns again to his audience to gloat.

'One doesn't ordinarily wake a man by clubbing his skull with an adjustable wrench.'

'I didn't think that the blow would kill him. I didn't mean to kill him.'

Nielsen shakes his head.

'That'll be all.'

The judge's got his head down and he's scribbling on his yellow notepad and the jurors watch the judge.

I watch the judge.

We all watch and wait for the judge.

And then we all look up at the public gallery where there's a madman hanging over the front rails and he's shouting, 'Hats off, strangers!' He shouts the same thing over and over until he's evicted by the usher.

When Perkins has his second round with me, it's all downhill. I've been four hours in the stand and I can hardly breathe with the sadness and all my answers are just yes or no or I don't know. He doesn't really give me a single chance to say any redeeming thing.

He tries for a while to make something of the fact that if I had wanted to kill Welkin I would have used a great deal more force and violence than I did. I was in the room alone with Welkin. I had plenty of time and I had the right weapon. If I'd wanted to kill him, if I'd been in a rage, or if I'd had a motive to kill him, I'd have beaten him more thoroughly and there'd have been more than a single blow. He makes a big fuss out of the single blow.

After I step down from the witness box, the judge asks the usher to have the key exhibit, the weapon, passed round for the jury to feel its 'heft and weight', which as far as I know are the same thing. I go back to the dock and watch. The passing round of the wrench wakes the jury up good and proper and they take their time with it, raising it and lowering, fast not slow, much as they think I must have done.

Gardam's lying on his cot, facing the wall. I tell him about my day in the box.

'I don't know why you're so surprised people don't care about you.'

'I just expected a bit more,' I say. 'Considering what's at stake.'

He turns round, sits up.

'You have to wait the whole weekend for your verdict.'

'I know it.'

'When I copped my first sentence,' he says, 'the magistrate was this really pretty thing. She tracked me down after I got out of Borstal. I was fourteen and she said she wanted to help me. She knew I'd get roughed up in that place. And I did. She was a real nice woman. But I didn't take her help.'

'Maybe she could help you now?'

'No. I wouldn't want her to see me. She was very pretty.'

I look across and see, in the dim light, the features of Gardam's face, softened and blurred. I see that he wasn't always as ugly. There would've been plenty of people willing to help him.

I'm woken on Monday morning for breakfast but the guard tells me the jury's still out deliberating, sequestered to a hotel in town, probably the Midlands, and I've got to wait for him to fetch me when they come back in. I might have to wait another day or two or even three. Just me alone in the cell while Gardam's up in his trial. Just me and the book about the deep-sea fish. The longer the jury takes, the better. That's what Perkins said. But I don't know how much more waiting I can stomach.

At noon the cell door's opened and I expect it to be lunch.

'Jury's coming back,' says the guard.

I stand from the cot and he cuffs me and takes me up the stone steps to the dock.

Perkins isn't here. He should be here. He should be here to talk to me. Everybody else is here. The public in the gallery and the journalists.

The usher goes to the door at the front of the courtroom next to the bench and he knocks three times then opens the door and the jury's called in. As they walk into the jury box they all take a good long look at me. They look at me as though it's the first time they've seen me.

Perkins arrives late and flustered, his black cape flapping, his wig on crooked. He apologises to the judge but doesn't look at me.

The judge turns to the jury and asks for their verdict and, as the foreman stands with the piece of paper in his hand, the same madman who was evicted from the courtroom last week stands up in the public gallery and shouts, 'The father eats sour grapes and the children's teeth are set on edge.'

I don't know whether the madman's on my side or not and I'm still thinking about him when the foreman of the jury says, 'We find the defendant guilty of murder.'

I almost don't hear it.

The courtroom empties fast and Perkins comes to see me in the dock.

'I'm very sorry, Patrick. I tried my hardest.'

I want to bawl but I fucking won't. I'll not let them see me cry.

I smile at Perkins. 'Yeah,' I say. 'You did.'

'Nobody saw it coming,' he said. 'Least of all me.'

'I did.'

He frowns, but says nothing.

I look away.

'I'm very sorry,' he says.

'Yeah. I know it.'

'We'll be adjourning for the sentencing tomorrow,' he says. 'Try and get some rest.'

Gardam's not in the cell and I've no idea if he's coming back.

I'm on edge, can't sit still, and can't get breathing properly.

At six o'clock the guard brings my dinner, a pie and chips.

'Where's Gardam?' I ask.

'He's been sent down. Gone in the van.'

'Where?'

'No idea.'

I can't eat. I want a strong drug for the misery and the pains. A stiff drink at the very least. A shoulder to cry on.

I keep getting up and down, going to the bars and looking down the corridor. Keep expecting Perkins to come and tell me he's spoken to the judge and I'm going to be released due to good behaviour, or on account of the fact that it's my first offence.

I can't stop still. Every movement outside sets my heart thumping with blasts of hope and fear. And there's the sickness too. I've had it since the first night in that cell after I was arrested and it feels now as though I'll have it for life.

The next morning there are about a dozen journalists. Unlike most people, they don't bow to the coat of arms when they walk in. They come and go, shaking the rain from their coats and umbrellas, and they talk. There should be a law against this kind of chatter when a man's about to be sentenced.

Perkins scribbles notes on his yellow pad and, when the judge enters the courtroom to deliver the sentence, he puts his hand to his forehead and looks up at the bench as though shielding his eyes from the sun.

I'm told to remain seated until asked to rise. Here's some of what the judge says:

Patrick James Oxtoby, you have been found guilty by a jury empanelled upon your trial in this court…

Murder is the most serious offence known to our criminal justice system, involving the intentional taking of the life of another person and the circumstances of this offence are such that I regard this as a serious instance of the crime of murder…

I now ask you to rise while I sentence you.

275

I stand and hold onto the wooden rail of the dock and close my eyes. I know what's coming, and still I hope, like an idiot hopes, for a miracle. As the judge speaks, my legs shake and the skin on my hands goes cold.

This is all I hear:

Taking all those matters into account...I sentence you, Patrick James Oxtoby, to life imprisonment...Please remove the prisoner.

The judge stands, opens the door behind the bench, and doesn't look back into the courtroom.

I'm carried down from the dock like a child from a car to a crib at night and then I'm taken out to the yard where the transit van, with its small high black windows, waits.

This is it.

It's over.

I'm so sick of being sick and so tired of being tired. I haven't even the energy for despair. There's nothing left.

The drive to the prison is slow and the rain pelts down steady and hard on the roof of the van and I'm glad of this noise that drowns out the voices of the other prisoners.

26

After about twenty minutes, the van stops inside the prison gates and an officer slides the door open.

The other four prisoners are uncuffed and taken out.

I'm told to wait.

'You're going into Cat A, D Wing,' says an officer. 'The rest of them's headed for remand.'

I wait.

Another officer, much younger than most, can't be more than nineteen, comes and uncuffs me.

'You can get out now.'

We're parked next to the yard.

I get out and he cuffs me again, hands behind my back.

It must be at least midday, but there are no prisoners outside. There are usually prisoners working the garden or doing a bit of exercise in the yard or on the football field.

Something's gone on.

I look up at the sky. It's pale and dull, and the air's cold enough for snow.

We're waiting, but I don't know what for.

'What's going on?' I say.

'There was an escape attempt last night,' he says. 'Admissions and investigations are all backed up. It's chaos.'

'Did they get out?'

'No.'

'Did they get far?'

'They got to the perimeter wall, then the homemade ladder broke.'

'How'd they plan to get over the wire?'

'They had ideas. I can't tell you any more.'

It's cold standing out here and the wind's picked up, but there's nothing to do but wait.

'I hate this stinking job,' he says.

'Me too,' I say.

He turns to me and smiles.

'You don't sound like you belong here,' he says.

'I don't.'

'First offence?'

'Yeah.'

'You're in D Wing, Cat A, so it must be at least armed robbery?'

'Yeah. It went a bit wrong.'

I wish it were this simple, that I were an armed robber.

'Aggravated then?'

'Yeah.'

'A ten stretch?'

'Yeah.'

'What were you after?'

'Jewels,' I say. 'Rubies, and fifty thousand in cash.'

He nods.

'There's a guy in here,' he says, 'by the name of Stan. He got as far as Portugal with two million from a bank haul, then he phones his girlfriend from the airport and she turns him in for the reward.'

'He'd want to kill her.'

'He did. Had somebody do it for him. A pal on the outside. Now Stan's a lifer. You'll meet him soon enough.'

I wish the two of us could go down the pub. I know a good one, a half a mile from here, The Red Lion, and it's next door to Riley's snooker hall. It'd be good and warm and we could get sausages and chips. We could play a few games and maybe even listen to a bit of music.

An officer comes out of the main building, walks towards us, stops halfway, gives the signal.

'That's us,' says the officer.

Everything happens as before. I'm taken to the admissions room where I'm given my kit and then to the Recess for a shower and then the infirmary. My blood pressure's taken and I'm checked for the clap and weighed.

The female nurse puts me straight on watch.

'You've lost too much weight,' she says. 'You'll be put on special.'

An officer takes me through the gates to my new cell.

'You'll be in till morning,' he says.

I tell him I want to appeal.

'Take it up with the deputy governor.'

'How do I see him?'

'You'll see him in a few days.'

'How long will it take to get an appeal?'

'How long's a piece of string?'

'But on average? Months? Years?'

'Ask your brief.'

'How do I get a new one?'

'Ask the deputy governor.'

I'm sent into my new cell.

My cell-mate's doing press-ups and he's doing them off the edge of his cot. He's swarthy, dark-skinned, has cropped hair and he's tattooed, hands, arms and neck.

'Hello,' I say.

He doesn't stop doing the press-ups, just looks across at me, then back down at the floor between his arms.

'I'm Harper,' he says.

I wouldn't have a hope in hell of defending myself against him.

'I'm Oxtoby.'

'Sounds like a fucking soup,' he says. 'Where'd you get a name like that?'

He keeps on with his press-ups and he's not at all short of breath.

'Off a tin,' I say.

'What you done?'

'Murder.'

'Same here. Double.'

I wouldn't mind knowing if he killed two people in one go.

'You?' he asks. 'How many you killed?'

He stops doing press-ups, stands, stretches his arms behind his back, sits on his cot.

'Just one. I killed one bloke.'

'First time?'

'Yeah.'

I sit on my cot.

'Welcome to life in hell,' he says. 'And relax. I'm not going to have you. Not my style. And we can't shit in our own nests, right?'

I think he's just told me he's not going to bugger or beat me.

I smile. 'Yeah. Right.'

This cell's as small as the cell in remand and it smells as they all do, of damp, smoke, sweat and piss. There are two cots, a bare metal desk, one metal chair with a slashed vinyl seat, a metal toilet, and a sink.

There's graffiti on the wall next to my cot, most of it below the line of the mattress. I lift the mattress to read it.

I have a habitual feeling of my real life having passed. I'm leading a posthumous life. John Keats, 1820. Died of TB.

'Did you write this?' I say.

'What's it say?'

I tell him.

'Not likely. Don't even know what it means. What's it mean?'

'I don't know.'

Harper gets off the cot, keeps on with his press-ups.

There's a pile of magazines on the desk. I go over to look at them.

Even though he's got his back to me, he knows what I'm doing.

'Help yourself,' he says.

I take a magazine to the cot and turn the pages. It's all about body building.

I put it back on the desk.

'I didn't think you'd last long with that,' he says. 'You don't look like you've ever lifted anything heavier than a cat.'

'Right,' I say.

I should get a bit fitter. It'd be a good way to kill some time and I might as well do what most of the blokes serving long stretches do.

'Is there a gym?' I say.

'Yeah, but it's real small and they won't give you the apps for it till you've served a fair bit of your stretch.'

I put the blanket over my head and try for sleep.

I drift off and end up sleeping a half-sleep of delirium, full of thoughts of the trial, the judge's red nose, the way he looked at me when he gave me the sentence, like he was just telling me the time, and that juror with the moustache who kept yawning.

I wake in the middle of the night with a mouth so dry it's stopped me from breathing.

I go to the sink, but I don't know if it's drinking water. A stench of sulphur comes out when I turn the tap on.

I get back into the cot.

The next time I wake, it's because the cell door's opened and there's a torch in my face.

Six screws have barged in and they've surrounded Harper's cot.

I sit up.

One of the screws gags Harper with a towel and says, 'Keep your trap shut!'

Harper struggles and another screw wraps a towel tight round his neck, another takes hold of his legs, and another takes both arms and pulls them tight behind his back. Another officer stands by the door and the sixth one packs Harper's belongings into a cardboard box.

I sit up.

'Don't move,' says the screw standing guard at the door. 'Get back into your cot.'

'What's going on?'

'Ghosting.'

'What?'

'He's leaving on the ghost train.'

I lie down and wait for them to leave.

I don't get back to sleep.

My cell door's not opened for slop-out and I'm not taken for breakfast.

I just lie on the cot, stare up at the low ceiling. There's no window.

I'm sick in the gut, the same way I was during the trial, the kind of sick I got when I was a kid and I'd gone on a fast-spinning ride after eating a sack load of sugar and threw up in front of Geoff and Daniel. Except this sick is a constant bitter sick, mixed with a fear that the sickness won't ever end.

But as I lie here, and even though I'm sick, I daydream Welkin's alive, that the jury gets called back to reverse their decision, that the judge's made a mistake, there's an appeal and I'm set free. I can't accept it. I can't quit the dreams of it all being reversed.

At 8 a.m. an officer comes. He's rake-thin, about fifty, dark-haired and he's got a comb-over.

'My name's Farrell,' he says. 'I'm taking you to see the chief officer.'

'What happened to Harper?'

'He's was taken to Scrubs.'

Wormwood.

'Let's go.'

We walk through four sets of gates, past the admissions and past the officers' mess.

He sends me in, locks the door behind.

The chief officer's behind his desk.

He's chubby and bald and wears a dark suit and a fat red tie.

'Sit down,' he says.

I sit.

'Thank you, sir.'

The prisoner who lays low should also be polite when he speaks to officers.

'Next week you'll be seeing the deputy governor and the welfare officer.'

'Thank you, sir.'

'But you need to start eating. You won't be taken off special-watch until you gain some weight.'

He reads something in my file.

'Thank you, sir.'

I rub my forehead.

'Do you need pain medication?'

'Yes, please, sir.'

'When the janitor comes with the trolley, I'll get him to give you some aspirin.'

'Is there any way I could get something stronger?'

He closes my file and stands.

'We'll review your case after you've seen welfare,' he says.

There's a gold cufflink on the floor by my feet. I reach down and pick it up.

I hand it to him.

'Ah,' he says. 'There it is.'

When I was a kid, I thought I was lucky. I often found things like coins and marbles, even a skateboard once. I was sure this meant that I was lucky, that I had special powers. I used to think that as long as I went on finding things I'd go on having special powers.

'I could probably find the other one for you, too,' I say.

He stands and heads for the door. 'Don't bother,' he says. 'I've got cufflinks up to my eyeballs.'

'What about an appeal?' I say.

He's waiting for me to get up. But I'm not moving. I'll wait for him to answer my questions.

'You'd better go now,' he says.

He opens the door. 'You need to go now.'

'I'm sorry, sir, but what about my appeal?'

'You need to take that up with the deputy governor.'

'Can I use the library?'

'You'll need special-leave and I'll have to check your record.'

You've got my fucking file. Why not check now?

'What about the gym, sir?'

'I'll get welfare to look into it.'

'Thank you, sir.'

Farrell takes me back to my cell.

'You'll get your breakfast brought in later,' he says.

He leaves, bangs me up.

I sit on my cot, nothing better to do than feel shit and sorry for myself.

I should have pleaded to manslaughter. I might have got five or six years. I could have been out of here before I'm thirty. Whenever I think of what's gone on, a constant and repetitive chain of thoughts, it's the desperate feeling of embarrassment that gets me most upset.

I've been a first-class idiot and, even though there's nobody in the cell, when I recall that night, going into Welkin's room, going back out to get the wrench, I turn red, a hot and raging shame crawls over my skin and it sickens me.

I sicken myself.

But thinking, any kind of thinking, it'll only make the whole thing worse than it already is. I've got to stop going over what's already happened and can't be reversed.

I get off the cot and do press-ups the way Harper did them. It's hard work, and I can't even manage a half-dozen, and when I stand up I'm dizzy. I lie prone on the cot, a sweat on me like I've done a hundred.

The kitchen screw comes with my breakfast.

'Keep the bowl and the spoon,' he says.

'Ta,' I say.

Both are brown and plastic.

'And here's your fork.'

I sit up, still light-headed.

'Ta.'

'Your first time?'

I wish it weren't so obvious.

'Yeah.'

'Good luck.'

I try to eat the porridge, but can't get through much of it. I get the gag reflex when I put the spoon in my mouth.

I lie down again and close my eyes.

The observation panel slides up and down during the night. It's the night-officer coming to check on me. This is what it means to be on special-watch. Sleep interrupted every two hours.

At 7 a.m., a screw opens the cell door.

'Get your breakfast,' he says.

There's a trolley outside and the prisoners on the landing are lined up to collect their trays, and it's noisy. About two dozen men talking and shouting at the tops of their lungs. No one says a word to me and I say nothing to them.

It's the same up on the twos and threes. Three landings, three floors, three lots of noisy cons getting their breakfast.

I take the food back into my cell and sit on my cot.

Breakfast is a bowl of cornflakes, an unripe banana and a cup of tea.

I get nowhere with the food and think about what I could be eating if I were still at the boarding house or with Georgia in the café or at home with my mother and father and Russell. A full English with sausages, bacon and eggs, hot buttery toast.

I had it good before. I didn't know it, but I know it now. But now that I know what was good before, all I get is shit.

A half-hour later, the same screw comes.

'Recess,' he says. 'Shower and slop-out.'

'I need to go on sick,' I say.

'What's wrong?'

'I'm sick.'

'Out of ten?'

'About a six, a seven.'

He shakes his head.

'You're not sick enough. Get out.'

The Recess is pretty much the same here as it was in remand, only there are more men and there are more screws standing watch and there are more older men here, probably lifers.

I shower and mind my own business, which isn't hard, since nobody says a word to me. A few look me over, but they look me over like they'd look at an ugly woman they can't be bothered with.

I'm taken back to my cell and banged up.

'Back in your cell then for the rest of the day,' says the screw. 'You're on basic.'

No privileges, no exercise yard, no association.

'Lunch at noon, tea at six.'

'How long am I on basic?'

'You'll have to ask the dep.'

The next morning, at 6.30, Farrell comes to my cell.

'Get up,' he says.

I sit up.

'There's a mental health thing going on,' he says. 'The Home Office wants six lifers to sign up.'

'Yeah?'

'If you sign up, you'll be seeing a psychologist about once or twice a month.'

Farrell smooths his thin black hair down flat on his chalky scalp.

'It's starting soon, in the next few days. Are you in? They need one more.'

I wonder if what I say to the psychologist will be off the record. If I say too much or the wrong thing, it could damage my appeal or chances of early parole.

'I haven't got all day,' he says. 'Are you interested or not?'

I've no idea how I'll pass the time and this might be a good way to get through a small part of it, might stop me from thinking so much. If I'm careful about what I say, it might help me get an appeal, get advice, get parole.

Anything's better than being banged up all day and night.

'All right.'

'Good.'

When evening chow arrives, I go out and line up and take a plate of beans and sausages, a cup of tea, take the tray back into my cell.

But I can't eat. I've got the same problem with the gag reflex and I've got a rotten sick gut. I wouldn't mind some coffee. I think I could keep that down. Strong coffee, and fresh white crusty bread, and jam and salty butter. Like in Georgia's café.

I kill a bit of time remembering what it was like to sit in the café and to chat to Georgia. I felt good with her. It felt good.

27

Next morning, Farrell comes to my cell.

I'm already awake and I think he's taking me to see the psychologist. This is what I hope for. Even if I can't say everything I want to say, it'll make me feel a whole lot better to talk to somebody.

'You're moving,' he says. 'Pack your kit.'

'Where am I going?'

'Same wing, different cell.'

'I'm staying on the ones?'

'Yeah. Same landing.'

I bundle my blankets, fetch my toothbrush, bowl and fork. I can't find my spoon.

We walk.

Farrell stops at a cell door near the end of the row.

'Who am I bunking with?'

He doesn't answer, doesn't look at me, just checks his reflection in the shiny black cell door, then shows me in.

'Get in,' he says. 'I haven't got all day.'

I go in.

My new cell-mate is Gardam.

Here he is, in my new cell, sitting up in his cot with two pillows behind his head.

'Hello,' I say, casual as hell.

'It's you, then, Ox,' he says, even more casual than me.

He smiles and puts his legs over the side of the cot as though he means to stand up to greet me, but he doesn't stand.

'I thought you might be dead,' I say.

'I couldn't manage it. Not yet.'

He sneezes and wipes his nose on his hand. His eyes are swollen and red.

'How long you been here?' I say.

'Three days. I got sent down for life.'

'Me too.'

I sit on my cot with a blanket over my shoulders, fold my arms round my chest for some extra warmth.

This cell's even colder than the other.

'Why isn't the heating on?'

'It is, it's just we're at the end of the row,' he says, 'a thousand miles from the boiler.'

'Shit.'

'Next door's the kit room,' he says, 'it used to be the condemned cell where they hanged the likes of us.'

I know. Dozens of men were executed here. When I was a boy, I used to love to hear the stories. I read all about them and the crimes they'd done.

Gardam tells me about the psychopath down the landing, a bloke called Smith. A documentary's just been made about him. He killed eight men, all about the same age as his father, the father who repeatedly raped him when he was a kid, all with red hair like his father. His crimes are like no other on record. Smith's not exactly a serial killer, because a serial killer's victims are usually women, but he's not quite a straightforward psycho either. According to Gardam, Smith said that what he did was revenge on his dead father's life, but he didn't mutilate the victims' bodies like most serial killers do. He killed them quickly. He just strangled them or knifed them.

'And,' says Gardam, 'he's the only one that a true crime book's been written about.'

Gardam tells me all the stuff I already know and I pretend to be hearing it for the first time.

He gets right pissed off if he's ignored.

He likes it when I ask him questions.

So I ask him lots of questions.

It passes the time and he smokes less when he's gabbing.

After lunch, the screw they call The Janitor comes down the hall with his trolley. At each cell he opens and closes the hatch and leaves pills on the narrow shelf.

A tot's been left in our hatch.

'These are mine,' says Gardam.

He empties the contents of the small white plastic cup into the palm of his hand. 'Right. Well, these red and white ones are mine.'

He gives me what's left, a single paracetamol.

'What do you take?'

'Valium,' he says. 'Two every night.'

He swallows the pills and I wonder why, if he's really so keen to die, he doesn't save them up for an overdose.

'Mind what you get hooked on,' he says. 'When the screws want to fuck you up, they just forget to bring your dose.'

After breakfast next morning, Farrell collects me from my cell. I'm seeing the psychologist. He takes me down past admissions and past the deputy governor's office. I get to see inside the officers' mess. They've got a pinball machine in there and a table piled up with games and magazines.

We stop at a room at the end of the corridor.

A woman meets us at the door.

She's in her mid-forties, with short red hair, cut in the style of a monk. She's got a knee-length red skirt, chocolate-brown stockings and a pink, v-neck jumper.

'Do you want me to sit in?' says Farrell.

'No,' she says, 'I'd like you to sit out.'

'Raise the alarm if you need to,' he says. 'I'm right outside.'

He leaves.

She extends her hand to me.

'Hello, Patrick. I'm Dr Forbes.'

'Hello, doctor.'

'I'm glad you decided to come,' she says.

I look at her breasts, tightly packed under that jumper, and a bolt of heat goes through me.

'Take a seat,' she says.

The room's small, dark and warm. Dr Forbes goes to her swivel chair behind the desk. I sit sideways on the chair opposite her, take a look round. There are two filing cabinets, a small bookshelf, and three more swivel chairs.

'I'm going to ask you a few questions about your background,' she says. 'Is that all right?'

'Yeah,' I say.

'And everything you tell me will be treated in the strictest confidence.'

'That's good,' I say. 'I was going to ask you about that.'

'Yes, that's important. I've a form here for you to sign and it sets out the guarantee of confidentiality.'

I read the form and sign it.

The window's small and barred but I can see the yard and beyond the yard the top of the high walls covered with circles of barbed wire. I wonder how the escape plan was going to deal with the wire.

I used to stand outside these walls and look up at the turrets and wonder if the murderers and bank robbers had cells up the very top. We thought of the prison as being like a castle.

'You have one sibling,' she says.

'A brother. Russell.'

'Where do you fit in?'

'I'm the youngest by seven years. I'm the runt.'

'Why do you call yourself the runt?'

'I'm a bit smaller than him,' I say. 'That's all.'

'But you're the bright one? Am I right?'

'Not really.'

Dr Forbes puts down her pen.

'Are you going to face me?' she says.

I'd rather not. Her top's tight across her breasts and I've got an erection.

I keep my legs crossed, turn round to face her.

'Okay,' I say.

'Is there anything in particular you'd like to talk about?'

'Not really.'

A few minutes go by in silence and Dr Forbes has her hands in her lap and looks at me. I suppose this is how it works. She waits for me to speak, but I want her to go first.

She looks at my dirty canvas shoes.

'I feel sick pretty much all the time,' I say.

'Do you need to see a doctor?'

She takes our her diary, flicks some pages.

'I don't think I've got any illness. It's just what's happened and the trial and my sentence.'

'Would you like to tell me how you feel?'

'I think about him every day,' I say. 'If that's what you want to know.'

293

'You can tell me anything at all,' she says. 'It's entirely up to you.'

'I think about what I did all the time,' I say. 'But I don't feel guilty or remorseful.'

'What then?'

'It's more like embarrassment, like when you lose something really important, leave it on a bus seat or something stupid like that. You know? That fear and shame that goes through you like poison.'

'Yes.'

'Well, I get that feeling of shame after doing something stupid, I get it hundreds of times a day.'

A long pause before she speaks. 'Do you think you can go on?'

'I'm not going to kill myself, if that's what you mean.'

She smiles. She's got a pretty smile.

'I meant, can you go on speaking. Can you tell me more?'

'All right.'

I tell her that, if I met Welkin again, I'd want to tell him stuff, like there's nothing wrong with wanting to save money to buy your own car and nothing wrong with looking at yourself in a mirror when you're wearing a hat.

'Was that one of the reasons you killed him?'

'What do you mean?'

'That you wanted to say things to him that you couldn't say?'

'That's probably part of the reason. Probably frustration.'

'Do you often feel frustrated?'

I want to stay in here with her, climb under the desk, listen to what the other prisoners say, and later I could go to sleep under her desk and she could go on with her reading or making notes.

'Probably. But I didn't mean to kill him. I didn't kill him out of frustration.'

She waits.

'I'd got into a habit of seeing everybody as an enemy,' I say.

'Do you know why?'

'Not really. I suppose it was a habit. Like in the shower how I always start with soaping under my armpits.'

'Were you sometimes paranoid?'

More silence while she waits for me, but I don't know what to say and dread I might cry.

'Perhaps you wanted to make him say sorry. You wanted him to apologise?'

'Did you read the police statement?'

'Yes,' she says, 'of course.'

'Nobody in court did. I don't even think the judge read it at all. He was a right cunt.'

'And the jury?'

'I think they had better things to do.'

'Are you angry about your conviction?'

I'm not interested in talking about anger, I get enough of that in the cell from Gardam.

There's another silence, a silence even longer than the one before, and the longer it lasts the hotter I get. The silence between us makes me high. I've never sat with somebody for so long without talk.

Dr Forbes stands.

'Our time's up,' she says. 'If you want, you can come back for five more sessions.'

I say nothing.

'It's up to you,' she says. 'You're not under any obligation, but I'd like to see you again.'

'I don't know,' I say.

She nods, but I haven't fooled her. She knows I'll be back.

'Think about it,' she says.

'All right,' I say. 'I will.'

It's late the next afternoon, a couple of hours before evening chow.

Gardam's with welfare and I'm sitting on my cot playing solitaire.

A screw comes to deliver a letter.

'Here,' he says.

I take it from him and see it's been opened.

Dear Patrick,

    I'm writing this letter to tell you that I don't hate you but like everybody else who cared about you, I'm still very shocked by what you did and I feel really sad for you.

    It must be awful in prison and I'm sorry you're in prison but I wonder if it might help you see the light and change for the better.

    I'm glad we didn't get married and it's strange that suddenly you change from somebody who can't make up his mind and you decide to make up your mind to do something dreadful and I'm glad I wasn't your victim. I'm sorry, but that's how it is. I do feel sorry for you and I don't hate you and you must be having a terrible time but I've met up with your mum a few times and she said (and my friends all said) I should tell you how I feel and that it might help me if I get all this off my chest.

    Sarah.

    p.s.

    You are in our prayers.

She's a monster, more malevolent than any of the nuts in here. And what gives her the right to use lies about a God she doesn't even believe in?

I go to the sink and douse my face with cold water.

Gardam comes in.

'What's wrong with you?'

I go to the cot and get the letter.

My hand shakes.

He takes the letter to his cot and takes his time reading it, mouthing the words slowly as he goes.

'Isn't she the one with the big scar on her face you was going to marry?'

'Birthmark.'

He reads the letter again.

'You shouldn't have wasted your time. She's a right fucking cow.'

I sit on my cot and Gardam comes over and sits next to me, puts his hand down near my leg.

I don't move away, wouldn't mind it if he touched me.

'Fuck her,' he says.

'It's like a joke,' I say. 'You couldn't make up something that awful.'

'Fuck her.'

He moves in closer, puts his hand on my leg.

'Fuck this place and fuck her.'

I stay awake most of the night, hot and tired, my eyes wide open, and I stare into the pitch.

The siren sounds for slop-out, but I don't line up for breakfast.

I go down past the trolley and line up for special-sick.

'What's wrong?' says Farrell.

'I can't sleep and I'm dizzy. I'm sick as a dog.'

'Do you have pills?'

'No.'

'Okay. Get in your cell and I'll collect you after breakfast.'

A half-hour after Recess, Farrell takes me to the nurse's office.

We cross the yard to get there, through the cold bright daylight.

I stop walking and look up at the clouds.

'Do you want a minute?' he says.

'Yeah. Thanks.'

He stands next to me, but turns away, gives me privacy.

I breathe in some fresh air, take it all in, pay close attention to the details, even the short, neat grass on the football pitch and then I close my eyes, listen to the birds a minute.

'I'm surprised there are birds,' I say.

'Because there are no trees?'

'Yeah.'

'They come for all the scraps of food you blokes chuck out the windows.'

'I didn't know the windows opened.'

'Some do. In the stores and kitchen and in the rec-room.'

'Right.'

'We'd better move along.'

The nurse is that tall bloke who dealt with me when I first got here, when I landed in remand, the one who stuck his finger up my arse.

Farrell stands inside the door and I sit at the nurse's desk.

'Oxtoby,' says the nurse. 'You look terrible.'

'That's how I feel.'

He asks me questions about what I've eaten, my bowel movements, my sleep, and my headaches.

'Any dizzy spells?'

'Yeah, when I stand up.'

He takes my blood pressure then talks to Farrell.

'He's got to stay in for a few days.'

'What is it?'

'Hypotension.'

The nurse takes me outside, across the yard, past the Seg. Unit where the nonces are, across to the other side of the prison, to the hospital.

It's a small red-brick block and outside there's an armed officer on guard. He takes a set of keys out of his pocket and lets us through.

This must be a newer part of the prison. The walls are gleaming white and there's a white polished floor with a yellow line showing the way to the wards and such. Where there's a red line and red arrow marked on the floor, we turn right and stop outside a room at the end of the corridor. The officer takes out a key and opens the single lock. There are no bars and only one bolt.

I go in with the nurse and the officer leaves.

It's a single ward and it's the size of at least two cells.

'You'll be checked every hour,' says the nurse, 'and that button on the wall beside your bed's the panic button.'

The single bed's bigger than the cot in my cell, and there's a thick mattress, a bedhead, blue blankets, big pillows with white pillowcases, a bedside table, a plastic jug for water, and there's a small bathroom with a shower and toilet.

It's like a hotel room compared to what I've been in.

'I'll have to get you on a drip and you need to put these pyjamas on,' he says. 'Leave your dirty kit on the end of the bed. We'll have it taken to the laundry.'

He goes out and locks the door.

I change into the clean, cotton pyjamas and sit with my back against the plumped white pillows. The air is fresh and soapy and there's a window looking out onto a garden with roses climbing up the wall across the way. This must be the governor's garden.

I feel like a king. Stevenson told me it was nice being in the hospital. I should ask where he is. He was good to me in remand. I didn't mind him in the end.

I know I'll sleep tonight. It's quiet in here. There's still the clanging of doors and shouting, but it's a more distant noise, not so bad.

I'll soon have myself drugged and, when I've had some good sleep and a few days in here, I'll be right again.

I look out the window and think I'll probably start up an exercise regime. I might get myself on the football team and go to the gym a few times a week. And, in here, I might make that phone call home. I'd be a lot more comfortable trying to talk to my mum here. If not the phone, then I'll get some pen and paper and write a letter.

About an hour later, the nurse comes with a tray of food. It's proper food, a meat pie and mashed spuds, must be from the officers' quarters.

'Do what you can with this,' he says.

He leaves.

I try a few mouthfuls, and it's tasty, but I can't manage more than a few bites.

The nurse comes back about twenty minutes later and he has the drip, a clear sac of fluid hanging off a pole.

'I've got to stick a cannula in,' he says.

He wheels the drip next to the bed then sits beside me and sticks a needle into the crook of my arm. A long needle goes in, deep in, and a tube's attached to the needle and the whole lot gets taped on and then the nurse opens the valve and the intravenous stuff starts feeding through.

'Can I have something to help me sleep?'

The nurse reaches into the pocket of his smock.

'Take these.'

He gives me two white pills.

'Are you going to eat?'

'I don't think I've got the stomach for it.'

He takes the tray.

'Could I make a phone call while I'm in here?'

'No, not from here.'

'Can I have a pen and some paper?'

'I'll see what I can get you.'

Even with the drugs, my sleep's full of trouble. In gaps between night-mares, I hear birds scratching at the infirmary window and dream that I eat one of them.

28

The nurse comes with my evening meal and the pen and paper I asked for.

'How are you feeling?'

'A bit better.'

'Any sleep?'

'A bit.'

He takes my blood pressure.

'It's still very low. I'm going to keep you on the drip. Try and eat some of this.'

He takes a silver domed lid off the plate and shows me my meal.

'Thanks,' I say.

'If you can't eat this, we'll put you on hospital food.'

'I'll eat it.'

It's a tasty pork pie, mash with real butter and hot carrots and peas. Just like room service in a hotel.

Soon after I've eaten, the nurse comes back.

'You did much better,' he says.

'Yeah, but I don't feel too great.'

He reaches under the bed and gets a brown kidney dish.

'Use this if you need it.'

'Thanks.'

He checks the drip, taps the needle a couple of times, then leaves.

I'm feeling good enough and clear-headed enough to write a proper letter home.

My dear family, Mum, Dad and Russell (and Julie and the twins),

I know it's going to be hard to forgive me for what I did, but here's an apology anyway. I am very sorry for what I did.

I'd really like it if somebody could come and see me in here. I know that's a lot to ask, but maybe if you think about how what I did was a big mistake and only took a second, and wasn't premeditated, you might have some sympathy. Also, I didn't want to kill Welkin. I can honestly say to you that I didn't even want to hurt him very badly.

I am still your son, your brother, and your friend, if you want. I am very, very sorry.

I've been an idiot, but I'm not the same now. If I was outside now, I could never do what I did again. I can't believe I did it at all, but I did, and I take responsibility, even if I think a life-sentence is harsh, I still think I deserve punishment.

Love, Patrick

After the letter, I fall into a deep sleep and when I wake I don't know where I am. There's sunlight coming in through the window and I can hear birds and when I sit up straight I can see into the garden.

The nurse comes to me with breakfast.

'Scrambled eggs,' he says.

I want to stay here in this hospital bed, get more sleep and write more letters. I owe one to Bridget and to Georgia and I definitely owe one to Welkin's parents.

The nurse takes my blood pressure. The eggs sit on the bed going cold.

'Your blood pressure's normal,' he says.

'But I'm not ready to go back,' I say.

'You'll have to go back as soon as you're well.'

'I still feel sick.'

'You'll be here another night. But you've stabilised.'

I fall asleep and I've no idea what time it is when I wake.

Farrell comes in with the nurse.

'Gardam's been passing round that letter you got,' he says, 'and the psycho's written you a consoling note.'

In this prison, population 856, there's only one psychopath and it's Trevor Smith, the one Gardam told me about.

Farrell gives me the note:

Dear Patrick, They call me the psycho but I wud not send you a letter like that one did. We have a code here when a man is right down we stick to him. Sounds like you tride real hard to be a good man and made just one mistake. And we think that you are down bad. Rest up and Get Well Soon. Trevor

I finish and smile.

'Not a bad bloke to have on your side,' says Farrell. 'When he's not out of action, he runs his landing.'

'What wing's he on?'

'He's on F, but he spends a lot of his time in the strongbox.'

I hand the note to Farrell.

'That's yours,' he says. 'Keep it.'

The nurse takes my blood pressure.

'A hundred and fifteen over seventy,' he says. 'You're on the mend now.'

'I don't feel a hundred percent,' I say.

'Take these and get some sleep.'

He gives me two more of those white pills and waits for me to take them.

They both leave.

I've forgotten to ask for more paper.

I want to sleep but I also want to enjoy the peace and clean and quiet of this room a bit longer.

I get up and go to the window and look out at the garden a while.

But the drugs are working on me, my eyelids are getting heavy, and I can't resist the bed.

I climb onto the soft mattress, stretch myself out, a good stretch, feel the crisp sheets under my back, fall into a deep sleep.

The nurse wakes me in the morning.

It's a much duller day and the room's dark.

'You're being shanghaied,' he says.

'Now?'

'Yeah.'

I'm not ready to go, but he takes the needle out of my arm, pulls it out rough, without any warning.

'What time is it?'

'Half past six,' he says. 'Better get dressed. I'll be back in a second.'

As soon as I stand I feel sick again and have to sit.

He comes back.

'Get dressed, Oxtoby. You've got one minute.'

I get dressed then fold the hospital pyjamas, put them neatly under the pillows.

He comes back.

'I got dizzy just then,' I say.

'That's because you've been in bed so long.'

Farrell comes to take me back to the cell.

'Let's go.'

I go into the cell and the stink of smoke and sweat hits me especially badly after the fresh air in the single ward.

Gardam's on my bed playing solitaire.

'Felt like a change of scenery,' he says.

He gets up and goes back to his own cot.

'What's it like in there?'

'I wish I could've stayed.'

'Thanks, Ox,' he says. 'I missed you, too.'

'I had a whole room to myself and a view.'

'Can you smoke in there?'

He reaches for his pouch of Drum. He's rolling his own now.

'I don't smoke,' I say.

'Oh yeah. Forgot.'

I sit on my cot, watch him roll and then light his fag.

'Are you better, or what?'

'Yeah. Not so dizzy.'

'Did you eat?'

'Yeah. Pies and casseroles and bread-and-butter pudding and ice-cream.'

'You fucking what?'

'Yeah. I got food from the officers' mess.'

'Could have brought me something.'

'Where would I stash pudding or casserole? In my socks?'

'You don't know anything.'

'Right.'

I go to the sink to wash my hands and he rolls another cigarette.

'Where's the soap?'

'I used it up,' he says. 'Get more on canteen tomorrow.'

'Right.'

'Want to play some poker?'

'Sure.'

We sit on his cot and play poker and he talks about his days while I was in the hospital. He tells me all about how he showed Smith the letter from Sarah, and how Smith wrote the note to me right there on the spot in his cell. He wants to know what I thought of the letter and whether I'm grateful.

'Yeah, thanks a lot. It really cheered me up.'

'Good.'

I let him win most of the hands, but after a couple of hours he smells a rat.

'Why do you keep raising and then folding when the pot gets really big? Why do you keep throwing in your hands?'

'I don't think they're any good.'

'How can three kings not be a good hand? If it's worth calling, it's worth raising and it's worth staying in for the turn.'

'There's too much that beats three kings, like a flush and a straight.'

'You don't know anything.'

'Right.'

'I don't know how you got into university.'

'Me neither.'

The next morning, I'm granted leave to visit the library. I can go every day with Farrell if I want, but I can't go to the yard until I've gained more weight and I can't join the football team for the same reason.

Farrell gives me a copy of my release form. Turns out I've been granted leave to use the library on the basis that I'm a *University-educated man with hopes to return to university upon release on licence*.

'Who wrote this?'

'I did,' he says.

'Thanks.'

Farrell's not like Johnson and he couldn't care less whether I'm grateful or not. He does the usual, puts his hands in his pockets, hitches up his trousers and, on the way out, checks his reflection in the shiny black cell door.

Next afternoon, after lunch, I'm taken to the library, a room about the size of three cells. It's down the other end of the landing, past the canteen, past the rec-room, past the work stores.

There are six bookcases and a couple of boxes piled with books waiting to be shelved, but it's warm and light, and there's no smoking allowed.

I'm the only one in here and I sit at the small table beside the radiator and get to reading a book about psychopaths that somebody's left behind.

Between the pages there are bits of tobacco and flecks of dried egg yolk.

On page 789 somebody's written: THIS IS ME! I'M A PSCYO. On page 811, in the same handwriting: THIS FUCKING BOOK IS ALL ABOUT ME! THEY SHOULD PAY ME ROYLTIES.

According to this book, *The Diagnostic and Statistical Manual of Mental Disorders*, the symptoms of psychopathy include: parasitic life-style, stealing, pathological lying, substance-abuse, financial irresponsibility, proneness to boredom, cruelty (especially towards animals in early life), running away from home, promiscuity, fighting, and lack of empathy.

I memorise as much as I can so as to use my brain a bit.

Back in the cell, just before the trolley with the evening cups of tea and cocoa, I run through the list with Gardam. He admits to all of the symptoms, even admits to having 'slightly' enjoyed killing his wife.

'What about remorse?' I say.

'I don't know, Ox,' he says. 'All I know is I want to die.'

'Do you really?'

'Yeah, I do fucking really. Fucking look at me. I'm a walking corpse.'

He re-lights his cigarette. He's bad at rolling and he can't keep the fags lit for more than a couple of puffs. From where I sit, and though I don't know much about tobacco, it looks like he doesn't unpack the tobacco enough.

He takes a puff, looks at me.

'Why don't you save up your Valium and take an overdose?' I say.

'First, you'd need about five hundred of them to top yourself. Second, they take the edge off day-to-day while I'm waiting to die. Third, if I miss a dose, I'll go off my nut and go into one.'

If he goes into one, it could be me he sticks with a shiv made out of a melted toothbrush.

'I get it,' I say. 'Best keep taking them.'

He crushes the cigarette that's gone out and starts over.

Next morning, five minutes before the first siren, an officer I've never seen before comes to the cell.

'You're to see the deputy governor,' he says. 'Get dressed.'

'Where's Farrell?'

'He's on sick leave.'

'Can I use the Recess first?'

'You're not at home now.'

'I know.'

'But I need to—'

He laughs. 'Shit?'

'Yeah.'

'Then say it. Say you need to shit.'

I won't say it. I get dressed while he watches, then make the bed.

'Fold your blankets.'

I do what I'm told and watching me do it puts a smile on his rotten face.

'Fold them neater.'

I do it again.

'Get out.'

The deputy governor's office is across the other side of the prison, at the back of the night officers' sleeping quarters. I get to walk across the yard again and it's the first clean air I've breathed since leaving the hospital.

The deputy governor's waiting at his door.

'Come in and take a seat,' he says. 'I hear you want to appeal.'

'Yes, sir. That's correct.'

'You'll have to see your brief. Give me his name, and I'll arrange for a phone call.'

With his foot, he opens and closes a small cupboard under his desk.

'Thank you,' I say. 'But I don't want the same one. I don't want Perkins. I want a new brief.'

'I'll get the ball rolling. But it'll take a while. You'll have to be patient.'

'Thank you.'

I look out the window to the small private garden. There are roses in a flowerbed and thick ivy climbing the walls.

'Although it's early days, your good behaviour in remand has earned you enhanced privileges. You'll be taken off basic and be free to use the yard for an hour every day and I'm giving you association privileges.'

There's an hour of association every night at eight o'clock and there's a TV, a pool table and a table tennis table in the rec-room.

'And I can still use the library?'

'Yes.'

'Thank you, sir.'

'And you'll eventually meet with the Board of Visitors who might favourably consider your circumstances.'

I can't believe what he's said.

I want to jump from my seat.

I want him to say it again.

My legs are light and happy as though they've been shot through with helium. The drugs from the infirmary are nothing compared to this.

The hour's come: I'll be entitled to parole, pardon, a reprieve.

I want to laugh but keep my voice low and steady.

'There's a good chance I'm going to be freed soon then?'

He kicks the cupboard door shut with his foot.

I stand up.

'Please sit down,' he says. 'I didn't say that.'

He has his finger over the panic button.

'You'd better sit down.'

I sit and put my hands on my lap.

'If your behaviour's impeccable, it's likely you'll meet with the Board of Visitors.'

'When?'

'It's up to the Home Office.'

'So I might be freed soon? Go out on licence?'

'No,' he says, 'you're in for murder. You won't be going out for a long time.'

This blow is like a dose of poison in my veins, a hot sharp shot through my legs and arms, through my bowels and bladder. I've a mind to release a hot flood of shit and piss right where I sit. They'll come and clean me, wrap me in a nappy, drug me, take me back to the infirmary, maybe even to the outside prison hospital for a few days.

But I don't piss or shit. I tighten the necessary muscles, bring my knees together.

'But you made it sound like I might get freed.'

'I didn't say that.'

'What's a long time, then?'

He hands me a colour pamphlet as though I'm buying a car, getting a loan from the bank.

'I can't tell you what a long time is,' he says. 'I want you to take this away with you and read it.'

He can't even be bothered to look at me.

'To be considered for licence, your conduct must be impeccable. Beyond reproach.'

'Yes, sir.'

'You mustn't commit any additional offences.'

'Of course, sir.'

'You mustn't participate in any riots or sit-ins or escape attempts.'

'Of course, sir.'

He's already finished with me and stands.

The door's opened by an officer.

I'm escorted back to my cell.

When I've finished reading the pamphlet, I give it to Gardam.

'You can't even have a passport when you're on licence.'

'I know,' I say. 'I've just read it.'

'And they can take the licence back off you whenever they like.'

And I've got to see a parole officer as often as the Home Office says so, and it's not likely I'll be considered for licence before I've served ten years.

'And you have to serve ten years first.'

'For fuck's sake,' I say. 'It's a whole lot better than being in here for life.'

'S'pose so,' he says.

'You'll be up for licence too, won't you?'

'No,' he says. 'Forgot to tell you something.'

'What?'

'I stuck a guy in remand. I got him in the preliminary artery. He lost the use of his right eye.'

'Right.'

'He was my cell-mate,' he says.

Gardam cackles. He wants me to ask if he's joking. He wants me to be impressed and he probably wants me to be nervous.

I'll show no interest.

My silence makes him sullen again.

'I wish they still hanged men for their crimes,' he says. 'I wish I was in America being lethally injected.'

'Maybe you should get some stronger medication,' I say.

'Maybe,' he says. 'But I don't think it'd make any difference.'

'Maybe it would.'

'I think if I met me,' he says, 'I'd probably kill me.'

'Right,' I say, but I don't know what he's talking about.

He laughs.

29

I see Farrell in the morning, and ask to use the phone.

'Do you have any money?'

'Yeah. Gardam gave me a few coins.'

'After breakfast,' he says.

At breakfast, I eat every scrap of slop served on my tray. I eat the cornflakes in the warm milk and the rubbery scrambled eggs and the small dog penises they call sausages.

I'm going to gain weight and get some energy for exercise in the yard and today I'm going to sign up to play on the football team and I'm going to put in an application for a cell transfer. Maybe see if I can get onto F Wing where Smith is.

Farrell comes to the cell after midday chow and flattens his hair with the palm of his hand. He behaves as though he can't be seen.

'I'm taking you to the phones now.'

I queue up and wait my turn and, by the time I get to a phone, I've only got two minutes left.

'Hello?'

'Mum, please don't hang up. It's Patrick.'

She doesn't miss a beat, speaks like a robot whose button's been pressed.

'Oh, Debbie,' she says. 'You've called at such a bad time. Could you call back tomorrow? At the same time?'

My father must be home on a rostered day off and she doesn't want him to know it's me on the phone.

'Okay,' I say.

She hangs up. What she's done is a good thing, a whole lot better than nothing. She wants to talk and she wants to do it in private.

My mood's good and I'm looking forward to tomorrow's chat.

Next day, Farrell takes me back to the phones at the same time and I stand in the queue for fifteen minutes listening to two cons begging for money and cross-examining their wives and girls about where they've been, why they didn't answer the phone last week and why they've not sent more fags and food.

I get my turn, stick the coins in.

'Hello.'

It's my mum. The sound of her voice floods my chest.

'It's me,' I say.

A pause.

'Did you get my letter?'

Silence.

'Mum?'

'Yes. I did. Thank you. Are you all right, Patrick? Is everything all right?'

'Yeah. I'm getting used to it. How are you?'

'I went back to work last week. Everybody looks at me a different way now, but I'm back on my feet and it's good to be working.'

'That's good you're back at work.'

'Yes. Do you work in there?'

'Listen, I don't have much time. When are you going to come

315

and visit?'

'I don't know if I'm ready yet.'

There's the sound of a chair scraping across the kitchen floor. She's talked about not being able to stand up and now she's got herself a seat. She's in the kitchen with the yellow walls and the blue tablecloth and the big fridge and the jars of jam and the loaves of fresh bread. I close my eyes and the idea of fetching a chair, this simple idea, and this simple choice, followed by a simple action, the thought of it makes me homesick and sorry for myself and my craving for freedom takes a hold of my stomach and twists it.

'Mum?'

'Yes, son.'

'I want to say I'm sorry.'

'Why did you do it?'

'I don't know.'

'How could you not know?'

'It happened in a split second.'

She's crying.

'I've just been starting to recover,' she says, 'but now the sound of your voice in that awful place.'

'So you won't come and see me?'

'I don't know.'

'Will you at least consider it?'

'I'm still very angry and upset. We're all very, very angry. We're very upset.'

The phone's beeping. I've hardly any time left.

'I understand,' I say. 'I don't blame you, but I want to say sorry in person and tell you what happened. Can't you come and visit me?'

'It breaks my heart. You've broken my heart.'

She's stopped crying.

'Just let me tell you what happened,' I say. 'Let me tell you in person.'

'Write another letter,' she says. 'Write a long letter and try and see if you can make some sense of it.'

Her voice has changed and she might as well be talking to the gas company.

I lower my voice. 'I'm saying all that's worth saying now. I'm saying sorry.'

She sighs, just like there's somebody wasting her time.

'I need to think about it,' she says.

A prisoner has come right up close behind me.

'Get the fuck off,' he says. 'You've got two seconds.'

I don't turn round to him.

'I have to go,' I say. 'Goodbye, Mum.'

'Goodbye.'

She hangs up.

I put the phone back in the cradle and walk away.

She doesn't want to know me. I'm short of breath and sick and being angry feels just as bad as feeling sad, maybe worse.

I don't bother going to the library when Farrell comes to fetch me. I stay in my cell the rest of the day, lie on my cot with my back to Gardam and fake sleep.

I'm only killing time till association at eight o'clock. It'll be my first time in a room with all the others from the landing and I need to get my head straight for it.

The cell door's opened at eight o'clock.

'Association,' says Farrell.

Gardam gets up too.

'You're not going anywhere,' says Farrell.

In the rec-room there's a small TV stuck on a black metal arm high on the wall, a dozen or so plastic chairs, a pool table and a table tennis table.

The room's full of smoke and, with all the shouting, the noise and stink is awful.

I sit in the only empty seat and face the TV.

A short, beefy bloke offers me a fistful of straws.

'Good luck,' he says.

The man who draws the shortest straw chooses what all the men will watch on TV for the next hour.

The winner selects a football match, but when it comes on I can't sit still and I'm the only one who hasn't got a chat going. I'm too conspicuous here.

I get up and pace by the back wall, still boiling hot from what my mother's said.

An old con comes to me.

'Show us what you're made of,' he says.

He wants me to play a game of pool with him.

His name's Harrison, he's about sixty, serving a five stretch for fraud.

We play four games and I win them all.

'You could turn pro,' he says.

'Maybe. I'll look into it.'

'There are tournaments between prisons, you know. You could win a few quid.'

He tells me how and when and where.

'You can sign up outside the canteen.'

I tell him I'll do it. I probably will.

Gardam's asleep and he's snoring.

I sit on my cot to read for a while but the stink of his ash is everywhere and I've got an urge to wash the whole place out with soap and water.

I take a cloth from the sink and soak it in soap and water and wash my face and hands, then take the cloth and douse it again and start washing the floor round Gardam's cot. I wipe up some of the ash and clear away the butts and dump the mess in the bucket.

He wakes and sits up.

'What you doing?'

'Cleaning.'

'Let the screws do it.'

'There's ash everywhere.'

'So?'

'It stinks.'

'What do you want me to do about it?'

'Nothing, but I want to clean a bit.'

He lies down again, rolls over on his side, says, 'Knock yourself out.'

I've spent the afternoon in the library, and then banged up again after evening chow for a couple of hours listening to Gardam talk about how he wants to die. Now it's time for association.

There's only one chair left, and it's in the back corner next to the pot plant and that's where Lumsden sits. Lumsden's in F Wing, so I rarely see him on the landing or at meals, but I've heard a bit about him and I've seen him in the library a couple of times. Yesterday he was playing cards with a bloke called Wiman.

Lumsden's not like the rest. He's about twenty-four and his thick blond hair is clean. He's got no stains on him, no tattoos, no cuts or bruises. Even though he's been inside for four out of a seven stretch for manslaughter, he's the picture of health.

He's got a cell to himself and always wears a clean, perfectly ironed uniform. And since he's on enhanced privileges because of good behaviour, he's even got pockets in his shirt as well as his trousers, and his shoes lace up and he's got a part-time job on Saturdays in the deputy governor's office.

He's sitting alone, staring straight ahead at the wall and, even though he's doing nothing but staring, he doesn't look bored and he

319

doesn't look afraid. He looks more like a free man than a prisoner.

I might ask for a cell transfer so as I can share with him.

I sit down beside him and he smells of soap, maybe even after-shave.

'Where's Wiman?' I say.

'He got paroled.'

He turns away to watch the pool game.

'Do you play?' I say.

'Not as well as you.'

'I'm not so good.'

'I watched you win four games straight yesterday.'

'I used to play snooker.'

'Are you still on special-watch?'

'Yeah, but not for long. I've gained seven pounds.'

He lowers his voice.

'Next time you play, you should lose a few games.'

'Why?'

'You're a sitting duck if you win every game.'

'Okay.'

He stands and goes to the pot plant in the corner. He takes a pencil out of his pocket and uses it to make a mark on the wall.

He sits down.

'A hardy ficus,' he says. 'It's grown seven inches in four years.'

'Right,' I say.

'I love that plant,' he says.

'How can you love a plant?'

'It's probably not love, but I care what happens to it. Sometimes they throw table tennis bats at it and I get furious. You've got to care about something.'

'Yeah.'

'If there was a dog in here, I'd care about that,' he says, 'but we can't have a dog. All we can get is a budgie after we've served eight years. So it's the plant.'

'Fair enough,' I say.

I turn away and he turns away. We pretend to watch the table tennis.

'Do you have a window in your cell?'

'Yeah,' he says, 'and I can open it a few inches.'

'Lucky.'

'It's down the end of the ones in F Wing. Near the library.'

I rub my leg and he stares at me doing it.

I stop rubbing my leg.

'The cue ball's going to go in-off the black,' I say.

The cue ball goes in-off the black.

'Good call,' he says.

Next day, I'm in the library and Farrell takes me away to the nurse for weighing.

The nurse, a short guy with acne, tells me I've not gained enough weight to be taken off watch, so I can't yet use the yard or join the football team.

I tell Gardam.

'Maybe you should eat my food,' he says. 'Maybe we could kill two birds with one stone.'

'I get fat and you get dead?'

'Yeah, that's it.'

But, when evening chow comes, cottage pie and chips, Gardam's forgotten all about it and eats so fast it's like he's in a race and he gives himself such a bad case of hiccoughs he nearly spews.

'So much for Gandhi,' I say.

'What?'

'Don't worry.'

At eight, I go to association and sit with Lumsden.

We face the pool table, to make it seem as though we're talking about the game.

It turns out Lumsden was an apprentice solicitor, not quite a solicitor, but almost.

I'm surprised. A con being a solicitor is the kind of thing that's likely to be widely known in here and I'd not heard it before. Gardam didn't tell me and he's pretty much told me everything else.

'How did it happen?' I say.

'The murder?'

'Yeah.'

'I was in my first year out of law school,' he says. 'I was working for a big city law firm.'

He looks back at the table.

'And I didn't really want kids,' he says. 'It was too soon.'

We pretend to watch the game.

'What happened then?'

'Not now,' he says. 'I'll tell you later.'

He offers me a cigarette.

'I don't smoke.'

He hands me the packet, 'Take one,' he says. 'I insist.'

There's a fag already poking out of the packet and that's the one I take.

'Stick it behind your ear,' he says.

Back in the cell, I wait for Gardam to turn away and then I take a look at the cigarette. Lumsden's written on it: *3 lib*. Takes me a few minutes to work out what it means. 3 p.m., library, probably. Tomorrow.

30

Next day, on the way back from breakfast, Farrell tells me I've got visitors coming.

Visiting hour is 3 p.m.

'Who?'

'The parents of your victim. Something arranged by welfare.'

'Why wasn't I told?'

'How would I know? Just be ready to go to the visiting room at three o'clock.'

'I don't think it's a good idea.'

'Well, they're booked in to come.'

'I don't think I should see them.'

'Up to you. But you're the one who'll be facing the Board of Visitors.'

Maybe this has something to do with Lumsden.

There's been a change. The old mess hall's been opened and that's where we'll all be having our meals from now on. Just like it was in remand.

There's a new governor, ex-Parkhurst, and he thinks eating

together, the men from three wings mixing together, will boost our morale.

We're taken across at noon.

Gardam sits next to me in the mess. I look for Lumsden and see him in the corner. He's sitting alone, but doesn't look as though he's in the least bit bothered about it. And he's got a big book on his lap and an expression on his face that's damned close to a contented smile.

Gardam finishes his food.

'You look nervous as hell,' he says. 'Why are you so scared of these Welkin people?'

'I killed their son.'

He shrugs. 'Still, you have to try and relax.'

'Can I have one of your pills?'

'All gone,' he says. 'But I'd give you one if I could.'

'Why are they coming?'

'Maybe they're doing that forgiveness thing that the shrinks always talk about.'

I give him my lunch, he takes it, gobbles it down.

'Your visitors are running late,' says the officer who takes me to the visiting room. 'You'll just have to wait.'

I sit in cubicle seven and hope they won't show. I've no idea what I'll do or say. It hasn't even started yet and my back's soaked with sweat.

They arrive fifteen minutes late, look at me a moment, then sit down, slow and calm.

They're both small. Welkin's height must've come from his grandparents.

My heart's pounding so hard I get to thinking they'll see the vein pumping in my neck.

I cover my throat with my hand.

Mrs Welkin's got a pretty, clear-skinned face and she wears a blue skirt and blue shirt. Mr Welkin also wears a blue suit, darker than hers.

They both take a telephone receiver and they put their free hands in their laps. They're not nervous. They've got the same confidence Welkin had. They don't fidget, and they look at me, as he did, right in the eyes, not blinking.

'We want to say a few things,' says Mrs Welkin.

'All right,' I say.

My lip's trembling.

'We know how unfair it must seem to you.'

'Seeing as you only hit him once.'

'But you wanted to hurt him.'

'So we wanted to meet you to tell you that we can understand if it seems unfair to you.'

'But you brought our son's life to an end and for this we think you should be punished.'

'We think you deserve to be punished.'

I shift in my seat and move the phone to the other ear.

'I understand how you feel,' I say.

'We don't expect you to say anything,' says Mrs Welkin.

I take a breath. 'I appreciate you coming,' I say.

There's silence a while, but it's not a comfortable silence like with Dr Forbes. Far from it.

They look at me and wait.

'I don't think it's unfair,' I say.

Mrs Welkin untwists the tangled phone cord.

I clear my throat.

'I don't think it's unfair. He'd still be alive if I hadn't hit him.'

'Yes,' says Mrs Welkin. 'That's right. He'd still be alive.'

Mrs Welkin wipes her eyes with the back of her sleeve. 'Where are my tissues, Derek?'

'I don't know, love. Maybe they're in your bag.'

'Can't you get them for me?'

'If you want.'

'Yes. Yes. Please.'

Mr Welkin finds Mrs Welkin's tissues and both of us watch while she wipes her eyes. She hasn't exactly cried. It's more like seepage, like she was full up.

'I'm sorry,' I say.

'We don't want an apology,' says Mr Welkin.

'We don't expect an apology,' says Mrs Welkin.

Mrs Welkin looks up at the clock.

'I liked him,' I say. 'Your son was a very nice man.'

'You don't have to say that,' says Mrs Welkin.'

'He wasn't perfect,' says Mr Welkin.

'He was more than me,' I say.

Mrs Welkin frowns.

'More perfect than me,' I say.

Mr Welkin sighs. 'It's a very sad situation,' he says. 'You seem like a good boy.'

The siren blares and Mr and Mrs Welkin get up and when they reach the door they wave goodbye and they smile.

They've smiled at me.

I smile back.

Gardam's sitting on his cot, knees up to his chest, and he's eating a bar of chocolate.

'How'd it go?'

'Not too bad.'

I sit on my cot and face him.

'What they say?'

'That they think it's unfair. That they feel bad for me.'

'They must be saints.'

'You're right. They must be.'

Gardam offers me some chocolate.

'No thanks.'

He wraps up what's left, puts it under his pillow.

'It'll melt there,' I say.

'Yeah.'

He takes it out and eats it.

'Are you doing association tonight?'

'Yeah.'

'Is it good?'

'Yeah, it passes the time.'

He lies down, face up to the ceiling.

'All I get is a cup of cocoa.'

Men who don't get association have an extra cup of cocoa brought to their cells at 8.30 p.m.

'Wish I hadn't knifed that guy in remand,' he says. 'Wish I wasn't such a cunt.'

'How long before you get off basic?'

'A year, maybe more. I wouldn't mind it so much, but I'm not like you. I've nothing to do to pass the time during the day.'

'Why don't I borrow some books for you?'

'Nah.'

'What kind of books do you like?'

'Cowboy stuff. Some comic books.'

'I'll get you some.'

'Nah.'

'Why not?'

'Takes me too long and I get bored. I've never finished one.'

'I could get somebody to send in some new cowboy books then. Maybe some comic books.'

'Who?'

I think straight away of Georgia.

'I used to know a really nice girl. Her name's Georgia. She might send me some.'

'You should ask her to come and see you, Ox.'

'I will.'

'What about your family? Still not talking to you?'

'I think they need more time.'

'That's rotten, that is.'

'Yeah.'

I eat the evening meal, every bit of the sausages, mash and peas.

In showers this morning, I noticed my stomach's starting to get plumper and I feel like I've got a bit more energy.

The cell door's opened and Farrell comes for me.

'Time for association,' he says.

As soon as I walk into the rec-room, I'm called to the pool table.

'Hey Oxtoby,' says Harrison. 'I won the last game. Table's mine. Want to challenge?'

'I don't have anything to play with.'

'You can cover it with an I.O.U.'

I lose two games and owe him a third of snout and now, more than ever, I've got to arrange for some money, or start work in one of the stores. I want to pay my debts and buy some extra food from the canteen.

Lumsden watches and, when I'm finished, I go to sit with him.

'I was in the library today,' he says. 'I waited.'

'I'm sorry,' I say. 'I had a visitor.'

I tell Lumsden about Welkin's parents.

'They were good to me.'

'They sound like nice people.'

'They are.'

He leans in close, whispers.

'Try again tomorrow. The library.'

'Okay,' I say.

328

Maybe he's got some inside information about my file from the deputy governor's office, some good news about my first meeting with the Board of Visitors.

Gardam's not in the cell. I ask the con next door what's happened.

'He cut himself. He's in the box.'

'How bad is it?'

'It wasn't bad enough for the hospital, so they've banged him up.'

Next day, I go to the library with Farrell and sit at the desk and read and wait for three o'clock.

Lumsden doesn't show.

I go on waiting for him, then get up and move books on the shelves, sit again and look at the clock.

I count the seconds and can't concentrate on reading.

He doesn't show.

I borrow a book and tell Farrell I want to go back to my cell.

I lie on my cot and read the book. It's written by an ex-con. The author was once homeless and it turns out he had a super high IQ and, when he landed in prison for a long stretch, he learnt to play chess and won a bunch of tournaments. It's a very good book.

I'm glad of the break from Gardam but I'm also a bit surprised how much time I spend thinking about him. I can see him in the box, probably with the suit on, strapped up. And I know they don't get a mattress or bedding in there, just a P.E. mat, and the food's bread and water, and I wonder what his state of mind must be like, how much worse he's gone and made it for himself.

At morning chow, I take Gardam's tray as well as mine. The con behind me notices.

'You can't do that,' he says.

'Right.'

'And, if you do, you'll have to give me the toast.'

'Okay.'

I do what he says.

'I'm Oxtoby,' I say.

'I know that,' he says. 'I'm Stanislavsky. Stan.'

The one whose girl grassed him up when he'd got all the way to Portugal.

'Right,' I say. 'You're the one who got the two million.'

'That's me.'

He shakes my hand. 'Thanks for the toast.'

I'm happy back in the cell. I've got two boiled eggs, two bowls of cornflakes and two bananas.

On a full belly, the day goes well.

I read more, can concentrate better, and don't feel like sleeping before evening chow and, when the meal comes, I take both trays, get two helpings of meat loaf and spuds, two bowls of jelly, two oranges and two cups of tea.

At eight I go to the rec-room and sit with Lumsden.

'You didn't turn up today,' I say. 'I was in the library at three.'

'Keep your voice down.'

'Right.'

'I'm sorry,' he whispers. 'It's a long story.'

He turns away.

'So what was it about?'

'I can't say now. Later.'

We watch the table tennis. Two men trounce their opponents and win a packet of fags. The fight's so fierce they might have been playing for their lives. The losers opt for doubling up, and you can see from a mile off they're going to lose again.

'You should write that long letter home,' says Lumsden. 'The one your mum asked for.'

'I don't want to beg.'

'I think you should consider it.'

'Yeah, but I don't want to push her.'

'What about your brother?'

'We were never that close. He's seven years older. I was only ten when he moved out of home.'

'Did you get along?'

'Not really. When we were alone in a room, we always ended up putting the TV on and turning it up loud. The only time we laughed together was when there was a comedian on the telly.'

'Then you should try your mum.'

He's probably right. It might be better sometimes to say something that isn't quite true than to say nothing at all. It might be best to make the first proper move, tell the story in a way that'll make some sense to her.

'Yeah,' I say. 'You're right.'

He looks at me. 'It took me a long time to ask my ex-wife for forgiveness,' he says. 'When I finally did, I felt a lot better.'

'What happened?' I say.

'With my wife?'

He looks down at the floor, then back at me. He's gone a bit red in the face.

'I smothered my son. He was five months old.'

'Jesus.'

'And my wife didn't forgive me, but I still felt a whole lot better for asking.'

He gives me another cigarette.

'Take this,' he says.

I put it behind my ear.

The siren goes.

31

Gardam's back in the cell.

I sit on my cot.

'They fucking put me in the strongbox.'

'I heard.'

'Didn't even stitch my wound.'

He bends over to get his pouch of tobacco from under the bed and, while his back's turned, I look at the cigarette Lumsden gave me, then put it under my pillow.

'They wouldn't do that to an animal,' he says.

He holds out his arm for me to see.

It's a small cut near the wrist, but deep. He squeezes the flesh round the wound and, sure enough, it bleeds.

I go to the sink, get the cloth.

'Is that the same cloth you used on the floor?'

'Yeah,' I say, 'but I washed it.'

'All right,' he says. 'Thanks.'

He takes the cloth and dabs at the wound.

I go back to my cot.

'What happened?' I say.

'I cut myself. Just a practice run, but lots of blood. I raised the alarm and they threw me straight in the box.'

'Why don't you get some help?'

'Don't fucking tell me I need help.'

'That's not what I meant.'

'What then?'

'Maybe get more drugs or something. See the nurse and ask for stronger meds.'

He gets up, reaches in under his bed.

He's got a can of baked beans.

'What I really need's a can opener so I can make a better knife out of this.'

'Why don't you have Johns get you one?'

His mate who works in the kitchen.

'They've got extra screws in there now. Every meal, every sandwich or bowl of fruit, a screw supervises the knives, and whenever they need a can opened it's done by the screw.'

'Hopkins' idea?'

The new governor.

'Yeah.'

'Wish I could help more,' I say.

'You do what you can.'

Strange thing to say.

'I'm going to sleep now,' he says. 'Don't do anything I wouldn't do.'

Next day, I go to the library.

The screw who's on library-watch stands by the table near the window reading a magazine. I go to the back corner of the library.

Lumsden's standing behind the tallest shelf, out of sight of the screw.

I go to him.

'Hello,' I say.

He says nothing, just walks behind me, swaps places. He's standing where I was just standing a moment ago, and I'm where he was standing just a moment ago.

'You look jumpy,' he says.

'Yeah?'

'I can probably guess why.'

'Why?'

'You don't know why we're here.'

'Not really.'

'Maybe you thought I was going to give you a kiss.'

Lumsden says this like a kid in the schoolyard. I should laugh as though he's made a joke.

'No,' I say.

'Well, I'm not. I want to give you my radio.'

He reaches into the bookshelf behind me and gets the radio out from behind some books. It's one of those small black portables, like old men take to the park for listening to race results.

'Here,' he says. 'This is yours.'

'Thanks, but don't you want it?'

'I have two.'

'Thanks.'

He steps closer, says, 'So, you were afraid I might kiss you?'

'Not really.'

'I've never done it. Have you?'

I put the radio down by my feet and clear my throat.

'No.'

He puts his hands in his pockets.

I'd have thought that, if somebody was going to say something serious like this, they'd take a lot longer to say it.

'Do you ever think of it?'

'Not really,' I say.

'But it gets lonely.'

'I'm not bent.'

'Nor am I,' he says.

I want my hands in my pockets like he has, but I can't copy him since I don't have pockets and, anyway, copying him would be just the same as touching him.

'Sometimes you want to do it though,' he says.

'Not really.'

The way he looks at me I might as well have said yes.

'But it's probably best not to do anything,' he says, stepping back.

I want to keep talking, don't want him to walk away, not yet, but I don't know how to deal with what he's saying.

'But just to think it,' I say. 'That's okay.'

I want to get at him, the way he's got at me.

'Yeah. Just to think about it,' he says.

'To only think about it.'

'Yes. To think about it and not to do it.'

'I agree.'

'Good.'

I've gone as far as I'll go, but he reaches for my hand.

'Relax,' he says, 'I just want to write down the name of my favourite station.'

'Okay,' I say.

He takes a biro out of his shirt pocket and tries to write on the back of my hand but the ink won't take because of my sweat. He pulls his shirtsleeve down and wipes my skin. When he's finished wiping, he doesn't let go.

He's holding my wrist.

'I have to go,' I say.

'Okay,' he says.

Still he doesn't let go.

'I'll see you later,' I say.

'Good,' he says.

I watch him leave and then I go to the law shelf and get a new book on the criminal law.

I take the radio back to my cell and put it under the bed and spend the rest of the day reading the new book and I underline the bits I want to ask Lumsden about.

At association I sit in the same spot, but Lumsden's not there. He doesn't show up.

I play some table tennis and watch some news on the TV.

Back in the cell, the lights are still on, but Gardam's asleep, or pretending to sleep, curled on his side, foetal position, facing the wall.

And then I see what he's done.

He's been bleeding and it's fresh, but maybe just a nose bleed. He's left some of the blood in the sink. He's left it there for me to see.

I go to his cot. 'Gardam?'

He doesn't move, but I think he's awake. His breath's too fast, too shallow for sleep.

'Gardam? You okay? There's blood in the sink.'

I shake his shoulder.

'Gardam. Wake up. There's blood in the sink.'

'Hum?'

'Wake up.'

He's a terrible actor. He turns round, uses his knuckles to wipe the sleep from his eyes, stretches his hands up, a really shit, fake yawn.

'What?'

'There's blood in the sink. Are you okay?'

He looks down at his wrist. He's got another cut there, long and thin, the blood still fresh, the skin raised round the wound, but it's not serious.

'I cut myself.'

'I can see.'

'Just another practice.'

336

He should get put in the psych unit.

'Do you want to go on watch?' I say. 'Do you want me to raise the alarm?'

'No fucking chance. I just want to be left in peace.'

'What did you use?'

He points to the corner of the cell, just beside the sink. 'The lid off the tin of baked beans.'

'Did you want to kill yourself?'

'Not yet, Ox. It was just a practice. I just wanted to see what it felt like and that.'

'Can I have it? Can I have the lid?'

'What for?' he says.

'I don't want you to keep it.'

He sits up and reaches for his tobacco.

'Mind your own business,' he says. 'What do you care?'

I stop and look at him, look at him properly, fix his gaze with my gaze, the way the Welkins do it. It's hard to do it without feeling a bit of extra emotion.

''Course I care,' I say.

He turns away.

I go to my cot, exhausted, sit with my legs over the side, watch him roll a fag.

'You can't wait to see the back of me,' he says. 'You'd get a transfer if you could.'

'That's not true.'

'Yeah it is. I heard you've made friends with that solicitor, Lumsden.'

'What of it?'

'He's a snob.'

'No, he's not.'

'And he's bent.'

'I don't think he is.'

'Wait and see. You'll learn the hard way. He's bent and he's the

337

Deputy Governor's pet. He's probably a grass, too.'

The lights go out.

I lie down, but don't undress. I might have to get up in the middle of the night.

When I get back from library next day, Gardam's on my cot with a letter.

'Here's another letter for you,' he says. 'I didn't read it.'

I go to my cot.

'Who's it from?' he says.

'I don't know.'

Gardam goes to the cell door and stands with his hands in his pockets.

Dear Patrick,

I'm sorry I haven't written sooner but I've been very busy and the time goes so fast. Don't think I haven't thought of you.

I'm certain that you didn't mean to hurt that man. I've been meaning to say this to you ever since it happened. I'm sorry I couldn't help you more in the trial. I hope you understand.

There's probably no point saying 'chin up', so I won't. But I want you to know that I'm on your side.

Your friend, Georgia

I read the last part, where she says she's on my side, probably a hundred times, then put the letter under my pillow, lie down and cover my face with a blanket, close my eyes, try not to make any noise.

Gardam comes over.

'What's it say?' he says. 'Who's it from?'

'An old friend.'

'Why've you got the blanket over your head?'

I take the blanket off.

'Was it a woman?'

'Yeah.'

'What's it say?'

'Nothing important.'

He sits on my cot and I get a fresh whiff of his ashy skin and breath. He should brush his teeth, drink some water, smoke less. But he refuses to do anything that's good for him, nothing but sleep.

He's probably afraid that, if he does anything other than sleep and talk of suicide, I'll not believe he wants to die. It seems nothing matters more to him than that I should believe he wants to die. This matters more, I think, than the idea of death itself.

'If it's nothing important, then why do you look like somebody kicked you in the head?' he says.

'She just made me want to get out of here.'

'Don't you always?'

I don't tell Gardam the truth. Truth is, now that I've been inside for a good while, I don't always think about my release, and I don't always want to get out.

I'm sometimes happier in here than I was out there. I'm under no pressure to be better in here and life's shrinking to a size that suits me more.

The siren sounds for association and I go out to line up.

Lumsden doesn't show again.

I wait a while and play a bit of table tennis, then go straight back to the cell.

Gardam's got the radio on and he's listening to country and western. I can't stomach it.

He smiles at me. 'This is good, this is.'

'What you listening to?'

'You can change it if you want. It's your radio.'

'I wouldn't mind.'

I tune it to the station recommended by Lumsden. It's classical music.

'That's fucking rank, that is.'

'Let's give it a bit of a chance,' I say.

'I'd rather stick pins in my eyes.'

'Just half an hour,' I say.

Gardam closes his eyes and he keeps them closed, lies still on his back, and doesn't light a cigarette for at least an hour.

He doesn't talk either.

We listen to Beethoven and Bach and Chopin and Schubert. I don't mind it.

He doesn't speak and doesn't smoke.

When we've got our cocoa, he comes and sits on my cot.

'Could we maybe listen to some news now?'

'Sure,' I say.

We listen to the BBC World Service, the nine o'clock news bulletin.

'I think she's probably really tall,' says Gardam.

'Who?'

'The woman on the radio.'

After lights out, I masturbate facing the wall, and Gardam pretends to sleep, and when it's his turn I do the same for him.

When I get back from the library next day, Gardam's sleeping with his head at the wrong end of the cot, no pillow and no blanket.

His eyelids flicker, probably dreaming.

He sometimes moves the cot away from the wall or moves his pillow to the other end of the bed, as though by changing positions he'll fool his body so that he can begin a fresh sleep.

I turn on the radio and Gardam wakes.

'I've a nickname for you, Ox. It came to me in a dream.'

'What?'

'I think I'll call you Miss Otis.'

He picks the sleep out of his eyes and wipes it on his trousers.

'Well, what do you think?'

'Nothing.'

'Do you know the song?'

'No.'

'Miss Otis regrets she's unable to lunch today.'

'What's it about?'

'It was on the radio last night.'

'I don't remember.'

'It's about a woman who killed a man, and she can't keep her lunch appointment. Or something like that.'

'What's Miss Otis got to do with me?' I say.

Gardam smiles. 'It came to me in a dream.'

'And you think I'm like a woman?'

'I didn't say that, did I? Did you hear me say that?'

'Why couldn't you find a sad song involving a man who can't make his appointment?'

'Forget about it,' he says.

Gardam's good mood is finished.

'I just thought you'd want a better name than Ox, seeing as you're more like a fucking rabbit than an ox.'

'Right,' I say.

'It's not even time for chow,' he says. 'Why the fuck did you wake me?'

'Sorry. Go back to sleep.'

He moves his pillow to the other end of the cot and within minutes he's snoring.

The siren sounds for evening chow and, as usual, Gardam and I sit together in the mess, but his eyes are so full of pus I can't look at him without being put off my food.

Lumsden's alone again and he's got that same book in his lap. He doesn't look at me.

I'll see him tonight.

A message gets passed along the ones. There's been a riot and a knifing in F Wing. Somebody's gone at a screw with a pair of bolt cutters.

We're all in lockdown.

'Wonder which one it was,' says Gardam.

'I hope it wasn't Johnson.'

'That fat bloke in remand?'

'He was all right.'

'I knew that Lumsden would fuck you up.'

'It's got nothing to do with Lumsden.'

Gardam puts the radio on, tunes it to country and western.

I read more of the book about the criminal law and start a letter to my mother.

After morning chow next morning, I'm taken to the nurse and weighed. It's the short fat nurse with acne.

'Okay,' he says, 'You should be taken off special-watch now.'

Farrell takes me back to the cell.

'When can I start using the yard?'

'You can go out today if you want.'

'Thanks.'

'I'll get you at eleven.'

At eleven, Farrell takes me out to the yard.

There's a small football field and a cricket pitch, but most of the men are walking back and forth on the tarmac, talking and smoking, just walking up and down in straight lines. And then there are the Wombles, that's what they call the men who collect the drugs that've been sent over the fence inside tennis balls. The guards see them but don't stop them.

I run two laps of the field and I plan to do more, but that's all I can manage.

When I'm done, I sit by the wall to check my pulse. It's way too high. I've got to get fitter and get my resting pulse down, probably down to near fifty-eight or sixty.

About halfway through the exercise hour, four men start playing football. When they stop for a break, I ask one of them if I can join in.

'Go fuck yourself,' he says.

'No problem,' I say.

I do more laps, run until I can't run any more.

For the rest of the hour I go on laying low, mind my own business and, when the exercise ends, go to the back of the line-up, walk inside with my head down.

In the cell, I wash up a bit at the sink, then sit on the cot, ready to read.

Gardam wakes.

'Morning,' I say.

'Fuck the morning.'

'You were in a good mood yesterday. What happened?'

'I remembered I want to die.'

I look at my book, but not for long.

'I have a knife,' he says.

He stands and comes over, stands right by my feet.

I put the book on my lap.

'I got hold of a blade,' he says.

'Yeah?'

'Maybe you could help me out?'

He sits down next to me.

'What do you want me to do?'

'I can't do it myself.'

'What?'

'I was thinking if I gave you the knife you could stick me in the middle of the night, stick the knife right in my preliminary artery or something. But you'd have to make sure you do it right. I don't want to end up like a cripple or in an iron lung or anything.'

I laugh a tight laugh.

'I'm serious,' he says.

'It's a stupid idea.'

'Why?'

'If I killed you, then I'd never get out of here.'

'You're wrong. I've thought it all out. We can make it look like self-defence. You just say that I attacked you and you fought back.'

He's sitting so close and I can smell his sweat and it smells like it's got diarrhoea mixed in with it.

'You knife me,' he says, 'and then put my body on the floor. And then you give yourself some defence wounds, like a small stab in the arm or something.'

'I don't think so,' I say.

He draws his fist back as though to strike, then lowers it.

'Not this time,' he says.

'Right,' I say.

'And I'm going to make some threats in your direction during chow. That way the whole thing is kind of set up.'

'I can't do it.'

He stands and goes to his cot, reaches under his mattress and takes out a knife.

'I got this off one of the screws,' he says.

It's a safety knife, the kind they use for cutting down suicides.

'How did you get it?'

He doesn't answer, just comes back to my cot, stands over me and flashes the knife through the air in front of my face. He smiles. *Flish, flish*, goes the knife.

'There's gonna be a cell search soon,' he says, 'so you'd better do me this favour quick.'

'I don't think so.'

'I'm going to leave this under the mattress,' he says.

'I can't do it,' I say.

He comes over again and stands in close.

I bring my teeth together.

'If you don't use the knife,' he says. 'I'll do some damage in another direction.'

'What's that supposed to mean?'

'It means maybe I won't use it on myself. Maybe I'll flip my lid and use it on somebody else.'

Gardam coughs, goes to his cot to get a cigarette. He sits with his back to the wall, puts the knife under his pillow and lights the cigarette. Then he lights another, and another.

I pretend to read.

'Don't worry, Miss Otis. I'm probably not going to come after you.'

The siren sounds for chow and we file out.

I go to association but Lumsden's not in the rec-room. I win three games of pool and get enough credit to pay off my debt to Harrison.

Back in the cell, Gardam's in a funk. He's not talking to me. He's got the radio turned up loud and he's chain-smoking.

I have a whole lot of trouble reading and when the lights go out I know straight away I've little hope of sleeping.

And that's how it is. I don't sleep.

32

When the morning siren goes, Gardam's up and waiting at the cell door.

He says nothing to me.

He doesn't get in line-up for the mess. He's going down the end of the landing to report for special-sick.

I hope he gets put in the psych unit so I can have some rest.

I eat both breakfasts and I'm just finishing off my second cup of tea when Farrell comes to get me.

'I'm afraid we're running late,' he says. 'There was a fire down in the store.'

'Late for what?'

'Your appointment with Dr Forbes.'

'Is that today?'

'Yes, but you've only got fifteen minutes.'

I'd thought I'd never see Dr Forbes again and I'm glad of the news. I've got a lot to get off my chest.

Dr Forbes is wearing a suit, all buttoned up, a white shirt underneath, and she's got black, flat shoes.

'Hello, Patrick. Take a seat.'

She sits and smiles at me and moves in closer to the desk, uncrosses and crosses her legs. 'Looks like you've gained weight.'

'Six pounds,' I say.

'That's good,' she says.

'I've been using the library,' I say. 'And I went out to the yard yesterday.'

'Do you feel better? You look better.'

I doubt it.

'Yeah.'

She waits for me to speak. I don't know where to start. There's Gardam and Lumsden, my family, and my appeal that's going nowhere. And the fuck-off I got yesterday in the yard. And there's Welkin.

'I think if I went to university now,' I say, 'I'd probably do a lot better.'

'Do you think you've changed then?'

'I think I have.'

'In what way?'

'I think I've got more patience or something, or maybe my expectations are just lower.'

'That's a good thing. So you might study something? Now or when you're out?'

'Nah. If I was free, I don't think I'd like studying at all.'

'Not necessarily.'

'That's how it is with me. I didn't live a proper life when I was free and I don't think it'd be any different if I got out.'

'Maybe that's not true.'

I look at the floor. My breath's got shallow.

'You look angry,' she says.

'I'm not.'

'What then?'

My mouth's full of the threat of tears and I can't speak. I feel like

347

I'm about to lose control.

But then, after a long gap, the silence between us starts to cover me, almost like being touched. The longer the stretch of silence, the more it feels like we're touching each other.

'Tell me more about your family,' she says. 'Have they been to see you?'

'No. I'm a fucking orphan now.'

I'm too agitated to sit.

'Patrick. You need to stay seated or I'll have to raise the alarm.'

I sit.

She takes a deep breath.

'Do you feel betrayed by your mother?'

I'm not sure if the truth will make any sense. The truth is, I thought I was rejecting my mother when I left home. I was sick of her poking and prodding and I didn't want her to interfere in my life and ask questions about Sarah. But it turns out she was the one doing the rejecting and it's just the same with my father.

'I think she hates me,' I say.

'Maybe she doesn't hate you. Maybe she needs time.'

'Or maybe she always hated me and I gave her the perfect excuse.'

'What about your father? Has he been in contact?'

'No.'

She turns the little clock on her desk to face me then scrunches up her nose.

'That's a pity,' she says. 'Our time's up.'

Gardam's not in the cell after chow and I find out he's been taken to the psych unit. He should be gone for at least two days.

I've some time alone and the radio's mine.

Within an hour, I already feel a bit better and I have a nice fantasy before I sleep. I'm sitting in a café and the table's covered in a white cloth. I order a bottle of wine and tuck a napkin into my collar. A woman with pale skin and long red hair comes to meet me for dinner and we're the only people in the café.

The waiter stands in the back corner, facing away from us. The woman wears a blouse and, when she's finished eating, she unfastens her buttons and slides her blouse down over her shoulder and she shows me one of her tits.

After the library, I go back to the cell. Farrell opens the cell door, as he usually does, but he doesn't look at himself the way he usually does. I know something's up.

'Get in,' he says, and then he shuts my cell door and leaves.

Two prisoners are sitting on my cot and I can't get out.

I've been inside a good while now and I've never been beaten. It's been so long that, until the fuck-off I got yesterday, I'd stopped even wondering about it.

But here it is.

'We need a word with you,' says Osborne, a lifer who killed his girlfriend.

'Okay.'

'We need you sorted,' says Platt, a short bastard serving fifteen for the manslaughter of his best friend who turned in some evidence.

I go to the gap between the desk and my cot.

'We've noticed the fuck-nest you've got going with that pansy Lumsden.'

'No I haven't.'

'Stink's got his eyes on you,' says Platt.

Peterson, nicknamed Stink, is the ugliest man in D Wing, a prison-bent ape serving life with no prospect of parole for murdering two prostitutes. His face is fat and looks like it's had grease rubbed over it.

'We've decided to give him access to twice-weekly buggery.'

'Unless you give us what we want.'

'What do you want?'

'The usual. Snout, cash. Whatever is yours is now ours.'

'I don't have anything.'

Platt pulls a belt out of his trouser leg. He's had it hidden there, tied on with a bit of rope and he runs his hand slow along the stiff leather, wraps the end of the belt round his left hand, takes a hook out of his pocket, thick and sharp, a small scythe.

He steps forward.

I want to call out for Smith. I should've got a transfer to F Wing. I should've seen the governor. I should've seen this coming.

'First,' says Osborne, 'Peterson buggers you senseless, takes you up the shitter good and proper. You'll probably bite your tongue in half. That's what happened to West, isn't it, Platt?'

'That's correct.'

'And then if we still don't get what we want,' says Osborne, 'this belt goes round your neck, and we pull real hard and, when your eyes are poking out of your stupid skull, we insert the hook right through your socket, and pull real hard and turn you blind.'

I step forward, no idea where I might get to, but I've got to move.

'You go fucking nowhere,' says Platt.

I take another step forward, make for the cell door.

The blow comes from behind, connects hard and fast, like a block of wood to the base of my skull and, when I'm going down, another blow to the top of my spine, a crack so hard, a pain so large it takes everything with it.

I wake in the infirmary next morning and, all things considered, I don't feel too bad. There's a drip in my arm giving me glucose and even though there's a shooting pain in the top of my head, a throbbing in my temples and at the base of my spine, I've slept a long time and I've woken feeling glad it's happened. This is my chance to get a transfer to F Wing.

The tall nurse is standing beside the cot. It's the same nurse, the one who looked after me last time, but there's something changed about him, something not right or normal.

'We meet again,' he says.

His pupils are dilated and he's got a terrible red rash across his neck.

He closes the door with his foot.

'You've been unconscious for twelve hours. We thought you might go into a coma.'

I can tell by the way he's talking and licking his lips that he's got a dry mouth. I don't know much about drugs, but it seems to me he's got a skull full of speed.

'I need a transfer,' I say. 'I want to go to F Wing.'

'You'll have to talk to the governor about that.'

'When can I see him?'

'I don't know.'

'I have to move. I want a transfer to F Wing.'

He looks at the door.

'What's the problem?'

He moves his chair in closer to the bed.

'They beat the crap out of me and sold my body.'

'Twice a week in Peterson's cell?'

'I need a transfer.'

'Some men wet themselves,' he says, 'some shit themselves, but you fainted. That's a first. Now they'll get every drop of your dosh.'

'I didn't faint. They knocked me out. And I don't have any dosh.'

'Do you want me to help you?'

'Yeah.'

He opens the door, checks the corridor and comes back.

I'm short of breath.

'Can they get away with this?'

'You don't know much, do you?'

I say nothing.

351

'I can help you. Do you want my help?'

'Yeah.'

He promises he'll arrange for a supply of cigarettes to pay off Platt and Osborne, but only enough for a couple of weeks. After that, I'll be on my own.

'All you have to do is let me watch while you do yourself.'

'What?'

'Just let me watch.'

'I'm not doing that.'

'Then I can't help you.'

'You'll stop me getting transferred if I don't?'

'Probably.'

'You want me to do it now?'

'Yeah. Now.'

I pull the sheet down and do myself and he watches.

When I've finished, he reaches in under the bed and gives me two packs of cigarettes.

'Hide these in your socks.'

'Right.'

'And take these pills. They'll make you feel a whole lot better.'

He leaves.

I take the drugs he gave me and sleep again and, when I wake, Farrell comes to take me back to the cell. Looks like he's got a wig on.

'Get dressed,' he says. 'It's time to go back.'

I get out of the bed and get dressed. I'm stiff and sore and I take my time doing it. He goes to the window and waits.

He turns round. 'Ready?'

'I need to see the governor.'

'You're on the list for review.'

'When? It's urgent.'

'All in due course.'

'It's bad enough I'm in here, I shouldn't even be in here. Don't I have any rights?'

'You'll see him. You're up for review.'

'And I need some money for the phone.'

'Have you not got any at all?'

'No.'

'You'd better get some sent in.'

He takes me to the cell.

Gardam's back from the psych unit and he's on his cot shuffling a pack of cards.

'How about a game of poker, Miss Otis?'

'I think I'll read.'

'Screw you, then.'

'I've just come out of the infirmary. I've taken a beating. My skull feels like it's about to crack open. Feels like a horse kicked me in the spine.'

I go to my cot, lie down and turn my back to him, take the packets out of my socks.

'Where'd you get those?'

'A loan from the nurse.'

'I'll bet he made you pay.'

'Right.'

'You got off pretty lightly though, Ox.'

He's forgotten about Miss Otis.

'I've got to get hold of some money.'

'Ask your family.'

'Yeah. I will.'

He shuffles the cards, looks at me.

'Could I borrow some money for the phone?'

'I'm empty,' he says. 'My sister owes me a bit, but she's on a holiday or something.'

'Right,' I say.

He sits on the floor, deals the cards.

'Want to play?'

I sit on the floor.

'I once won a motorbike with a straight flush,' he says. 'It was one of the best nights of my life.'

We play and the only talk is talk of the game. We play with matches and it's as boring as hell.

I want to quit.

'Why doesn't the king of hearts have a moustache?' I say. 'All the others do.'

'Who cares? Just deal.'

'I can't be bothered.'

I move to stand and he throws the empty matchbox at me.

'What the fuck kind of question is that anyway? How the fuck would I know why the king of hearts doesn't have a moustache?'

'Relax,' I say. 'I was only making conversation.'

'Who gives a fuck? What's your fucking problem?'

He goes to his cot and lifts the mattress.

'It's okay,' I say. 'I'm sorry. Just go ahead and deal another hand.'

He drops the mattress.

'You fucking deal, then,' he says.

My hands sweat on the cards.

He sits back down.

A half-hour before the morning siren, Farrell wakes me. My head hurts even more than it did yesterday. I should've stayed in the infirmary.

I sit bolt up.

'Platt's coming for you again,' he says. 'You better get what he's asked for.'

'I've got two packs of cigs.'

'Okay. Give them to me.'

'Why?'

'I'll hand them over.'

'Right.'

'But these won't buy you much time.'

'How long do I have?'

'A week at most.'

After showers, I stop Stan on the landing and ask to borrow some phone money. He gives me fifty pence in exchange for some pool tips and then I catch up to Farrell and ask him if he'll take me to the phones.

'Are you going to get what they need?'

'Yeah. And what about the governor and my transfer?

'I wouldn't get my hopes up about a transfer if I were you.'

He takes me straight to the phones after Recess.

He throws another man off the phone.

While I dial the number, he stands in close, tidies his black hair, puts it behind his waxy white ears.

My father answers.

'Hello, Dad.'

'Please be quick, son.'

'I need some money. It's a matter of life and death.'

'For drugs?'

'No, for protection.'

'How much?'

'About two hundred pounds. And I'll pay you back.'

'How?'

'I've got plans for when I get out. When I get out, I'll—'

He hangs up.

Gardam's in the cell.

'They won't put me back in psych. They say I'm crying wolf.'

'Right.'

'I'll show them.'

'You do that,' I say.

I lie prone on my cot all day, don't bother with the library, don't bother with anything. I don't bother with the yard, and I don't bother with association. My head's sick again, my gut too. I sleep in snatches, don't eat the meals.

When the evening tea and cocoa comes, Gardam gets me a cup of tea.

'Drink this at least,' he says. 'I've put four sugars in it.'

'No thanks.'

'I'll fucking toss it then.'

'Why don't you drink it?'

''Cos I made it for you.'

I take the tea and it feels pretty good on my tongue. I turn away from him and shed a few more tears.

Two days later, I'm on the cot. The money order's arrived by first class with this note.

Dear Patrick,

After this lot, I can't send you any more money. Your mother and I are emigrating next month and we don't have any more to spare. I hope this money helps you out of the new trouble you're in.

I've also included a couple of mechanics magazines you left in your room.

Your father.

++

After tea, I stop Farrell outside the cell.

'I've got a money order,' I say. 'I need it cashed.'

'Give it here,' he says. 'I'll take care of it.'

He's going to take the whole lot to pay off Platt and Osborne and leave me with nothing.

'Do I get to see any of it?'

'I'll see what I can do.'

'I just want some coins for the phone.'

He reaches into his trouser pocket.

'Use this.'

He gives me two pounds and some coins.

'I need a bit more. I've got to call my brief.'

He gets three more notes and some coins from his pocket. I've got just over five quid now. That's it.

'Fucking great,' I say.

He laughs. 'Mind your language.'

I miss Johnson.

It's time for association and Lumsden's putting more pencil marks on the wall next to the plant.

I sit away from him, up close in front of the TV and wait for him to finish. I don't want to go over straight away and make it too conspicuous. I've got to stall a while.

After about twenty minutes I go over to his place by the back wall.

He says nothing.

The news comes on the TV and we both pretend to watch.

'Thanks for the radio,' I say.

'You already thanked me.'

His mood's no good.

We hardly speak. We say a few words, that's all. A bit of small talk about the stabbing in F Wing. It wasn't Johnson who got stabbed.

The siren sounds and we walk together.

In line-up, there's a delay. One of the gates won't open. Lumsden stands close and our shoulders touch. He has me in the stomach again.

He moves so that the back of his hand touches mine and I let him do it, and our hands stay like this, and we wait like this for the gates to open.

There's nothing wrong with this, not in here. I'll take it.

From him, I'll take it. Not from anybody else, but from him I'll take it.

'Goodbye, Ox,' he says. 'See you later.'

I don't like the way he says this, makes too much of it, makes it too obvious. It should happen if it's going to happen, but without the chat.

'Yeah,' I say.

I watch him turn the corner for F Wing. His canvas shoes are brand new.

Gardam paces next to his cot and chain-smokes, lighting one cigarette from another. He flicks ash on the floor, doesn't bother to use a tray.

He stops pacing and turns to me.

'What's your fucking problem?'

'I don't have a problem.'

'Good.'

I lie down and put a pillow over my head. He sits on the end of my cot.

'Did you hear about the bloke in H Wing who slit his wrists?'

'No?'

'Well, he did. He used a blunt razor. Must have took him hours to cut through.'

Gardam tries to light another cigarette but his lighter fluid's run out.

'Fuck.'

He bashes the lighter on his knee, on the edge of the cot, then on the floor.

'Fuck.'

The very last thing I want is more smoke in the air, but if he doesn't get a light he'll be awake all night.

He might reach for the knife.

'Don't you have any matches?' he says.

'No.'

But I know Farrell has some.

I go to the door and slide open the observation panel and call out for him.

'Are you fucking crazy?' says Gardam.

I've been shouting for about ten minutes.

Farrell comes.

'This better be good,' he says.

'Gardam needs some matches,' I say.

He laughs. 'Gardam can wait.'

'He can't,' I say. 'He hasn't had a smoke since breakfast and he's about to cut up.'

He opens the cell door, but makes me wait, then he reaches into his pocket and takes out a box of matches.

'Give me twenty,' he says.

'On top of the two hundred?'

'Yeah.'

'No.'

He laughs, gives me the box, bolts the door.

But he comes straight back.

'You're seeing the head-shrinker again tomorrow.'

'What time?'

'After breakfast.'

'Thanks.'

'Don't mention it.'

Gardam takes the matches.

'I owe you,' he says.

'Good. Find me a topnotch QC, get me an appeal, get Georgia in here for a contact visit and get my family to forgive me.'

'Anything else?'

'Quit smoking.'

The siren sounds and the lights go out. We're banged up till morning.

33

Dr Forbes is wearing a green dress and she's got a red band in her hair and red shoes. She looks like the funny and smart Irish girl who worked in the local pub, the one I chatted to for about a month, before I met Sarah.

'Hello,' she says. 'Take a seat.'

I sit and she sits.

'Hello, doctor.'

I like saying that.

'Is there anything you'd like to talk about?'

'Nothing special.'

She looks at me and waits.

'My dad sent me some money and two mechanics magazines.'

I take the folded note out of my pocket and show her.

'The kisses he's put on look more like crucifixes.'

'That was probably only a reflex,' she says. 'There's a great deal that people do out of habit, unconsciously, without thinking.'

She reads this bit of the letter out loud: *Your mother and I are emigrating next month and we don't have any more to spare.* 'How did that make you feel?'

'A bit shocked,' I say, 'but also a bit like that's the end of that then. It might be better that they're overseas, then we can both blame that for the fact that they don't come and see me. I think my dad's just acting on his gut.'

'Do you want to know where they're going?'

'It'll be Australia. My mum loves the idea of Australia.'

She waits for more but I don't want to say anything more about them.

'Do you think what you did was a reflex? A gut reaction like your father's? The night you killed?'

She's getting a bit carried away here with the psychology.

'I don't know,' I say. 'I don't know what I thought before I did it and don't remember anything except that I wanted him to wake up.'

'Do you feel sad about what happened?'

I look under the desk at her legs.

'Yeah. I told you before.'

'I'd like to hear more.'

'Like what?'

'Has the death changed you?'

'Not really. What do you mean?'

'Is there anything different about the way you think or feel?'

'I just think the same thoughts over and over. Like a fucking cow chewing his cud.'

'I think that's pretty normal,' she says. 'Can you tell me what the thoughts are?'

Her foot swings back and forth, the heel of her red shoe slipping from her ankle. Her stockings shine above her knee.

'Patrick?'

I clear my throat.

'I can give you one example of how I feel,' I say.

'Okay.'

'Last night when I got into bed, I thought about Welkin. When I moved my legs across the part of the sheet I'd made warm with my body, I thought, the sheets will stay cold when you're dead. He'll stay cold. He's cold and dead.'

'How did you feel when you read all the reports in the paper about him?'

'I didn't read them.'

She frowns.

If Dr Forbes stood now and went to the door I'd follow her and we'd go down the hall and nobody would stop us because she'd tell them not to follow us and they'd listen to her and she'd take me outside, through the gates, out beyond the prison walls. We'd get in her car and drive to the sea and on the way we'd stop at a roadside café and in the car I'd put my hand on her leg just above where the hem of her skirt is.

'Patrick?'

'Yeah,' I say. 'Even if I didn't kill him I'd probably have found another nail.'

She lifts her chin.

'My grandfather gave me a good winter coat when I turned sixteen,' I say. 'And in less than three months or something I'd ripped it in three places on three nails. No, two nails and some barbed wire. If there's a nail, I'll find it.'

Dr Forbes puts the lid on her pen and puts the pen on her desk.

I want to tell her about Gardam, but I can't rat on him and I can't tell her about Farrell, Osborne and Platt either. But maybe I can tell her about Lumsden.

'Is this coat important to you?'

'No.'

'When did you last wear it?'

'I was wearing it when I arrived at the boarding house and I didn't want to take it off and put it on the coat-rack.'

We're silent again. I look at her hands.

'Is there anything else you want to tell me?'

If I start on Lumsden I'm not sure I'll like what comes out.

'No.'

After a minute, she stands.

'Our time's up,' she says. 'Will you come back?'

'I mightn't bother,' I say.

She laughs. 'I'll see you in a few days.'

Lumsden doesn't show up for association and I can't risk asking anybody if they know where he is.

I sit alone in front of the TV and watch a football match replay. But I don't care about the score and can't concentrate.

If Lumsden's been sent on the ghost train, there'd have been talk. If he's been sent to the infirmary, or hospital, there'd have been talk of that, too. And if he was up for parole, somebody would've been taking bets.

Back in the cell, I can't sleep and, in the morning, my eyes sting with tiredness, and I'm hungry, but can't eat.

Farrell comes to the cell to see if I want to go to the yard or to the library and I tell him I want the library. He comes back a half-hour later and I go with him to the library and sit at the table next to the radiator and listen to two men from D Wing talking cricket and football with the other officer.

Lumsden doesn't come.

I read, but take nothing in. I put my head in my hands.

At the other table there's an old con with a newspaper over his lap. He's stroking his dick through his trousers.

Back in the cell, Gardam's smuggled in bits of potato and meat and he gives them to me. He's got these morsels wrapped in tissue paper and the paper's stuck to everything.

'No thanks,' I say.

'I thought you were in training for the football team.'

'Yeah, but I'm not hungry.'

He drops the food in the toilet and stares into the bowl, but doesn't flush.

'Do you think the fish out in the ocean will eat this?'

'Probably.'

'Probably?'

'Yeah, I think they will. I think they'll love it. They'll be grateful.'

This makes Gardam strange. He smiles and nods and, when he flushes the toilet, a rush of colour travels up his neck, some pink in his usually grey face.

'Yeah,' he says. 'They probably will be very grateful.'

I read for a while, then take a nap.

When I wake, Gardam's got his head in the toilet, his arms wrapped round the seat like a hug.

'What's wrong?' I say.

'Sick as a dog. What do you think?'

I go to him.

He pukes again, just liquid, and lots of it.

'He told me it'd kill me.'

'What?'

He turns round, wipes his mouth on his hand, sits with his back against the toilet.

'Johns. He said if I swallowed this stuff he gave me I'd be dead in five seconds.'

'What was it?'

'I didn't ask, did I? It didn't work and now I've got this cramp so bad.'

'I'd offer you a glass of water, but—'

'We've no glasses.'

'Right.'

Gardam recovers enough to go to his cot.

When he seems right again, I get the chat going.

'Do you know if anybody off F Wing's been paroled or transferred recently?'

'Don't think so. But I wouldn't know.'

'How would you go about finding out?'

'Don't ask me. You're the one who goes to association every night. Ask somebody there.'

'It's no big deal.'

He goes back to the toilet, chucks again.

Next night, Lumsden's not in the rec-room.

On the way back to the cell, I look at the notice board. There's a list of men due to see Welfare tonight, but he's not one of them. Maybe his name was just left off the list. Maybe he's working extra hours in the Deputy Governor's office this week, or maybe he's doing one of those stupid creative writing workshops.

I'll see him tomorrow.

At breakfast next day, there's no sign of Lumsden and I get to thinking he must be gone. I bend over, put my head between my knees.

Gardam puts his hand on my back and then a screw comes.

'You going to be sick or what?'

'No,' I say.

'Did you take some of that ratsack shit too?'

'No.'

'Do you need the infirmary?'

'No.'

'Then sit up and be a fucking man.'

He goes back to his post at the door.

'What's up?' says Gardam.

'Nothing.'

Next day, I go to the library.

Lumsden's not there.

I sit for an hour and wait for him and then I get an idea to go to the place in the bookshelf where he'd kept the radio for me.

There's a note, addressed to me.

I sit at the desk beside the radiator.

My heart pounds.

My dear friend, Patrick,

    I hope you'll forgive me for not telling you that my parole has come through.

    I had a meeting with the Board of Visitors last week, but I couldn't tell you. I worried that the unsaid would get said, that there'd be pressure for us to act.

    There was no easy way to say goodbye and in the end I didn't have the guts to say it.

    As you probably know, ex-prisoners can't visit prison, which is cruel enough, but I've just learnt that I won't be allowed to write to you either.

    But I have an idea:

    Everyday, when you wake, you'll think of me and you'll keep thinking of me while you're dressing and washing and eating your breakfast.

    I'll do the same.

    Think whatever you want.

    Every morning, wherever I am, whatever I'm doing, I'll have an appointment with you, you'll have an appointment with me.

    See you in a few years.

    Your friend, Derek Lumsden

I read the note about a dozen times, sometimes faster, sometimes slower, forwards then backwards.

I read it over until the siren goes.

Gardam's sitting up in his cot and he's got both pillows behind his head.

I sit right down beside his feet.

'Do you have any Valium?' I say.

'No.'

'Can you get me some?'

'Yeah, in a few days. Probably Friday.'

'I need something now.'

'What's wrong, Ox?'

'I need sleep. I haven't slept in days.'

'If I give you one, will you do me that favour?'

'No. I can't do it.'

'Then I can't help you. Get off my cot and get off my fucking feet.'

'Give me my pillow then.'

Before he hands the pillow over, he wipes his face with it.

34

Today's my last appointment with Dr Forbes.

Farrell collects me at eleven.

When we get to her office door, she greets me and smiles and puts her hand on my elbow and she does it all in full view of Farrell.

He leaves.

'Take a seat,' she says.

She sits behind her desk and I sit forward in my chair, put my elbows on my knees.

'How are you?' she says.

I think for a minute.

'Can you tell me what it's like outside?' I say.

'What do you mean?'

'I just want you to describe something.'

'Would you like to stand by the window and look out?'

'No,' I say. 'I get to see the yard during exercise. I just want you to describe the outside for me.'

'Anything?'

'Yeah.'

We both look at the window.

A pigeon wants to sit on the windowsill but can't because the bars are too close together and he's too fat to squeeze through.

'Well,' she says, 'it was drizzly this morning.'

'What about last night? Was there a full moon or a half-moon? What kind of moon? What did you do? Did you go anywhere?'

'I can't tell you about my personal life.'

'Okay, then describe something. The city at night-time or anything like that.'

'I haven't been in the city at night lately and I haven't even looked at the night sky. Not lately.'

'Make it up then. Or try to remember.'

She faces me, thinks a minute, and her shoe slips from her foot. She doesn't put it back on. She just leaves the shoe where it's fallen, under the desk.

'I was coming home from a dinner party in the countryside a few nights ago,' she says, 'and the moon was a strange orange colour. It was full, and it was big and orange.'

'What did you have to eat?'

'Salmon and…I can't honestly remember.'

'What about the sun? Was it in or out this morning? Does the sun come into your bedroom in the morning?'

'Not often.'

'Was it cloudy this morning when you woke up? What kind of sky was it?'

'I'm sorry, Patrick,' she says. 'I feel a bit foolish. I suppose I wasn't paying enough attention.'

'Neither did I,' I say. 'I never paid enough attention.'

She smiles. 'I was about to say I'll tell you more next time, but this is our last session.'

'I know,' I say.

I move back in the chair, try to relax a bit.

She opens the desk drawer and removes a parcel wrapped in brown paper.

'This is for you,' she says. 'You can open it now or open it later.'

'I want to open it now.'

She laughs. 'But it's already been opened twice, unwrapped once and then re-wrapped.'

'Yeah,' I say. 'The censors.'

She's given me a small framed picture, a painting.

I was hoping for some food.

'Thanks,' I say.

'Aren't you going to look at it?'

'Yeah.'

'It's a print of one of my favourite paintings,' she says. 'It's by Isaac van Nickele. It's one of his paintings of the interior of Saint Bavo cathedral. It was painted in the late seventeenth century.'

'I can't take it,' I say. 'It'll just get slashed or stolen.'

'I want you to take it.'

'My cell mate's a suicidal maniac. He'll probably try and eat it, and choke to death on the frame.'

'Then you write to me and I'll send you another. It's just a print.'

I look at it, take my time.

It's a picture of three priests dressed in robes and they're standing in a dark passageway and there's another man, in the distance, down the other end of the passageway, and he's in brighter clothes. He's walking toward the priests, or walking away. It's hard to tell.

'It really makes you look at it,' I say.

'Yes,' she says.

'Why'd you give me this?'

'I think that your situation is not unlike the situation of the priests in the cloisters, you are somewhere dark but—'

'—but, if I look closely,' I say, 'I'll see other things, like this light here to the right, the small orange lamp on the wall and the light coming through a door, or is it a window? At the very back of the corridor, there's light.'

'Yes, at the front or at the back,' she says.

'There's a way out?' I say.

'Yes,' she says. 'There's freedom.'

I put the picture on the desk, calm and slow.

'That's complete fucking rubbish,' I say.

But she's not the least bit ruffled. She's no pushover.

'Do you remember you told me you had a terrible day at school because you woke with a squashed ear?'

'It wasn't that,' I say. 'It was because I realised my ears were a bit too big for my head and I was mad because nobody else in my family has big ears.'

'That's right,' she says. 'And don't you think that now you won't let the small things get you down so much? When you get out on licence?'

She's smart, but she's missed the point of what's wrong with people. She's missed the very point. People never get on with what they've got. They don't like things enough and barely even notice things in the first place.

'I'll probably make the same mistakes,' I say.

'But not as much perhaps, and not—'

'No. Not exactly the same mistakes. I'll make different ones.'

I take the picture off the desk and look at it.

She checks the time.

'Is there anything finally that you want to talk about?' she says.

I want to talk about Gardam and Lumsden, but there's too much to say and I don't want to be in the middle of something important and then be stopped by the clock.

I stand up.

She doesn't raise the alarm.

I go over to her, stand at the side of her desk.

She stands and her shoulders go up and down with the deep breaths she takes.

'Are you okay?' she asks.

'Would it be all right if I gave you a hug?'

She thinks. Takes a good look at me.

'Yes,' she says. 'All right.'

I don't know how to do what I want to do.

'Move in,' she says, 'bring me to you.'

I hold her now, not too hard, but close, really warm and really very close, and the mood of being wrapped round her, it's a mood and feeling so great I want to bawl.

She takes a step back.

I let go.

'Okay?' she asks.

I turn away and wipe my face with the heel of my hand.

'How are you?' she says.

'Happy,' I say. 'Thanks.'

She closes her eyes and we stand in silence.

There's an officer outside.

The key turns in the door.

Farrell's come to get me.

Nothing more gets said and I'm taken back to my cell.

Gardam's sleeping.

I go quietly to my cot but, when I sit, he wakes.

'What time is it?'

'Nearly time for chow.'

He groans.

He doesn't ask me about Dr Forbes.

He never has.

'Do you know that men executed in the electric chair have to

373

wear nappies?' he says.

I get up and go to sit on the cot next to him.

'How are you?' I say.

I'm sitting close, but he doesn't move away.

'What do you mean, how am I?'

'Do you still have that knife?'

'Yeah.'

'Give it to me then. I'll put you out of your misery.'

'When?'

'Tonight.'

'You serious?'

'Why not? That's what you want, isn't it?'

He swallows. 'Yeah.'

'Right then, give it to me.'

He gets the knife from under the mattress, gives it to me.

'When?' he says.

'I can't give you an exact time. It'll be a surprise.'

'Right then.'

'I'll do it while you sleep.'

'Tonight then?'

'Yeah, tonight.'

We go to chow together but he doesn't speak. He's got nothing to say. But he eats. He eats every morsel. He eats the sausages and peas and potatoes and he looks slowly round the mess hall like a man who wants to remember a good place he might not visit again, like a man looking over a place that he might miss.

'Are you sure?' I say.

'Yeah, let's get on with it.'

'And you're ready?'

'Yeah. Ready for martyrdom.'

I laugh.

374

We return to our cell and lie on our cots.

And still he doesn't speak.

My mouth's dry and my heart hammers hard, must be the same for him, worse.

Before lights out, I check again.

'Are you sure you want this?'

'Yeah.'

'If you want to change your mind, better do it now.'

He goes to the desk, sits and looks up at the wall, smokes one cigarette after another.

We get undressed after lights-out and I sneak a look at his body in the darkness.

He's very thin now and his shoulders are rounded and his stomach's bloated from the meal. From side-on, he looks like a pig that's been stood up after hanging belly down from a spit.

We get into our cots, get under our blankets, and I wonder if the other men get dressed and undressed in front of each other without shame, or whether, like me and Gardam, they undress in the dark and dress with their backs turned to each other.

He doesn't sleep, just as I don't sleep, stays awake, just as I stay awake.

It's like I thought it would be.

Dark hour, after slow dark hour, we stay awake and pretend to sleep.

I wait and he waits.

And then, not long before sunrise, I get up and go quietly to his cot.

I crouch down beside him, hold the knife over his chest, make sure my grip is tight.

He turns onto his back and opens his eyes.

'Close your eyes,' I say.

He goes on looking at me, doesn't blink.

'Close your eyes.'

He won't close his eyes.

'Do you want me to stick this knife in you or what?'

He closes his eyes and I can feel the panic coming off him in fumes.

His breath's fast and shallow.

'What do you want?' I say.

He doesn't answer, just moves across on the cot, turns to face the wall, makes room for me.

I think, then put the knife down.

I get in under the blankets.

I move in close and put my hand on his chest, press down. His awful heart speeds up, then slows a bit.

He's relaxing now and he's put his hand over mine.

'I'd better go back to my cot,' I say.

'Right,' he says. 'Okay then.'

He takes hold of my fingers.

I don't go.

I'm warm and sleepy here.

I might as well stay.

'Okay?' I say.

'Yeah,' he says. 'Okay.'

I let my head sink to its rest, but leave my hand on his chest and I feel when he goes under with me, deeper and calmer.

I breathe as he breathes.

Acknowledgments

Very special thanks to my friend, Julian Owen, who stepped in when this book was in a terrible state. Julian worked very hard to help me make it better and I owe him—his intelligence and his talent, as both a writer and an editor—an enormous debt.

For the same reason, I also thank my dear friends, Stewart Muir and Carolyn Tétaz. I owe them both huge thanks for their smart and patient editorial advice on the awful and wrong-footed early drafts of this novel.

For their wonderful editorial help and steadfast guidance, I also thank my agent, Deborah Rogers, at Rogers Coleridge & White, and my chief editor at Text Publishing, the brilliant Michael Heyward.

Very special thanks also to Jamie Byng, my publisher at Canongate Books, for continuing to make it possible for me to pay the bills and for his unflinching enthusiasm and faith.

I'd like also to thank Anya Serota, my editor at Canongate Books, Penny Hueston, my second editor at Text Publishing, Michael E. Halmshaw, David Sime and Steve Jones, all of whom provided invaluable editorial and critical feedback during the final stages of editing.

For their generous advice about criminal law and procedure, I'd like to thank Alistair Webster QC, Suzanne Goddard QC, Guy Gozem QC, Tim Storrie, Michael Hayton and Andrew Nuttall. Because I have sometimes ignored their advice (for the sake of dramatic tension, economy and atmosphere) the criminal law and procedure described in these pages is sometimes true-to-life and sometimes not.

And finally, I'd like to acknowledge the late Tony Parker for his tremendous book, *Life After Life: Interviews with Twelve Murderers* (Secker & Warburg, 1990) which gave me the idea for this novel.